Dora Noyes DeSautel

ła? kłcaptíkʷł

Dora Noyes DeSautel on her couch in her living room (December 1970)
Dora Noyes DeSautel splitting wood in her yard (early 1960's)
(Photos courtesy Adrian Holm)

UM

OCCASIONAL PAPERS IN LINGUISTICS NO. 15, 2002

Dora Noyes DeSautel ła? kłcaptíkʷł

Edited by
ANTHONY MATTINA
and
MADELINE DESAUTEL

With a Biographical Note by
ADRIAN HOLM

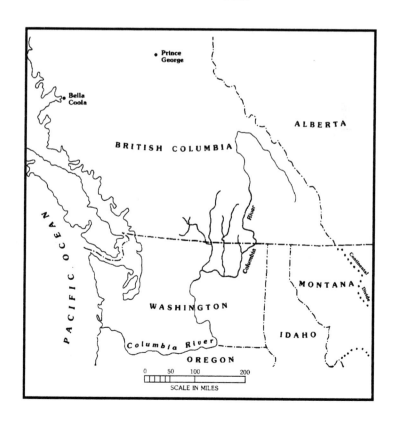

First Published May 2002

UMOPL — A series dedicated to the study
of the Native languages of the Northwest.

SERIES EDITORS
Anthony Mattina, University of Montana (mattina@selway.umt.edu)
Timothy Montler, University of North Texas (montler@unt.edu)

Address all correspondence to:
          UMOPL — Linguistics Laboratory
          The University of Montana
          Missoula, MT 59812

Anthony Mattina & Madeline DeSautel
          Dora Noyes DeSautel ła? kłcaptík"ł
          UMOPL No. 15

ISBN 1-879763-15-X

Library of Congress Control Number: 2002103000

CONTENTS

PART I - INTRODUCTION

PART II - THE INTERLINEARIZED TEXTS

PREFACE

p‿isl'əx̌l'áx̌t, p‿isnəqsílxʷ,

k‿ʷu‿púta?ntəp kʷu‿ł‿nk'ʷak'ʷíntp axá? iksq'y'ám i?‿nxa?xnúsc
t‿sˤ'aˤ'ác'. axá? t‿sˤ'aˤ'ác' yəwyáˤwt sck'ʷul's Dora DeSautel.

matlán na?ł sˤamtíc'a? na?ł i?‿sənk'ʷłk'ʷúl'əm na?ł sx̌əlpúla?xʷ,
yəwyáˤwt i?‿scq'áy'səlx ks?a?úms.

inx̌mínk ikscúnəm límləmt a?‿ck'ʷəl'k'ʷúl'əm la‿nsílxcən,
nqílxʷcnəm, k'əl yaˤyáˤt i?‿sck'ʷúl'səlx. k'ʷəc'k'ʷác't isck'ˤáw mi
niˤíp cxʷəlxʷált a?‿nqílxʷcəntət, i?‿cáwtət. ta?lí kən‿climt.

spəkʷk'ʷálqs

Callum F. Crawford.

by

Adrian Holm

[Anthony Mattina's Note: Adrian Holm is the eldest of Dora's eight grandchildren. She and her sister Robin were raised by Dora from infancy. Adrian is named after Dora's only son, Adrian, who was killed in World War II.

Adrian Holm received her library training at Eastern Washington University. She worked for seven years in the 70s at the JFK Library (periodicals department) at the time when the library was re-cataloging the collection, from the Dewey decimal to the Library of Congress classification.

After Adrian and her husband Jeff had a baby in 1980, they decided to return to the Colville Reservation and raise him there. Currenly Adrian Holm manages the three sites of the Tribal Resource Centers in Inchelium, Keller and Nespelem, an environment she pre-dilects. She enjoys cataloging and working with the patrons, slowly building the Indian material collections as the budget permits.

Growing up, Adrian and her sister Robin would discuss things with their grandmother, and when they came across something neither of them understood, Dora would tell them to go find out. Adrian attributes to these exchanges her love of library work, the looking for answers, the digging for information. She recently wrote "Who would have thought I would be cataloging my grandmother's material! Full circle. Isn't life interesting?"]

Dora Noyes was born April 1, 1902 and died December 10, 1982.

Dora was born around the Oroville, Washington area. She never knew her father, Peter Noyes, until she was a teenager. Dora moved to the Inchelium area where her father lived with his wife, Belle and their two daughters, Nellie and Margie and two sons, Peter (Jr.) and Tom. Dora's mother, Rosalie Hayward, died of wood alcohol poisoning; she drank it to get drunk not realizing what it would do to her. Rosalie liked to drink. Dora must have been around five or six years old at this time. Her favorite playmate was her cousin, Margaret, called Maggie, who was a year younger than Dora.

Before Rosalie's death, Dora remembered a time when she and her mother would go to Canada and visit relatives up there. Her mother would pack a few clothes, homemade bread or fry bread with fried deer meat and a couple jars of water. They would stop on the way and eat. Rosalie would hobble the horse and sometimes they would camp under a tree. Dora saw her mother in a dress one day, and then realized her mother was a woman. Until that time, she thought her mother was just like the uncles gender-wise. She said she must have been around three, almost four when she recalls the dress episode. Rosalie would break horses with her brothers and she liked hunting, tanning deer hides and making moccasins and gloves that she would sell to a store in Oroville. Twenty-five cents for a pair of gloves is what the store in Oroville would pay. Rosalie would sell these leather goods, what took her most of the winter months to make. With the money she would buy flour, baking powder, lard, slab bacon, thread, needles and things for winter. Dora said her mother was a hard worker. She never did say if her uncles had worked as hard. They did contribute to the house, they hunted deer, birds, fished and were busy with the horses and cows. At Christmas Rosalie would buy candy with about 10 cents that they had saved.

After Dora's mother died, there were only her maternal grandmother and her uncles, grown men. There were other distant relatives in the Oroville area but they had families of their own. Dora never really talked much about them except the cousin's family she had spent much time with. Dora said her grandmother had arthritis bad to the point of not being able even to walk without help. I don't recall if two or three years passed from the time of Rosalie's death to the point when Dora and Maggie were removed from the home. Dora remembers some people coming to see her grandmother. They told the grandmother that being in a house with young men just wasn't proper for very young girls. Made no difference if they were uncles. The "authorities," as Dora called them, came one day soon after the talk with the old grandmother and took Dora and Maggie away to boarding school. Dora never saw her grandmother again. Only one uncle had come to visit them at the school at two different times. She doesn't know when her grandmother died as no one wrote to tell her or Maggie.

Dora learned the basics of writing, reading and arithmetic. Dora called them the 3-R's. At the school, the students, girls especially, learned to cook and sew, besides what they got from books. Boys learned about woodshop and fixing things. (I never knew what things, and I don't think Gram was quite sure either). When I was growing up, Dora would tell Robin and me interesting stories of what boarding school was like for her and Maggie. They couldn't speak Indian at the school, only English. Luckily, Dora and Maggie came from a home that had three languages, English, Indian and French. So it wasn't quite so hard on them when it came to English as it was for some Indian kids. Dora came back to the Oroville area when she was about fifteen or sixteen. Most of the family she knew had either died or moved away. Dora moved to Inchelium to be near her father, Pete Noyes, and cousins that lived in the area. Pete welcomed his daughter, but her stepmother, Belle, didn't. At least that is what Dora said about her stepmother, and being "a coastal Indian and a fish eater." Dora also had another sister, Cecilia Pichette (Pichette is her married name) and another brother, Jim Thomas. These siblings lived in the Inchelium area and both came from different mothers. Pete Noyes, from all the stories I heard both from families and his contemporaries when I was growing up, was a man who loved women. Therefore, all the relatives I now have, are thanks to him.

Dora was married three times, first to John Adolph, whom she married in the Catholic church and had three children with him. These are in birth order: Mary Francis, a baby girl who died in infancy; Adrian Louis, a son who died in the Pacific Campaign during World War II. He was servicing on the aircraft carrier USS Princeton when the Japanese bombed it. Modesta Mary, the youngest daughter, was born January 20, 1925. Modesta married George Louis Fry (born January 16, 1921). Modesta had eight children, five girls and three boys. Modesta's son, Gilbert Merle, died October 1977, in a motorcycle accident just a month before his 21st birthday. Of Modesta's children, Robin and Adrianna (she prefers to be called Adrian and spells it so) were raised by Dora. Flo(rence) Peone Fry raised Gloria Jean (who prefers Jeannie), Modesta's mother-in-law. James Thomas, Juanita Marie, Gilbert Merle, Mary Francis and Ray Anthony were all raised in their parents' home. Dora lived just a short distance from her daughter for many years.

Dora must have been 17 or 18 when she married John(nie) Adolph, a Colville Indian. Dora told me they used to drink and "drinking is hard on a marriage." They divorced when John started beating Dora when they were drinking. I don't know the period here, but my mother tells me she doesn't remember her father being in the home. After the divorce, Dora lived with a man called Willie Stransgar for a few years. Modesta liked Willie. He made toys for her and her brother using pieces of wood and cans. Times were hard and they didn't buy any toys from the store.

This was the Depression era. Modesta and her brother were little kids during this time. Dora took jobs planting and weeding the neighbors' gardens, washing their clothes, etc. There wasn't much money around and Mom recalls her mother bringing home sacks of vegetables in payment. One story is quite funny, I'll share it here. At this time Maggie was married and had two daughters. Dora had always been afraid of cows. Dora and Maggie were passing their neighbor's place when Maggie saw the milk cow in the pasture. They went home, got a bucket and went to the pasture. Maggie caught the cow and had Dora hold on to it so Maggie could milk the cow in it. Dora said the cow didn't care that they were taking her milk and she was friendly for a cow. They never did tell the neighbor they stole milk for their kids.

Dora's second husband was Al Picard (Colville Indian). They were married a few years and drinking became a problem in this relationship too. This would have been during the late 1930's to early 1940's, I don't know the exact time.

Dora's third and last marriage was to Elmer Desautel (Spokane Indian). They had periods of separation but never divorced and drinking was also a problem in their marriage. Dora had stopped drinking in the late 1940's, I don't know the exact time. Nevertheless, I do recall a time, during the summer, of Gram being drunk. There were just Jeannie and I, so that must have been around 1948 or 1949. Our brother wasn't born yet. Elmer continued to drink and I remember the quarrels they had because of the drinking. Dora wouldn't let him in the house to drink or come home drunk. They were apart more than they were together. Elmer died in Colville, Washington at the hospital in August 1975. Elmer was born in 1898. Dora didn't go to his funeral. It took place on the Spokane Reservation, she didn't seem to care that he died and she wasn't going to "go that far to attend his funeral." She never did go visit his grave or any of the previous husbands' burial places. She outlived them all.

Dora liked making quilts and she made many for family and friends. Each grandchild had quilts from her. I still have a couple of tops she gave me and said, when I received them, that I could put them together when I have time. Meaning to finish them, which includes the top, batting and lining. Dora taught me to sew. She would tell me stories about the boarding school and how they taught. Dora learned to crochet at the school. During Lent, which is the Catholic Church time of penitence and fasting, Dora would have little sewing projects for me to do. Growing up, Lent was a time for sewing. She also learned to crochet and in the evening she would crochet lace on the pillowcases, dish towels and some of the wash clothes. One year, I must have been about seven or eight, Dora took a gingerbread man cookie cutter and traced the image on flour sack towels. I learned to embroider by working on these every evening. Another Lenten time, I embroidered a set of pillowcases that had flowers and ribbons in the design. She would then crochet lace on these pillowcases. Dora showed me how to make clothes. She had an old Singer treadle sewing machine. All the quilts she made were sewn on this machine. I learned how to sew using it. Dora taught me how make patterns and how to dress my cats. I had a doll, but dressing my cats was more fun. Learning how to finish buttonholes, cuffs and collars, French seams, how to line jackets/coats. I had very well dressed cats. She taught me how sleeves with cuffs must look when finished and how a placket must look. Dora took a strip of cloth and cut a row of slits and I learned how to put in a placket that had no puckers and was even. It took about seven or eight plackets until I could do one with no mistakes. If I did one that didn't pass her inspection, I had to remove all the stitches carefully and do it over again until it looked nice. My cats were not impressed by the pains that were taken in making their fine wardrobe that fit in shoe boxes. The boarding school did teach Dora a lot of skills in needlecraft which she loved to pass on to her daughter and grand-daughters.

Dora had an Indian accent when she talked. When I was growing up I never noticed it. After I had left home for college, my grandmother called me one time in the middle of the week to tell me some important news of family. When I heard her speak, I noticed the enunciation. Dora never pressed me to learn our Indian language. When I would ask about some words, she would tell me. She said what she spoke as a child wasn't quite the same as what was being used by Indians around Inchelium. Dora said that is what happens when there are too many languages to grow up with, they get mixed up.

Dora had an Indian name. My sister, Jeannie, said it had to do with a mother grizzly bear. I remember Uncle Jim would say, "How is Grizzle Bear?", when he would come to visit. And she would say, "Oh, fine". My grandmother's last years were spent in Inchelium, the town she came to as a young woman. She enjoyed telling stories about her childhood and the mischief that she and Maggie would get into. Robin and I heard only couple sad stories about the boarding school but most of them were about the fun she and Maggie had. When Dora's health started to fail due to the cancer, her mind went back to the past. She would ask about people she knew when she was young. She would ask how her cousin was doing. Maggie had preceded Dora by about twenty years.

Tony Mattina started coming to visit my grandmother and study the language from her. Dora told me, "I don't know why he would want to visit me. I'm not smart and I don't know all the words." She worried that Mr. Mattina would be wasting his time and the University's money talking to her. Dora looked forward to his visits and was happy that someone wanted to save the language.

My grandmother would be very happy that the work she did with Mr. Mattina will be shared with her Tribe. That her words will live on and be enjoyed by the language students of the Tribe and the Linguistics Department at the University of Montana. Yes, Gram would be very happy.

Adrian L. (Fry) Holm

August 23, 2000

PART I

INTRODUCTION

THE PEOPLE
THE RECORDING OF THE NARRATIVES
THE EDITING OF THE NARRATIVES
GRAMMATICAL NOTES
REFERENCES CITED

INTRODUCTION

THE PEOPLE. Speakers of Colville-Okanagan comprise several socio-political groups united by mutually intelligible dialects of a common language. The geographic area they occupy consists of the north-south expanse of the Okanagan valley in British Columbia from what is now Enderby through Kelowna, Penticton, Oliver and Osoyoos, and in Washington State through Oroville, Omak, and Okanogan; the Similkameen and Methow valleys in British Columbia and Washington State respectively; the north-south expanses of the Sanpoil and Kettle rivers, and the area west of the Columbia river as far as the bend around Wilbur, Washington. The details of the phonological and lexical differences between the various dialects remain to be spelled out, but the widespread movement of individuals and families within the Colville-Okanagan territory, and similarly widespread intermarriage, make difficult the identification of discrete dialects. Dora Noyes DeSautel was born near the international border, and lived most of her adult life near Inchelium, Washington. Like many other Colville-Okanagans she adopted the local dialect variety.

THE RECORDINGS OF THE NARRATIVES. I began working with Dora Noyes DeSautel[1] in 1970, my third summer in Inchelium. I had been introduced to Dora by Madeline DeSautel. The first recording I have of Dora DeSautel is a conversation, much of it in English, some of it in Colville, with two other participants, Madeline, and Pete Seymour. That took place in Madeline's house, Seylor Valley Road, the afternoon of June 16, 1970. The conversation served as a warm up, after which Dora told five stories, four cəpcaptík^{w}ɬ (myths, legends--singular captík^{w}ɬ) and an ethnographic account.[2] The titles she gave to the four cəpcaptík^{w}ɬ are: Skunk & Fisher; Coyote, Bear, & Kingfisher; Frog & Crane; and Coyote, Muskrat, & Bear.

A year and a month later, on July 14, 1971 I recorded part I of her version of a European tale, which she called The Three Boys. She finished her narrative six days later, on July 20, 1971. That same day she told me and I recorded her versions of three more cəpcaptík^{w}ɬ: Coyote Juggles His Eyes; Chipmunk & Grandma Rabbit; and Two Girls & Their Uncle. The last one is a long narrative that incorporates several Colville mythic episodes.

I did not return to Inchelium for any extended periods in 1972 or 1973. I spent the summer of 1974 there, transcribing, mostly with Madeline

---

[1] All the while I knew her, she was known to me simply as Dora DeSautel.

[2] The ethnographic account, and two versions of a European tale will be part of an anthology of Colville authors that I hope to complete in the next few years.

DeSautel, but also with Dora, tapes that I had recorded in previous years. I recorded very little that summer, but on June 21, 1974, I did tape Dora's last captíkʷɬ Mosquito; on June 27 I taped the second version of the narrative she called The Three Boys; and on August 7 I taped another brief text of European origin, the story of a girl whose hands are chopped off by her father at the instigation of the jealous step-mother.

I transcribed the recordings of Dora's narratives either with Dora's help, or, more commonly, with Madeline DeSautel's help. We finished the transcriptions of the first two stories in 1971 (Coyote Juggles His Eyes, and Chipmunk & Grandma Rabbit), and of the others in 1974 and 1975.

This collection contains the eight cəpcaptíkʷɬ she recorded, hence the title I have given it, Dora's Legends, and keeps them in the order in which she recorded them: four narratives recorded in 1970 (Skunk & Fisher; Coyote, Bear, & Kingfisher; Frog & Crane; and Coyote, Muskrat, & Bear); three narratives recorded in 1971 (Coyote Juggles His Eyes; Chipmunk & Grandma Rabbit; Two Girls and Their Uncle); and the narrative recorded in 1974 (Mosquito). The CD that accompanies this collection contains all the stories, each in a track. The order of the tracks differs from the order of the printed stories as follows: the first story in the book is the last track of the CD. This is because when I recorded Skunk and Fisher the microphone malfunctioned, and the quality of that recording is poor. Because I don't want the CD to start with a defective track, I put it at the end, after the others. Otherwise the order of the tracks on the CD matches the printed stories. The length of each track is indicated in the notes that accompany the free translations, along with a synopsis of the story, and some brief explanations and mention of cognate versions that can be found in the ethnographic literature.

THE EDITING OF THE NARRATIVES. Free translations of all the texts are provided. These diverge from the interlinear translations that Madeline DeSautel and I worked out during the transcription of the tapes only in minor ways--an occasional pronoun change, an (English) grammatical correction, a choice of words. We have chosen to add nothing that is not in the original, and the translations are not always easy to follow. Some editors have proposed that elaborations and explanations incorporated in the story correlate with the fieldworker's acquaintance with the culture ("the less the fieldworker knows, the more information will be explicit" Dauenhauer and Dauenhauer 1999:7), and if this principle is at work in Dora's narratives then I must have been entirely inconspicuous, and Madeline the sole audience. The same editors also propose a corollary correlation, that while "outsiders tend to find the versions with most explanation and detail to be most satisfying and coherent[, f]rom the indigenous point of view, the best versions are the most laconic" (ibid.). The appreciation of Dora's texts hinges crucially on the familiarity one has with Colville culture. What John Updike said about the reaction of one unfamiliar with the Tibetan pantheon arrayed on a *thank-la*, can also be said about these texts of those unfamiliar with Colville: "We do not know the language, the code of mythology and tradition, and feel oppressively confused ... while an equally populous mural of, say, the Last Judgment or the battle of Waterloo quickly sorts itself out. There is always a code, and oral narrative disconcertingly assumes that we know it" (1984:119). The texts provide an entry into the Colville world, and in this volume I provide some general information and some annotations that should help readers begin to enter this unfamiliar world.

The world of the captík"ł is populated by animal people, monsters, and animated objects such as combs and paint powder. It is Coyote's task to rid the world of monsters, and he has been given special powers to accomplish this task. Some creatures have special powers such as that of transforming themselves into other creatures or instantly transporting themselves to other places, of dying and resurrecting. Creatures are not all good or all bad. Strange events take place, such as magic disembowlments and removals of anuses. Elements such as snot and feces can be turned into creatures and even ingredients for food. All these facts are recoverable from the texts, as are the attributes and characteristics of the animal people: Magpie is a tattletale; Frog is ugly but makes a good wife; Coyote is horny, foolish, selfish, conceited, and a destroyer of man-eaters; Gopher is Coyote's pitiful wife.

The free translations of Dora's cəpcaptík"ł comprise the next section, each following my introductory synopsis. Readers who want to get a sense of what these stories are like should read the translations more than once. I have annotated them to the extent that I think necessary for their literal understanding, and any interpretive errors therein are solely mine.[3] The numbers in parentheses, in increments of five, correspond to the numbers that precede each utterance in the interlinearized texts.

SKUNK AND FISHER (7m:38s). Dora narrated this and the next three stories on June 16, 1970. This is the story of a grandmother who sends two granddaughters to be Fisher's wives. Fisher is a good hunter and a desirable husband. When the women arrive at Fisher's, Skunk, who lives with Fisher, tries to take advantage of the fact that Fisher is away hunting, and take the women as his own wives. The women cleverly reject him, and when Fisher finds out what has happened, a struggle ensues between the two men, in which Skunk manages to kill Fisher. The women again find ways of rejecting Skunk, and trap him under a boulder. Skunk manages to free himself by quartering himself and throwing out each body piece, and then reassembling his body pieces and reconstituting himself. He does so, except for his anus, which has been plucked by Raven and taken elsewhere. Skunk then looks for his anus, finds it, reinstalls it, and tries to spray everyone with it, managing only to spray Raven.

(1) There were people, an old lady, and her grandchildren [granddaughters], Squirrel and Chipmunk. The grandmother said to them, "go

---

[3] Unless otherwise indicated the annotations are Mattina's.

to Fisher's[4]." (5) It's not far from there. They started to go. They went and they got there, but there was nobody there. There were two food caches, (10) one cache over there. And one stinks, but the other doesn't. And they were going to crawl in there.

Skunk[5] came back, going piqʷ, and Chipmunk started to laugh.[6] Skunk went to the cache, and they were sitting there. He grabbed them, and they tickled him. They tickled him and he laughed. (20) He rolled around there, and then he said "I'm tired." He put them there in the cache. He put their legs up just like they had good knees.[7] Then Fisher got back. He said to his friend, "you haven't cooked." (25) "You're not my boss that I cook for you!" And Fisher cooked and they ate. He was alone.

The next daylight his partner [Fisher] said, "I'm going back hunting." (30) He took a rock and threw it. Roll, roll, roll, roll, he's gone.[8] He [Skunk] brought out his women. They tickled him, and he laughed. (35) And then he said "I'm going to follow my partner." And Fisher was hiding outside the door. He followed behind Skunk. Fisher was sitting there, and he took his women. (40) They said to him, "we were coming for you, but then he took us." They came out, went outside the house. And they burned the house. (45) Gee it burned.

Skunk was already over on top. He looked, and gee the fire! He ran down the hill. "Goodness my women, goodness my women." (50) He ran, got there, there was nothing. It was all burned. He cried, and looked around for tracks. They sprinkled ashes on the tracks, and he tracked them. (55) He went to st'aʔt'aʔpústn.[9] They say that long time ago there is water there. He tipped his head to drink, and there were people there,[10] sitting on the rock. He sprayed them. (60) He [Skunk] did something to him [Fisher], he [Fisher] fell down and died. And he took his women.

He asked [Chipmunk], "where is your house?" She said, "in that stump." He said, "it's too small." (65) He asked Squirrel, "where is your house?" She said, "in that split rock." He said, "over there is OK." (70) They crawled in there. As soon as they went in there they tickled him.[11] They tickled him a long time, and Skunk went to sleep. (75) They slept and in the morning he woke up.

He was pinched in the rock because Ground Squirrel had done that. And he said, "move over a little bit." He said, "move over

---

[4] To be his wives. Fisher is a good hunter.

[5] Skunk and Fisher, both men, live together.

[6] They were supposed to wait quietly until Fisher got back.

[7] I don't know what this means, and I didn't think of asking.

[8] He's pretending to have gone hunting, but he's hiding and watching.

[9] The name of a place.

[10] He sees their reflection.

[11] To put him to sleep and get him pinched under the rock.

Chipmunk.[12]" But nothing, because the rock was there. (80) He looked around, the women were gone, there is only rock. He can't get out, the rock has him pinched. He broke his foot.[13] There is a little hole there,[14] and he threw it outside, (85) with his hand and his foot. And Stink Bug.[15] He threw that too. As soon as he threw it Raven flew by. He saw that, and wondered what it was. (90) He grabbed it and he left.[16] He [Skunk] got his body out; there was no Stink Bug, just a hole. He took some grass, went like that, and put it in that hole.[17]

(95) He went looking for them. He said, "they are dancing at Addy." So he went there. He went, and it took him a while to get there. Those gathered there are all sitting, (100) gathered, those that are going to dance. The chickadees, everything there, it's full of people. Maybe the Magpies too. (106) They were examining that Stink Bug.[18] One would take it, and pass it to somebody else, they all looked at it. Then he [Skunk] came. He said, "plug all the holes, (110) the air might go out of my story, I have a story, it might ooze out." They plugged the holes. He said, "plug them tight, tight. My story is very good, and it might ooze out." (115) They plugged the holes good and tight. He said, "I came, I came, I came down." He did like that, turned around. That Stink Bug was stuck in the anus, and it squirted out. (120) Then he turned a bit, and he said, "I came, I came, I came down.[19]" They ran, the deer ran out, everyone ran, ran away.[20] (125) Raven is laying there, he has a big nose. The air went in his nose, as he lay there. He said, "cut it off, cut it off!" Nobody paid attention to him, (130) they all ran away. He thought if they cut his nose off then he won't smell that. And that's the end of the story.

The story is remarkably similar to the story told by Michel Brooks in the summer of 1930, collected by W. B. C. [Walter Cline?] and published in Spier 1938, pp. 210-212. According to Spier "Michel Brooks, Southern Okanagon, aged 55, was born of a Canadian mother (Northern Okanagon ?). He remembers the old life as a little boy. His father and grandfather told him much of the old ways" (Spier 1938, p. 4).

---

[12] Skunk thought it was the girl sleeping close to him.

[13] To free himself.

[14] This is his anus. Skunk is tearing his body apart piece by piece and throwing it outside the cave.

[15] This probably refers to the anus.

[16] Skunk has just lost his anus.

[17] In place of the anus.

[18] Skunk's anus.

[19] Skunk gets his anus back, but it's not clear how to me.

[20] Those who couldn't run away would be sprayed and die.

COYOTE, BEAR, & KINGFISHER (6m:29s). This was the second of four stories narrated June 16, 1970. Coyote visits Bear. To feed his guest, Bear harmlessly cuts off his wife's breast, and seasons it with feces. The food is delicious. Then Coyote visits Kingfisher who dives in the river and procures fish with which he feeds his guest. Bear visits Coyote who tries to replicate what Bear had done to feed him, but fails and hurts his wife instead. Bear scolds him that he should not try to adopt someone else's ways. Kingfisher visits Coyote who tries to replicate what Kingfisher had done to feed him. He tries to dive, but lands on the ice and dies, making himself pitiful in the process. Kingfisher provides fish for Coyote's family, and Coyote seems to remain unaware of his foolish attempts to be who he isn't and do what he can't.

(1) There are people. Coyote and Gopher and their children, four boys. And they have names, I don't know them. (5) Squirted Legs, and Yellow Legs, and Straight Legs. These are his children from Gopher.

They were sitting around, and Coyote said: "I'm going to go to my brother Bear." And he went. (10). He went, got there, sat down and he said to her, Bear told his wife, "you better feed your visitor." She said, "and what'll I feed him, I haven't got anything." Then he took his knife, sharp; (15) he walked over to his wife, took her [breast] and cut it off. He put his hands on the ashes, did like that, and it was healed.

He put that down there. He started to cook it in the bucket, a pot. He put it in the water, and boiled it. (20) He put things in the water, saskatoons, things, he shat in there. He put it there, and Coyote said, "I'm not going to eat any of that, it's too..." He [Bear] turned around, and he [Coyote] put his finger there easy and sucked. Goodness, it's good. (25) He ate and ate, and then Bear said to him, "take the rest back to your children." He went back. He went and gave it to Gopher and they ate.

A few days after that he said: (30) "I'm going over to my brother Kingfisher." So he went to Kingfisher. He went and got there and Kingfisher said, "feed your visitor." She said, "and what?" He said, "the water is near, fish." (35) So he flew high on top of his tipi, he flew from there. He went c'arrrrr,[21] he jumped in the water.

In a while she told his children, "go help your father with the fish." The boys went out and they helped him. They put the fish down. (40) She cooked and she fed them. She didn't do anything to some. She cooked just some. They got done eating and Kingfisher said: "it's best you take this to your children." (45) Then Coyote went back home.

They were sitting down, and they looked there. Gee, Bear was coming. Bear came in. Coyote said to her: (50) "give your visitor something to eat." And Gopher said, "and what'll I feed him?" He took

---

[21] The sound Kingfisher makes.

the knife and did that[22] to Gopher. And it's nothing but her skin. He went like that and cut it. (55) She hollered, "alalalala, I'm afraid!" She fell on her back, fainted. He [Bear] told him [Coyote], "leave her alone, you're abusing your [wife]." And he [Bear] cut it [his own] and put down the ...[23]; He put his hand on the ashes, did like that, and it healed. He said, "I'm going back home." (60) And Bear went back. He said, "that's our way of doing things.[24]" He went back. Coyote said, "that's what we wanted to do..." (65) They ate, they fixed it and cooked it.

A few days later he looked, gee! Kingfisher is coming. He grabbed his children; he tied their hair up.[25] (70) He tied all of them. Gopher didn't have any hair; just a little, and he did like that and tied it. Gee, she has big cheek pockets; and that thing tied there. (75) He got there, and he said, "you better cook." She said, "I don't have anything." Coyote climbed the tent pole. He climbed and went c'arrrr. (80) He climbed and looked, and sure enough; the water is far and he doesn't know [how]. He jumped and fell on the ice. Not in the water, but here on the ...; he fell on this side. (85) He fell on the ice. He passed out.

They waited and waited, and then she told her children, "go look." They went there. (90) They looked. He was lying on the ice. They took him by the arms and dragged him to his house. And that yellow that you see on the ice, it's yellow; must be pee. (95) That's where he fell.

Kingisher flew there. He flew and kicked the ice and went under. He grabbed a bunch, and lay them down. (100) He went back home. Coyote was lying there. Then he came to, cleared up. He looked, gee there is lots of fish there. He said, "that's what we wanted to do...[26]" (105) Gopher started to cook. That's all, the end of the story.

Several versions of either or both of these episodes in which Coyote tries to imitate Bear's and Kingfisher's ways can be found. See, for example, "Bungling Host" told by Cecile Brooks in the summer of 1930, collected by May Mandelbaum, and published in Spier 1938, pp. 233-234, which is a variant of the Kingfisher episode of the present tale. We are told that "Cecile Brooks, about 58 years old, was born at the time of the great earthquake (1872 ?). Wife of Michel Brooks[27] by the levirate. (Her first husband had been a cousin of Michel's and a son of Lucy Joe's.) Kalispel by birth, but married into the Kartar branch of the Okanagon at a rather early age (about fourteen). There got rather full technological training as well as some insight into the functioning of the social and religious order, and traditions about the tabus of menstruation and so forth, which were for the

---

[22] Cut her breast off.
[23] Not clear.
[24] Implying Coyote shouldn't try to imitate him.
[25] To make them look like Kingfisher's children.
[26] He doesn't realize Kingfisher got the fish.
[27] See the previous text.

most part no longer practiced. Very able and intelligent. Distinguished very carefully between customs of the Okanagon and those she knew of the Kalispel." (Spier 1938, p. 4). Another version of the Kingfisher episode is "Bungling Host" in Ray 1933, pp. 177-78. The version that most resembles Dora's is "Coyote Imitates Bear and Kingfisher" (Mourning Dove 1933, pp. 223-228).

FROG & CRANE (2m:56s). This was the third story told on June 16, 1970, and is the story of a woman deemed undesirable who finds a husband. Crane is a desirable man, and women regularly offer themselves to him. He sends each away, and as each departs, she is given a basket of gifts by Crane's grandmother, with whom he apparently lives. Frog, warty, fat, and bow-legged, offers herself to Crane, who takes her. This narrative may be a variant of "Crane and Louse" told by Michel Brooks,[28] and collected by W. B. C. [Walter Cline ?] (Spier 1938, p. 237). The editor ends the tale with the annotation that "Michel had forgotten the rest of the story, but says that Crane finally got a louse for a wife."

(1) There were people. They were there, not just a few, lots, a group, lots of them. There were pretty women, girls. (5) They get ready, bathe and comb their hair, and then they go there [to Crane].[29] To Crane, yes. They go there and Crane has a grandmother there. They get there, and they go there, and they go in.

She [the grandmother] started bundling up dry meat and things. (10) As soon as she [the girl] comes out, she gives it to her, and she leaves again. And then another one arrives, and she goes in. A little while she comes out. "k^wára k^wára grandmother.[30]" He sends them away. (15) The women are all gone. He refuses all. Then Frog goes there. She has braids, and she's fat and ugly. (20) She's bow legged and has a big belly. She went over there and said... The women laughed and they said, "what is she going to do over there?" She went and got there and said to the old lady, (25) "where is Crane?" She said, "over there." So she went in there. She was there, and the old lady got the meat and wrapped it. She said, "she'll be there a while, and any time she'll come back out." (30) But she was gone a long time. Then it was morning. Sure enough he took Frog.

So Crane told them. He woke up and came out, looked around the camp. (35) All the people are awake. He said, "k^wára k^wára I'm going to the head of the circle and stay there.[31]" Frog stayed there, stayed there for good. He took her. (40) And that's why Crane likes Frog and eats them.

---

[28] See "Skunk and Fisher".

[29] To offer themselves as wives.

[30] I think this anticipates the noise that Frog makes (sw'arák'xən).

[31] I don't know why Crane would say that.

COYOTE, MUSKRAT, & BEAR (10m:25s). This is the last of the four narratives Dora tape recorded June 16, 1970. A man-eater has killed the four sons Coyote has from Gopher. Muskrat, Coyote's son not by Gopher, offers to avenge their deaths, and does, killing Grizzly's daughter. Coyote gloats over Muskrat's success, and Grizzly seeks out Coyote to exact her own revenge. With the help of his special powers Coyote eludes Grizzly who remains scorned.

(1) Coyote lived there with his children. He has four children from Gopher, and one is his distant child, whachamacallit Muskrat. His sons, boys, (5) would go and they'd get to Grizzly.[32] When the boys get there she motions to her daughter,[33] "go on." The daughter goes across the creek, (10) she goes on a little hill. She goes there, and the boy, Coyote's son, goes by there. She bites them on the head, she kills them. And the old lady always fixes[34] the arrow heads with things, (15) with anything, with bark, and puts it there. And they'd be shooting with bark; The four of them, yes.

(20) Muskrat told his father, "I am going, because she has killed my brothers." His father said to him, "don't go, it's too [dangerous]. Don't, you're the only [son I have] left," Coyote cried. (25) He went. He stuck arrow heads in his belt, and he left the rest stuck on the arrows. He went and the old lady said to him, "put those there." (30) He leaned them outside and went in. Her daughter was sitting there, she [her mother] told her, "go on now." Then she went out.

She went across the stream and climbed the hill. She told him "go, look there. (35) Go kill that [bear] for a rug for me to lie on. Go kill it." Muskrat went out and took his arrows. He looked at them, it's just bark. He threw them away. (40) He took them [the good arrow heads], and put them there. He went. She said, "go from below. You'll shoot and he [the bear] will roll down." He didn't pay any attention to her. He crossed and went up the hill. (45) He got on top, from above, and did like that. He looked at her. She smiled, and he shot her. He skinned her and cut her head off. Then he went back, and crossed back there on the boat.

(50) He threw the hide there, "take your rug." He had her head stuck under his arm. He jumped in the water, dived in and swam across. He went and got to his father and said: (55) "take that girl's head." Coyote took it, and he poked it with something, a stick, and hung it up. He put pitch on the fire, and it started to burn. It was black. (60) He was monkeying around laughing, and that's when the mother went inside,

---

[32] The boy wants to propose for the daughter.
[33] She is going be used as bait. She disables the visitor's arrow points, turns into a grizzly, and kills the man.
[34] The line says that the old lady disables the arrow points, but it's the daughter who does so as she goes out.

right in the house. Gee, her daughter's head is there, getting black. She's
going to kill Coyote. Coyote said p'əs p'əs p'əs kʷƛ'up, p'əs p'əs
p'əs kʷƛ'up, p'əs p'əs p'əs kʷƛ'up.[35] (65) They grabbed Grizzly, and
he [Coyote] took the stick to stir the fire with and stuck her in the
bottom with that poker. They [his powers] said "hurry up, we are
getting dry, we're going to let go." Coyote ran away. (70) He ran, and
Grizzly is chasing him. They went. He said [to his powers], "hurry up,
hurry up! I want to be a thornbush, a thornbush." So he turned into a
thornbush. [The bear] came running. The thorn bush scratched her
thighs. (75) She went down, went like that. Coyote is standing there,
"wa··, wa, wa, wa. I scratched Grizzly's ass." "a·· now I'm going to kill
you." She started to climb, she went up the hill, Coyote's gone. (80)
There is a little hill there, and he went around there. He said, "hurry
up!" He did his magic, p'əs p'əs kʷƛ'up. There he made the ... There
were some women pit cooking something. She went around, and there
were some women. (85) She [Grizzly] said, "have you seen Coyote?"
They said "no, we've been cooking here. Come and eat." She said,
"no!" She didn't know what to do, then she said OK, and she went over
there, and she ate. (90) She did that to her dress; She put things there,
she stuffed it. She went on.

She's full and she walks slowly. She did that, they're gone, there is
nobody. (95) Coyote was standing there, "wa··, wa, wa, wa. That was
my dung and you ate it." She did like that, gee, her mouth is full. She
did like that, and she threw it away. (100) It's all shit. She said to him,
"now for sure I'm going to kill you." She chased him again. She chased
him, and there is a hole in the ground, something lives there, I guess.
Coyote jumped in there. (105) He jumped in there and stayed there and
then she came. She did like that, and went there, and sat there by the
hole. She felt her dress. She sat there doing like that. Coyote went like
that, she still sat there. (110) She won't leave. [You could hear] the
people, saying "come, come, we're going to move. We're going to
move, come." The dogs started to bark. (115) She was listening. I guess
that's his place down there. She said, "that must be his house there."
She left, walked away. Coyote crawled out (120) and ran to his house.
She chased Coyote, and was about to catch him. He turned into
something, thorn bushes. And he scratched her thighs. (125) She said
"that's just like Coyote. If I knew that was Coyote I'd go in and bite his
head. I am too ashamed. Maybe it's somebody else." He said, "she
chased me, and was going to kill me." (130) He went around a little
hill.

There were women there pit cooking.[36] She ate there. That's only
Coyote's shit she ate. "If I knew that was him I'd kill him, I'd bite his
head." (135) If she bites his head he'd die.

---

[35] He is calling his powers.
[36] The narrator is repeating the end of the story.

A version of this story is "Coyote and Grizzly-Bear," published in Boas 1917, pp. 79-80. James A. Teit, who edited the story, tells us that it was "related by Red-Arm (KwElkwElta'xEn). He was an old man who belonged to Nespelim, which is also the name of the western division of the Sanpoil. He was related to the Okanagon, and frequently came as far north as the head of Okanagon Lake. He said the stories he related were common to the Nespelim and Lower Okanagon of Okanagon River, and he thought probably to all the Sanpoil; i.e., to the Sanpoil tribe, and to that part of the Okanagon tribe on the Okanagon River, particularly those living in the United States" (Boas 1917, p. 65.). I also recorded Pete Seymour's version of the story on August 8, 1968, and that story awaits publication in a separate collection of Seymour's *captíkʷɬ*.

COYOTE JUGGLES HIS EYES (6m:01s). This is the first of three stories Dora told on July 20, 1970. In this story as Coyote is juggling his eyes Raven steals them and leaves him blind. Coyote stumbles around until he distracts a bird, gouges out his eyes and puts them in his own eye sockets regaining his eyesight. The bird's grandmother outfits the boy with kinnickkinnick berry eyes, and he, too, regains his sight. Coyote wantonly kills some baby pheasants and moves on. Wherever Coyote goes people transform themselves and otherwise shun him. Eventually the pheasants' parents avenge their babies' deaths by killing Coyote. Coyote remains dead about a year, when his cousin Fox brings him back to life by stepping over his remains. He comes back to life claiming to have been asleep, while Fox insists he's been dead.

(1) Coyote was going. He took his eyes out and he threw them up in the air. And he said, 'come back in' and his eyes came back in. (5) Then Raven flew by and he took his eyes. He [Coyote] said, "slip in!" and nothing happened. He was blind. He was going, walking around any old place, to the water, (10) to the creek, he didn't find anything. There was brush, and he asked it, "what are you?" It told him, "I am a grey willow." (15) And he said, "I'm getting close to the river." Then he went on, and there was brush. He said, "what are you?" It told him, "I am a rose bush." "My, I am not near the water." (20) He traveled on, there was some more brush. He said, "what are you?" It said, "I am a red willow." Well, now I'm near the water." And he fell in the water, and he drank.

(25) There was a bird flying around there. He said, "come here you little boy. Look at the stars, the little stars." He looked up high. The boy came and then said, "where?" (30) "Look there up high." He looked there, and he [Coyote] gouged his eyes out. Then he put them in his own eyes. And the boy started crying, and he ran away, and he cried. And Coyote went on.

(35) Then the boy's grandmother said to him, "come here, I'll make you some eyes from these kinnickkinnick berries, I'll give them to you." And that's why his eyes are red.

(40) Coyote went, and there were baby pheasants running around there, in their tipi, their house. Coyote got there, and he asked them, "where are your father and your mother?" (45) And he said, "gone, they've left." He scraped the cinders away, and put the little birds there on the fire, the little ones. They died. And he put them.[37]

(50) He went on. He went to another living place, and went in. There was nothing there but combs lying around there, because the people had turned themselves into combs. He took one, and was going out, but there are people there. (55) They combed him, gee he hollered, and threw the comb away. Then he went on. He went into a little living place. He went in there. (60) My, nothing but rouge powder. He took some, started picking it out, and did like this [she motions rubbing as if to rub out the color]. These other People had turned themselves into baby painting powder.[38] "I'll take this one." (65) He stuck it under his clothes. He was just about to leave when they grabbed him and threw him on the ground. They shat on him. They shat on him, and that upset his stomach. (70) Then he threw up, and then he went on.

He went up a little hill. Well, lo and behold, the birds that had the baby chicks had come back, and their children were dead. They went. (75) They went up that little trail, and there they hid.[39] The man told her, "I'll whack him on the head with the wing. If he won't fall off the rock then you whack him with the wing. (80) Then he'll fall off and die." Then they went there. Coyote was coming along, he wasn't thinking. All of a sudden the bird flew (85) and whacked him on the head. "Goodness," he said, "I pretty near fell." He had just said that when he got whacked by the mother. Then he fell over the bank, he fell down, and died.

He lay there, maybe it was a year that he lay there. (90) His older brother came by there, some relative, maybe Fox. His partner came by. He gathered the remains that were scattered about, and the hair. He gathered them, and piled them up. Then he stepped over them. Coyote woke up. (95) Goodness, "I lay here, and I fell asleep. I've been stuck." He [his partner] told him, "you haven't been asleep, you were dead." "No, I've been sleeping." He told him, "look, these are your worms, they're still crawling around." Then they went away. (100) That's all I know. Do you know more?

---

[37] Not clear.

[38] This is Madeline DeSautel's comment.

[39] They want to ambush Coyote.

This tale includes the motif that is called "the eye juggler"[40]. The published Colville version I am familiar with is Mourning Dove's more complete story of how Coyote loses and regains his eyes, which she also titled "Coyote Juggles His Eyes" (Mourning Dove 1933, pp. 141-147).

CHIPMUNK & GRANDMA RABBIT (7m:48s). This is second of three stories Dora told July 20, 1970, and may be the best known of all the Colville myths. Chipmunk, who lives with his grandmother, goes berry picking. A giant man-eater sees him and wants to eat him. Chipmunk barely escapes and runs to his grandmother who hides him under a clam shell. Giant follows him, finds him thanks to Meadowlark's tattle-taling, and eats him. The grandmother gathers Chipmunk's remains, brings him back to life, and plans to take revenge on Giant. As if to oblige, Giant returns to admire the grand-mother's light skin. Giant is promised that he, too, can have light skin, if he jumps into a fired fueled by pitch. Giant falls for the ruse, is kept in the fire with some poles, and dies. His eyes pop out and turn into Owl, a mere scarecrow who frightens children but is otherwise harmless.

(1) There lived Rabbit and her grandson Chipmunk. In the morning Chipmunk went out and picked kinnickkinnick berries. He picked and said, "one berry ripe, (5) two berries ripe, three berries ripe." Then something broke, he heard it break, he did like that, looked there, and he saw Giant coming over. He climbed on a tree. He threw away the berries he'd picked (10) and climbed on a tree there.

Giant came closer and said to him, "come here, come over here, my little nephew." And the Chipmunk said, "ah, ah, I don't have any uncle!" "Come here, my grandchild." (15) And the Chipmunk said, "ah, ah, I have no grandma." It did no good to say things. Then Chipmunk said [to Giant], "take your basket, and cover your head with it; then I'll come down." (20) So Giant covered up its head. He [Chipmunk] said, "keep it covered, I am coming down." He came down, ran away, was gone. He was going to go over there, but he got scratched by Giant. He got scratched on his back.

(25) Then [Giant] sucked on his hands, "this boy is really good meat!" Chipmunk got away, ran to his grandma. (30) He way saying, "sna? sna? sna?." He must have been trying to say snína?. She picked up a clam shell that was lying there, and covered him. She hid him there, and said to him, (35) "you hide there, don't come out." She hid him there under a pillow.[41] Then Meadowlark landed there, and she [the grandma] told her, "don't tell, don't say anything, don't tell [Giant]. (40) I'll give you this medallion." She put the medallion on Meadowlark, who stayed there. Then that Giant got there. He asked, "did that little boy get here?" She [grandma] told him, "no, I haven't seen him."

---

[40] Motif J1423 in Thompson 1955.
[41] Not clear whether it was a clam shell or a pillow.

(45) Meadowlark said, "the clam shell." There it lay. [Giant] opened that clam shell, sure enough the boy way lying there. He took him and said,[42] "what do you like, cousin?" (50) She said, "the leg." "What do you like, cousin?" She said, "the arm." "What do you like, cousin?" She said, "the little leg." (55) "What do you like, cousin?" "The arm." "What do you like, cousin?" She said, "the body." "What do you like, cousin?" (60) She said, "the head." "What do you like, cousin?" "The ears." Then he took the heart and he swallowed it, "nˤam nˤam nˤam, (65) this boy tastes good." Then he quit, he left.

The old lady cried. She gathered up the hands, feet, everything. She took the kinnickkinnick berries and made a heart for him. (70) She stepped over him, and he got well. Meadowlark flew. "Give back that locket, don't you take that, you tattle tale." She left, flew away. She [grandma] told the boy, "you keep hiding, (75) don't pick berries any more. I am going to kill this Giant." Then Giant came back, and said, "gee, but you are white, my friend. How come you're so white?" (80) She said, "because I gathered pitch from bark and wood pitch, then I dug a big hole and I put that [pitch] there, I set it on fire, and I jumped in. Go get some of that pitch, (85) some gum pitch." He took his basket, put the pitch in it, and then he poured it in, and put the wood pitch on. It was a big hole. (90) Rabbit set it on fire and it started to burn. Rabbit jumped back and forth [over the fire]. She told him, "now you." "I might burn." (95) She said to him, "no, come, you'll get white." He jumped there, fell in. She told her grandson, "take that forked stick we made." They pushed him down, the boy also pushed down on his leg. (100) "náˑnənənənə, I am burning, náˑnənənə I am burning, friend." She told him, "no, you're going to be white. You'll jump in the creek and you'll be white like me." They poked him into the ground, and he died. (105) His eye popped out, and a bird flew from there and flew to tx̌ásəmqən Mountain, I don't know where; It flew to tx̌ásəmqən and lit there, and went "hm hm, hm hm." She said to him, "the next generation of People you'll be a scarecrow, owl." (110) The other of his eyes popped out. It lit on c'isəlín mountain. It went "hm hm, hm hm." She said to him, "when the next generation comes you'll be just a scarecrow." (115) That's it, that's all I know. The end of the story.

Published versions of this myth include "Chipmunk and the Cannibal Woman," told by Cecile Brooks, collected by May Mandelbaum, and published in Spier 1938, pp. 228-229. Mourning Dove's version of the story is titled "Chipmunk and Owl-Woman" (Mourning Dove 1933, pp. 51-59). A text that includes a variant of the present text is "Chipmunk, Coyote, and the

---

[42] Giant is dismembering the boy and giving out parts to eat, but I think Giant is eating them.

dangerous beings, Owl Sisters" told by William Burke in August 1930 and published in Ray 1933, pp. 165-67. A partial variant was collected by Marian K. Gould, titled "Chipmunk and Meadow-Lark" and published in Boas 1917, pp. 105-106. Also published, but without identification of its author, is "Owl and Chipmunk" (Coyote and the Colville, pp. 59-65). Another version (unpublished, to my knowledge) is that told in February or March of 1972 by Cecelia Condon, a Methow Colville then in her late sixties, and written down by Steve Mannenbach.[43]

TWO GIRLS & THEIR UNCLE (21m:27s). This is the third of three stories Dora told July 20, 1970. In this story two girls are instructed by their uncle, a hunter, not to look as they throw into the water animal bones and materials used in the butchering. The girls eventually violate the interdiction discovering that the bones had turned into beads. The uncle finds out and abandons the girls, notwithstanding the grandmother's sorrow. The grandmother also abandons them, and the girls embark on a journey that causes first one and then the other sister to become pregnant by abnormal means. Sea Gull impregnates the younger woman first, by giving her some food, which she eats in spite of her sister's warning not to. The older sister tells Sea Gull that he ought to take responsibility for his child and wife, and moves on, only to meet with her own abnormal impregnation. First Rabbit catches an unchaste glimpse of the woman, then his brother Lynx is exposed as the one who had fathered her child.[44] The people kill Lynx and abandon mother and child. Lynx's remains ask his wife to be gathered, stepped over, and covered until he can come back to life. Lynx comes back to life, hunts, and provides well for his family, while the group that had abandoned them has no luck, except for some meager successes of Rabbit. The people have hardly anything to eat and resort to stealing tallow, even, and try to conceal what little food they have. Lynx generously invites the group to return, and offers to feed everyone. The people return, gather, and

---

[43] At the time Mannenbach was a student in the Folklore Program at Indiana University. The manuscript is a term paper with detailed contextual information, including descriptions of the transcription process from a tape recorded text, and of the audience. Of some interest is the author's observation that "the number three reappears twice... In the sequel to the first tale, there are three sisters. Coyote ate three times ... Coyote used his power three times ... [and] spent 'about three months' in the badger hole. Other tale texts collected from this region also have the number three appearing many times. In one tale three trees appear ... In another tale, Coyote travels for three days, catches three salmon three times, and cuts the salmon into three parts ... The 'third day' and for 'three days' are periods of time suspension ... The number three appears to often act as a formula ..." (Mannenbach 1975, pp. 5-6). The number three also figures prominently in Mourning Dove 1933.

[44] This motif recurs in several Colville myths.

each holds the woman and Lynx's child. As they take turns holding the child, a pair of hands appears through the folds of the tent and asks to hold the child. The people comply, and the child is kidnapped and disappears. Lynx and his wife set out to find their son, and do so find him after a long period. He has been reared by a giant, here referred to as Ape. The boy and his parents conspire to kill Ape with the help of other creatures, and succeed. After Ape is killed the boy realizes how much he misses his adoptive mother, and by magic turns his natural mother into Robin, his natural father into Pheasant, and himself into Loon. Loon embarks on a journey of his own, and reaches some folks. He is covered with scabs, but a girl looks after him and he turns strong and desirable, with a full head of beautiful hair.

(1) There lived some people, a grandmother, two little girls, and their uncle. And when their uncle killed something he said to them, "take these bones and throw them in the water." (5) And they threw them in the water, and other things, fir boughs.[45] He said to them, "close your eyes when you throw the bones and the fir boughs in the water." That's when they butcher the meat. (10) "The fir boughs, throw them too in the water." And they threw them in the water. And they don't go where he told them not to go.

Then they grew up, (15) and they went there. Maybe they played in the water, and they saw them, goodness, jewels.[46] They took them. They made earrings and put necklaces on, (20) they played in all kinds of ways with them. Then their uncle saw them.[47] He told his mother, "I'm going to throw them away. They are big, yet they don't mind." (25) Then he went, he left. Little ways from there he went into the ground.[48]

They played there, and only their grandmother is still sitting there. They got back. (30) There was nothing else, all gone, nothing, they had moved, they went away. There was just she [the grandmother] sitting by the fire. She told them, "look, you are disobedient, and your uncle threw you away for ever, and now I'm going to leave too." (35) They cried, they said to her, "don't go," and they grabbed her. There was a rock lying there, and a hole there, and the old lady went under it. She fell in there. They started to go in there, (40) but she [a spider] brought them out and they went out. The grandmother must be a spider.

They were hanging around. The fire went out. They took whatever they had there, (45) and they left, they walked, went any old place. They went long ways, they camped, and started again. They went, and camped, and [went again]. Then Sea Gull must have seen them coming, (50) and he said to them, "go below and cross there." So they crossed

---

[45] Used when butchering.

[46] Beads.

[47] Saw that they had violated his interdiction.

[48] To a different place.

there. And the older sister said to her, "when he gives us things to eat, don't eat anything."

(55) They got there and Sea Gull said to them, "I'm cooking so you can eat." It's fat. And the oldest one didn't eat, but the young one dipped her finger in it (60) and she ate, she put it in her mouth. They stayed there a while, then they went. She said, "we are going to our aunt." Then they went, and there is a gulch there. The oldest one ran down and from there got on top to the other side. (65) She told her little sister, "hurry, come here." She ran down there, and at the bottom she sat down. Her baby went, "awáˁ, awáˁ." She had had a baby. The older sister ran down. (70) She told her, "now you stay here, don't go with me." She said, "come here Sea Gull, look, you got a baby." He said, "if it's a boy take care of it, but if it's a girl throw it in the water." (75) She said, "no, come here, that's your wife, take her."

She [the older sister] started to go. She went, and then she stepped over a log laying there. Rabbit said, "your sister-in-law's legs are white white.[49]" She hit him on the nose with her cane. (80) He put his hand on his nose, and ran away. Then she went on.

It took her a long time to get there. Her aunt was splitting wood outside the tipi. (85) She split it with a bone, a horn. She sat on the log. Her aunt couldn't split it,[50] then she saw her niece sitting on the log. (90) She took her in her house. She laced up the tipi. Her little sister had stayed at Sea Gull's for good. She stayed there, and all at once the older one got a baby. Goodness, her aunt got mad. (95) She was mad at her, she tore down the lacing.

She said to them,[51] "any time you come and hold the baby, and the baby goes, awá, awá, awá," she said, "whoever makes it stop crying (100) that must be his father." So they started holding the baby, all of them, the Bear, the Grizzly, the Coyote. Everybody held the baby. Then Rabbit held it, and for a little while it stopped,[52] and then it cried again. (105) And then it was Lynx's [turn]. Lynx held the baby and that's when it stopped [crying]. Then her aunt stripped her [niece]; she took her things, and she had nothing. (110) Her baby was there. And then they killed Lynx. They kicked him and he fell down. Then they rubbed him on the ground, and there is only his skin left. (115) Everything was laying there, they killed him. Bear came and he rubbed his feet, "because you got a baby."

He [Lynx] sat there, dead. And then the woman cried and cried. (120) and then Magpie came. She said, "oh my dear!" She took a patch of old moccasin and covered her up. Then Raven came and said, (125)

---

[49] He was hiding behind the log and caught an immodest glimpse of the girl.
[50] Not clear.
[51] She called a meeting of all the people to find out who the father was.
[52] Rabbit had some part in the events--his brother Lynx is the father.

"what's the matter?" Then he threw it[53] to one side, and Magpie said, "oh my dear." They stayed there a few days, (130) then that hair laying there[54] said, "gather me up, and then step over me." Then she gathered it up, and stepped over it. And he got well, came to life. He said to her, "now I am going to sing." (135) And he started to sing.

And there is nobody, they all had packed and gone; but nobody can kill deer, no. In no time and little Rabbit killed a little one, but the others nothing.[55] (140) They are starving. They dried deer, fat, any-thing, the fat on the rump, what's there. And then Magpie came and went under the tent.[56] (145) She said, "he [the boy] is wheeling some-thing made of tallow.[57]" He pecked it.[58] And then his mother ran over there, and whacked her on the head, and she'd say, "oh my dear." (150) She said to her, "don't hide there, I might hurt you, come in." She said to her, "come in and I'll feed you." She gave her some meat, something, some fat. Then Magpie went back. (155) She has children, four children. She puts in their hands something to eat. And one of them said, "my, yours is black and mine white.[59]" (160) My, and they cried. Raven ran in and took it from them. Then he went away and fed his children. Next day Magpie went, and lay under the flap again, (165) and she fed her that honey, and she came back home, covered it with something, with moss, and fed them again. The first time she gave her while tallow; (170) the last time he got hold of the meat, "oh, mine is black, yours white.[60]" Raven was listening and ran in there. Magpie put some moss in her children's hands.[61] He [Raven] said, "what are you doing, what's the matter with you?" (175) She said, "they are eating some moss." Raven went out, went back. But he was listening there, he hadn't gone to his house. Their mother told them, "be quiet, don't holler, and eat." She put it in their hands. (180) "Oh, mine is white and yours is black!" Raven ran back in in, took it away from them and left again. And Raven said, "I'm going over there.[62]"

So he went and went under there in the house, in the tules. The little boy passed by there. (185) He was wheeling his wheel, it's all tallow. He pecked it, and broke it in two. The little boy started to cry, and said, "that darned thing took my wheel." (190) His mother came out there

---

[53] Not clear.

[54] Lynx's remains.

[55] The group that left has nothing; Lynx and his group do manage to get food.

[56] Not clear.

[57] Their son is play with a toy made of tallow.

[58] They are starving, and looking for anything to eat.

[59] They are just playing, but the noise alert Raven.

[60] I think Dora is repeating what happened.

[61] To pretend that they had nothing good to eat.

[62] To Lynx's place.

and hit Raven on the head. She hit Raven over the head and he lay dead there, fainted. She ran back in her house, she took the soup and poured it on him.[63] Raven lay there, then woke up. (195) He took that, it was nothing but fat. He put it in his basket, and then he went back. He went and, "goodness, that woman sure pleased me." So he fed his children, he cut it up and fed them. His children started eating. (200) And he could feel the air. She touched it [the food], it's his guts that the children are eating. He took it away and put it back where it belongs. That was the last time he went back there.

(205) They [the people] said, "we are just starving to death." And Lynx started to sing and it started to snow. He went hunting. He told them, "you better move back over there. I'll feed you." (210) And they moved over there. And the boy[64] said, "we're going to hold the baby." So they took the baby and they held the baby. It was getting late and dark, and all of a sudden two hands stuck through the tent. (215) And [a voice] said, "I want to hold it, I want to hold the child." They gave it to him, and he threw it in his basket, and he left, ran away with it. That's the Ape. They cried, (220) they couldn't find him. They said, "we are going to look for nothing.[65]"

Lynx and his family walked away. They walked and went long ways. They got to an old lady (225) who was there. The old lady told them, "when I was a little girl Ape kidnapped me, and look, you can see I'm old. Your boy is hunting.[66] (230) There is a log across the road. You can hide a little ways from there, and maybe you'll see your boy. He's grown up." Then the boy came along (235) and his parents said to him "here, we are here." He kept on going,[67] and said, "tomorrow I'll come back." He just kept going, didn't stop there. It wasn't long that Ape came by. (240) And he crossed too. He said [to the boy], "what made you twist your foot sideways? You turned your foot there.[68]" "That thing there, a pheasant. I was going to shoot it but it flew away." That's what he said. (245) They slept, they went to bed.

The parents arranged it, they paid the little wiggle worms, the wood worms, the crawfish there in the water, they paid them [to rig the log so that] Monster falls in the water. (250) In the morning the boy came by again and crossed again. Right behind him the other one [Ape] was hurrying and got there. He got to the edge of the water and said, "where did you cross?" He said, "over on that log." (255) He ran on the log, he was in the middle of the log when it broke. The wood worms had eaten

---

[63] Not clear how it happens, but the food turns out to be Raven's guts.

[64] Dora probably misspoke, because it's the people who want to hold Lynx's baby.

[65] Meaning, we've lost him.

[66] She knows what happened.

[67] So as not to let Ape know his parents are there.

[68] Ape had noticed that the boy had moved in an unusual way.

it. He fell in the water and the crawfish grabbed him, the wiggle worms. The wiggle worms grabbed him and pushed him under water. (260) They did that, and he cried and died.

Then they went on, they went a long way, and they saw a lake. Their son took his clothes off, he jumped in the water and swam. (265) Gee, his mother is Robin.[69] She was hollering [robin noises]. His father was rolling around in the dirt, he's a pheasant, he's rolling around. (270) Their son kept on going. He'd go under water and he'd say, "xʷuxʷuxʷuxʷú, xʷuxʷuxʷú." That's Loon['s call]. They called and called him, but he's gone. I guess his parents must have died, I don't know. (275) He kept going that way. He swam, and got out of the water on the other side. There are people there, several people. He got there. Loon has speckles. And then they turned into something, scabs. (280)

There's a little girl, and her mother told her, "go over to your aunt, look, there's company." The girl went over there, she said, "I want to get a piece of fire." And she looked at the man. He's nothing but sores. (285) She went back, and told her mother, "gee, the man is nothing but sores and my aunt is combing him." She went there and told her younger sister, "you should throw him away, he's too scabby." Her partner didn't pay attention. (290) Then the little girl went back. The man didn't have any more scabs, he had shed them, had bathed and thrown them away. Gee, his hair is long, and the woman is combing it. The girl ran over, said, (295) "my aunt is combing that man. His hair is sure nice." She went there, and said, "give it here, I'll comb him." She said, "no, he's got too much scab, you can't comb him." (300) Then they got ready. They said, "we are going to gather and have a contest." And they gathered there, and they shot at targets with arrow heads. And Loon won. (305) And they didn't tell stories.[70] Some swam, others did nothing. They didn't win, Loon won.

This story comes close to being what, perhaps infelicitously, scholars have called a cycle, a complex of myths found in a particular culture. Typical of such complexes is that episodes have neither a fixed order nor specific endings or beginnings. Opening and closing formulas are the signals narrators give that, respectively, they have started and ended their performances. In Dora's Two Girls and Their Uncle one can recognize a number of well-known mythic episodes. For example, beginning approximately at sentence 76, the story matches (portions of) a narrative by John Tom, interpreted by Bob Covington, titled Wildcat, Magpie and Raven, and published in Ray 1933. The story line of Dora's narration can be summarized as follows: two girls who live with their uncle and grandmother violate their uncle's interdiction and are sent away. One marries Sea Gull, the other ends

---

[69] In other versions of the myth it is made clear that it is the son who turns his parents into these (or other) creatures.

[70] Not clear why Dora is saying this.

up impregnated by Lynx. Lynx's son is then kidnapped by Ape who rears the boy. The boy's parents manage to kill Ape, but the boy transforms himself into Loon and his parents into Robin and Phesant. Several of these episodes are cognate with various other Colville narratives. Thus the secret impregnation of the girl by Lynx is a story in itself, versions of which I have recorded from Pete Seymour and from Madeline DeSautel.

MOSQUITO (3m:55s). This story was recorded June 21, 1974. It is the last of the cəpcaptík"ł Dora DeSautel told me and I recorded on tape.[71] I know of no published versions of the myth, a story in which little boy Mosquito discovers that Cricket was going to kill the whole Mosquito camp. When he reports what he has heard, Mosquito is not believed, and the whole camp is killed, except for the boy who had gone to hide in the sweat house. The boy travels on and is offered blood pudding by a woman who intends to kill him since she apparently views him as a man-eater. She so succeeds and transforms Mosquito into the relatively harmless pest we know today.

(1) The Mosquito group was camped at ..., there is a lake there. And they camped there. And then Cricket came (5) and he was going to kill them all. The Crickets hid there in the lake.

[The Mosquito told] little boy Mosquito, "go get some water." And he went and dipped the water. (10) He took the water, stood up straight, and very near there somebody said, "take him, grab him by the arm, kill him." They were whispering. (15) He went back and he told his big brothers: "there are people there; [they said] grab him by the arm and kill him. And one said, 'no, wait a little while.'" (20) His older brother said to him, "are you scared, you are talking nonsense." So Mosquito went into the sweat house there. And he went to sleep. He slept and the Crickets came.

(25) They got there and they killed them all. They killed them all. Only the little boy that was sitting in the sweat house is left alive. He woke up, gee, they're all gone, killed. He went to the lake, and there there were those jointed weeds. (30) He took the jointed weeds,[72] split them lengthwise, and he stuck a stick there.[73]

He sat down in there, then he paddled. He went, he said [singing] "oh my brothers, the Crickets stepped on my belly. (35) Oh my brothers, the Crickets stepped on my belly.[74]" From the top of the hill came a woman. She said, "Mosquito, Mosquito, come here. I am going to feed

---

[71] The following week we did record The Three Boys, a European story a version of which she had told me three years earlier.

[72] I don't know what weeds Dora is referring to.

[73] Dora explained that this is to keep the weed open--is he making a boat?

[74] I am not familiar with this motif, but there is a story where Deer steps on Cricket's belly, and the song that accompanies the story is well known to the Okanagan people.

you some blood pudding." He tied his boat and went there, (40) climbed the hill. The woman told his [her?] brother,[75] "go and put in the ground these sticks that are whittled to a sharp end. Drive them into the ground, and while he is eating untie the boat."

(45) The boy went and drove the stick in the little trail. He untied his boat and put down the basket with the blood pudding. He ate it, and he set down another one. He ate it, gee, he was full to a bursting point. (50) He said, "gee, partner, your boat came untied." Gee, he ran out of there and ran down the hill. Those sharp sticks, they were stuck in the ground. He kicked him, he fell down, his body got poked, and he died.

The Mosquito hummed, flew from there. (55) He said, "when the next generation of people comes you won't be a man eater; you'll only bite any which critter. The end of the story.

GRAMMATICAL NOTES. In this section I sketch the inflectional categories of the language as mapped by the person markers. In the process I briefly discuss some of the analytical problems that confront the linguist.

PERSON MARKING. Okanagan has four main sets of person reference markers: the kn‿ set (intransitive), the i(n)- set (possessive), the -(í)n set (transitive subject), and the (transitive) object set.

The **kn‿** set consists of clitics (marked with the ligature), and a suffix:

kn‿	first singular	**kʷu‿**	first plural
kʷ‿	second singular	**p‿**	second plural
ø	third singular	**ø ...-lx**	third plural

These markers accompany stems that in English translate as intransitive verbs, nouns, and adjectives.

kn‿ʔitx. *I slept.*
kʷ‿sqilxʷ. *You are an Indian / a person.*
ʔayx̌ʷt (axáʔ). *This one is tired.*

A subset of these markers, identical in all persons except for 1sg **kʷu‿**, co-occurs with the possessive set of person markers, and is reserved for double possessives and verb nominalizations.

The possessive set has two subsets, one used with nouns and psych verbs, and the other with verb nominalizations. I abbreviate members of the form-er *1in, 2in, 3in*; and members of the latter *1i, 2i, 3i* in a fashion that captures the phonology of the forms: verb nominalizations never have the nasal in the first and second persons, while nouns and psych verbs do, except for stems that begin in **s** and kin terms that begin in **ɬ**:

i(n)-	first singular	**-tt**	first plural
a(n)-	second singular	**-mp**	second plural
-s / -c	third singular	**-s-lx / -c-lx**	third plural

which yield such forms as
an-lʔíw *your father*

---

[75] Not clear.

in-x̌mínk *I like / want it*

which, in turn, may combine with members of the **kn‿** set (**kʷu‿** subset) to yield forms such as

kʷu‿an-lʔíw *I am your father.*

kʷ‿in-x̌mínk *I like / want you (you are my wanting).*

kʷ‿i-ks-ʔam-ɬt-ím an-lʔíw *I am going to feed your father.*

the last of which is the nominalization of a future (**ks-**) possessor applicative (**-ɬt**) verb form (see below--root **ʔam**, *feed*), in which the suffix **-(i)m**, sometimes referred to as the antipassive, is required.

The transitive subject set, often called the ergative set, consists of the following suffixes (parentheses abbreviate stressed and unstressed variants):

-(i)n	first singular	**-(i)m / -t**	first plural
-(i)xʷ	second singular	**-(i)p**	second plural
-(i)s	third singular	**-(i)s-lx**	third plural

These markers follow the object markers, which, in turn, follow one of several obligatory transitive markers (see below).

The (transitive) object set consists of the following markers (one proclitic and suffixes):

kʷu‿	first singular	**kʷu‿...-m**	first plural
-s / -m	second singular	**-ɬ(úl)m**	second plural
-Ø	third singular	**-Ø ... -lx**	third plural

Because third person object markers and third person intransitive subject markers are **Ø**, Salishan languages are often characterized as split ergative systems. The allomorphy of the second singular object is transitivizer-dependent. The disambiguation of number in the first person object is accomplished by the suffix **-m** and such forms are interpreted as 3rd indef subject - 1pl object:

kʷu‿sp'-nt-is *He whipped me.* (-nt transitivizer)

kʷu‿sp'-nt-im *They whipped us / We were whipped.*

-(i)m occurs also with **Ø**, and the interpretation of these forms can be indefinite subject, or passive:

sp'-nt-is *3rd person whipped 3rd person.*

sp'-nt-im *3rd person indef whipped 3rd person / 3rd person was whipped.*

WORD CLASSES. Aspectual criteria can be established to distinguish word classes, and, as expected, these may derive forms of other classes--nouns can derive verbs and verbs can be nominalized, for example (N. Mattina 1996). A prototypical noun like **kʷilstn** *sweat lodge*, culturally relevant and categorially marked (**-tn** *instrumental*), derives a verb with **-m**:

kn‿kʷilstn-m *I sweat bathed.*

Similarly, **qʷacqn** *hat* derives **qʷacqn-m** *wear a hat* (intransitive); **ntx̌ʷx̌ʷqin** *noon* derives **ntx̌ʷx̌ʷqin-m** *do lunch* (intransitive).

Analogously **qiʔs** *to dream* (intransitive) derives **s-qiʔs** *a dream*, and the latter form can be inflected with possessive markers and interpreted as a possessive noun form, or as a nominalized verb form.

Most Okanagan stems can also be transitivized (see below).

NOMINAL AND PRONOMINAL ARGUMENTS. Scholars have argued that Salishan languages are pronominal argument languages: a form like **wik-nt-xʷ**
You saw it. is a full sentence with a third person object (**Ø**), and second
person subject (**-xʷ**). In this interpretation, any object expressed in nominal
form is an adjunct, not a (nominal) argument. The claim is countered with
the suggestion that in applicative sentences like
    kʷu‿tq-łt-is in-kílx. *He touched my hand.*
the noun phrase **in-kílx** *my hand* functions as one of the arguments of the
possessor applicative verb form **kʷu‿tq-łt-is** *He touched my ...* and this
argument is not, and cannot be, referenced in pronominal form on the verb.
    Intransitive forms are most often also analyzed as fully predicative.
    kn‿xʷuy. *I went.*
    kʷ‿ilmíxʷm *You are a boss.*
    kʷ‿x̌ast *You are fine.*
In these sentences, the clitics **kn‿** and **kʷ‿** are the subjects, and the word
to which the clitics are attached are the predicates. Third person forms have
Ø subject person marking, and forms like **sql'tmíxʷ** have been analyzed as
full predications that should be translated as something like *He is a man* or
It's a man. In the stream of discourse such words can function as predicative
elements. The normal way to express either of the isolated propositions *He's
a man,* and *It's a man.* is with utterances like **ixí? sql'tmíxʷ** *That's a man,*
or **sql'tmíxʷ ya?x̌ís** *That one over there is a man*; that is, by juxtaposing
(in either order) the stem **sql'tmíxʷ** and a deictic stem (**ixí?, ya?x̌ís**). In
traditional terms these sentences would be analyzed as exocentric equa-
tional constructions consisting of a subject and a predicate. The participant
persons **kn‿** and **kʷ‿** are pronominal subjects; third person forms can be
analyzed as having a nominal subject of the classes mentioned, which, in
context, can be deleted. Another complication for the interpretation of all
full words as predicative is presented by the different markings for morphological and syntactic plurals: the morphological plural of **citxʷ** *house* is the
reduplicated form **ct-citxʷ** *houses*, while the syntactic plural of the same
form is **citxʷ-lx (ixí?)** *(Those) are houses.*
    In recent times, when scholars are preferring to view all constructions to
have heads (or centers, in the old terminology) the question is raised as to
what constitutes the head of such a sentence as **kn‿sql'tmíxʷ**. Most common is the hypothesis that the verb is the head of the sentence (here it would
be the predicate nominal), but because the identification of head with lexical
head can be dispensed with, just as abstract features within the Inflection or
Agreement nodes have been proposed to head sentences, and just as the
determiner has been proposed to head Determiner Phrases, so can **kn‿** be
proposed to head the sentence **kn‿sql'tmíxʷ**. An utterance like **xʷuy** *He
went*, then, can be viewed as the abbreviation of **xʷuy ixí?** *That one went,*
and analyzed either as having a null subject, or as requiring a third person
nominal subject which undergoes deletion in the appropriate circumstances.

OTHER **kn‿**, **i(n)-**, AND **-(í)n** PARADIGMS. Beside the constructions already discussed, Okanagan uses **kn‿** inflection in a number of forms derived by means of prefixes, suffixes, and circumfixes. Among these forms are:

kn‿ PARADIGMS.
To-Be nouns (**kn‿kɬ**-noun)
    kɬ-ilmíxʷm snkʼlip. *Coyote will be chief / is chief-to-be.*

kɬ- *have* forms (**kn‿kɬ**-noun)
    kn‿kɬ-qʷacqn *I have a hat.*

inchoatives (**kn‿**verb**+-ʔ-** before stressed vowel)
    kn‿cʼ-ʔ-ax *I got ashamed.* (root **cʼax**)

patient forms (**kn‿** verb**+VC₂**)
    kn‿tʼkʼʷ-akʼʷ *I fell.* (Cf **tʼkʼʷ-nt** *put something down*)

get patient forms (**kn‿** **c+**verb)
    uɬ ilíʔ kn‿c-lakʼ *I was in jail a long time* (cf. **lkʼ-nt** *tie something*)

habitual / durative forms (**kn‿c+**verb)
    kn‿c-nqilxʷ+cn-m *I (regularly) talk Indian.*
    (Cf. kn‿nqilxʷ+cn-m *I talked Indian*)
    kn‿c-málx̌aʔ *I (regularly) lie.*
    (Cf. kn‿málx̌aʔ *I lied*)

imperfective forms (**kn‿s**-verb-**(mi)x**—compare with the forms that follow)
    kn‿s-kʼʷlʼ+cn+cut-x *I am cooking.*
    s-ʔitx-x pit *Pete is sleeping.*
    kn‿s-qʼyʼ-mix *I am writing.*

imperfective of present relevance forms (**kn‿sc**-verb-**(mi)x**—compare with imperfective forms given above)
    kn‿sc-kʼʷlʼ+cn+cut-x *I have been cooking.*
    sc-ʔitx-x pit *Pete has been sleeping.*
    kn‿sc-qʼyʼ-mix *I have been writing.*

inceptive forms (**kn‿ks**+verb-**(mí)xaʔx**)
    kn‿ks-λʼaʔ+λʼaʔ-míxaʔx *I'm going to look for something.*
    kn‿ks-xʷúy-aʔx *I'm going (away).*

past perfect forms (**kn‿ksc+**verb)

kn‿ksc-k'ʷul' ta‿nc'aqk^w *I have some sour dough bread made / I have made some sour dough bread.*

kn‿ksc-nik' *I have some cut / I have cut some.*

i(n)- PARADIGMS.

durative / intent forms (**i+s**+verb)

s-q'sápi^ʔ-s ilí^ʔ i-s-ilí^ʔ *I lived there a long time.* (root **ilí^ʔ** *there*, lit. *long-time there I-there*).

perfective forms (**i+sc**+verb)

in-x̌ást i-sc-^ʔítx *I slept well* (my-good my-having-slept).

future forms (**i+ks**+verb)

lut a-ks-x^wúy *Don't go.*

k^w‿i-ks-(s)íw-m *I'll ask you.*

future imperative forms (**i+kc**+verb)

lut a-kc-náq'ʷ *You will not steal.*

x̌ast a-kc-k'ʷúl'-m *You will work well.*

future applicative forms (i-ks-verb-t-m)

k^w‿i-ks-may'-xít-m ... *I am going to tell you* ...

-(í)n PARADIGMS. All forms that take transitive person markers also take a (di)transitivizer. Okanagan has two transitivizers, **-nt** and **-st**; a causative **-st**; and three applicatives **-łt, -x(í)t, -túłt.**

-nt is the transitivizer that accompanies most stems:

wik-nt-x^w *You saw it.*

ƛ'a^ʔ-nt-ín *I fetched it.*

One verb takes **-t, ^ʔam-t-ín** *I fed him.* Several verbs take **-st**:

pul-st-n *I beat him up.*

q^wl+q^wil-st-m-s *He talks to you.*

The causative is **-st**:

^ʔayx̌^wt-st-m-n *I made you tired* (Cf. **k^w‿^ʔayx̌^wt** *You are tired*).

Customary transitive forms are marked with the circumfix **c-...-st**:

c-wik-st-n *I always see it.*

Three suffixes prepare stems for transitivization:

-nu(n)[76] *manage to* (most common added to stems with **-C2** reduplication)

tałt i?‿x̌s+s+nu-nt-x̌ʷ *You did well* (**x̌ast** *good*).

talí? x̌ast i?‿kʷ'l'+ł'+nu-nt-x̌ʷ *You did / got it done very well.*

tałt x̌ast i?‿kʷ'l'+nu-nt-x̌ʷ *You did very well.* (Cf. **kʷul'-nt-x̌ʷ** *You fixed it.*)

-min, often as the circumfix **k-/t-...-min** with intransitive stems:

k+pulx+m(n)-nt-s-n *I'll camp with you.* (Cf. **kn‿pulx** *I camped.*)

t+x̌ʷuy+m(n)-nt-s-n *I went up to you.* (Cf. **kn‿x̌ʷuy** *I went*; **x̌ʷuy-st** *take st to*).

tałt ?ayx̌ʷt+m(n)-nt-s-n *I am tired of you.* (Cf. **kn‿?ayx̌ʷt** *I am tired*; **?ayx̌ʷt-st-n** *I made him tired.*)

else with some change in the meaning of the stem:

c'q'-nt-ix̌ʷ *You hit it*; c'q'+mi-nt-x̌ʷ *You threw it.*

-xixm, with changes (not fully understood) to the roles of the arguments of the verb as well as to the meaning of the verb:

kʷłn+xixm-st-x̌ʷ *You lent it out to her.* (Cf. **kʷuł-nt-x̌ʷ** *You borrowed it.*)

-łt is the possessor applicative:

uc kʷu‿wik-łt-x̌ʷ i-sqʷsí? *Did you see my son?* (Cf. **uc kʷu‿wik-nt-x̌ʷ** *Did you see me?*)

-x(i)t is the benefactive applicative:

kʷu‿q'y'-xit-s t‿i-ks... *He wrote the X for me.* (Cf. **q'y'-nt-is** *He wrote it.*)

-tułt with changes to the roles of the arguments:

kʷu‿?am-tułt-x̌ʷ i?‿spapáʕła? *You fed me to the monster.* (Cf. **kʷu‿?am-t-ix̌ʷ** *You fed me*; **kʷu‿?am-łt-ís i-sqʷsí?** *You fed my child.*)

---

[76] The underlying form **-nun** is confirmed by such forms as **kʷ‿i-ks-ƛ'l-nún-m** *I'm going to kill you.*

REFERENCES CITED

Boas, Franz, ed. 1917. *Folk-tales of Salishan and Sahaptin tribes.* Collected by James A. Teit, Livingston Farrand, Marian K. Gould, Herbert J. Spinden. Ed. by Franz Boas. Lancaster, Pa, and New York, American Folklore Society.

Dauenhauer, Nora Marks and Richard Dauenhauer 1996. "The paradox of talking on the page: Some aspects of the Tlingit and Haida experience." In *Talking on the page. Editing aboriginal oral texts.* Ed. Laura J. Murray and Keren Rice. University of Toronto Press.

Mannenbach, Steve 1975. MS. "Colville and Makah Indian oral texts & commentary."

Mattina, Nancy J. 1996. *Aspect and category in Okanagan word formation.* PhD dissertation, Simon Fraser University.

Mourning Dove 1933. *Coyote stories.* Ed and illus. Heister Dean Guie, with notes by Lucullus V. McWhorter (Old Wolf) and a foreword by Chief Standing Bear. Caldwell, Idaho, Caxton Printers.

NA 1971. *Coyote and the Colville.* Material collected and prepared by Eileen Yanan, Editorial Supervision John E. Andrist. Published by St Mary's Mission, Omak Washington, June 1, 1971.

Ray, Verne F. 1933. "Sanpoil folk tales." In *Journal of American Folklore* Vol 46, pp. 129-187.

Spier, Leslie, ed. *The Sinkaietk or Southern Okanagon of Washington.* By Walter Cline, Rachel S. Commons, May Mandelbaum, Richard H. Post, and L. V. W. Walters. General Series in Anthropology No. 6. Contributions from the laboratory of anthropology. George Banta Publishing Company, Menasha, Wisconsin.

Thompson, Stith 1955. *Motif-index of folk-literature.* Revised and Enlarged Edition. Indiana University Press.

Updike, John 1984. Book review column, "Three tales from Nigeria." *The New Yorker.* April 23. Pp. 119-129.

PART II

THE INTERLINEARIZED TEXTS

INTRODUCTORY NOTES
ABBREVIATIONS AND SYMBOLS
THE TEXTS
GLOSSARY

INTRODUCTORY NOTES

These notes explain some of the conventions used in the interlinearized texts. The texts are broken up into sequentially numbered discourse-cohesive units that match, roughly, sentences, including coordinate constructions. The interlinearization consists of four lines: the surface phonetics; the segmentation of the line into stem and inflectional affixes, where the boundaries between stem and inflectional affixes are marked by hyphens; a morpheme gloss line; and a free translation line. Stem-internal morpheme breaks are marked with plus signs (+) and represent boundaries significant in derivation or word-formation.

Material included in curly brackets {} represents one of the following: an unfinished utterance; as much as I could provide of the reconstruction of an unintelligible utterance; an interjection either of the speaker or of a listener; or a response to a listener's interjection.

Material included in square brackets [] represents an insertion provided by the editors.

A single length mark (·) represents grammatically significant length (of resonants), in preference to a representation with geminate symbols, while a double length mark (··) signals rhetorical length. [unf] abbreviates unfinished and [unint] unintelligible.

The texts are followed by a glossary, which contains a list of all the stems and inflectional affixes found in the text, their glosses, the skeletal make-up of the lexical roots, and the sentence number of their first occurrence in each of the texts. Stem-internal derivational and word-forming morphs are marked with + (the plus sign), but the morphs themselves are not listed in the glossary. Thus, for example, ɬ- *back, again*, is not an entry in the glossary, but the nine stems that begin with it can easily be found. The titles of the texts are abbreviated as follows: SF Skunk and Fisher; CN Coyote, Bear, & Kingfisher; FC Frog & Crane; CMB Coyote, Muskrat, & Bear; CE Coyote Juggles His Eyes; CR Chipmunk & Grandma Rabbit; GU Two Girls and Their Uncle; M Mosquito.

As a result of the often idiosyncratic laryngealization of resonants, and because I have chosen not to regularize the forms, the glossary contains many entries in pairs the transcriptions of which differ with regard to laryngealization, as in m+mátk'ya? and m+m'átk'ya? *blood pudding*. I have left my transcriptions transparent with regard to other indeterminacies, for example yaʕ+p and yaʕ'+p arrive pl; ʕ'an' and ʕ'an *Magpie*, and the near-homophonous interjection.

Labels followed by the raised caret (^) abbreviate the prefixal part of a circumfix. Labels preceded by the raised caret (^) abbreviate the suffixal part of the circumfix. Except for ^ 3e4obj, I list only the labels followed by the caret. The hyphen (-) marks inflectional affixes; the plus sign (+) marks derivational morphemes or word-internal word-formation boundaries; the double hyphen (=) marks lexical affixes.

Label	Elaboration and notes
1erg	First singular ergative. Suffix -(í)n. The suffix has a variant -ˤán in forms that undergo pharyngeal movement. The parenthesized material (here and elsewhere) occurs with weak stems (suffix-stressed forms).
1i	First singular possessive. Prefix i- (cf. in-) (used with verb nominalizations).
1in	First singular possessive. Prefix in- (cf. i-) (used with nouns and psych verbs).
1kn	First singular intransitive. Clitic kn‿, kn‿ set.
1kʷu	First singular intransitive. Clitic kʷu‿, kʷu‿ subset of kn‿. 1. In possessor applicative forms. 2. With i(n)- forms.
1obj	First singular object. Clitic kʷu‿ (with transitivizer).
2erg	Second singular ergative. Suffix -(í)xʷ. The suffix has a variant -ˤáxʷ in forms that undergo pharyngeal movement.
2i	Second singular possessive. Prefix a- (cf. an-) (used with verb nominalizations).
2in	Second singular possessive. Prefix an- (cf. a-) (used with nouns and psych verbs).
2kn	Second singular intransitive. Clitic kʷ‿, kn‿ set (and kʷu‿ subset).
2kʷu	Second singular intransitive. Clitic kʷ‿, kʷu‿ subset of kn‿. 1. In possessor applicative forms. 2. With i(n)- forms.
2obj	Second singular object. Suffix -s (with -nt and -ɬt transitivizers). Suffix -m (with -st and -x(í)t transitivizers).
^ 3e4obj	Third subject (with first plural object). Suffix -(í)m (with clitic kʷu‿ and transitivizer).

3erg	Third person ergative. Suffix -(í)s. The suffix has a variant -ʕás in forms that undergo pharyngeal movement.
3i	Third person possessive. Suffix -s (cf. 3in). The suffix has a variant -c after stems ending in ł or s (used with verb nominalizations).
3in	Third person possessive. Suffix -s (cf. 3i). The suffix has a variant -c after stems ending in ł or s (used with nouns and psych verbs).
4erg	First plural ergative. Suffix -(í)m. The suffix has a variant -t after -s or -m 2nd object.
4i	First plural possessive. Suffix -tt (cf. 4in). The suffix has a variant -t after stems ending in t (used with verb nominalizations).
4in	First plural possessive. Suffix -tt (cf. 4i). The suffix has a variant -t after stems ending in t (used with nouns and psych verbs).
4kn	First plural intransitive. Clitic kʷu‿. kn‿ set (and kʷu‿ subset).
4obj	First plural object (with third subject). Clitic kʷu‿ (with transitivizer and -(í)m).
5erg	Second plural ergative. Suffix -(í)p.
5in	Second plural possessive. Suffix -mp. The suffix has a variant -p after stems that end in m (used with nouns and psych verbs).
5kn	Second plural intransitive. Clitic p‿. kn‿ set (and kʷu‿ subset).
5obj	Second plural object. Suffix -ł(úl)m (with transitivizer).
agInst	Agent / Instrument. Proclitic t‿.
art	Article. Clitic i(ʔ)‿ with variants a(ʔ).
benf	Benefactive. Suffix -x(í)t, forms conjugated with the -(í)n set.
caus	Causative. Suffix -st, forms conjugated with the -(í)n set.
cisl	Cislocative. Prefix c+
cust ^	Customary. Circumfix c-...-st. These forms are conjugated with the -(í)n paradigm. The circumfix has a variant s-...-st before stems that begin with c.

dub	Dubitative. Particle uc.
dur(^)	Durative. Prefix s-; circumfix in the 1st plural only: kʷu‿s-...-s. Else conjugated with the i- paradigm. The prefix has a variant ł- before stems that begin with ł, and a variant Ø- before stems that begin with s.
emph	Emphatic.
evid	Evidential. Particles nakʼʷm, t'i?.
fut	Future. Particle mi.
futCust ^	Future customary. Circumfix ks+c-...-st, forms conjugated with the -(í)n set.
futI	Future intransitive. Prefix ks-, forms conjugated with the i- set. The prefix has a variant kł- before stems that begin with ł- *back, again.*
futT ^	Future transitive. 1. Circumfix ks-...-m, forms conjugated with the i- set. 2. Circumfix ks-...-y' in forms with third person subject (3i); 3. Circumfix ks-...-transitivizer, usually, though not always in forms with plural subjects (and ergative markers).
gpat	Get patient. Prefix c-, forms conjugated with the kn‿ set.
hab	Habitual. Prefix c-, forms conjugated with the kn‿ set. The prefix has a variant s- before stems that begin with t('), c(').
incp ^	Inceptive. Circumfix ks-...-(míx)a?x, forms conjugated with the kn‿ paradigm. The circumfix has the variant k-...-(míx)a?x before stems that begin with ł, the variant s-...-(míx)a?x in 2sg and 2pl forms, and the variant ks-...-x after stems that end in a?.
inten	Intent. Prefix s-, forms conjugated with the i- set. The prefix has a variant ł- before ł- *back, again.*
intj	Interjection.
ipftv ^	Imperfective intransitive. Circumfix s-...-(mí)x, forms conjugated with the kn‿ paradigm. Has a variant Ø-...-(mí)x before stems that begin with ł. These forms translate as progressive.
ipftvp ^	Imperfective intransitive with present relevance. Circumfix sc-...-(mí)x, forms conjugated with the kn‿ paradigm. Translates as *have been X-ing.*
ipimptv	Intransitive plural imperative. Suffix -wy.

isimptv	Intransitive singular imperative. Suffix -x. The suffix has a variant -x^w after stems that end in x^w.
ɬt	Transitivizer (possessor applicative). Suffix -ɬt.
m's	Man's.
negfac	Negative factual. Particle t'.
nt	Transitivizer. Suffix -nt.
onom	Onomatopoeic.
pftv	Perfective. Prefix sc-, forms conjugated with i- paradigm.
pl	Plural. Suffix -lx.
pl_name	Place name.
psv	Passive. Suffix -(í)m, forms conjugated with -(í)n paradigm. The suffix has a variant -ʕám in forms that undergo pharyngeal movement.
subord	Subordinate. Particle ɬ.
tpimptv	Transitive plural imperative. Suffix -y with stems that take -nt transitivizer. Suffix -sk^{w}y with stems that take -st transitivizer.
tsimptv	Transitive singular imperative. Suffix -(í)k^w with stems that take -nt transitivizer. Suffix -sk^w with stems that take -st transitivizer.
w_X	with X.
X_dim	Diminutive form of X.
X_inch	Inchoative form of X.
X_pl	Plural form of X.
X_sg	Singular form of X.
X_st	X something.
X_w	X with.

1. cwix   i?   sqilxʷ
   c   -wix   i?   s+qilxʷ
   hab-live   art person
   There were people;

2. ixí?   i?   pəptwína?xʷ   uɬ   ksən?am?ím·a?t
   ixí?   i?   p+ptwína?xʷ   uɬ   k   -s+n+?am+?ím·a?t
   that   art old_woman   and have -grandchildren

   stətáq   la?ɬ   qʰʷəqʰʷc'w'íya?
   s+t+taq   la?ɬ   qʰʷ+qʰʷc'w'íya?
   Squirrel   and   Chipmunk

   an old lady, and she had grandchildren, Squirrel and Chipmunk.

3. ixí?   cúntəm   ixí?   t   stəmtíma?s
   ixí?   cu -nt -m   ixí?   t   s+tm+tíma?   -s
   then   tell -nt -psv that   aglnst grandmother -3in
   and the grandmother told them;

4. p   ksxʷúya?x   k'əl cər'túps
   p   ks   -xʷuy -a?x   k'l cr't+ups
   5kn incp^ -go -   ^incp   to   Fisher
   "Go to Fisher's."

5. lut t'a   lkʷut   itlí?
   lut t'   lkʷ+ut itlí?
   not negfac   far   from_there
   It's not far from there.

6. ixí?   itlí?   sxʷúy'ysəlx
   ixí?   itlí?   s -xʷuy'+y-s -lx
   then   from_there   dur -go_pl -3i -pl
   They started to go.

7. xʷú··y'ylx {uɬ}   uɬ   i?ˁápəlx   ik'lí?
   xʷuy'+y -lx   uɬ   y?aˁ+p -lx   ik'lí?
   go_pl -pl   and   arrive -pl   there
   They went and they got there;

8. uɬ   lut   t'a   kswit   ilí?
   uɬ   lut   t'   k   -s+wit   ilí?
   and   not   negfac   there_be -anybody   there
   but there was nobody there.

9. uɬ   ilí?   i?   xəlína?,   ?asíl   i?   xəlína?
   uɬ   ilí?   i?   xl+ína?   ?asíl   i?   xl+ína?
   and   there   art cache   two   art cache
   There were food caches there, two;

38

10. k'a?x̌ís   i?   x̌əlína? {uł}
    k'a?+x̌ís   i?   x̌l+ína?
    over_there art cache
    a cache over there;

11. uł   i?   naqs way' q?yax̌ʷ, uł   i?   naqs náx̌əmł lut
    uł   i?   naqs way' qy'ax̌ʷ uł   i?   naqs nax̌mł   lut
    and art one   well smell and art one   but   not
    and one stinks, but the other doesn't.

12. ixí?   ik'lí?   sx̌ʷúysəlx   uł
    ixí?   ik'lí?   s   -x̌ʷuy -s -lx uł
    then   there   dur -go   -3i -pl and

    ksk'əłppíl'xa?xəlx {uł}
    ks   -k'ł+p+pil'+x   -a?x   -lx
    incp^ -crawl_under -^incp -pl
    And they were going to crawl under.

13. ixí?   scx̌ʷuys   sənkstíya?   uł   t'i?   piq'ʷ
    ixí?   s -c+x̌ʷuy -s   s+n+kstíya?   uł   t'i?   piq'ʷ
    then   dur -come -3i skunk   and   evid onom

    piq'ʷ   piq'ʷ
    piq'ʷ   piq'ʷ
    onom   onom
    Skunk came back, going "piq̓ʷ."

14. ixí?   uł   sʕ'ayncúts   axá?   q'ʷəq'ʷc'w'íya?
    ixí?   uł   s -ʕ'ay+ncút -s axá?   q'ʷ+q'ʷc'w'íya?
    then   and   dur -laugh   -3i this   Chipmunk

    ʕ'ayncút   q'ʷəq'ʷc'w'íya?
    ʕ'ay+ncút q'ʷ+q'ʷc'w'íya?
    laugh   Chipmunk
    Chipmunk started to laugh, Chipmunk laughed;

15. uł   ik'lí?   {k'əłqc'íkstəm} i?   k'əl   x̌lína?
    uł   ik'lí?   k'ł+qc'+ikst -m   i?   k'l   x̌l+ína?
    and   there   ?   -mdl art   to   cache
    and they [were hiding] in the cache,

16. uł   ilí?   k'łk̓ʷlíwtəlx
    uł   ilí?   k'ł+k̓ʷl+iwt   -lx
    and   there   sit_pl_under -pl
    and they were sitting there.

17. ixí?   kəm'əntíməlx   t   sənkstíya?
    ixí?   km' -nt -im   -lx t   s+n+kstíya?
    then   take -nt -psv -pl aglnst Skunk
    And Skunk grabbed them.

18. {kiw} ixí?   uł   ʕəyʕáynksəlx
    kiw   ixí?   uł   ʕay+ʕáyn+k -s   -lx
    yes   then   and   tickle   -3erg -pl
    And they tickled him.

19. ʕəyʕá·˙ynksəlx   nt'aʔ   uɬ   ʕ'ayncút
    ʕay+ʕáyn+k -s   -lx   nt'a   uɬ   ʕ'ay+ncút
    tickle   -3erg   -pl   intj   and   laugh
    They tickled him and he laughed;

20. uɬ   k'ʷəlk'lwís   ilí·˙ʔ   uɬ   hoy   cut   way'   kən   ʔayx̌ʷt
    uɬ   k'ʷlk'+lwis   ilíʔ   uɬ   hoy   cut   way'   kn   ʔayx̌ʷ+t
    and roll_around   there   and   well   say   yes   1kn   tired
    he rolled around there, then he said, "I'm tired."

21. {ixíʔ uɬ}   ik'líʔ   iʔ   k'əl x̌línaʔ   sk'əlcníɬ   -c
    ik'líʔ   iʔ   k'l   x̌l+ínaʔ   s+k'l+cniɬ   -c
    there   art   to   cache   to_the_side -3in

    k'ɬpəpílxsts
    k'ɬ+p+pilx   -st   -s
    enter_under   -caus   -3erg
    He put them under there the cache.

22. ixíʔ   sc'əl'c'əl'qínxnəms   kəm'   x̌əsx̌əsqínxən
    ixíʔ   s -c'l+c'l+qin+xn+m   -s   km'   x̌s+x̌s+qin+xn
    that   dur -stick_legs_up   -3i   or   good_knees
    He put their legs up just like he had good knees;

23. c'əl'c'əl'qínxnəm   məɬ axáʔ   ɬckicx   cər'túps
    c'l+c'l+qin+xn+m   mɬ   axáʔ   ɬ+c+kic+x   cr't+ups
    stick_legs_up   and this   arrive_cisl_again   Fisher
    he put the legs up, and then Fisher got back.

24. cus   iʔ   sl'ax̌ts   uɬ   lut   kʷ   t'
    cu -s   iʔ   s+ɬ'ax̌+t -s   uɬ   lut   kʷ   t'
    tell -3erg art friend   -3in   and   not   2kn   negfac

    k'ʷəl'cəncút
    k'ʷl'+cn+cut
    cook
    He said to his friend, "You haven't cooked."

25. nak'ʷáʔ   kʷ   inilmíxʷəm   mi
    nak'ʷ+a   kʷ   in -ylmixʷm   mi
    not   2kʷu 1in -chief   fut

    ck'ʷaʔk'ʷúl'stmən
    c   -k'ʷaʔ+k'ʷúl' -st   -m   -n
    cust ^   -work   - ^ cust -2obj   -1erg
    "You're not my boss that I work for you."

26. ixíʔ   uɬ   ilíʔ   k'ʷəl'cəncút   cər'túps   uɬ   ʔaɬʔíɬn
    ixíʔ   uɬ   ilíʔ   k'ʷl'+cn+cut   cr't+ups   uɬ   ʔaɬ+ʔíɬn
    then   and   there   cook   Fisher   and eat_pl
    And Fisher cooked and he ate.

27. uɬ   aɬíʔ   knaqsmísaʔt
    uɬ   aɬíʔ   k+naqs+mísaʔt
    and   so   alone
    He was alone.

28. ixíʔ   x̌lap,   uɬ   cúntəm   iʔ t
    ixíʔ   x̌la+p   uɬ   cu -nt -m   iʔ t
    then   morning and   tell -nt -psv art agInst

    sl'ax̌ts
    s+l'ax̌+t -s
    friend -3in

    The next daylight his partner said:

29. way'   ixíʔ   iɬəɬpíx̌əm
    way'   ixíʔ   i -ɬ   -ɬ+pix̌+m
    yes   then   1i -inten -hunt_again

    "I'm going back hunting."

30. nák'ʷʷəm   kʷis   iʔ xƛ'ut k   c'əq'mís
    nak'ʷʷm   kʷi   -s   iʔ xƛ'ut kiʔ c'q'+mi   -s
    evid   take -3erg   art rock   rel throw   -3erg

    He took a rock and threw it.

31. t'iʔ   lu   lu   lu   lu   uɬ   nis
    t'iʔ   lu   lu   lu   lu   uɬ   nis
    evid   onom   onom   onom   onom   and   gone

    Roll, roll, roll, roll, he's gone.

32. ixíʔ   ckəm'ntís   iʔ sm'am'ʔíms
    ixíʔ   c+km'   -nt -is   iʔ s+m'a+m'ʔím   -s
    then   take_cisl -nt -3erg art women   -3in

    He brought out his women.

33. ixíʔ   ʕayʕáynksəlx
    ixíʔ   ʕay+ʕáy+nk -s   -lx
    then   tickle   -3erg -pl

    They tickled him.

34. ilí··ʔ   ʕayncú··t
    ilíʔ   ʕay+ncút
    there   laugh

    They did that, he laughed.

35. uɬ   ixíʔ   cut   way'   iksənʔúcxnəm
    uɬ   ixíʔ   cut   way'   i   -ks   -n+ʔuc+xn   -m
    and   then   say   yes   1i -futT ^ -track   - ^ futT

    isl'áx̌t
    i   -s+l'áx̌t
    1in -friend

    And then he said "I'm going to follow my partner."

36. nák'ʷʷəm   iʔ l   tk'əmkn'íɬxʷ   ilíʔ {t'ə}
    nak'ʷʷm   iʔ l   t+k'm+kn'+iɬxʷ   ilíʔ
    evid   art in outside   there

    cwíkʷmiʔst   cər'túps
    c   -wikʷ+miʔst   cr't+ups
    hab -hide   Fisher

    And Fisher was hiding outside the door.

37. ixí?   sənkxáms   sən?úcxəns   sənkstíya?
    ixí?   s   -n+kxa+m -s   s   -n+?uc+xn -s   s+n+kstíya?
    then   dur -go_on_foot-3i   dur -track   -3i skunk
    He followed behind Skunk.

38. ilí··?   cər'túps   k'əłmu··t   ixí?   scxʷuys
    ilí?   cr't+ups   k'ł+mut   ixí?   s -c+xʷuy -s
    there   Fisher   sit_sg   that   dur -come -3i
    Fisher was sitting there, he came.

39. kəm'əntís   i?   sm'am?íms
    km'   -nt -is   i?   s+m'a+m?ím   -s
    take   -nt -3erg   art   women   -3in
    He took his women.

40. cúsəlx   k'   anwí   kʷu   łə
    cu -s   -lx k'   anwí   kʷu   ł
    tell -3erg   -pl to   you   4kn   subord

    scxʷuyx
    s   -c+xʷuy -x
    ipftv^ -come   -^ ipftv^
    They told him, "We were coming for you;

41. uł   ałí?   kʷu   kəm'əntím
    uł   ałí?   kʷu   km'   -nt -im
    and   so   4obj   take   -nt -^3e4obj
    and then he took us."

42. ixí?   uł   i?   k'əł?ácəcqa?lx {uł}
    ixí?   uł   i?   k'ł+?ác+c+qa?   -lx
    then   and   the   exit_from_under   -pl
    Then they came out.

43. ?ácəcqa?lx   k'əl   tk'əmkn'íłxʷ
    ?ác+c+qa?   -lx   k'l   t+k'm+kn'+iłxʷ
    go_out_pl   -pl   to   outside
    They went outside the house;

44. ki? k'əłtk'ʷípc'a?səlx   ixí?   i?   citxʷ
    ki? k'ł+tk'ʷip+c'a?   -s   -lx   ixí?   i?   citxʷ
    rel set_fire   -3erg -pl   that   art house
    and they burned the house.

45. nt'a ki?   uláp
    nt'a ki?   wla+p
    intj rel   burn
    Gee it burned.

46. nák'ʷəm   k'ałá?   sən'kstíya?   way'   qilt
    nak'ʷm   k'ałá?   s+n+kstíya?   way'   qil+t
    evid   on_that_side   skunk   finish top

    k'ałá? {k'əl}{k'a qilt}
    k'ałá?
    on_that_side
    Skunk was already over on top.

47. ɬˢ'ác'əm   nt'a   i   suláps
    ɬ+ˢ'ac'   -m   nt'a   i?   s -wla+p -s
    look_at_again -mdl intj art dur -burn -3i
    He looked, and, gee, the fire.

48. nt'a   xi   suckl'ípəms
    nt'a   ixí?   s -wckl'+ip+m   -s
    intj   then   dur -go_downhill   -3i
    He ran down the hill.

49. nákna   t   ism'am?ím,   nákna   t
    níkxna?   t   i -s+m'a+m?ím   níkxna?   t
    goodness   ?   1in -women   goodness   ?
    ism'am?ím
    i -s+m'a+m?ím
    1in -women
    "Goodness my women, goodness my women."

50. xʷət'pəncú··t   k'li?   ɬkicx,   lut_stim'
    xʷt'+p+ncut   ik'lí?   ɬ+kic+x   lut̄_s+tim'
    run   there arrive_again   nothing
    He ran, got there, there was nothing.

51. uɬ   cyaˢ'   uláp
    uɬ   c+yaˢ'   wla+p
    and   lots   burn
    It was all burned.

52. ixí?   sc'qʷa··qʷs   uɬ   ixí?
    ixí?   s -c'qʷ+aqʷ   -s   uɬ   ixí?
    that   dur -cry   -3i   and   then
    λ'a?λ'?úsəms   i? sxʷúytən
    λ'a?+λ'?+ús+m -s   i? s+xʷuy+tn
    look_for   -3erg art track
    He cried, and he looked around for tracks.

53. {xi?} i? t   qʷəlmín uɬ   npq'ʷúsəs   ixí? i?
        i? t   qʷl+min uɬ   n+pq'ʷ+us -s ixí? i?
        art aglnst ashes   and sprinkle -3erg that art
    sxʷúytən
    s+xʷuy+tn
    track
    They sprinkled ashes on the tracks.

54. ixí?   sən?úcxəns
    ixí?   s -n+?uc+xn   -s
    then   dur -track   -3i
    He tracked them.

55. [s]xʷu··ys   uɬ   i? k'əl   st'a?t'á?pu?stn
    s- xʷuy -s   uɬ   i? k'l   s+t'a?+t'á?p+w's+tn
    dur go   -3i and art to   place_name
    He went to st'a?t'á?pu?stn.

56. ilíʔ {iʔ sútən}   iʔ   ksiwɬkʷ   q'sápiʔ
     ilíʔ   iʔ   k   -siwɬ+kʷ   q'sápiʔ
     there   the there_be   -water   long_ago

     scutx
     s   -cut   -x
     ipftv ^   -say   - ^ ipftv
     They say there's water there long time ago.

57. ilíʔ   nt'əpqsám,   uɬ   nkʷlutí··tkʷ
     ilíʔ   n+t'p+qs+a+m   uɬ   n+kʷl+wt+itkʷ
     there   tip_head   and   live_in_water
     He tipped his head to drink, there were people there.

58. nákʷʼəm   iʔ   k'əl xƛ'ut   ilíʔ   tkʷlutí[sxən]
     nakʷʼm   iʔ   k'l   xƛ'ut   ilíʔ   t+kʷl+wt+isxn
     evid   art   to   rock   there   sit_pl_on_rock
     They were sitting on the rock.

59. ixíʔ   p'əc'ntáˤs
     ixíʔ   p'c'   -nt -aˤs
     that   squirt   -nt -3erg
     He sprayed them.

60. t'əxʷ   mat   xkists   ixíʔ   kiʔ
     t'xʷ   mat   x+ki   -st -s   ixíʔ   kiʔ
     evidently   maybe   do_something -st -3erg   that   rel

     cyaxʷt   uɬ   ƛ'lal
     c+yaxʷ+t   uɬ   ƛ'l+al
     fall_cisl -fall   and   dead
     He did something to him, he fell down and died.

61. ixíʔ   uɬ   ckəm'ntís   iʔ   {niˤíp   ƛ'lal
     ixíʔ   uɬ   c+km'   -nt -is   iʔ   n+yˤ'+ip   ƛ'l+al
     then   and   take_cisl   -nt -3erg   art   still   dead

     kiw}   ixíʔ   uɬ   ckəm'ntís
     kiw   ixíʔ   uɬ   c+km'   -nt -is
     yes   then   and   take_cisl   -nt -3erg

     iʔ   sm'am'ʔíms
     iʔ   s+m'a+m'ʔím   -s
     art   women   -3in
     And he took {Still dead? Yes.} his women, then he took his women.

62. cus   anwí   k'aʔkín'   ancítxʷ
     cu -s   anwí   k'aʔ+kín'   an -citxʷ
     tell -3erg   you   where_to   2in -house
     He asked, "Where is your house?"

63. cut t'əxʷ   ya   nx̌ʷəx̌ʷc'úsaʔ
     cut t'xʷ   ya   n+x̌ʷ+x̌ʷc'+úsaʔ
     say evidently   art   stump
     She said, "In that stump."

64.   cut   way'   myaɬ   kʷəkʷyúmaʔ
       cut   way'   myaɬ   kʷ+kʷy+úmaʔ
       say   yes   too_much   small
       He said, "It's too small."

65.   cut   k'aʔkín'   anwí   ancítxʷ
       cut   k'aʔ+kín'   anwí   an -citxʷ
       say   where_to   you   2in -house
       He asked, "Where is your house?"

66.   cut t'əxʷ   aʔ   cənsq'íw's   iʔ   l   xƛ'ut
       cut t'xʷ   aʔ   c   -n+sq'+iw's   iʔ   l   xƛ'ut
       say evidently   art hab-split   art in   rock
       She said, "In that split rock."

67.   {ixíʔ   stətáq}
       ixíʔ   s+t+taq
       that   Squirrel
       This is Squirrel.

68.   {kiw}
       kiw
       yes
       Yes.

69.   cut   -   ik'líʔ   way'
       cut   ik'líʔ   way'
       say   there   OK
       He said, "Over there is OK."

70.   ixíʔ   uɬ   npəpəlxúlaʔxʷəlx
       ixíʔ   uɬ   n+p+plx+úlaʔxʷ -lx
       then   and   crawl_in   -pl
       They crawled in there.

71.   ik'líʔ   uɬ   way'   t'iʔ   k'əɬpəpílxəlx   məɬ   ixíʔ
       ik'líʔ   uɬ   way'   t'iʔ   k'ɬ+p+pilx   -lx   mɬ   ixíʔ
       there   and yes   evid   enter_under   -pl   and   that
       ʕayʕáynksəlx
       ʕay+ʕáy+nk -s   -lx
       tickle   -3erg   -pl
       As soon as they went in there they tickled him.

72.   ʕayʕáynksəlx   ilí··ʔ   uɬ   ʔitx
       ʕay+ʕáy+nk -s   -lx   ilíʔ   uɬ   ʔit+x
       tickle   -3erg -pl   there   and   sleep
       They tickled him a long time, and he went to sleep.

73.   {sənkstíyaʔ}
       s+n+kstíyaʔ
       skunk
       Skunk.

74.   {kiw}
       kiw
       yes
       Yes.

75. ʔatxílxəlx   uɬ   x̌lap   iʔ   qiɬt
    ʔatx+ílx   -lx uɬ   x̌la+p   iʔ   qiɬ+t
    sleep_pl -pl and   morning   art awaken
    They slept and in the morning he woke up.

76. uɬ   aláʔ   ck'ip' {iʔ}   iʔ   xƛ'ut aɬíʔ
    uɬ   aláʔ   c   -k'ip'   iʔ   xƛ'ut aɬíʔ
    and   here   gpat -pinch art rock   so

    taʔx̌ílsts   stətáq
    taʔx̌íl   -st -s   s+t+taq
    do_a_certain_way -st -3erg Squirrel
    He was pinched in the rock because Ground Squirrel had done that.

77. ixíʔ   uɬ   scuts   k'aɬáɬxaʔx   way'
    ixíʔ   uɬ   s -cut   -s k'aɬáɬxaʔ -x   way'
    then   and   dur -say -3i a_ways   -isimptv yes
    And he said, "Move over a little bit."

78. cut   k'aɬáʔx   qʼʷəqʼʷc'w'íyaʔ
    cut   k'aɬáʔ   -x   qʼʷ+qʼʷc'w'íyaʔ
    say   on_that_side -isimptv Chipmunk
    He said, "Move over Chipmunk."

79. uɬ   lut,   aɬíʔ   xƛ'ut   ilíʔ
    uɬ   lut   aɬíʔ   xƛ'ut   ilíʔ
    and   not   so   rock   there
    But nothing, because the rock there.

80. ixíʔ   sƛ'aʔƛ'ʔúsəms   uɬ   t'iʔ   k'aw iʔ
    ixíʔ   s -ƛ'aʔ+ƛ'ʔ+ús+m -s uɬ   t'iʔ   k'aw iʔ
    then   dur -look_for   -3i and evid gone art

    smamʔím   kmax   ixíʔ   iʔ   xƛ'ut {iʔ}
    s+ma+mʔím kmax   ixíʔ   iʔ   xƛ'ut
    women   only   that   art rock
    He looked around, the women are gone, there is only rock.

81. {xiʔs} lut   xkínəm   aɬíʔ   mi ʔácqaʔ cyax̌
           lut   x+ʔkin -m   aɬíʔ   mi ʔácqaʔ c -yax̌
           not   how   -mdl because fut go_out hab-?

    iʔ k'ip's   iʔ xƛ'ut
    iʔ k'ip' -s   iʔ xƛ'ut
    art pinch -3erg   art rock
    He can't get out, the rock has him pinched.

82. ixíʔ   təlntís   iʔ sc'uxáns
    ixíʔ   tl   -nt -is   iʔ s+c'w'+xan   -s
    then   break -nt -3erg art animal_hind_leg -3in
    He broke his foot.

83. məɬ   k'aʔx̌ís   ixíʔ   cx̌əx̌áq
    mɬ   k'aʔ+x̌ís ixíʔ   c -x̌+x̌aq
    and   over_there there hab-empty_dim
    And there is a little hole there;

84. ilí?   uɬ   ik'lí?   k'əɫc'əq'mís   k'əl tk'əmkn'íɬxʷ
     ilí?   uɬ   ik'lí?   k'ɬ+c'q'+mi -s   k'l t+k'm+kn'+iɬxʷ
     there   and   there   throw   -3erg   to   outside
     and he threw it there outside,

85. ho·y   uɬ   i?   kilxs,   uɬ   i?   sc'u?xáns {xi? uɬ i?}
     hoy   uɬ   i?   kilx -s   uɬ   i?   s+c'w'+xan   -s
     well   and   art   hand   -3in   and   art   animal_hind_leg   -3in
     and his hand and his foot.

86. stim's   ixí?   ha   sw'ar'íps
     stim'   -s   ixí?   ha   s+w'ar'+íps
     what   -3in   that   inter   Stink_Bug
     And what's that, Stink Bug

87. ixí?   ik'lí?   [nixʷ]   c'q'mís   ixí?
     ixí?   ik'lí?   nixʷ   c'q'+mi -s   ixí?
     that   there   also   throw   -3erg   that
     He threw that there too.

88. mat   ik'lí?   c'əq'mís   ki   t'i   t'uxʷt   yútəlxʷ
     mat   ik'lí?   c'q'+mi -s   ki?   t'i?   t'uxʷ+t   yutlxʷ
     maybe   there   throw   -3erg   rel   evid   fly   Raven
     As soon as he threw it there Raven flew by.

89. a?   wiks,   nwa?lílsəms   stim' {a?}
     a?   wik -s   n+wa?l+íls+m   -s   stim'
     art   see -3erg   admire   -3erg   what
     He saw that, and wondered what it was.

90. ixí?   c'əlxəntís   ixí?   snisc,
     ixí?   c'lx   -nt -is   ixí?   s   -nis   -c
     that   hook   -nt -3erg   that   dur -gone   -3i
     He grabbed it and he left.

91. {?a}   ?á··cqa?sts   i?   sqiltks
           ?ácqa? -st   -s   i?   s+qil+tk-s
           go_out -caus   -3erg   art   body   -3in
     He got his body out;

92. uɬ   lut   k'am   t'a   ksw'ar'íps   t'i
     uɬ   lut   k'am   t'   k   -s+w'ar'+íps   t'i?
     and   not   except   negfac   there_be   -Stink_Bug   evid
     cənɬx̌ʷíɬc'a?
     c   -n+ɬx̌ʷ+íɬc'a?
     hab -hole
     there was no Stink Bug, just a hole.

93. ixí?   ckm'ám   i?   t   st'?i?
     ixí?   c+km'a   -m   i?   t   s+t'?i?
     that   take_cisl   -mdl   art   obj_itr   grass
     He took some grass;

94. ta?x̌í··lsts   uɬ   ixí?   nəq'ʷməntís
     ta?x̌íl   -st -s   uɬ   ixí?   n+q'ʷm -nt -is
     do_a_certain_way   -st -3erg   and   that   put_in -nt -3erg
     He went like that and put it in that hole.

95. ixíʔ   sən̓ʔúcxəns
    ixíʔ   s   -n+ʔuc+xn -s
    then   dur -track   -3i
    He went looking for them.

96. cut way'   ik'líʔ   stər'qmíx { k'əl}   k'əl {Addy}
    cut way'   ik'líʔ   s   -tr'q   -mix   k'l
    say yes   there   ipftv ^ -kick - ^ prg at

    sk'awílaʔx
    s+k'awílaʔx
    Addy
    He said, "They are dancing at Addy."

97. ik'líʔ   xʷuy
    ik'líʔ   xʷuy
    there   go
    He went there.

98. xʷu·y,   uɬ   taʔlí   mat   q'q'sápiʔ   ki   kicx
    xʷuy   uɬ   taʔlíʔ   mat   q'+q'sápiʔ kiʔ kic+x
    go   and very_much maybe little_while rel arrive
    He went and it took him a while to get there.

99. uɬ   axáʔ {iʔ} kʷlíwt   iʔ   siyaʕ'míx   ilíʔ
    uɬ   axáʔ   kʷl+iwt iʔ   s   -yaʕ' -mix   ilíʔ
    and   this   sit_pl   art ipftv ^ -gather - ^ ipftv   there
    Those gathered there are all sitting;

100. ciyáʕ'   iʔ   stim'
     c+yaʕ'   iʔ   stim'
     lots   art thing
     everything gathered.

101. {iʔ kstər'qmíxaʔx}
     iʔ   ks   -tr'q   -míxaʔx
     art incp ^ -kick   - ^ incp
     The ones that are going to dance.

102. kiw
     kiw
     yes
     Yes.

103. həɬc'əsqáqnaʔ   itíʔ   həɬstím'   ilíʔ   uɬ
     hɬ=c'sqáq+naʔ   itíʔ   hɬ=stim'   ilíʔ   uɬ
     group=Chickadee   that   group=thing   there   and

     nqʷíc'təlx
     n+qʷic'+t   -lx
     full   -pl
     The Chickadees, everything there, full of people.

104. {t'əxʷ_mat həɬsʕ'án'}
     t'xʷ_mat   hɬ=   s+ʕ'an'
     maybe   group= Magpie
     Maybe the Magpies too.

105. kiw
kiw
yes
Yes.

106. {ixíʔ uɬ}   ixíʔ   kʷˠənkʷˠínsəlx   ixíʔ   iʔ {iʔ}
ixíʔ   kʷˠn+kʷˠin -s   -lx   ixíʔ   iʔ
then   study   -3erg   -pl   that   art

sw'ar'íp
s+w'ar'+íps
Stink_Bug
They were examining that Stink Bug.

107. t'iʔ   knaqs   ɬkʷˠi··s,   məɬ   itlíʔ
t'iʔ   k+naqs   ɬ+kʷˠi   -s   mɬ   itlíʔ
evid   one_person take_again -3erg   and   from_there

xʷˠíc'xəms   uɬ   nxƛ'pnúsəlx
xʷˠic'+x+m   -s   uɬ   n+xƛ'+p   -nu   -s   -lx
give_to   -3erg and   complete -manage   -3erg   -pl
One would take it, and pass it to somebody else, they all looked at it.

108. ixíʔ   skicx
ixíʔ   s   -kic   -x
then   ipftv ^ -reach_st/b - ^ ipftv
Then he came.

109. cut   nq'ʷˠəmq'ʷˠmúsənt   iʔ   ciyáʕ   cx̌əqx̌áq {cəm'}
cut   n+q'ʷˠm+q'ʷˠm+us -nt   iʔ   c+yaʕ   c   -x̌q+x̌aq
say   plug_hole   -nt   art   all   hab-hole
He said, "Plug all the holes;

110. cəm'   xuxwáp   ism'aʔm'áy',   kən
cm'   xw+xwa+p i   -s+m'aʔ+m'áy'   kn
maybe   deflate   1in -story   1kn

ksm'aʔm'áy'
k   -s+m'aʔ+m'áy'
have   -story
the air might go out of my story, I have a story.

111. cəm'   itíʔ   xuxəwáp
cm'   itíʔ   xw+xwa+p
maybe   from_that   deflate
It might ooze out."

112. ixíʔ   nq'ʷˠəmq'ʷˠmú··səlx
ixíʔ   n+q'ʷˠm+q'ʷˠm+us   -s   -lx
then   plug_hole   -3erg   -pl
They plugged the holes;

113. uɬ   cut   xc'əmstíp,   taʔlíʔ
uɬ   cut   xc'+m   -st   -ip   taʔlíʔ
and   say   tight   -caus -5erg   very_much

xc'əmstíp
xc'+m   -st   -ip
tight   -caus -5erg
He said, "Plug them tight, tight.

114.ta?lí?   xast   iksm'a?m'áy'   cəm'
    ta?lí?   xas+t   i -k   -s+m'a?m'áy' cm'
    very_much good   1i -to_be -story   maybe

    xuxəwáp
    xw+xwa+p
    deflate
    My story is very good, and it might ooze out."

115.ixí?   nq'^wəmq'^wmúsəlx
    ixí?   n+q'^wm+q'^wm+us   -s   -lx
    then   plug_hole   3erg -pl

    xəc'mstísəlx
    xc'+m -st   -is   -lx
    tight   -caus -3erg -pl
    They plugged the holes good and tight.

116.ixí?   scuts   kən   cx^wuyax^wú··y   kən
    ixí?   s -cut -s   kn   c+x^wuy+a+x^wúy kn
    then   dur -say -3i   1kn come   1kn

    cx^wuyax^wú··y   kən   cyayúx^wt
    c+x^wuy+a+x^wúy   kn   c+ya+yúx^wt
    come   1kn   fall_cisl
    He said, "I came, I came, I came down."[1]

117.{t'a ki} ta?x̌íləm   p'əlk'məncút
           ta?x̌íl   -m   p'lk'+mncut
           do_a_certain_way -mdl   turn_around
    He did like that, turned around;

118.k   cənlp'x̌^wúps   ixí? i?   t   sútən   [i? t]
    ki? c -n+lp'x̌^w+ups   ixí? i?   t   sutn   i? t
    rel hab -stuck_in_anus   that art agInst thing   art agInst

    sw'ar'íps
    s+w'ar'+íps
    Stink_Bug
    That thing, Stink Bug was stuck in the anus;

119.ixí?   p'əc'əntáˤməlx
    ixí?   p'c'   -nt -aˤm   -lx
    that   squirt -nt -psv   -pl
    and it squirted out;

120.məł   k'la? xəlkməncút
    mł   ak'lá? xlk+mncut
    and   here   turn
    and then he turned a bit;

---

[1] Madeline DeSautel commented that the storyteller is dragging her story.

121. məɬ   cut   kən   cxʷuyaxʷúˑy   kən   cxʷuyaxʷúˑy
     mɬ   cut   kn   c+xʷuy+a+xʷúy   kn   c+xʷuy+a+xʷúy
     and   say   1kn   come   1kn   come

     kən   cyayúxʷt
     kn   c+ya+yúxʷt
     1kn   fall_cisl

     And he said, "I came, I came, I came down."

122. nt'aˑ   ixíʔ   sxítmiʔstsəlx {iʔ}
     nt'a   ixíʔ   s -xít+miʔst -s -lx
     intj   that   dur -run   -3i -pl

     They ran.

123. ɬíx̌ʷptəlx   ixíʔ   həɬsƛ'aʔcínəm
     ɬix̌ʷp+t   -lx   ixíʔ   hɬ=   s+ƛ'aʔcínm
     slipped_away -pl   that   group= Deer

     The Deer ran out.

124. ciyáˤ   iʔ   stim'   xítmiʔstəlx   yilyáltəlx
     c+yaˤ   iʔ   stim'   xít+miʔst -lx yl+yalt   -lx
     all   art thing   run   -pl run_away -pl

     Everyone ran, ran away.

125. ilíˑʔ   ck'əɬt'ákʷ   yútəlxʷ
     ilíʔ   c -k'ɬ+t'ak'ʷ   yutlxʷ
     there   hab-lay_under Raven

     Raven is laying there;

126. aɬíʔ   sílxʷaʔ   iʔ   sənp'sáqstəns
     aɬíʔ   sílxʷaʔ   iʔ   s+n+p's+aqs+tn -s
     so   big   art nose   -3in

     he has a big nose;

127. nxuxupáqs   nt'aˑ   ck'əɬt'ak'ʷ
     n+xw+xw+p+aqs   nt'a   c -k'ɬ+t'ak'ʷ
     air_in_nose   intj   hab-lay_under

     the air went in his nose, he was lying there;

128. uɬ   ixíʔ   cut   laq'ísˑ   laq'ísˑ
     uɬ   ixíʔ   cut   laq'ís   laq'ís
     and   then say   cut_off   cut_off

     he said, "Cut it off, cut it off."

129. ixíʔ   uɬ   lut t'   q'aʔílsəmsəlx
     ixíʔ   uɬ   lut t'   q'aʔ+íls+m   -s   -lx
     that   and   not negfac pay_attention -3erg   -pl

     And nobody paid attention to him;

130. ixíʔ   ylyáltəlx
     ixíʔ   yl+yalt   -lx
     then   run_away   -pl

     they all ran away.

131. nstils   n'ín'w'iʔ   k'əɬník'ɬtsəlx   iʔ
     n+st+ils   n'ín'w'iʔ   k'ɬ+nik' -ɬt -s   -lx iʔ
     think   a_while,   cut_out -ɬt -3erg -pl art

sp'sáqsc
s+p's+aqs -c
nose   -3in
He thought if they cut his nose off;

132.uɫ   way'   ɫə   ksqiʔxʷnúy's {iʔ}
uɫ   way'   ɫ   ks   -qy'xʷ -nu   -y'   -s
and   yes   subord futT^ -smell -manage -^futT -3erg
then he won't smell that.

133.ixíʔ   uɫ   way'   nc'ayxʷápəlqs
ixíʔ   uɫ   way'   n+c'ayxʷ+áplqs
that   and   finish end_of_story
And that's the end of the story.

COYOTE, BEAR, AND KINGFISHER

1. cwix   iʔ   sqilxʷ
   c -wix   iʔ   s+qilxʷ
   hab-live   art   person
   There are people.

2. ixíʔ {a·}   sənk'l'íp   uɬ   ʕalapúl   uɬ   iʔ
   ixíʔ   s+n+k'l'+ip   uɬ   ʕalapúl   uɬ   iʔ
   that   Coyote   and   Gopher   and   art

   sqʷəsqʷasíʔasəlx
   s+qʷs+qʷasíʔa -s -lx
   children   -3in -pl
   Coyote and Gopher and their children;

3. kmúsməs {iʔ s}   iʔ   tuʔtw'ít
   k+mus+ms   iʔ   tw'+tw'it
   four_persons   art   boys
   four boys.

4. uɬ   t'əxʷ   kskʷəskʷíst,   lut   t'a
   uɬ   t'xʷ   k   -s+kʷs+kʷist   lut   t'
   and   evidently   have   -name_pl   not   negfac

   cmistín
   c   -my   -st   -in
   cust ^ -know - ^ cust -1erg
   And they have names, I don't know them;

5. p'aʕc'əlqʷáʕw'stxən,   uɬ   tkʷər'kʷər'ákstxən,   uɬ
   p'aʕc'+lqʷ+aʕw'st+xn   uɬ   t+kʷr'+kʷr'+akst+xn   uɬ
   Squirted_leg   and   Yellow_leg   and

   ttiɬtáɬlqʷ
   t+tiɬ+taɬ+lqʷ
   Straight_Leg
   Squirted Legs, and Yellow Legs, and Straight Legs.

6. ixíʔ   iʔ   sqʷəsqʷasíʔas   təl'   púl'laʔxʷ   {kiw}
   ixíʔ   iʔ   s+qʷs+qʷasíʔa -s   tl'   púl'+laʔxʷ   kiw
   that   art children   -3in   from   Gopher   yes
   These are his children from Gopher.

7. ixíʔ   uɬ   kʷlíwtəlx,   uɬ   ixíʔ   scuts
   ixíʔ   uɬ   kʷl+iwt -lx   uɬ   ixíʔ   s -cut   -s
   that   and   be_home   -pl   and   then   dur -say   -3i

   sənk'l'íp {cut way' kən}
   s+n+k'l'+ip
   Coyote
   They were sitting around, and Coyote said;

53

8. sənk'líp   cut   way'   kən ksx*ʷ*úya?x {k' ił}   k'
    s+n+k'l'+ip   cut   way'   kn ks   -x*ʷ*uy -a?x   k'
    Coyote   say   well   1kn incp ^   -go   - ^ incp   to

    iłqáqca? {k'əl}   k'əl   skəmxíst
    i -ł+qá+qca?   k'l   s+kmxist
    1in -older_brother to   Bear
    Coyote said: "I'm going to go to my brother Bear."

9. ixí?   uł   sx*ʷ*uy[s]
    ixí?   uł   s -x*ʷ*uy   -s
    then   and   dur -go   -3i
    And he went.

10. x*ʷ*u··y,   kicx   uł   mut   uł   xi?   cúntəm
    x*ʷ*uy   kic+x   uł   mut   uł   ixí?   cu -nt -m
    go   arrive   and   sit_sg   and   then   tell -nt -psv
    He went, got there, sat down and he said to her;

11. t   skəmxíst   cus   i?   təkłmílx*ʷ*s
    t   s+kmxist   cu -s   i?   tkłm+ilx*ʷ*   -s
    aglnst   Bear   tell -3erg art   wife   -3in
    Bear told his wife:

12. way'   aks?amnám   askícəc
    way'   a -ks   -?amná -m   a -s+kic+c
    well   2i -futT ^ -feed - ^ futT   2in -visitor
    "You better feed your visitor."

13. cut ałí? t   stim'   mi ?amtín,   lut kən
    cut ałí? t   stim'   mi ?am -t -in   lut kn
    say so aglnst   what_thing fut feed -nt -1erg   not 1kn

    t'a   ks[tim']
    t'   k -s+tim'
    negfac   have -thing
    She said, "And what'll I feed him, I haven't got anything."

14. ixí?   uł   ta?x̌ílsts   i?
    ixí?   uł   ta?x̌íl   -st -s   i?
    then   and   do_a_certain_way   -st -3erg   art

    n'ín'k'mən's,   x̌*ʷ*əyx̌*ʷ*áyt
    n'i+n'k'+mn'-s   x̌*ʷ*y+x̌*ʷ*ay+t
    knife   -3in   sharp
    Then he took his knife, sharp;

15. uł   xí?   tx*ʷ*uyms   i?   təkłmílx*ʷ*s   uł   xi?
    uł   ixí?   t+x*ʷ*uy+m   -s   i?   tkłm+ilx*ʷ*   -s   uł   ixí?
    and   then   go_for   -3erg   art   wife   -3in   and   then

    xa?   k*ʷ*iłts   uł   k'əlník'əłts
    axá?   k*ʷ*i   -łt -s   uł   k'ł+nik' -łt-s
    this   take   -łt -3erg   and   cut_out -łt-3erg
    he walked over to his wife, took her [breast] and cut it off.

16. ixí?   ntqúsəs {i?}   i?   q*ʷ*əlmín   uł   xi?
    ixí?   n+tq+us   -s   i?   q*ʷ*l+min   uł   ixí?
    then   put_on   -3erg   art   ashes   and   then

ta?x̌ílsts   uɬ   t'i?   x̌ast
ta?x̌íl   -st -s   uɬ   t'i?   x̌as+t
do_a_certain_way -st -3erg   and   evid   good

He put his hands on the ashes, did like that, and it was healed.

17. ixí?   t'ək'ʷɬtím   ilí?
    ixí?   t'k'ʷ-ɬt   -im   ilí?
    then   put_down   -ɬt-psv   there

    He put that down there.

18. ixí?   sk'ʷəl'cəncúts   i   l   [ɬək]cín   t'əx̌ʷ
    ixí?   s -k'ʷl'+cn+cut   -s   i?   l   ɬk+cin   t'x̌ʷ
    then   dur -cook   -3i   art in   bowl   evidently

    stim'   i?   {x̌əc}cín
    stim'   i?   ɬk+cin
    something art bowl

    He started to cook it in the bucket, a pot.

19. ilí?   nt'k'ʷitk̓ʷs   uɬ   nɬəx̌ʷpúsəs {uɬ}
    ilí?   n+t'k'ʷ+itk̓ʷ   -s   uɬ   n+ɬx̌ʷp+us -s
    there   throw_in_water -3erg   and   boil   -3erg

    He put it in the water, and boiled it.

20. ixí?   nutnítk̓ʷs {i}   i   t   sútən, i   t
    ixí?   n+wtn+itk̓ʷ   -s   i?   t   sutn   i?   t
    then   put_in_water   -3erg   art obj_tr thing art obj_tr

    síya?,   i   t   stim',   np'c'ʕatk̓ʷs
    síya?   i?   t   stim'   n+p'c'+aʕtk̓ʷ   -s
    saskatoons   art obj_tr something   squirt_in_water -3erg

    He put things in the water, saskatoons, things, he shat in there.

21. ixí?   ilí?   utəntís,   uɬ   ixí?
    ixí?   ilí?   wt   -nt -is   uɬ   ixí?
    then   there   put_down -nt -3erg   and   then

    scuts   sənk'l'íp
    s -cut   -s   s+n+k'l'+ip
    dur -say -3i Coyote

    He put it there, and Coyote said:

22. lut itlí?   t'   iks?íɬən,   way'   maɬ [unf]
    lut itlí?   t'   i -ks   -?iɬn   way'   maɬ
    not from_there negfac 1i -futl   -eat   yes   too_much

    "I'm not going to eat any of that, it's too..."

23. k'a?x̌ís {ɬn}   p'əlk'məncút   xi?
    k'a?+x̌ís   p'lk'+mncut   ixí?
    over_there   turn_around   then

    ta?x̌ílsts   alá?   ttəqəntís
    ta?x̌íl   -st -s   alá?   t+tq   -nt -is
    do_a_certain_way -st -3erg   here   touch_dim -nt -3erg

uɬ   ixíʔ   c'ums
uɬ   ixíʔ   c'um   -s
and   that   suck   -3erg

He [Bear] turned around, and he [Coyote] put his finger there easy and sucked.

24. níkna   way'   t'iʔ   x̌ast
    níkxnaʔ   way'   t'iʔ   x̌as+t
    goodness   yes   evid   good

    Goodness, it's good.

25. xiʔ   ilíʔ   ʔíˑɬən   uɬ   xiʔ   cúntəm   t
    ixíʔ   ilíʔ   ʔiɬn   uɬ   ixíʔ   cu -nt -m   t
    then   there   eat   and   then   tell -nt -psv aglnst

    skəmxíst
    s+kmxist
    Bear

    He ate and ate, and then Bear said to him:

26. way'   ɬxʷuystxʷ   ixíʔ   k'   asqʷəsqʷasíʔa
    way'   ɬ+xʷuy+st   -xʷ   ixíʔ   k'   a -s+qʷs+qʷasíʔa
    yes   take_st_back   -2erg   that   to   2in -children

    "Take the rest back to your children."

27. ixíʔ   təɬxʷúys
    ixíʔ   ɬ   -ɬ+xʷuy   -s
    then   dur -go_back   -3i

    He went back.

28. ɬxʷuy   uɬ   xiʔ   xʷíc'əɬts   ʕalapúl   uɬ
    ɬ+xʷuy   uɬ   ixíʔ   xʷic' -ɬt   -s   ʕalapúl   uɬ
    go_back   and   then   give -ɬt -3erg   Gopher   and

    ʔaɬʔíɬən[lx]
    ʔaɬ+ʔiɬn -lx
    eat_pl -pl

    He went and gave it to Gopher and they ate.

29. ixíʔ   mat   k'ʷən'ásaʔq't   uɬ   xiʔ   scuts
    ixíʔ   mat   k'ʷn'+ásaʔq't   uɬ   ixíʔ   s -cut   -s
    then   maybe   few_days   and   then   dur -say   -3i

    A few days after that he said:

30. kən   ksxʷúyaʔx   k'   iɬqáqcaʔ   k'əl
    kn   ks   -xʷuy -aʔx   k'   i -ɬ+qá+qcaʔ   k'l
    1kn   incp^ -go   -^incp   to   1in -older_brother   to

    c'ris
    c'ris
    Kingfisher

    "I'm going over to my brother Kingfisher."

31. ixíʔ   sxʷuys   k'əl c'r[is]
    ixíʔ   s   -xʷuy   -s   k'l c'ris
    then   dur -go   -3i   to Kingfisher

    So he went to Kingfisher.

32. x̌ʷuy   uɬ   kicx   uɬ   c'ris   cut   way'   ʔamnánt
    x̌ʷuy   uɬ   kic+x   uɬ   c'ris   cut   way'   ʔamná -nt
    go   and   arrive   and   Kingfisher   say   well   feed   -nt

    askícəc
    a -s+kic+c
    2in -visitor
    He went and got there and Kingfisher said, "Feed your visitor."

33. cut   uɬ   aɬíʔ   t   stim'
    cut   uɬ   aɬíʔ   t   stim'
    say   and   so   obj_itr   what
    She said, "And what?"

34. cut   way'   t'i   k'ík'aʔt   iʔ   siwɬkʷ   n'u
    cut   way'   t'iʔ   k'í+k'aʔt   iʔ   siwɬ+kʷ   n'u
    say   yes   evid   near   art   water   a_while

    t   qáqx̌ʷəlx
    t   qa+qx̌ʷ+lx
    obj_itr fish
    He said, "The water is near, fish."

35. ixíʔ   t'ux̌ʷt   uɬ   k'a   nwist   iʔ   k'a   np'ƛ'əmqsíɬx̌ʷ
    ixíʔ   t'ux̌ʷ+t   uɬ   k'   n+wis+t   iʔ   k'   n+p'ƛ'm+qs+iɬx̌ʷ
    then   fly   and   to   high   art   to   tipi_top

    itlíʔ   uɬ   t'ux̌ʷt
    itlíʔ   uɬ   t'ux̌ʷ+t
    from_there and   fly
    So he flew high on top of his tipi, he flew from there.

36. t'iʔ   c'ar··   uɬ   nɬət'pmítkʷ
    t'iʔ   c'ar   uɬ   n+ɬt'p+m+itkʷ
    evid   onom   and   jump_in_water
    He went c'arrrr, he jumped in the water.

37. ixíxiʔ   uɬ   cus   iʔ   sqʷəsqʷasíʔas
    ix+íxiʔ   uɬ   cu -s   iʔ   s+qʷs+qʷasíʔa -s
    in_a_while   and   tell -3erg   art   children   -3in

    x̌ʷuyx   kənxít   ya   lʔíwmp   way'   iʔ
    x̌ʷuy -x   kn+xit   ya   lʔiw   -mp   way'   iʔ
    go   -isimptv   help   art   m's_father -5in well   art

    qáqx̌ʷəlx
    qa+qx̌ʷ+lx
    fish
    In a while she told his children, "Go help your father with the fish."

38. ixíʔ   sʔácəcqaʔs   iʔ   tuʔtw'ít   uɬ   xiʔ
    ixíʔ   s -ʔác+c+qaʔ -s   iʔ   tw'+tw'it   uɬ   ixíʔ
    then   dur -go_out_pl -3i art   boys   and   that

    kənxítsəlx
    kn+xit -s   -lx
    help   -3erg   -pl
    The boys went out and they helped him.

39. alá?   kłpək^wntísəlx   i?   qáqx^wəlx
    alá?   kł+pk^w   -nt-is   -lx   i?   qa+qx^w+lx
    here   put_down   -nt-3erg -pl   art   fish
    They put the fish down.

40. ixí?   k'^wəl'cəncút   uł   ?amtí[s]
    ixí?   k'^wl'+cn+cut   uł   ?am   -t   -is
    that   cook   and   feed   -nt   -3erg
    She cooked and she fed them.

41. uł   i?   k'^wiƛ't   lut   t'   xkists
    uł   i?   k'^wiƛ'+t   lut   t'   x+ki   -st   -s
    and   art   others   not   negfac   do_something   -st   -3erg
    She didn't do anything to some.

42. kmax   i?   k'^wiƛ't   k'^wəl'[cəncúts]
    kmax   i?   k'^wiƛ'+t   k'^wl'+cn+cut   -s
    only   art   others   cook   -3erg
    She cooked just some.

43. ixí?   wi?wi?cínəlx,   uł   ixí?   cúntəm   t
    ixí?   wy'+wy'+cin   -lx   uł   ixí?   cu -nt-m   t
    that   finish_eating_pl   -pl   and then   tell -nt-psv aglnst

    c'ris
    c'ris
    Kingfisher
    They got done eating and Kingfisher said:

44. way'   xast   ł   kəm'ntíx^w   k'   asq^wəsq^wsí?a
    way'   xas+t   ł   km'   -nt   -ix^w   k'   a -s+q^ws+q^wasí?a
    yes   good   if   take   -nt   -2erg   to   2in -children
    "It's best you take this to your children."

45. ixí?   łəłx^wúys   sənk'l'íp
    ixí?   ł   -ł+x^wuy   -s   s+n+k'l'+ip
    then   dur -go_back   -3i   Coyote
    Then Coyote went back home.

46. {ixí? ilí?}   k^wlí··wtəlx   uł   ixí?   sˁ'ác'əms   k'la?
                  k^wl+iwt -lx   uł   ixí?   s -ˁ'ac'+m   -s   ak'lá?
                  sit_pl   -pl   and then   dur -look   -3i   here
    They were sitting down, and they looked there.

47. níkna   way'   uł   txa   ck'a?ítət {s}   skəm'xíst
    níkxna?   way'   uł   txa   c+k'a?ít+ł   s+kmx+ist
    goodness   yes   and   ?   get_near_cisl   Bear
    Gee, Bear was coming.

48. ixí?   cən?úłx^w {uł}   skəm'xíst
    ixí?   c+n+?úłx^w   s+kmx+ist
    then   enter_cisl   Bear
    Bear came in.

49. cúntəm   t   sənk'l'íp
    cu -nt-m   t   s+n+k'l'+ip
    tell -nt-psv aglnst   Coyote
    Coyote said to her:

50. way' {uɬ}   aks?amnám   askícəc
    way'   a -ks -?amná -m   a -s+kic+c
    yes   2i -futT ^ -feed - ^ futT 2in -visitor
    "Give your visitor something to eat."

51. ixí?   scuts   ˤalapúl uɬ t   stim' mi
    ixí?   s -cut -s   ˤalapúl uɬ t   stim' mi
    then   dur -say -3i Gopher and obj_tr what fut

    ?amtín
    ?am -t -in
    feed -nt -1erg
    And Gopher said, "And what'll I feed him?"

52. {cúntəm}   ixí?   uɬ   ixí?   kʷis   i?
    cu -nt -m   ixí?   uɬ   ixí?   kʷi -s   i?
    say -nt -psv then and   that take -3erg art

    n'ín'k'mən'   ixí?   ta?x̌əlx̌ílsts   ˤala[púl]
    n'i+n'k'+mn' ixí?   ta?+x̌l+x̌íl -st -s ˤalapúl
    knife   then   do_that_pl -st -3erg Gopher
    He took the knife and did that to Gopher.

53. {ixí?} uɬ   aɬí? kmax síp'i?s
          uɬ   aɬí? kmax síp'i? -s
          and   so only hide   -3in
    And it's nothing but her skin.

54. ixí? ckʷíɬtəm   ta?x̌íɬ[təm]   məɬ ixí? ník'ɬtəm
    ixí? c+kʷi -ɬt -m   ta?x̌í -ɬt -m   mɬ ixí? nik' -ɬt-m
    then take_cisl -ɬt -psv do_that -ɬt -psv and that cut -ɬt-psv
    He went like that and cut it.

55. alalalala kən   nx̌iɬ   cqqink   λ'lal
    alalalala kn   n+x̌iɬ   cq+q+ink   λ'l+al
    onom   1kn   afraid   fall_on_back dead
    She hollered, "alalalala, I'm afraid!" She fell on her back, fainted.

56. {ixí? cu}   cúntəm   way'   ci?skʷ
             cu -nt -m   way'   ci? -skʷ
             tell -nt -psv yes   stop -tsimptv

    ckʷníkstəmstxʷ   a [unf]
    c   -kʷn+ikst+m   -st   -xʷ   a
    cust ^ -abuse   - ^ cust -2erg art
    He [Bear] told him [Coyote], "Leave her alone, you're abusing your..."

57. ixí? cniɬc   k'əɬník's   uɬ ilí?   t'kʷəntís
    ixí? cniɬ+c k'ɬ+nik' -s uɬ ilí?   t'kʷ   -nt-is
    then (s)he cut_out -3erg and there put_down -nt-3erg

    i? [unf]
    i?
    art
    And he [Bear] cut it [his own] and put down the ...;

58. ntqúsəs   iʔ   qʷəlmín   uɬ
    n+tq+us -s   iʔ   qʷl+min   uɬ
    put_on   -3erg   art   ashes   and

    taʔx̌ílsts   uɬ   x̌əstwílx
    taʔx̌íl   -st -s   uɬ   x̌s+t+wilx
    do_a_certain_way -st -3erg   and   get_well
    He put his hand on the ashes, did like that, and it healed.

59. ixí··ʔ   ixíʔ   cut   way'   ixíʔ   iɬəlx̌ʷúy
    ixíʔ   ixíʔ   cut   way'   ixíʔ   i   -ɬ   -ɬ+x̌ʷuy
    then   then   say   yes   then   1i   -inten -go_back
    He said, "I'm going back home."

60. uɬ   ixíʔ   ɬəɬnisc {sən}   skəmxíst
    uɬ   ixíʔ   ɬ   -ɬ+nis   -c   s+kmxist
    and   then   dur -gone_again   -3i   Bear
    And Bear went back.

61. cut   aɬíʔ   mnímɬtət   nk'ʷúl'məntət   ixíʔ
    cut   aɬíʔ   mnimɬ+tt   n+k'ʷul'+mn   -tt   ixíʔ
    say   because   us   custom   -4in   that
    He said, "That's our way of doing things."

62. ixíʔ   ɬəɬnísc
    ixíʔ   ɬ   -ɬ+nis   -c
    that   dur -gone_again   -3i
    He went back.

63. ixíʔ   scuts   sənk'l'íp
    ixíʔ   s   -cut   -s   s+n+k'l'+ip
    then   dur -say   -3i   Coyote
    Coyote said:

64. aɬíʔ   ilíʔ {ks}   kʷu   kstiʔx̌ílaʔx   kiʔ [unf]
    aɬíʔ   ilíʔ   kʷu   ks   -tiʔx̌íl -aʔx   kiʔ
    because   there   4kn   incp^   -do_so   -^incp   rel
    "That's what we wanted to do..."

65. ixíʔ   uɬ   sʔaɬʔíɬənsəlx,   k'ʷúl'səlx   ixíʔ,
    ixíʔ   uɬ   s -ʔaɬ+ʔíɬn -s   -lx   k'ʷul'   -s   -lx   ixíʔ
    then   and   dur -eat_pl -3i -pl   fix   -3erg -pl   that

    k'ʷəl'cəncútəlx
    k'ʷl'+cn+cut -lx
    cook   -pl
    They ate, they fixed it and cooked it.

66. xi··ʔ   uɬ   k'ʷənʔásaʔq't   uɬ   ʕ'ác'əm
    ixíʔ   uɬ   k'ʷn'+ásaʔq't   uɬ   ʕ'ac'   -m
    then   and   few_days   and   look_at -mdl
    A few days later he looked, gee!

67. níkna   way'   axáʔ   t'əcx̌ʷúy   c'ris
    níkxnaʔ   way'   axáʔ   t'c   -x̌ʷuy   c'ris
    goodness   yes   this   actCisl -go   Kingfisher
    Kingfisher is coming.

68. nt'a   kəm'əntís   i? sqʷəsqʷasí?as
     nt'a   km'   -nt -is   i? s+qʷs+qʷasí?a -s
     intj   take   -nt -3erg art children   -3in
     He grabbed his children;

69. ixí?   nlək'u?súsəs
     ixí?   n+lk'+w's+us   -s
     then   tie_in_middle -3erg
     he tied their hair up.

70. cyaˤ   cənlək'u?sústs
     c+yaˤ   c   -n+lk'+w's+us -st   -s
     all   cust^ -tie_in_middle -^cust -3erg
     He tied all of them.

71. ˤalapúl   ałí? lut   t'a   kłqəpqíntən
     ˤalapúl   ałí? lut   t'   kł   -qp+qin+tn
     Gopher   so   not negfac have   -hair
     Gopher didn't have any hair;

72. kʷˈəkʷˈína? ixí? uł ta?x̌ílsts   alá?
     kʷˈ+kʷˈína? ixí? uł ta?x̌íl   -st -s   alá?
     small   then   and do_a_certain_way -st -3erg   here

     uł   lk'łtís
     uł   lk' -łt -is
     and tie -łt -3erg
     just a little, and he did like that and tied it.

73. ní··kna   ałí? cənqʷa?qʷ?ípna?   ak'lá?
     níkxna?   ałí? c -n+qʷa?+qʷ?+ípna? ak'lá?
     goodness so   hab-cheek_pocket   here
     Gee, she has big cheek pockets;

74. uł   náx̌əmł   cənlək'u?sús
     uł   nax̌mł   c -n+lk'+w's+us
     and   but   hab-tie_in_middle
     and that thing tied there.

75. ik'lí?   kicx   ixí?   scuts
     ik'lí?   kic+x ixí?   s -cut   -s
     there   arrive that   dur -say   -3i
     He got there, and he said:

76. way'   aksk'ʷúl'cnəm
     way'   a -ks   -k'ʷul'+cn -m
     yes   2i -futT^ -cook   -^futT
     "You better cook."

77. məł   cut   ałí? lut kən t'a   kstim'
     mł   cut   ałí? lut kn   t'   k -s+tim'
     and   say   so   not 1kn negfac have -thing
     She said, "I don't have anything."

78. ixí?   i? stk'iwlx   sənk'l'íp   k'a nwist
     ixí?   i? s -t+k'iw+lx s+n+k'l'+ip k' n+wis+t
     then   art ? -climb   Coyote   to high
     Coyote climbed the tent pole.

79. tk'iwlx   uɬ   c'ar··   {ki}
    t+k'iw+lx   uɬ   c'r   kiw
    climb   and   onom   yes
    He climbed and went c'ar··.

80. k'la··ʔ   után   tk'iwlx   kiʔ   ʕác'əs   way'   lut
    ak'láʔ   wtan   t+k'iw+lx   kiʔ   ʕ'ac' -s   way'   lut
    here   placed   climb   rel   look_at -3erg   yes   not

    nákʷəm
    nakʷm
    evid
    He climbed and looked, and sure enough;

81. maɬ   lkʷut   iʔ   siwɬkʷ   uɬ   lut   t'a
    maɬ   lkʷ+ut   iʔ   siwɬ+kʷ   uɬ   lut   t'
    too_much   far   art   water   and   not   negfac

    cmistís
    c   -my   -st   -is
    cust^ -know -^cust -3erg
    the water is far and he doesn't know [how].

82. *unint*   cərqməncút   kiʔ   kɬt'kʷkʷíkən'
              crq+mncut   kiʔ   kɬ+t'kʷ+kʷ+ikn'
              jump   rel   fall_on_ice
    He jumped and fell on the ice.

83. lut   k'aʔx̌ís   iʔ   k'əl siwɬkʷ   uɬ   t'iʔ   axáʔ   i   l [unf]
    lut   k'aʔ+x̌ís   iʔ   k'l   siwɬ+kʷ   uɬ   t'iʔ   axáʔ   iʔ   l
    not over_there   art   to   water   and   evid   this   art   in
    Not in the water, but here on the ...;

84. ck'láʔ   kiʔ   t'kʷakʷ
    c+k'laʔ   kiʔ   t'kʷ+akʷ
    this_way   rel   land_flat
    he fell on this side.

85. ilíʔ   kɬt'kʷkʷíkən'
    ilíʔ   kɬ+t'kʷ+kʷ+ikn'
    there   fall_on_ice
    He fell on the ice.

86. ixíʔ   uɬ   sƛ'lals
    ixíʔ   uɬ   s -ƛ'l+al -s
    then   and   dur -dead -3i
    He passed out.

87. k'əɬʔí··msəlx   uɬ   xiʔ   cus   iʔ
    k'ɬ+ʔim -s   -lx uɬ   ixíʔ   cu -s   iʔ
    wait_for -3erg   -pl and   then   tell -3erg   art

    sqʷəsqʷasíʔas
    s+qʷs+qʷasíʔa -s
    children   -3in
    They waited and waited, and then she told her children:

88. xʷúywi ʕ'ác'ənti {ya}
    xʷuy -wy ʕ'ac' -nt-y
    go -ipimptv look_at -nt-tpimptv
    "Go look."

89. ik'líʔ ixíʔ sxʷúy'səlx {ki}
    ik'líʔ ixíʔ s -xʷuy -s -lx kiw
    there then dur -go -3i -pl yes
    They went there.

90. k'li‥ʔ ʕ'ác'əsəlx
    ik'líʔ ʕ'ac' -s -lx
    there look_at -3erg -pl
    They looked.

91. nt'a ilí‥ʔ ckəłt'k'ʷíkən
    nt'a ilíʔ c -kł+t'k'ʷ+ikn'
    intj there hab-lie_on_ice
    He was lying on the ice.

92. ixíʔ ckəm'km'áx̌səlx uł ckʷákssəlx
    ixíʔ c+km'+km'+ax̌ -s -lx uł ckʷa+ks-s -lx
    then take_pl_cisl -3erg -pl and drag -3erg -pl

    k'əl citxʷs
    k'l citxʷ -s
    to house -3in
    They took him by the arms and dragged him to his house.

93. uł ixíʔ iʔ kʷriʔ a cwikstxʷ i
    uł ixíʔ iʔ kʷriʔ a c -wik -st -xʷ iʔ
    and that art yellow art cust ^ -see - ^ cust -2erg art

    l sxʷúyənt t'iʔ kʷriʔ
    l s+xʷuy+nt t'iʔ kʷriʔ
    in ice evid yellow
    And that yellow that you see on the ice, it's yellow;

94. ixíʔ mat [tkiʔ]
    ixíʔ mat tkiʔ
    that must pee
    must be pee.

95. {kiw}
    kiw
    yes
    yes.

96. ilíʔ ałíʔ kiʔ t'k'ʷakʷ
    ilíʔ ałíʔ kiʔ t'k'ʷ+akʷ
    there because rel land_flat
    That's where he fell.

97. ixíʔ c'ris t'uxʷt {uł} k'laʔ
    ixíʔ c'ris t'uxʷ+t ak'láʔ
    that Kingfisher fly here
    Kingisher flew there.

98. uɬ   t'uxʷt   uɬ   kɬtər'qíkiʔs   ixíʔ   uɬ   nʔuɬxʷ
    uɬ   t'uxʷ+t   uɬ   kɬ+tr'q+íkiʔ -s   ixíʔ   uɬ   n+ʔuɬxʷ
    and   fly   and   kick_ice   -3erg   then   and   enter
    He flew and kicked the ice and went under.

99. km'a··m   uɬ   ixíʔ   ilíʔ   kɬqmíɬtməlx
    km'a   -m   uɬ   ixíʔ   ilíʔ   kɬ+qmi   -ɬt-m   -lx
    take   -mdl   and   that   there   lay_st_down   -ɬt-psv   -pl
    He grabbed a bunch, and lay them down.

100. ixíʔ   ɬəɬnísc
     ixíʔ   ɬ   -ɬ+nis   -c
     that   dur -gone_again   -3i
     He went back home.

101. axáʔ   sənk'líp   ilíʔ   ct'a··k'ʷ
     axáʔ   s+n+k'l'+ip   ilíʔ   c   -t'ak'ʷ
     this   Coyote   there   hab -put_down
     Coyote was lying there.

102. ixíʔ   mat   mipnús,   nx̌əlpús
     ixíʔ   mat   my+p   -nu   -s   n+x̌l+p+us
     that   maybe   learn   -manage   -3erg   aware
     Then he came to, cleared up.

103. ʕ'ác'əs   ik'líʔ   níkna   qáqxʷəlx   a
     ʕ'ac'   -s   ik'líʔ   níkxnaʔ   qa+qxʷ+lx   a
     look_at -3erg   there   goodness   fish   art

     ckɬután
     c   -kɬ+wtan
     hab -lie_on
     He looked, gee there is lots of fish there.

104. cut mʕ'an   ilíʔ   kʷu   ksx̌ílaʔx   kiʔ [unf]
     cut mʕ'an   ilíʔ   kʷu   ks   -x̌il   -aʔx   kiʔ
     say interj   there   4kn   incp ^   -act_so - ^ incp   rel
     He said, "That's what we wanted to do..."

105. ixíʔ   skʷəl'cəncúts   ʕalapúl {ki}
     ixíʔ   s   -kʷl'+cn+cut   -s   ʕalapúl kiw
     then   dur -cook   -3i   Gopher yes
     Gopher started to cook.

106. ixíʔ   way',   ilíʔ   nc'ayxʷápəlqs
     ixíʔ   way'   ilíʔ   n+c'ayxʷ+áplqs
     that   all   there   end_of_story
     That's all, the end of the story.

FROG AND CRANE

1. cwix   i?   sqilx^w

c -wix   i?   s+qilx^w

hab-live   art person

There were people.

2. t'əx^w   lut   kmax   sk'^wək'^wína?s,   k'əłx̌^wíl·   ilí?

t'x^w   lut   kmax   s -k'^w+k'^wína? -s   k'ł+x̌^wil+l ilí?

emph not   only   dur -small   -3i   lots   there

k^wlíwt[əlx],

k^wl+iwt -lx

live   -pl

They were there, not just a few, lots.

3. ałí? {nəqnəqsílx^w} {kiw}   x^w?ítəlx

ałí? nq+nqs+ilx^w   kiw   x^w?it   -lx

so neighbor_pl   yes   many   -pl

{MD A group?} {DD Yes}, lots of them.[1]

4. uł   ixí?   axá? {i?swi?wi?}   i?   swi?wi?númtx   i?

uł   ixí?   axá?   i?   s+wy'+wy'+numt+x i?

and   that   this   art handsome_pl   art

smam?ím {i?} i?   sk'^wúmalt   scútxəlx

s+ma+m?ím   i?   s+k'^wúma+lt   s   -cut   -x   -lx

women   art virgin   ipftv ^ -say   - ^ ipftv -pl

There were pretty women, girls.

5. məł   x̌cməncú··təlx, cáˁwlxəlx, txáməlx   məł   xi?

mł   x̌c+mncut -lx caˁ^w+lx -lx txa+m -lx mł   ixí?

and   get_ready   -pl bathe   -pl comb -pl and   then

sx^wúy'səlx   ik'lí?

s -x^wuy -s -lx ik'lí?

dur -go   -3i -pl there

They get ready, bathe and comb their hair, and then they go there [to Crane].

6. {k'əl   sk^wrxán}   {kiw}

k'l   s+k^wr+xan   kiw

to   Crane   yes

To Crane, yes.

7. k'li?   x^wuylx   məł xi?   ilí?   kstəmtíma?

ik'lí?   x^wuy -lx mł ixí?   ilí?   k   -s+tm+tíma?

there   go   -pl and that there   have -grandmother

---

[1] MD abbreviates Madeline DeSautel, and identifies this as her interjection. DD abbreviates Dora DeSautel.

65

skʷərxán
s+kʷr+xan
Crane
They go there and Crane has a grandmother there.

8. ik'lí?   yáˁ'pəlx   məɬ axá? ta?   xʷuylx   ak'lá?
   ik'lí?   yaˁ'+p   -lx   mɬ axá? atá?   xʷuy   -lx ak'lá?
   there arrive_pl -pl and this here go   -pl here

   nppílxəlx
   n+p+pilx   -lx
   enter_pl -pl
   They get there and they go there and they go in.

9. məɬ xi? sk'əlk'əlkíc'a?s   i? sɬiqʷ i? x̌əw'áw' i?
   mɬ   ixí? s -k'l+k'lk+íc'a? -s i? s+ɬiqʷ i? x̌w'+aw' i?
   and that dur -bundle   -3i art meat art dried   art

   stim'
   stim'
   thing
   She started bundling up dry meat and things.

10. axá? t'i? c'ácqa?   məɬ ixí? xʷíc'əɬts   məɬ
    axá? t'i? c+?ácqa? mɬ ixí? xʷic' -ɬt -s   mɬ
    this evid come_out and that give -ɬt -3erg and

    ɬnis {ixí? uɬ i?}
    ɬ+nis
    gone_again
    As soon as she comes out she gives it to her and she leaves again.

11. way' itlí?   i? knaqs   ckicx   məɬ   way'
    way' itlí?   i? k+naqs   c+kic+x mɬ   way'
    well from_there art one_person arrive_cisl and yes

    k'li? n?uɬxʷ
    ik'lí? n+?uɬxʷ
    there enter
    And then another one arrives, and she goes in.

12. t'i?   ixíxi?   məɬ   way' [c'ácqa?]
    t'i?   ix+íxi?   mɬ   way' c+?ácqa?
    evid in_a_while and yes   come_out
    A little while she comes out.

13. kʷára kʷára stəmtíma?
    kʷára kʷára s+tm+tíma?
    onom onom grandmother
    "kʷára kʷára grandmother."

14. {may'} ma?mísəlx
          ma?+mí -s   -lx
          send_away -3erg -pl
    He sends them away.

15. ho··y   uɬ   c'sap   iʔ   smamʔím
    hoy   uɬ   c'sa+p   iʔ   s+ma+mʔím
    finish   and   gone   art women
    The women are all gone.

16. {yayáʕt   lutsts}   {kiw}
    yaʕ+yáʕ+t   lut+st   -s   kiw
    all   refuse   -3erg   yes
    He refuses all, yes.

17. ixíʔ   uɬ {ta}   sw'ar'ák'xən   k'liʔ   xʷuy
    ixíʔ   uɬ   s+w'ar'ák'+xn   ik'líʔ   xʷuy
    then   and   Frog   there   go
    Then Frog goes there.

18. uɬ   aɬíʔ   cktəɬtəɬpínaʔ
    uɬ   aɬíʔ   c   -k+tɬ+tɬp+ínaʔ
    and   so   hab -braids
    She has braids;

19. sic²   itlíʔ   q'ʷuc't   k'sus
    sic   itlíʔ   q'ʷuc'+t   k's+us
    ?   from_there   fat   ugly
    she's fat and ugly;

20. sic itlíʔ   ctk'ʷərk'ʷərc'áqstxən   uɬ   st'pink
    sic itlíʔ   c   -t+k'ʷr+k'ʷrc'+aqst+xn   uɬ   s -t'p+ink
    ?   from_there hab-bow_legs   and   hab-fat_belly
    she's bow legged and has a big belly.

21. k'liʔ   után,   uɬ   ixíʔ   scuts
    ik'líʔ   wtan   uɬ   ixíʔ   s -cut   -s
    there   placed   and   that   dur -say   -3i
    She went over there and said;

22. iʔ   smamʔím   ʕ'ayʕ'ayncútəlx   uɬ   cútəlx
    iʔ   s+ma+mʔím   ʕ'ay+ʕ'ay+ncút -lx   uɬ   cut -lx
    art   women   laugh_pl   -pl   and   say -pl
    The women laughed and they said:

23. uɬ   ixíʔ   kskstím'aʔx   ik'líʔ
    uɬ   ixíʔ   ks   -k+stim'   -aʔx   ik'líʔ
    and   that   incp ^ -do_what   -^ incp   there
    "What is she going to do over there?"

24. ixíʔ xʷu··y uɬ   kicx   uɬ   cus {iʔ}   ixíʔ iʔ   pəptwínaʔxʷ
    ixíʔ xʷuy uɬ   kic+x   uɬ   cu -s   ixíʔ iʔ   p+ptwínaʔxʷ
    that go   and   arrive and   tell -3erg   that art old_woman
    She went and got there and asked the old lady:

25. k'aʔkín'   skʷərxán
    k'aʔ+kín'   s+kʷr+xan
    where_to   Crane
    "Where is Crane?"

---

² sic has causal import, and its use here is not clear.

26. cut   ik'lí^ʔ   k'a[łáʔ]
    cut   ik'lí^ʔ   k'ałáʔ
    say   there   on_that_side
    She said, "Over there."

27. ixíʔ   uł   k'liʔ   nʔułx^w
    ixíʔ   uł   ik'líʔ   n+ʔułx^w
    that   and   there   enter
    So she went in there.

28. ilí··ʔ, ilíʔ   uł   axáʔ   iʔ   pəptwínaʔx^w
    ilíʔ   ilíʔ   uł   axáʔ   iʔ   p+ptwínaʔx^w
    there there and   this   art old_woman

    ckəm'ntís   iʔ   słiq^w   uł   kəlk'íc'aʔs
    c+km'   -nt -is   iʔ   s+łiq^w uł   k+lk'+íc'aʔ -s
    take_cisl -nt -3erg art meat and   wrap   -3erg
    She was there, and the old lady got the meat and she wrapped it.

29. way' ilíʔ   cut   way'   xiʔmíx mi   łc'ácqaʔ
    way' ilíʔ   cut   way'   xiʔ+míx mi   ł+c+ʔácqaʔ
    yes there say   yes   whatever fut come_out_again
    She said, "She'll be there, any time she'll come back out."

30. ixíʔ   k'á··wcənlx
    ixíʔ   k'aw+cn   -lx
    that   stop_talking -pl
    She was gone a long time.

31. ho··y uł   šlap
    hoy   uł   šla+p
    well   then   morning
    Then it was morning.

32. ixíʔ   uł   nak^wəm ixíʔ ł   k^wis   ixíʔ {s}
    ixíʔ   uł   nak^wm ixíʔ ł   k^wi   -s   ixíʔ
    that   and   evid   that subord take -3erg that

    sw'ar'ák'xən
    s+w'ar'ák'+xn
    Frog
    Sure enough he took Frog.

33. ixíʔ   scuts   k^wərxán, qiłt   uł   c'ácqaʔ
    ixíʔ   s -cut -s k^wr+xan qił+t   uł   c+ʔácqaʔ
    then   dur -say -3i Crane   awaken and come_out
    So Crane told her, he woke up and came out.

34. ixíʔ sƛ'aʔƛ'ʔúsəms   uł   ałíʔ   ixíʔ
    ixíʔ s -ƛ'aʔ+ƛ'ʔ+ús+m -s uł   ałíʔ   ixíʔ
    that   dur -look_for   -3i and   because that

    cənxlák
    c -n+xlak
    hab-be_in_circle
    He looked around the camp.

35. cya··ˤ   cqíɬəɬ   way'   iʔ   sqilxʷ
    c+yaˤ   c -qiɬ+ɬ+t   way'   iʔ   s+qilxʷ
    all   hab-wake_up   well   art person
    All the people are awake.

36. uɬ   ixíʔ   scuts   kʷára   kʷára   kʷára   k'a
    uɬ   ixíʔ   s   -cut   -s   kʷára   kʷára   kʷára   k'
    and   that   dur -say -3i   onom   onom   onom   to

    np'ƛ'mqsíɬxʷ   mi   kən   t'ql'i··mx
    n+p'ƛ'm+qs+iɬxʷ   mi   kn   t'ql+imx
    tipi_top   fut   1kn   move
    He said, "kʷára kʷára kʷára I'm going to the head of the circle and stay
    there."

37. {axáʔ iʔ}   t_ˤ'ip   ilíʔ   lut t'a   ɬxʷuy
                 t_n+yˤ'ip   ilíʔ   lut t'   ɬ+xʷuy
                 continuously   there   not negfac go_back

    sw'ar'ák'xən
    s+w'ar'ák'+xn
    Frog
    Frog stayed there for good.

38. ilíʔ   t_ˤ'ip   mut
    ilíʔ   t_n+yˤ'ip   mut
    there   continuously   be_home
    She stayed there.

39. ixíʔ   uɬ   nak'ʷəm   skʷnims
    ixíʔ   uɬ   nak'ʷm   s   -kʷni+m -s
    that   and   evid   dur -take   -3i
    He took her.

40. uɬ   cut   ixíʔ   itlíʔ   sc'x̌ilx   ka
    uɬ   cut   ixíʔ   itlíʔ   s+c   -ʔx̌il   -x   ka
    and   say   that   from_there   ipftvp^-do_like-^ipftvp   rel

    cx̌minks {iʔ}   iʔ   skʷərxán   {iʔ
    c   -x̌m+ink-st   -s   iʔ   s+kʷr+xan   iʔ
    cust^-like   -^cust -3erg   art Crane   art

    sw'ar'ák'xən}   {kiw}   ksc'iɬsts
    s+w'ar'ák'+xn   kiw   ksc   -ʔiɬ -st   -s
    Frog   yes   futCust^   -eat-^cust -3erg
    And that's why Crane likes Frog and eats them.

1. cwix   sənk'l'íp   uɬ   iʔ   sqʷəsqʷasíʔas
    c -wix   s+n+k'l'+ip   uɬ   iʔ   s+qʷs+qʷasíʔa   -s
    hab-live   Coyote   and   art children   -3in
    Coyote lived there with his children.

2. sənk'l'íp   aɬíʔ {ka}   kmúsəms   iʔ
    s+n+k'l'+ip   aɬíʔ   k+mus+ms   iʔ
    Coyote   so   four_persons   art

    sqʷəsqʷasíʔas   təl'   ʕalapúl
    s+qʷs+qʷasíʔa   -s   tl'   ʕalapúl
    children   -3in   from   Gopher
    He has four children from Gopher;

3. uɬ   knaqs   ixíʔ   skləkʷtíɬts {iʔ}   iʔ   sútən   iʔ
    uɬ   k+naqs   ixíʔ   s+k+lkʷt+ilt   -s   iʔ   sutn   iʔ
    and   one_person   that   distant_child   -3in   art   thing   art

    {sʕ'an'íxʷ} {sʕ'an'íxʷ}
    s+ʕ'an'íxʷ   s+ʕ'an'íxʷ
    Muskrat   Muskrat
    and one is his distant child, whachamacallit Muskrat.

4. ixíʔ   sqʷsiʔs   uɬ   axáʔ   iʔ   tuʔtw'it {xʷu}
    ixíʔ   s+qʷsiʔ -s   uɬ   axáʔ   iʔ   tw'+tw'it
    that   son   -3in   and   this   art boys
    His son, boys.

5. axáʔ   iʔ   tuʔtw'it   xʷu··ylx   məɬ yáʕpəlx   iʔ   k'əl
    axáʔ   iʔ   tw'+tw'it   xʷuy   -lx   mɬ   yaʕ+p   -lx   iʔ   k'l
    this   art boys   go   -pl and   arrive_pl   -pl art to

    ixíʔ   səmx̌íkn
    ixíʔ   s+mx̌+ikn
    that   Grizzly
    The boys'd go and they'd get to Grizzly;

6. aɬíʔ {ks}   kst'əmkʔíɬt   uɬ   sqílxʷəlx   c'x̌iɬt
    aɬíʔ   k -s+t'mkʔ+iɬt   uɬ   s+qilxʷ -lx   c+ʔx̌iɬ+t
    because   have -daughter   and   person -pl like

    mnímɬtət
    mnimɬ+tt
    us
    because she has a daughter, and they are people like us.

7. uɬ   náx̌əmɬ   t'i   kicx   iʔ   tuʔtw'ít
    uɬ   nax̌mɬ   t'iʔ   kic+x   iʔ   tw'+tw'it
    and   but   evid   arrive   art boys
    When the boys get there,

8. məł   ixí?   ta?x̌ílsts   i? {stəmtəm}
   mł   ixí?   ta?x̌íl   -st -s   i?
   and   that   do_a_certain_way -st -3erg   art

   st'əmk?ílts
   s+t'mk?+ilt -s
   daughter   -3in
   she motions to her daughter:

9. xʷuyx   way'
   xʷuy   -x   way'
   go   -isimptv   yes
   "Go on."

10. ixí?   məł axá?   xʷuy   ixí?   i? st'əmk?ílts   uł
    ixí?   mł   axá?   xʷuy   ixí?   i? s+t'mk?+ilt -s   uł
    then   and this   go   that   art daughter   -3in and

    ni?ák'ʷ
    n+y?ak'ʷ
    cross
    The daughter goes across the creek;

11. məł   ixí?   {st}[sxʷuys   k'a cəm'm'áq'ʷ]
    mł   ixí?   s   -xʷuy   -s   k'   c+m'+m'aq'ʷ
    and   that   dur -go   -3i to   hillock
    and she goes on a little hill.

12. uł   atá?   xʷuy,   uł   atá?   ixí? i? tətwít   i? sqʷsi?s
    uł   atá?   xʷuy   uł   atá?   ixí? i? t+tw'it i? s+qʷsi? -s
    and   here   go   and   here   that art boy   art son   -3in

    sənk'l'íp   atá?   xʷuy
    s+n+k'l'+ip   atá?   xʷuy
    Coyote   here   go
    She goes there, and the boy, Coyote's son, goes by there.

13. məł   k'ʷ?ápqəs,   [ixí?]   λ'əlλ'l[nús]
    mł   k'ʷ?+ap+q   -s   ixí?   λ'l+λ'l -nu   -s
    and   bite_head   -3erg   that   dead_pl-manage   -3erg
    She bites them on the head, she kills them.

14. uł   ixí?   i? pəptwína?xʷ   tə_nyʕ'ip   i?
    uł   ixí?   i? p+ptwína?xʷ   t_n+yʕ'+ip   i?
    and   that   art old_woman   continuously   art

    sənululmúsa?stən   ck'ʷul'sts   i?
    s+n+wl+wl+músa?s+tn c   -k'ʷul' -st   -s   i?
    arrow_points   cust ^   -fix   - ^ cust -3erg art

    t   sútən   i? t
    t   sutn   i? t
    obj_tr thing   art obj_tr
    And the old lady always fixes the arrow heads with things;

15. t'əxʷ   xi?míx   ilí?   stim',   i? k'i?lílxʷ   məł
    t'xʷ   xi?+míx   ilí?   stim'   i? k'y'l+ilxʷ   mł
    evidently whatever   there   something   art tree_bark   and

utəntís
wt   -nt -is
put_down -nt -3erg
with anything, with bark, and puts it there.

16. uɬ   itíʔ   a   ct'aˤpstísəlx   iʔ
     uɬ   itíʔ   a   c   -t'aˤp -st   -is   -lx   iʔ
     and   from_that   art cust^ -shoot -^cust -3erg   -pl   art

     t   k'iʔlílxʷ
     t   k'y'l+ilxʷ
     agInst   tree_bark
     And they'd be shooting with bark;

17. uɬ   λ'əxʷəntís,   k'awsts   ixíʔ   iʔ
     uɬ   λ'xʷ   -nt -is   k'aw -st   -s   ixíʔ   iʔ
     and kill_many -nt -3erg   gone -caus -3erg   that   art

     tuʔtwít
     tw'+tw'it
     boys
     and she killed them, she finished the boys.

18. {ixíʔ   iʔ   kmúsəms}
     ixíʔ   iʔ   k+mus+ms
     that   art four_persons
     The four of them.

19. {kiw}
     kiw
     yes
     Yes.

20. ilíʔ   kicx   sˤ'an'íxʷ   uɬ   cus   ya   lʔiws
     ilíʔ   kic+x   s+ˤ'an'íxʷ   uɬ   cu -s   ya   lʔiw   -s
     there   arrive   Muskrat   and tell -3erg   art m's_father -3in
     Muskrat got there, and told his father:

21. {iks}   kən   ksxʷúyaʔx   aɬíʔ   myaɬ
             kn   ks   -xʷuy   -aʔx   aɬíʔ   myaɬ
             1kn   incp^   -go   -^incp because   too_much

     kʷu   λ'xʷɬtis {iʔ sqʷəsqʷəs}   iʔ   sútən
     kʷu   λ'xʷ   -ɬt   -is   iʔ   sutn
     1poss   kill_many -ɬt -3erg   art thing

     isənsínca?
     i   -sn+sínca?
     1in -younger_brothers
     "I am, I am going, because she has killed my brothers."

22. ixíʔ   uɬ   cúntəm   i   ta   lʔiws,   way'
     ixíʔ   uɬ   cu -nt -m   iʔ   t   lʔiw   -s   way'
     then   and tell -nt -psv   art agInst m's_father -3in   yes

     lut   aksxʷúy,   way'   maɬ   cəm'
     lut   a   -k+s   -xʷuy   way'   maɬ   cm'
     not   2i -futl   -go   yes   too_much maybe
     His father told him, "Don't go, it's too, maybe."

23. way'   lut,   way'   k'am   knaqs   iʔ,   k'am   kʷ
    way'   lut   way'   k'am   k+naqs   iʔ   k'am   kʷ
    well   not   yes   except   one_person   art   except   2kn

knaqs
k+naqs
one_person
Don't, the only one, you're the only [son] left."

24. ixíʔ   sc'qʷaqʷs {sən}   sənk'l'íp {kc'qʷa··}
    ixíʔ   s -c'qʷ+aqʷ -s   s+n+k'l'+ip
    then   dur -cry   -3i   Coyote
Coyote cried.

25. ixíʔ   uɬ   axáʔ   sxʷuys
    ixíʔ   uɬ   axáʔ   s -xʷuy -s
    then   and   this   dur -go   -3i
He went.

26. uɬ   axáʔ   iʔ   la   nyq'pálqstəns   ilíʔ
    uɬ   axáʔ   iʔ   l   n+yq'p+alqs+tn -s   ilíʔ
    and   this   art   in   belt   -3in   there

k'əɬq'a'ntís   iʔ   {sənululmúsaʔstən} {kiw}
k'ɬ+q'a' -nt -is   iʔ   sənululmúsaʔstən
stick_in-nt -3erg   art   s+n+wl+wl+músaʔs+tn

iʔ   sənululmúsaʔstən
iʔ   s+n+wl+wl+músaʔs+tn
art   arrow_points
He stuck the arrow heads in his belt;

27. uɬ   iʔ   k'ʷiƛ't   way'   ilíʔ   ckutután   iʔ   k'əl
    uɬ   iʔ   k'ʷiƛ'+t   way'   ilíʔ   c -k+wt+wtan   iʔ   k'l
    and   art   rest   yes   there   hab -put_on   art   on

cq'ílən
c'q'+iln
arrow
and he left the rest stuck on the arrows.

28. [uɬ]   xʷuy   uɬ   cúntəm   ixíʔ   iʔ   t   pəptwínaʔxʷ
    uɬ   xʷuy   uɬ   cu -nt-m   ixíʔ   iʔ   t   p+ptwínaʔxʷ
    and   go   and   tell -nt-psv   that   art   aglnst   old_woman
He went and the old lady said to him:

29. way'   aláʔ   mi   utəntíxʷ
    way'   aláʔ   mi   wt   -nt -ixʷ
    yes   here   fut   put_down   -nt -2erg
"Put those there."

30. uɬ   ilíʔ   kɬaʔɬaʔqís   i   l   tk'əmkn'íɬxʷ   uɬ
    uɬ   ilíʔ   k+ɬaʔ+ɬaʔ+qí   -s   iʔ   l   t+k'm+kn'+iɬxʷ   uɬ
    and   there   lean_on   -3erg   art   in   outside   and

nʔuɬxʷ
n+ʔuɬxʷ
enter
And he leaned them outside and went in.

31.
ilíʔ	mut	iʔ	st'əmkʔílts,		cus
ilíʔ	mut	iʔ	s+t'mkʔ+ilt	-s	cu -s
there	sit_sg	art	daughter	-3in	tell -3erg

xʷuyx	way'
xʷuy -x	way'
go -isimptv	yes

Her daughter was sitting there, she told her, "Go on now."

32.
ixíʔ	uɬ	axáʔ	xʷuy	ʔácqaʔ,	uɬ
ixíʔ	uɬ	axáʔ	xʷuy	ʔácqaʔ	uɬ
then	and	this	go	go_out	and

Then she went out.

33.
ixíʔ	uɬ	xʷuy	niʔákʷ	uɬ	[x̌íƛ'əm]
ixíʔ	uɬ	xʷuy	n+yʔakʷ	uɬ	x̌iƛ'+m
that	and	go	cross	and	climb

She went across the stream and climbed the hill.

34.
ixíʔ	scuts			xʷuyx		ʕ'ác'ənt		yaʔx̌ís
ixíʔ	s -cut -s	xʷuy -x				ʕ'ac' -nt		yaʔx̌ís
that	dur -say -3i	go	-isimptv			look_at -nt		over_there

She told him, "Go, look there;

35.
kʷu	akspúlɬtəm
kʷu	a -ks -pul -ɬt -m
1kʷu	2i -futT^ -kill_one -ɬt -^futT

iksxʷípəlp
i -k -s+xʷip+lp
1i -to_be -rug

go kill that for a rug for me to lie on.

36.
xʷuyx,	pulskʷ
xʷuy -x	pul -skʷ
go -isimptv	kill_one-tsimptv

Go kill it."

37.
uɬ	xaʔ	ʔácqaʔ	sʕ'an'íxʷ	uɬ	km'əntís		iʔ
uɬ	axáʔ	ʔácqaʔ	s+ʕ'an'íxʷ	uɬ	km' -nt -is		iʔ
and	this	go_out	Muskrat	and	take -nt -3erg		art

c'q'íləns
c'q'+iln -s
arrow -3in

Muskrat went out and took his arrows.

38.
uɬ	taʔ	ʕ'ác'əs,	nákʷəm	kmax	sútən,
uɬ	atáʔ	ʕ'ac' -s	nakʷm	kmax	sutn
and	this	look_at -3erg	evid	only	thing

k'iʔlílxʷ
k'y'l+ilxʷ
tree_bark

He looked at them, it's just bark.

39. ixí?   x̌ʷəlx̌ʷílsts
    ixí?   x̌ʷl+x̌ʷil -st -s
    that   discard -st -3erg
    He threw them away.

40. axá?   atlá?   ckəm'əntís   uɫ   k'li?
    axá?   atlá?   c+km'   -nt -is   uɫ   ik'lí?
    this   from_here take_cisl -nt -3erg and   there

    nututəntís
    n+wt+wt   -nt-is
    put_pl_obj -nt-3erg
    He took them, and put them there.

41. itlí?   sxʷuys,   cut   a   ck'əwtímatks
    itlí?   s -xʷuy -s   cut   a   c+k+?wt+íma?tk   -s
    from_there   dur -go -3i   say   art below_cisl   -3in

    mi kʷ xʷuy
    mi kʷ xʷuy
    fut 2kn go
    He went; she said, "Go from below.

42. itlí?   t'aʕpəntíxʷ   məɫ   ck'ʷilk'
    itlí?   t'aʕp -nt -ixʷ   mɫ   c+k'ʷilk'
    from_there   shoot -nt -2erg   and   rolling_cisl
    You'll shoot and she'll roll down."

43. uɫ   axá?   lut t'   q'a?ílsməntəm
    uɫ   axá?   lut t'   q'a?+íls+m   -nt -m
    and   this   not negfac pay_attention -nt -psv
    He didn't pay any attention to her.

44. ni?ákʷ   uɫ   xi?   sx̌íλ'əms
    n+y?akʷ   uɫ   ixí?   s -x̌iλ'+m -s
    cross   and   that   dur -climb -3i
    He crossed and went up the hill.

45. sqi··lts, {təl'}   təl'   w'íw'a?st   uɫ
    s -qil+t   -s   tl'   w'í+w'a?st   uɫ
    dur -top   -3i   from   high_dim   and

    ta?x̌ílsts,   alá?   ʕ'ác'əs   way'
    ta?x̌íl   -st -s   alá?   ʕ'ac' -s   way'
    do_a_certain_way -st -3erg   here   look_at -3erg yes
    He got on top, from above and did like that, he looked at her.

46. ixí? uɫ i?, ik'lí? ʕ'ác'ntəm,   t'ət'úm'səm,   ixí?
    ixí? uɫ i? ik'lí? ʕ'ac' -nt -m   t'+t'um'+s -m   ixí?
    that and art there look_at -nt -psv   little_smile -mdl that

    t'aʕpəntím
    t'aʕp -nt-im
    shoot -nt-psv
    He looked at her, she smiled, and he shot her.

47. kck̓ʷíc'aʔntəm   iʔ t   síp'iʔs,   uɬ   ixíʔ
    k+ck̓ʷ+íc'aʔ   -nt -m   iʔ t   síp'iʔ -s   uɬ   ixíʔ
    pull_cover_off -nt -psv   art obj_tr hide   -3in   and then

    nk't'úsəs
    n+k't'+us   -s
    cut_off_head   -3erg
    He skinned her and cut her head off.

48. ixíʔ   ɬəɬxʷúys
    ixíʔ   ɬ -ɬ+xʷuy   -s
    then   dur -go_back   -3i
    Then he went back.

49. uɬ   i   ǀ   stáɬəm uɬ   ɬniʔákʷ   ik'líʔ
    uɬ   iʔ   ǀ   s+taɬm uɬ   ɬ+nyʔakʷ   ik'líʔ
    and   art   in   boat   and   cross_again   there
    And he crossed back there on the boat.

50. xiʔ   c'q'əmíɬts   ixíʔ   iʔ síp'iʔ
    ixíʔ   c'q'+m -ɬt-is   ixíʔ   iʔ síp'iʔ
    then   throw   -ɬt-3erg that   art hide
    He threw the hide there:

51. kʷint   aksxʷípəlp
    kʷin   -t   a   -k   -s+xʷip+lp
    take   -nt 2in -to_be   -rug
    "Take your rug."

52. ixíʔ   náx̌əmɬ iʔ c'ásyqəns
    ixíʔ   nax̌mɬ iʔ c'asy+qn   -s
    then   but   art head   -3in

    k'əɬq'aʔáx̌nəms
    k'ɬ+q'ʔ+ax̌n   -m   -s
    stick_under_arm   -m_nt   -3erg
    He had her head stuck under his arm.

53. ixíʔ   nɬət'pmítkʷ   k'a   nyx̌ʷtitkʷ   úɬiʔ
    ixíʔ   n+ɬt'p+m+itkʷ   k'   n+yx̌ʷt+itkʷ   uɬ+iʔ
    that   jump_in_water   to   in_water   and_then

    sk'rams   niʔákʷ   xiʔ   c'q'əmíɬtəm
    s -k'ra+m -s   n+yʔakʷ   ixíʔ   c'q'+mí -ɬt -m
    dur -swim   -3i   cross   then   throw   -ɬt -psv

    cúntəm   kʷint   axáʔ   aksxʷípəlp
    cu -nt -m   kʷin   -t   axáʔ   a   -k   -s+xʷip+lp
    say -nt psv   take   -nt   that   2in -to_be -rug
    He jumped in the water, dived in and swam across.

54. xʷu·y uɬ kicx   iʔ k'a lʔiws   uɬ   xiʔ cus
    xʷuy   uɬ kic+x iʔ k'   lʔiw   -s   uɬ   ixíʔ cu -s
    go   and arrive art to   m's_father -3in and that tell -3erg
    He went and got to his father and said:

55. k^wint   axáʔ   iʔ c'ásyqəns   xíʔ   [iʔ tkəɬmílx^w]
    k^win -t   axáʔ   iʔ c'asy+qn -s ixíʔ iʔ tkɬmilx^w
    take -nt this   art head   -3in   that art woman
    "Take that girl's head."

56. ixíʔ   k^wis   sənk'l'íp
    ixíʔ   k^wi -s   s+n+k'l'+ip
    that   take -3erg Coyote
    Coyote took it;

57. uɬ   atáʔ ɬəwʔɬtís   iʔ t   sútən i   t
    uɬ   atáʔ ɬw'   -ɬt -is   iʔ t   sutn   iʔ t
    and this poke -ɬt -3erg art agInst thing art agInst

    sx̌əxc'íʔ   uɬ   kɬəx̌^wpəntís
    s+x̌+xc'iʔ uɬ   k+ɬx̌^wp -nt -is
    stick   and   hang_up -nt -3erg
    and he poked it with something, a stick, and hung it up.

58. uɬ   xiʔ   iʔ t   sútən iʔ t   sƛ'ƛ'úk^waʔ
    uɬ   ixíʔ   iʔ t   sutn   iʔ t   s+ƛ'+ƛ'úk^waʔ
    and then art agInst thing art agInst wood_pitch

    kp'əntís   úɬiʔ   suláps
    kp'   -nt -is   uɬ+iʔ   s -wla+p -s
    place_on -nt -3erg and_then dur -burn -3i
    He put something, pitch, on the fire, and it started to burn;

59. uɬ   t'iʔ   q'^ʷaˁy ixíʔ
    uɬ   t'iʔ   q'^ʷaˁy ixíʔ
    and   evid black that
    and it was black.

60. ilíʔ   c'ax̌əlwís   sˁ'ayncúts {kiw}
    ilíʔ   c -ʔax̌l+wis   s -ˁ'ay+ncút -s
    there hab-fool_around dur -laugh   -3i
    He was monkeying around laughing;

61. ki   k'a   nʔuɬx^w   ixíʔ   iʔ tum'   k'əl
    kiʔ   k'   n+ʔuɬx^w ixíʔ   iʔ tum'   k'l
    rel   to   enter   that   art woman's_mother ?

    nʔaɬx^wípəntəm
    n+ʔaɬx^w+ip -nt -m
    go_inside -nt -psv
    and that's when the mother went inside, right in the house.

62. nt'a iʔ   st'əmkʔílts   iʔ   c'ásyqəns {a cult} a
    nt'a iʔ   s+t'mkʔ+ilt -s iʔ   c'asy+qn -s   a
    intj art daughter   -3in art head   -3in   art

    cután,   a   cq'^ʷʔuɬ
    c -wtan   a   c -q'^ʷ+ʔ+uɬ
    hab-placed art hab-black
    Gee, his daughter's head is there, getting black.

63.   ixíʔ   kspulsts   sənk'l'íp
        ixíʔ   ks   -pul   -st -s   s+n+k'l'+ip
        then   futT ^ -kill_one   -st -3erg   Coyote
        She's going to kill Coyote.

64.   uɬ   ixíʔ   cut sənk'l'íp   p'əs   p'əs   kʷƛ'up p'əs
        uɬ   ixíʔ   cut s+n+k'l'+ip p's   p's   kʷƛ'up p's
        and   then   say Coyote   onom   onom   onom   onom

        p'əs   kʷƛ'up   p'əs   [p'əs   kʷƛ'up   p'əs   p'əs   kʷƛ'up]
        p's   kʷƛ'up   p's   p's   kʷƛ'up   p's   p's   kʷƛ'up
        onom   onom   onom   onom   onom   onom   onom   onom
        Coyote said, "p'əs p'əs p'əs p'əs kʷƛ'up."

65.   ixíʔ   uɬ {iʔ}   kʷísəlx   səmx̌íkən
        ixíʔ   uɬ   kʷi   -s   -lx s+mx̌+ikn
        that   and   take   -3erg   -pl Grizzly
        They grabbed Grizzly.

66.   ixíʔ   kʷis   ixíʔ   q'aʔlqʷsísəlp'tən
        ixíʔ   kʷi   -s   ixíʔ   q'aʔ+lqʷs+íslp'+tn
        then   take   -3erg   that   fire_rod
        So he took the stick to stir the fire with;

67.   ixíʔ   nɬuʔɬuʔú··psəs   atáʔ   ɬuʔɬuʔtán
        ixíʔ   n+ɬw'+ɬw'+ups -s   atáʔ   ɬw'+ɬw'+tan
        then   poke_anus   -3erg   this   poker
        then he stuck her in the bottom with that poker.

68.   cut way'   xʷustx   way'   uɬ   kʷu   x̌əw'x̌w'áw',
        cut way'   xʷust   -x   way'   uɬ   kʷu   x̌w'+x̌w'+aw'
        say yes   hurry   -isimptv   yes   and   4kn   dry_pl

        kʷu   kɬəwɬwníkstaʔx
        kʷu   k   -ɬw+ɬwn+ikst   -aʔx
        4kn   incp ^   -let_go_pl   - ^ incp
        They said, "Hurry up, we are getting dry, we're going to let go."

69.   xʷət'pəncút   [sənk'líp]
        xʷt'+p+ncut   s+n+k'l'+ip
        run   Coyote
        Coyote ran away.

70.   qí··cəlx   uɬ   xiʔ   kíləntəm   t   səmx̌íkən
        qic+lx   uɬ   ixíʔ   kil   -nt -m   t   s+mx̌+ikn
        run   and   that   chase -nt -psv   agInst Grizzly
        He ran, and Grizzly is chasing him.

71.   xʷu··ylx, {uɬ}   cut   xʷístwi,   xʷístwi,
        xʷuy   -lx   cut   xʷist   -wy   xʷist   -wy
        go   -pl   say   walk   -ipimptv   walk   -ipimptv

        way' {kən}   kən   ksútən
        way'   kn   k   -sutn
        yes   1kn   to_be   -thing
        They went, he said, "Hurry up, hurry up, I want to be a something;

72. iʔ sxʷaxʷankíɬp   way',   iʔ sxʷaxʷankíɬp
    iʔ s+xʷaʔ+xʷaʔ+nk+íɬp   way'   iʔ s+xʷaʔ+xʷaʔ+nk+íɬp
    art thornbush   yes   art thornbush
    a thornbush, a thornbush.

73. ixíʔ   kʼʷulʼlʼ_t   sxʷaxʷankíɬp
    ixíʔ   kʼʷulʼ+l̄ʼ_t   s+xʷaʔ+xʷaʔ+nk+íɬp
    that   turn_into   thornbush
    So he turned into a thornbush.

74. uɬ   itíʔ   cxʷətʼpəncút,   ixíʔ {cʼəlcʼəlx̌}
    uɬ   itíʔ   c+xʷtʼ+p+ncut   ixíʔ
    and   from_that run_cisl   that

    cʼəlcʼəlxwʼáqstxəntəm   ixíʔ   t
    cʼl+cʼlx+wʼ+aqst+xn -nt -m   ixíʔ   t
    scratch_thigh   -nt -psv   that   aglnst

    sxʷaʔxʷaʔnkíɬp
    s+xʷaʔ+xʷaʔ+nk+íɬp
    thornbush
    [The Bear] came running, the thorn bush scratched her thighs;

75. kʼlaʔ   kʼa yxʷut {kʼa yxʷut}   kiʔ ɬ
    akʼláʔ   kʼ yxʷ+ut   kiʔ ɬ
    here   to below   rel ?

    taʔx̌íləm   aláʔ
    taʔx̌íl   -m   aláʔ
    do_a_certain_way -mdl here
    She went down, went like that.

76. ilí··ʔ   ʔakswíx   sənkʼlʼíp   wa··   wa   wa
    ilíʔ   ʔaks+wíx   s+n+kʼlʼ+ip   wa   wa   wa
    there   stand   Coyote   onom   onom   onom

    wa   ncʼəlcʼəlxʔú··psən   səmx̌íkən
    wa   n+cʼl+cʼlx+ʔ+ups   -n   s+mx̌+ikn
    onom   scratch_bottom   -1erg   Grizzly
    Coyote is standing there, "wa··, wa, wa, wa I scratched Grizzly's ass."

77. a··   sic   kʷ   ikspúlstəm
    a   sic   kʷ   i   -ks   -pul   -st -m
    intj   then   2kʷu   1i -futT ^ -kill_one -st - ^ futT
    "a·· now I'm going to kill you."

78. ixíʔ   ɬəɬtkʼíwləxs   ikʼlíʔ {kiw}
    ixíʔ   ɬ -ɬ+t+kʼiw+lx   -s   ikʼlíʔ
    that   dur -climb_again -3i   there
    She started to climb.

79. uɬ   x̌í··λ̓əm unint, nis   sənkʼlíp
    uɬ   x̌iλ̓+m   nis   s+n+kʼlʼ+ip
    and   climb   gone   Coyote
    She went up the hill, Coyote's gone.

80. ixí?   a   cmaq'ʷ   uł   ik'lí?   txlak'
    ixí?   a   c+maq'ʷ   uł   ik'lí?   t+xlak'
    that   art mountain   and   there   go_around
    There's a little hill there, and he went around there.

81. ixí?   cut   way'   xʷústwi,   way'
    ixí?   cut   way'   xʷust   -wy   way'
    that   say   yes   hurry   -ipimptv   yes

    q'ʷastínkəm   p'əs   p'əs   kʷλ'up, p'əs   p'əs
    q'ʷast+ínk   -m   p's   p's   kʷλ'up p's   p's
    Coyote_magic -mdl   onom   onom   onom   onom   onom

    kʷλ'up
    kʷλ'up
    onom
    He said, "Hurry up," he did his magic, "p'əs p'əs kʷλ'up."

82. ilí?   k'ʷúl'əm   i?
    ilí?   k'ʷul'+m   i?
    there   build   art
    There he made the.

83. ilí?   kʷliwt   i?   sm'am?ím
    ilí?   kʷl+iwt   i?   s+m'a+m?ím
    there   sit_pl   art women

    scəlkípx   t'əxʷ
    s+c   -lkip   -x   t'xʷ
    ipftvp ^ -pit_cook   - ^ ipftvp   evidently

    sc'kinx
    s+c   -?kin   -x
    ipftvp ^ -indef   - ^ ipftvp
    There were some women pit cooking something.

84. t'i?   txlak',   nt'a   xa?   kʷliwt   i?   sm'am?ím
    t'i?   t+xlak'   nt'a   axá?   kʷl+iwt   i?   s+m'a+m?ím
    evid   go_around   intj   this   sit_pl   art women
    [Grizzly] went around, and there were some women.

85. cut   uc   atá?   wíkəntp   sənk'l'íp
    cut   uc   atá?   wik -nt-p   s+n+k'l'+ip
    say   dub   here   see -nt-5erg   Coyote
    She said, "Have you seen Coyote?"

86. cútəlx   lut,   cut {cut}   lut,   alá?   kʷu
    cut -lx   lut   cut   lut   alá?   kʷu
    say -pl   not   say   not   here   4kn

    scəlkípx,   cxʷuyx   kʷ
    s+c   -lkip   -x   c+xʷuy -x   kʷ
    ipftvp ^ -pit_cook   - ^ ipftvp   come -isimptv   2kn

    s?íłnx
    s   -?iłn   -x
    ipftv ^ -eat   - ^ ipftv
    They said, "no," said, "No, we've been cooking here, come and eat."

87. ixí?   cut   lut
    ixí?   cut   lut
    that   say   not
    She said no.

88. t'i?   wim'   uł   ixí?   scuts   way'
    t'i?   wim'   uł   ixí?   s -cut   -s   way'
    evid   in_vain and   that   dur -say -3i OK
    She didn't know what to do, then she said OK.

89. ixí?   itlí?   sutáns,   ixí?   s?íłəns,   ?í··łən
    ixí?   itlí?   s   -wtan   -s   ixí?   s -? iłn -s   ?iłn
    that   from_there   dur   -placed -3i   that   dur -eat   -3i eat
    Then she went over there, and she ate, she ate.

90. ixí?   ta?x̌ílsts   i?   łəłáxʷs   alá?
    ixí?   ta?x̌íl   -st -s   i?   ł+łaxʷ   -s   alá?
    that   do_a_certain_way   -st -3erg art   dress   -3in   here
    She did that to her dress.

91. uł   ixí?   nutəntí··s,   uł   alá?   nq'a?q'a?ntí··s
    uł   ixí?   n+wt   -nt -is   uł   alá?   n+q'a?+q'a?   -nt -is
    and   that   put_in -nt -3erg   and   here   stick_in_pl   -nt -3erg
    She put things there, she stuffed it.

92. uł   ixí?   itlí?   sxʷuys
    uł   ixí?   itlí?   s   -xʷuy   -s
    and   then   from_there   dur   -go   -3i
    She went on.

93. ałí?   mq'ink   uł   k'ək'a?lí?
    ałí?   mq'+ink   uł   k'+k'a?lí?
    because   satiated   and   slow
    She's full and she walks slowly.

94. {k'lan} ta?x̌íləm   t'i?   k'aw,   lut
            ta?x̌íl   -m   t'i?   k'aw   lut
            do_a_certain_way   -mdl   evid   gone   not

    i?   t'a   kłswit {kiw}
    i?   t'   kł   -swit
    art   negfac   there_be   -anybody
    She did that, they're gone, there is nobody.

95. sənk'l'íp   way'   ilí··?   ł   k   ?akswíx   wa··
    s+n+k'l'+ip   way'   ilí?   ł   ki?   ?aks+wíx   wa
    Coyote   yes   there   ?   rel   stand   onom

    wa   wa   wa
    wa   wa   wa
    onom   onom   onom
    Coyote was standing there, "wa··, wa, wa, wa.

96. xa?   ałí?   inmník   úłi?   kʷu   ?iłtxʷ
    axá?   ałí?   in -mnik   uł+i?   kʷu   ?ił -łt -xʷ
    this   so   1in -shit   and_then   1kʷu   eat -łt   -2erg
    That was my dung and you ate it."

97. taʔx̌ílsts,   níkna   iʔ
    taʔx̌íl   -st -s   níkxnaʔ   iʔ
    do_a_certain_way -st -3erg   goodness   art

    splímcəns   nakʷʼəm   qʼʷicʼt
    s+plim+cn -s   nakʷʼm   qʼʷicʼ+t
    mouth   -3in evid   full
    She did like that, gee, her mouth is full.

98. taʔx̌ílsts   aláʔ   xiʔ *unint*
    taʔx̌íl   -st -s   aláʔ   ixíʔ
    do_a_certain_way -st -3erg   here   that
    She did like that;

99. yaˤyáˤt   taʔx̌ílsts   aláʔ,   uɬ   xiʔ
    yaˤ+yáˤ+t   taʔx̌íl   -st -s   aláʔ   uɬ   ixíʔ
    all   do_a_certain_way -st -3erg   here   and   that

    x̌ʷəlx̌ʷílsts
    x̌ʷl+x̌ʷil -st -s
    discard -st -3erg
    she did like that, and she threw it away.

100.{yaˤyáˤt   mnik}   {kiw}
    yaˤ+yáˤ+t   mnik   kiw
    all   shit   yes
    All shit, yes.

101.cus   ˤapnáʔ kʷ   ikspúlstəm
    cu -s   ˤapnáʔ kʷ   i -ks   -pul   -st -m
    tell -3erg   now   2kʷu   1i -futT^ -kill_one -st -^futT

    ta_uníxʷ
    ta_wnixʷ
    for_sure
    She told him, "Now for sure I'm going to kill you."

102.ixíʔ   ɬkíləntəm
    ixíʔ   ɬ   -kil   -nt -m
    that   again   -chase -nt -psv
    She chased him again.

103.kí··ləntəm   məɬ   ixíʔ   cənɬx̌ʷúlaʔx̌ʷ   mat
    kil   -nt -m   mɬ   ixíʔ   c -n+ɬx̌ʷ+úlaʔx̌ʷ   mat
    chase   -nt -psv   and   that   hab-hole   maybe

    stimʼ   ilíʔ   aláʔ   kɬcitxʷ
    stimʼ   ilíʔ   aláʔ   kɬ   -citxʷ
    something   there   here   have   -house
    She chased him, and there is a hole in the ground, something lives
    there, I guess.

104.ikʼlíʔ   nɬətʼpmúlaʔx̌ʷ   sənkʼlíp
    ikʼlíʔ   n+ɬtʼp+m+úlaʔx̌ʷ   s+n+kʼlʼ+ip
    there   jump_in_hole   Coyote
    Coyote jumped in there.

105.ik'lí? nłət'pmúla?xʷ   uł ilí··? uł xi? cxʷuy
   ik'lí? n+łt'p+m+úla?xʷ   uł ilí?   uł ixí? c+xʷuy
   there jump_in_hole   and there and that come
   He jumped in there and stayed there and then she came.

106.alá?   ta?x̌íləm   məł t'i? ik'lí? ki
   alá?   ta?x̌íl   -m   mł t'i? ik'lí? ki?
   here   do_a_certain_way -mdl   and evid there rel

   ilí?   smuts   k'əł?amtíp
   ilí?   s -mut   -s k'ł+?amt+íp
   there dur -sit_sg -3i sit_by_door
   She did like that, and went there, and sat there by the hole.

107.ixí?   sm'a?m'ásəlqsəms
   ixí?   s -m'a?+m'ás+lqs+m -s
   that   dur -feel_dress   -3i
   She felt her dress.

108.ilí··? mut, st'a?c'x̌í··ls   a
   ilí?   mut   s -t'a?+c+?x̌il -s a
   there sit_sg dur -do_like   -3i art
   She sat there doing like that.

109.sənk'líp   ta?x̌íləm,   t_ʕip
   s+n+k'l'+ip ta?x̌íl   -m   t_n+yʕip
   Coyote   do_a_certain_way -mdl continuously

   ilí?   mut
   ilí?   mut
   there sit_sg
   Coyote went like that, she still sat there;

110.{kʷa} lut ksəlkʷílxa?x
         lut ks   -lkʷ+ilx -a?x
         not incp^ -leave   -^incp
   she won't leave.

111.ixí?   uł   scuts   way'
   ixí?   uł   s -cut   -s way'
   then   and dur -say -3i OK
   Then he said;

112.t'a·· i?   sqilxʷ
   nt'a   i?   s+qilxʷ
   intj   art person
   [You could hear] the people;

113.cxʷú··ywi,   cxʷúywi,   way' way' kʷu
   c+xʷuy -wy   c+xʷuy -wy   way' way' kʷu
   come   -ipimptv   come   -ipimptv   yes   well 4kn

   ks?ímxa?x,   kʷu ks?ímxa?x
   ks   -?imx   -a?x   kʷu ks   -?imx   -a?x
   incp^ -move -^incp   4kn incp^ -move -^incp
   "Come, come, we're going to move.

114.kʷu ks?ímxa?x, way' cxʷúywi, uł i?
   kʷu ks -?imx -a?x way' c+xʷuy -wy uł i?
   4kn incp^ -move -^incp yes come -ipimptv and art

   kəkəw'ápa? u?hám
   k+kw'ápa? w+?+ham
   dog bark_inch

   We're going to move, come," and the dogs started to bark.

115.[ixí?] k'ək'níya?
   ixí? k'+k'níya?
   that listen

   She was listening.

116.way' mat ilí? nákʷəm ixí? mat
   way' mat ilí? nakʷm ixí? mat
   well maybe there evid that maybe

   təmxʷúla?xʷs ik'lí?
   tmxʷ+úla?xʷ -s ik'lí?
   land -3in there

   I guess that's his place down there.

117.cut nakʷm way' mat ixí? i? citxʷs ilí? {kiw}
   cut nakʷm way' mat ixí? i? citxʷ -s ilí?
   say evid yes maybe that art house -3in there

   She said, "That must be his house there."

118.k'la? nis xʷist
   ak'lá? nis xʷist
   here gone walk

   She left, walked away.

119.uł xi? xa? cən?acq?úla?xʷ sənk'líp
   uł ixí? axá? c+n+?acq?+úla?xʷ s+n+k'l'+ip
   and then this crawl_out_of_ground Coyote

   So Coyote crawled out;

120.uł ixí? sxʷət'pəncú·ts [k'əl citxʷs]
   uł ixí? s -xʷt'p+ncut -s k'l citxʷ -s
   and then dur -hurry -3i to house -3in

   he ran to his house.

121.kí··ləntəm sənk'l'íp
   kil -nt-m s+n+k'l'+ip
   chase -nt-psv Coyote

   She chased Coyote;

122.uł ksənkəcn'íkəntəm
   uł ks -n+kcn+ikn -t -m
   and futT^ -overtake -nt -psv

   and was about to catch him;

123.uł xi? {i?} k'ʷul'l'_t {sútən, t} sxʷa?xʷa?nkíłp
   uł ixí? k'ʷul'+l̄'_t sutn s+xʷa?+xʷa?+nk+íłp
   and that turn_into thing thornbush

k'ʷul'l'̲ t   sxʷa?xʷa?nkíłp
k'ʷul'+l̄'̲ t   s+xʷa?+xʷa?+nk+íłp
turn_in̄to   thornbush

and he turned into something, thorn bushes.

124.uł   ixí?   c'əlc'əlxw'á·qstxəntəm {i?}
    uł   ixí?   c'l+c'lx+w'+aqst+xn -nt -m
    and   that   scratch_thigh   -nt -psv

And he scratched her thighs.

125.uł   ixí?   scuts   tałt   put   c'x̌iłt   sənk'líp
    uł   ixí?   s   -cut -s tał+t   put   c+?x̌ił+t   s+n+k'l'+ip
    and that   dur -say -3i surely   just like   Coyote

ilí? {a c}
ilí?
there

She said, "That's just like Coyote."

126.ca?kʷ cmistín   sənk'líp   uł   kən
    ca?kʷ c   -my   -st   -in   s+n+k'l'+ip uł   kn
    if   cust^ -know -^cust -1erg   Coyote   and 1kn

n?ułxʷ   uł   k'ʷ?ápqən   uł   way'
n+?ułxʷ   uł   k'ʷ?+ap+qn   uł   way'
enter   and bite_head   and finish

If I knew that was Coyote I'd go in and bite his head.

127.uł   ałí?   mał   kən   c'?ax
    uł   ałí?   mał   kn   c'+?+ax
    and   so   too_much   1kn   shame_inch

I am too ashamed.

128.mat   ití?   switx
    mat   ití?   swit   -x
    maybe that   somebody   -?

Maybe it's somebody else."

129.cut ixí? {uł}   kʷu   ki··ls   məł   kʷu
    cut ixí?   kʷu   kil   -s   mł   kʷu
    say that   1obj   chase -3erg   and   1obj

kspulsts
ks   -pul   -st -s
futT^ -kill_one   -st -3erg

He said, "She chased me, and was going to kill me."

130.uł   xi?   txlak'   ixí?   ta   cmaq'ʷ
    uł   ixí?   t+xlak'   ixí?   t   c+maq'ʷ
    and   that   go_around   that   obj_itr   mountain

And he went around a little hill.

131.ilí?   səck'ʷəl'cəncútx   i?   sm'am?ím
    ilí?   s+c   -k'ʷl'+cn+cut   -x   i?   s+m'a+m?ím
    there ipftvp^ -cook   -^ ipftvp art women

səcəlkípx
s+c   -lkip   -x
ipftvp ^ -pit_cook - ^ ipftvp
There were women there pit cooking.

132. ixí?   uɬ   ?íɬən   ilí?
     ixí?   uɬ   ?iɬn   ilí?
     then   and   eat   there
     She ate there.

133. kmax ixí?   sənk'l'íp   ɬa   kɬmnik[1]   uɬ   i?
     kmax ixí?   s+n+k'l'+ip ɬa?   kɬ   -mnik uɬ   i?
     only   that   Coyote   one_that have -shit and art

     ?iɬs
     ?iɬ -s
     eat -3erg
     That's only Coyote's shit she ate.

134. caʔkʷ cmistín   way'
     caʔkʷ c   -my   -st   -in   way'
     if   cust ^ -know - ^ cust -1erg yes

     ikspúlstəm   ikskʷʔápqən
     i   -ks   -pul   -st -m   i   -ks   -kʷʔ+ap+qn
     1i -futT ^ -kill_one   -st - ^ futT 1i -futl -bite_head
     "If I knew that was him I'd kill him, I'd bite his head."

135. caʔkʷ kʷʔápqən uɬ   λ'lal
     caʔkʷ kʷʔ+ap+qn uɬ   λ'l+al
     if   bite_head and   dead
     If she bites his head he'd die.

---

[1] The construction ɬaʔ kɬ- marks third person possessive: *s/he who has*; *his/her*, as in the title of this volume.

1. cxʷu··y   sənk'l'íp,   uɬ   wiks   iʔ {uɬ}
    c -xʷuy   s+n+k'l'+ip uɬ   wik -s   iʔ
    act-go   Coyote   and   see -3erg art
    Coyote was going and he saw...

2. kəm'əntís   iʔ   stk'ʷλ'k'ʷλ'ústəns   məɬ k'a
    km'   -nt -is   iʔ   s+t+k'ʷλ'+k'ʷλ'+us+tn   -s   mɬ   k'
    take -nt -3erg   art eyes   -3in and to

    nwist   ʔiskʷləms
    n+wis+t   ʔiskʷl+m   -s
    high   pitch   -3erg
    He took his eyes out and he threw them up in the air;

3. məɬ   cut   kaslípx̌ʷəx̌ʷx̌ʷəx̌ʷ
    mɬ   cut   kas+lipx̌ʷ+x̌ʷ+x̌ʷ+x̌ʷ
    and   say   slip_in
    and he said, "come back in!"

4. məɬ   ɬcənlípx̌ʷəm   iʔ   stk'ʷλ'k'ʷλ'ústəns
    mɬ   ɬ+c+n+lipx̌ʷ   -m   iʔ   s+t+k'ʷλ'+k'ʷλ'+us+tn -s
    and   slip_in_cisl_again -mdl art eyes   -3in
    And his eyes came back in.

5. itíʔ   t'uxʷt   iʔ {iʔ} yutlxʷ   uɬ   kəm'ɬtím   iʔ
    itíʔ   t'uxʷ+t   iʔ   yutlxʷ   uɬ   km'   -ɬt -im   iʔ
    from_that   fly   art   Raven   and   take -ɬt -psv   art

    stk'ʷλ'k'ʷλ'ústəns
    s+t+k'ʷλ'+k'ʷλ'+us+tn   -s
    eyes   -3in
    Then Raven flew by and he took his eyes.

6. uɬ   cut   lípx̌ʷəx̌ʷəx̌ʷ t'i   lut_stim'
    uɬ   cut   lipx̌ʷ+x̌ʷ+x̌ʷ t'iʔ   lut_s+tim'
    and   say   slip_in   evid   nothing
    He said, "Slip in," and nothing happened.

7. nák'ʷəm   knəm'qín
    nak'ʷm   k+nm'+qin
    evid   blind
    And he was blind.

8. məɬ   xʷu··y   itíʔ   cxʷilwís,
    mɬ   xʷuy   itíʔ   c -xʷy+lwis
    and   go   from_that   act -wander
    He was going, walking around any old place;

9. uɬ   iʔ   k'əl {cəc}   síwstaʔx,
    uɬ   iʔ   k'l   siwst+aʔx
    up_to   art to   drinking_water
    to the drinking water;

10. iʔ   k'əl   cəcw'íxaʔ,   uɬ   lut   t'a
    iʔ   k'l   c+cw'íxaʔ   uɬ   lut   t'
    art   to   little_creek   and   not   negfac

    ckaʔkícsts
    c   -kaʔ+kíc   -st   -s
    cust^   -find   -^cust -3erg
    to the creek, he didn't find anything.

11. ixíʔ   uɬ {iʔ iʔ}   ya əct'kʷt'ákʷ
    ixíʔ   uɬ   ya c -t'kʷ+t'akʷ
    there   and   art act -brush
    There was brush.

12. məɬ   cus,   kʷ   stim'   anwí
    mɬ   cu -s   kʷ   stim'   anwí
    and   tell -3erg   2kn   what   you
    And he asked him, "What are you?"

13. cúntəm   t'əxʷ   kən   páx̌ʷpəx̌ʷɬp {a kən}
    cu -nt-m   t'xʷ   kn   pax̌ʷ+px̌ʷ+ɬp
    tell -nt-psv   evidently   1kn   pussy_willow
    He told him, "I am a grey willow."

14. cut   kən   páx̌ʷpəx̌ʷɬp
    cut   kn   pax̌ʷ+px̌ʷ+ɬp
    say   1kn   pussy_willow
    He said, "I'm a grey willow."

15. uɬ   cut, way' nak'ʷəm kən   k'aʔítət   iʔ   k'əl cəcw'íxaʔ
    uɬ   cut way' nak'ʷm   kn   k'aʔít+t   iʔ   k'l c+cw'íxaʔ
    and say well evid   1kn   get_near art to little_creek
    And he said, "I'm getting close to the river."

16. uɬ   itlíʔ   xʷu··y məɬ ixíʔ   əct'ákʷ
    uɬ   itlíʔ   xʷuy mɬ ixíʔ   c -t'ákʷ
    and   from_there go and then act -brush
    Then he went on, and there was brush.

17. cus,   anwí   kʷ   stim'
    cu -s   anwí   kʷ   stim'
    tell -3erg   you   2kn   what
    He said, "What are you?"

18. cúntəm   t'əxʷ   kən   skʷəkʷʔíɬp
    cu -nt-m   t'xʷ   kn   s+kʷ+kʷʔ+iɬp
    tell -nt-psv   evidently   1kn   rose_bush
    He told him, "I am a rose bush."

19. níkna   way'   nák'ʷəm lut kən t'   k'aʔítət iʔ
    níkxnaʔ   way'   nak'ʷm lut kn t'   k'aʔít+t iʔ
    goodness   well   evid not 1kn negfac get_near art

    k'əl siwɬkʷ
    k'l siwɬ+kʷ
    to water
    "My, I am not near the water."

20. itlí?   xʷu·· y,   məɬ   itlí?   ya ct'əkʷt'ákʷ
    itlí?   xʷuy   mɬ   itlí?   ya c -t'kʷ+t'akʷ
    from_there go   and   from_there art act -brush
    He traveled on, there was some more brush.

21. cus   anwí   kʷ   stim'
    cu -s   anwí   kʷ   stim'
    tell -3erg you   2kn   what
    He said, "What are you?"

22. cut t'əxʷ {kən} cut   kn   stəkcxʷíɬp
    cut t'xʷ   cut   kn   s+tkcxʷ+íɬp
    say evidently   say   1kn   red_willow
    He said, "I am a red willow."

23. way' nákʷəm   kən   k'a?ítət   i?   k'əl siwɬkʷ
    way' nakʷm   kn   k'a?ít+t   i?   k'l   siwɬ+kʷ
    yes   evid   1kn   get_near   art to   water
    "Well, now I'm near the water."

24. ixí?   uɬ   nixʷítkʷ   ik'lí?, uɬ   si··w'st
    ixí?   uɬ   n+yxʷ+itkʷ   ik'lí?   uɬ   siwst
    then   and   fall_in_water   there   and   drink
    And he fell in the water, and he drank.

25. uɬ   ilí?   i? skəkˤáka? ct'əxʷtəlwís
    uɬ   ilí?   i? s+k+kˤáka? c -t'xʷt+lwis
    and   there   art bird   act -fly_around
    There was a bird flying around there.

26. cus,   cxʷuyx   ak'lá? kʷ tətw'ít
    cu -s   c+xʷuy -x   ak'lá? kʷ t+tw'it
    tell -3erg come -isimptv   here   2kn boy
    He said, "Come here you little boy.

27. ˤác'ənt   i? skʷkʷúsənt,   i? scəcˤásənt
    ˤac' -nt i? s+kʷ+kʷusnt   i? s+c+caˤsnt
    look_at -nt art stars   art little_stars
    Look at the stars, the little stars."

28. {ak'lá? ɬn} ak'lá? ˤác'əm   k'a nwist
                 ak'lá? ˤac' -m   k'   n+wis+t
                 here   look_at -mdl to   high
    He looked up high.

29. ixí?   cxʷu··y i? tətw'ít, uɬ ilí?   cus   k'a?kín
    ixí?   c+xʷuy i? t+tw'it uɬ ilí?   cu -s   k'a?+kín'
    then   come   art boy   and there   tell -3erg where_to
    The boy came and then said, "Where?"

30. k'la?   ˤác'ənt,   k'a nwist
    ak'lá? ˤac' -nt   k'   n+wis+t
    here   look_at -nt   to   high
    "Look there up high."

31. k'liʔ　　ʕʼác'əs,　　　　kə　nc'ənc'ənq'úsəs
    ik'líʔ　　ʕʼac'　-s　　　　kiʔ　n+c'n+c'nq'+us -s
    there　　look_at -3erg　　rel　gouge_eyes　　-3erg
    He looked there, and he gouged his eyes out.

32. ixíʔ　　nləpləpx̌ʷəntís　　　　　　iʔ　　k'əl
    ixíʔ　　n+lp+lpx̌ʷ　-nt　-is　　　iʔ　　k'l
    then　　slip_in　　-nt　-3erg　　art　　on

    stkʷˈʔk̓ˈʷλ̓ústəns
    s+t+kʷˈλ̓'+k̓ˈʷλ̓'+us+tn　　-s
    eyes　　　　　　　　　　　　　-3in
    Then he put them back in his eyes.

33. uɬ　　ixíʔ　　axáʔ　iʔ　tətw'ít　cəcʕáypəm,　　məɬ
    uɬ　　ixíʔ　　axáʔ　iʔ　t+tw'it　ca+cáʕyp+m　mɬ
    and　　then　　this　art　boy　　cry　　　　　　and

    xʷət'pəncút,　　uɬ　　c'qʷaqʷ
    xʷt'+p+ncut　　uɬ　　c'qʷ+aqʷ
    run　　　　　　and　　cry
    And the boy started crying, and he ran away, and he cried.

34. uɬ　　itlíʔ　　sxʷuys　　　　sənk'l'íp
    uɬ　　itlíʔ　　s　-xʷuy　-s　s+n+k'l'+ip
    and　　from_there dur -go　-3i　Coyote
    And Coyote went on.

35. axáʔ　iʔ　tətw'ít　cúntəm {iʔ}　iʔ　t
    axáʔ　iʔ　t+tw'it　cu -nt-m　　iʔ　t
    this　art　boy　　tell -nt-psv　art　aglnst

    stəmtímaʔs,
    s+tm+tímaʔ　-s
    grandmother　-3in
    And then the boy's grandmother said to him:

36. cxʷuyx,
    c+xʷuy -x
    come　-isimptv
    "Come here.

37. axáʔ iʔ　təl　skʷəlsíɬməlx　　mi　k'ʷúl'xtmən
    axáʔ iʔ　tl　s+kʷl+s+iɬmlx　　mi　k'ʷul' -xt　-m　　-n
    this　art from kinnickkinnick　fut　make -benf -2obj -1erg

    t　　　akstkʷˈʔk̓ˈʷλ̓ústən
    t　　　a　-k　　-s+t+k̓ˈʷλ̓'+k̓ˈʷλ̓'+us+tn
    obj_tr　2in -to_be -eyes
    I'll make you some eyes from this here kinnickkinnickberry.

38. xʷíc'xtmən
    xʷic' -xt　-m　　-n
    give　-benf -2obj -1erg
    I'll give it to you."

39. uɬ   itlí?   t'i   kʷəlkʷíl   i?   stkʷᵂəƛ'kʷᵂƛ'ústəns
     uɬ   itlí?   t'i?   kʷl+kʷil   i?   s+t+kʷᵂƛ'+kʷᵂƛ'+us+tn -s
     and   from_there   evid   red   art   eyes   -3in
     And that's why his eyes are red.

40. uɬ   axá?   xʷu··y   sənk'l'íp,
     uɬ   axá?   xʷuy   s+n+k'l'+ip
     and   this   go   Coyote
     Coyote went.

41. uɬ   ilí?   i?   cəcám'a?t {i?}   i?   sw'əsw'ˤás   ilí?
     uɬ   ilí?   i?   c+cám'+a?+t   i?   sw'+sw'+aˤs   ilí?
     and   there   art   small   art   pheasant   there

     əcxətxítmi?st
     c   -xt+xít+mi?st
     act -run_around
     And there were baby pheasants running around there;

42. i   l   sp'əc'níɬxʷsəlx,   t'əxʷ   i   l   cítxʷsəlx
     i?   l   s+p'c'n+iɬxʷ   -s -lx   t'xʷ   i?   l   citxʷ   -s -lx
     art   in   tipi   -3in -pl   emph   art in   house   -3in -pl
     in their tipi, their house.

43. ik'lí?   kicx   sənk'líp
     ik'lí?   kic+x   s+n+k'l'+ip
     there   arrive   Coyote
     Coyote got there;

44. uɬ   cus   k'a?kín   anl?íw   uɬ   askʷúy
     uɬ   cu   -s   k'a?+kín'   an -l?iw   uɬ   a   -s+kʷuy
     and   tell -3erg where_to   2in -m's_father   and   2in -mother
     and he asked them, "Where is your father and your mother?"

45. uɬ   cut   k'aw,   súxʷxʷəlx
     uɬ   cut   k'aw   suxʷ+xʷ   -lx
     and   say   gone   leave_pl   -pl
     And they said, "Gone, they've left."

46. ixí?   ?a··qᵂs   i?   qʷəlmín
     ixí?   ?aqᵂ   -s   i?   qʷl+min
     then   scrape   -3erg   art   ashes
     He scraped the cinders away.

47. ilí?   ixí?   npkʷúsəs   ixí?   i?   skəkˤáka?
     ilí?   ixí?   n+pkʷ+us   -s   ixí?   i?   s+k+kˤáka?
     there   then   put_on_fire -3erg   that   art   bird

     ilí?   i?   cəcám'a?t
     ilí?   i?   c+cám'+a?+t
     there   art   small
     He put the little birds there on the fire, the little ones.

48. t'i?   ƛ'axʷt,
     t'i?   ƛ'axʷ+t
     evid   dead_pl
     They died.

49. ilíʔ   ɬqəmís   ilíʔ {pəkʷs} pəkʷəntís
     ilíʔ   ɬq+mi -s   ilíʔ   pkʷ   -nt -is
     there   put   -3erg   there   pour_solids -nt -3erg
     And he put them (back ?) there in a bunch.

50. ixíʔ   itlíʔ   sxʷuys
     ixíʔ   itlíʔ   s -xʷuy   -s
     then   from_there   dur -go   -3i
     He went on.

51. xʷuy {ɬi}   ik'líʔ   k'a cwix,   nʔuɬxʷ
     xʷuy   ik'líʔ   k' cwix   n+ʔuɬxʷ
     go   there   to live   enter
     He went to another living place, went in.

52. ciʕ'áʔ   stəxmín   ilíʔ   əcqəmqmín,
     c+yaʕ'   s+tx+min   ilíʔ   c -qm+qmin
     lots   comb   there   act -lie
     And there there was nothing but combs;

53. uɬ   aɬíʔ   ixíʔ   iʔ   sqilxʷ   k'ʷúl'səlx {kɬ}   t
     uɬ   aɬíʔ   ixíʔ   iʔ   s+qilxʷ   k'ʷul'   -s   -lx   t
     and   because   that   art   person   make   -3erg   -pl obj_tr

     stəxmín
     s+tx+min
     comb
     lying around there, because the people had turned themselves into combs.

54. {ixíʔ}   itlíʔ   kʷnim,   uɬ   ksʔácqaʔx {xiʔ}
     itlíʔ   kʷni -m   uɬ   ks -ʔácqaʔ -x
     from_there   take   -mdl   and   incp^ -go_out -^incp

     ciʕ'áʔ   nákʷəm   sqilxʷ   ixíʔ
     c+yaʕ'   nak'ʷm   s+qilxʷ   ixíʔ
     lots   evid   person   there
     He took one, and was going out, but there are people there.

55. ixíʔ   txəntísəlx,   nt'a   cacacá··ʕ,
     ixíʔ   tx -nt -is   -lx   nt'a   ca+ca+cáʕ
     then   comb -nt -3erg   -pl   intj   holler
     They combed him, gee he hollered;

56. ik'líʔ   sc'q'mis   iʔ   stəxmín
     ik'líʔ   s -c'q'+mi   -s   iʔ   s+tx+min
     there   ? -throw   -3erg   art   comb
     he threw the comb away.

57. ixíʔ   itlíʔ   sxʷuys,
     ixíʔ   itlíʔ   s -xʷuy   -s
     then   from_there   dur -go   -3i
     Then he went on.

58. uɬ   way'   ɬənʔúɬxʷ   ilíʔ   t'əxʷ   aʔ
     uɬ   way'   ɬ+n+ʔuɬxʷ   ilíʔ   t'xʷ   aʔ
     and   well   enter_again   there   evidently   art

cəw'íw'aʔx
c   -w'í+w'aʔx
act -living_place_dim
And went again into a little living place.

59. ik'líʔ   cən?úɬxʷ
    ik'líʔ   c+n+?uɬxʷ
    there   enter_cisl
    He went in there.

60. nt'a··   nák'ʷʷəm   ilíʔ   kmax   túl'mən
    nt'a   nak'ʷm   ilíʔ   kmax   tul'+mn
    intj   evid   there   only   paint_powder
    My, nothing but rouge powder.

61. ixíʔ   úɬiʔ   kəm'əntís   iʔ
    ixíʔ   uɬ+iʔ   km'   -nt -is   iʔ
    then   and_then   take   -nt -3erg   art
    He took some;

62. nk'ʷʷaʔk'ʷʷí··nəm,   məɬ   aláʔ   taʔxílsts,
    n+k'ʷʷaʔ+k'ʷʷín -m   mɬ   aláʔ   taʔxíl   -st -s
    pick   -mdl   and   here   do_a_certain_way -st -3erg
    and started picking out, and did like this;⌐

63. məɬ   itlí··ʔ
    mɬ   itlíʔ
    and   from_there
    then another one.[2]

64. way'   axáʔ   ikskʷním
    way'   axáʔ   i   -ks   -kʷni   -m
    well   this   1i   -futT^ -take   ^futT
    "I'll take this one."

65. ixíʔ   k'əɬq'ʔálqsəms
    ixíʔ   k'ɬ+q'ʔ+alqs   -m
    that   stick_under_clothes   -mdl
    He stuck it under his clothes.

66. put   ksʔácqaʔx   kiʔ   kʷən·úsəlx, {iʔ}
    put   ks   -ʔácqaʔ -x   kiʔ   kʷn -nu   -s -lx
    just   incp^ -go_out - ^incp   rel   take -manage -3erg-pl
    He was just about to leave when they grabbed him.

67. nɬc'úlaʔxʷəmsəlx   ilíʔ
    n+ɬc'+úlaʔxʷ+m   -s   -lx ilíʔ
    throw_on_ground -3erg -pl there
    They threw him on the ground.

---

[1] The narrator made the motions of trying to rub out the paint.
[2] Madeline DeSautel explained that the people turned themselves into painting powder.

68. ixíʔ   kp'uʔqísəlx {λ'a}
    ixíʔ   k+p'w'+qi -s   -lx
    then   shit_on   -3erg -pl
    They shat on him.

69. kp'uʔqísəlx,   uɬ   ixíʔ   stk'síls {uɬ xi}
    k+p'w'+qi -s   -lx uɬ   ixíʔ   s -t+k's+ils
    shit_on -3erg -pl and then   act -bad_stomach
    They shat on him, and that upset his stomach.

70. ilíʔ   witk'x, uɬ   itlíʔ   xʷuy
    ilíʔ   witk'x uɬ   itlíʔ   xʷuy
    there vomit and   from_there go
    Then he threw up, and then he went on.

71. ixíʔ   xʷuy [iʔ t]   w'íw'aʔst
    ixíʔ   xʷuy iʔ t   w'í+w'aʔst
    then   go   art obj_itr high_dim
    He went up a little hill.

72. uɬ   nákʷəm   axáʔ ɬcyˤáp   aʔ
    uɬ   nakʷm   axáʔ ɬ+c+yaˤ+p   aʔ
    and   evid   this   arrive_here_again art

    ksqʷəsqʷasíʔa   iʔ skəkáˤkaʔ
    k   -s+qʷs+qʷasíʔa   iʔ s+k+kˤákaʔ
    have -children   art bird
    Well [lo and behold], the birds that had the baby chicks came back.

73. uɬ   way'   λ'axʷt   iʔ sqʷəsqʷasíʔasəlx
    uɬ   way'   λ'axʷ+t iʔ s+qʷs+qʷasíʔa -s -lx
    and   yes   dead_pl art children   -3in -pl
    Their children were dead.

74. ixíʔ   sxʷúysəlx
    ixíʔ   s   -xʷuy   -s -lx
    then   dur -go   -3i -pl
    They went.

75. uɬ   ixíʔ   a   cq'q'áx̌   iʔ xəwíɬ ilíʔ,   uɬ
    uɬ   ixíʔ   a   c -q'+q'ax̌ iʔ xwiɬ ilíʔ   uɬ
    and   then   art act -clearing art road   there and

    ɬk'əl'lílxəlx
    ɬ+k'l'+l+ilx -lx
    hide_again -pl
    They went up that little trail, and there they hid.

76. cúntəm   iʔ t   sqəl'tmíxʷ,
    cu -nt-m iʔ t   s+ql't+mixʷ
    tell -nt-psv art aglnst man
    The man told her,

77. n'ín'w'iʔ   t   incá   ɬc'ápɬx̌ənmən
    n'ín'w'iʔ   t   in+cá ɬc'+apɬ+x̌n+m -n
    a_while,   aglnst I   hit_with_wing -1erg
    "When I whack him on the head with the wing,

78. mi lut yaxʷt   ixíʔ {ta}   iʔ t   xƛ'ut   yaxʷt,
    mi lut yaxʷt   ixíʔ   iʔ t   xƛ'ut   yaxʷt
    fut not fall   that   art from   rock   fall
    (if) he won't fall off the rock,

79. mi t   anwí   ɫc'ápɫx̌ənməntxʷ,
    mi t   anwí   ɫc'+apɫ+x̌n+m -nt -xʷ
    fut aglnst   you   hit_with_wing -nt -2erg
    then you whack him with the wing;

80. məɫ {n}   k'aʔx̌ís   yaxʷt   mi ƛ'lal
    mɫ   k'aʔ+x̌ís   yaxʷt   mi ƛ'l+al
    and   over_there fall   fut dead
    then he'll fall off and die."

81. ixíʔ   itíʔ   sxʷúy·səlx
    ixíʔ   itíʔ   s -xʷuy -s -lx
    that   from_that   dur -go   -3i -pl
    Then they went there.

82. itíʔ   cxʷu··y   sənk'l'íp,
    itíʔ   c+xʷuy   s+n+k'l'+ip
    from_that   come   Coyote
    Coyote was coming along;

83. lut t'a   cənstílsəm,
    lut t'   c   -nst+ils -m
    not negfac   act -think   -mdl
    he was't thinking.

84. kʷm'iɫ   kiʔ   ct'uxʷt   ixíʔ   iʔ   skəkáˤkaʔ
    kʷm'iɫ   kiʔ   c+t'uxʷt   ixíʔ   iʔ   s+k+kˤákaʔ
    suddenly   rel   fly_cisl   that   art   bird
    All of a sudden the bird flew;

85. kiʔ ɫc'ápɫx̌ənməntəm
    kiʔ ɫc'+apɫ+x̌n+m -nt -m
    rel hit_with_wing -nt -psv
    and whacked him on the head.

86. k'ík'əm,   níkxnaʔ   scutx   uɫ   k'ík'əm
    k'i+k'm   níkxnaʔ   s   -cut   -x   uɫ   k'i+k'm
    nearly   goodness   ipftv^ -say   -^ipftv   and nearly

    iksyáxʷt
    i -ks   -yaxʷt
    1i -futl -fall
    "Goodness," he said, "I pretty near fell."

87. put ilíʔ   tixʷk'únəm   kiʔ ɫc'ápɫx̌ənməntəm   iʔ
    put ilíʔ   tixʷ+kʷún+m   kiʔ ɫc'+apɫ+x̌n+m -nt -m   iʔ
    just there talk   rel hit_with_wing -nt -psv   art

    t   túm'təm'
    t   tum'+tm'
    aglnst   mother
    He had just said that when he got whacked by the mother.

88. ixí?   syax^wts   ixí?   i? t   xλ'ut, uł
    ixí?   s -yax^wt -s ixí?   i? t   xλ'ut   uł
    then   dur -fall   -3i that   art from   rock   and

    nłəc'c'úla?x^w,   uł   λ'lal
    n+łc'+c'+úla?x^w uł   λ'l+al
    hit_ground   and   dead
    Then he fell over the bank, and he fell down, and died.

89. ilí?   əct'ák'^w,   mat   nək^wspíntk   ilí?
    ilí?   c+t'ak'^w   mat   nk'^w+s+pin+tk   ilí?
    there   lay_cisl   maybe one_year   there

    sct'ak'^ws
    s- c+t'ak'^w   -s
    dur -put_down -3i
    He lay there, maybe it was a year that he lay there.

90. {xi?xa?}   [i]tí?   cx^wuy ixí?   łqáqca?s,
               ití?   c+x^wuy ixí?   ł+qá+qca?   -s
               from_that come   that   older_brother -3in

    stim's   x̌^wʕáylx^w
    stim'   -s   x̌^wʕ+ilx^w
    thing   -3in Fox
    His older brother came by there, some relative, maybe Fox.

91. ití?   cx^wuy, syúmcəns   ití?   cx^wuy {ixí? cun}
    ití?   c+x^wuy s+yum+cn -s ití?   c+x^wuy
    from_that come   partner   -3in from_that come
    Then his parther came by.

92. ixí?   ?ú··lu?łtəm {i?} láq^wmi?st ałí?   ixí?   sútən   i?
    ixí?   ?ul+w' -łt-m   láq^w+mi?st ałí?   ixí?   sutn   i?
    that   gather -łt-psv lay_about because that   thing   art

    spumt
    s+pumt
    fur
    He gathered the remains/things that were scattered about, the hair.

93. ?ú··lu?səs   uł   ilí?   tx̌^wayqs,   ixí?
    ?ul+w's -s   uł   ilí?   t+x̌^wayq -s   ixí?
    gather -3erg and   there pile   -3erg   that

    tk^wítxnəms
    t+k^wit+xn+m   -s
    step_over   -3erg
    He gathered them, and piled them up, he stepped over them.

94. ixí?   uł {i?} cqiłt   sənk'l'íp
    ixí?   uł   c -qił+t   s+n+k'l'+ip
    that   and   act -awaken   Coyote
    Coyote woke up.

95. ná··kna?,   alá?   kən   łq'ilx,   kən   ?itx,   uł   kən
    níkxna?   alá?   kn   łq'+ilx   kn   ?it+x   uł   kn
    goodness   here   1kn   lie   1kn   sleep   and 1kn

nyaˁ'pəncút
n+yaˁ'+p+ncút
stuck
"Goodness, I lay here, and I fell asleep, I've been stuck."

96. cúntəm   lut kʷ t'ə   sʔítxəx,   kʷ λ'lal
    cu -nt-m   lut kʷ t'   s   -ʔitx -x   kʷ λ'l+al
    tell -nt-psv not 2kn negfac ipftv ^ -sleep - ^ ipftv 2kn dead
    [Fox] told him, "You haven't been asleep, you were dead."

97. lut, way'   kən   sʔítxəx
    lut way'   kn   s   -ʔitx   -x
    not yes   1kn   ipftv ^ -sleep - ^ ipftv
    "No, I've been sleeping."

98. cúntəm   ˁ'ác'ənt,   ixíʔ   anmˁámlaʔ,   pútiʔ
    cu -nt-m   ˁ'ac' -nt ixíʔ   an -máˁ+mlaʔ pút+iʔ
    tell -nt-psv look_at -nt that 2in -maggots   still
    cʔakʷʔakʷtl'ílx
    c   -ʔakʷ+ʔakʷt+l+ílx
    act -crawl_around
    He told him, "Look, these are your worms, they're still crawling
    around."

99. ixíʔ   itlíʔ   sxʷúy'səlx
    ixíʔ   itlíʔ   s   -xʷuy -s -lx
    then   from_there dur -go   -3i -pl
    They went away.

100.ixíʔ   uɬ   way'   a   cmistín
    ixíʔ   uɬ   way'   a   c   -my   -st -in
    that   and   all   art cust ^ -know -st -1erg
    That's all I know.

101.uc   anwí   itlíʔ   cmistíxʷ
    uc   anwí   itlíʔ   c-   my   -st -ixʷ
    dub   you   from_there cust ^ know   -st -1erg
    Do you know more?

1. cwíxəlx   həɬspəpl'ína?   uɬ   i?
   c -wix -lx   hɬ   -s+p+pl'+ína?   uɬ   i?
   act -live -pl   group -Rabbit   and   art

   sən?ímats   q'ʷəq'ʷc'w'íya?
   s+n+?íma?t -s   q'ʷ+q'ʷc'w'íya?
   grandchild -3in   Chipmunk
   There lived Rabbit and her grandson Chipmunk.

2. uɬ   ixí?   x̌lap   məɬ   ixí?   sxʷuys
   uɬ   ixí?   x̌la+p   mɬ   ixí?   s -xʷuy -s
   and   then   morning and   then   dur -go -3i

   q'ʷəq'ʷc'w'íya?
   q'ʷ+q'ʷc'w'íya?
   Chipmunk
   It was morning and Chipmunk goes.

3. [məɬ] ixí?   sq'ʷəl'íw'ms   tə   skʷlis
   mɬ   ixí?   s -q'ʷl'+iw'm -s t   s+kʷlis
   and   that   dur -berry_pick -3i obj_itr kinnickinnick
   He would pick kinnickinnik berries.

4. q'ʷəl'í··w'm məɬ   cut   p'i?p'ay'áqa? knaqsú··s,
   q'ʷl'+iw'm mɬ   cut   p'y'+p'ay'áqa? k+naqs+ús
   berry_pick and   say   ripe   one_berry
   He picked and said "One berry ripe;

5. p'i?p'ay'áqa? tk'aslú··s,   p'i?p'ay'áqa? tka?ɬlú··s
   p'y'+p'ay'áqa? t+k+?asl+ús   p'y'+p'ay'áqa? t+ka?ɬl+ús
   ripe   two_berries   ripe   three_berries
   two berries ripe, three berries ripe."

6. t'i   qax̌ʷ··, níxəl' qax̌ʷ,   ta?x̌íləm,
   t'i?   qax̌ʷ nixl   qax̌ʷ   ta?x̌íl   -m
   evid break hear   break do_a_certain_way -mdl
   Something broke, he heard it break, he did like that;

7. məɬ ik'lí? ʕác'əs,   uɬ nákʷəm   ixí? spəpʕáta?
   mɬ ik'lí? ʕ'ac' -s   uɬ nakʷm   ixí? s+pa+páʕɬa?
   and there look_at -3erg and evid   that Ape[1]

   t'əcxʷúy
   t'c   -xʷuy
   actCisl -go
   looked there, he saw Giant coming over.

8. ixí?   stk'íwləxs,
   ixí?   s -t+k'iw+lx -s
   that   dur -climb   -3i
   He climbed on a tree.

---

[1] This is the monster Sasquatch.

9. c'q'mis i? scqᶦʷl'íw'sc,
   c'q'+mi -s i? sc+qᶦʷl'+iw's -c
   throw -3erg art picking -3in
   He threw the berries he'd picked;

10. ixí? stk'íwəlxs i? k'la? cc'əl'c'ál'
    ixí? s -t+k'iw+lx -s i? ak'lá? c -c'l+c'al
    then dur -climb -3i art here act -trees
    and climbed on a tree there.

11. ixí? cxʷuy spəpˤáɬa?, uɬ cus
    ixí? c+xʷuy s+pa+páˤɬa? uɬ cu -s
    then come Ape and tell -3erg
    Giant came closer and said to him:

12. cxʷuyx, cxʷuyx ak'lá? kʷ
    c+xʷuy -x c+xʷuy -x ak'lá? kʷ
    come -isimptv come -isimptv here 2kʷu

    isɬəɬw'ílt
    i -s+ɬ+ɬw'+il't
    1in -nephew_dim
    "Come here, come over here, my little nephew."

13. ixí? scuts qᶦʷəqᶦʷc'w'íya? hahá kən lut kən
    ixí? s -cut -s qᶦʷ+qᶦʷc'w'íya? hahá kn lut kn
    then dur -say -3i Chipmunk intj 1kn not 1kn

    t'a ksəsí?
    t' k -s+si?
    negfac have -uncle
    And the Chipmunk said, "Ahah, I don't have any uncle."

14. t'əxʷ cxʷuyx ak'lá? kʷ isən?íma?t
    t'xʷ c+xʷuy -x ak'lá? kʷ i -s+n+?íma?t
    emph come -isimptv here 2kʷu 1in -grandchild
    "Come here, my grandchild."

15. ixí? scuts qᶦʷəqᶦʷc'w'íya? hahá lut kən t'a
    ixí? s -cut -s qᶦʷ+qᶦʷc'w'íya? hahá lut kn t'
    then dur -say -3i Chipmunk intj not 1kn negfac

    kstəmtíma?
    k -s+tm+tíma?
    have -grandmother
    And the Chipmunk said "Ahah, I don't have no grandma."

16. wi··m' cus
    wim' cu -s
    in_vain tell -3erg
    It did no good to say things.

17. ixí? scuts qᶦʷəqᶦʷc'w'íya?
    ixí? s -cut -s qᶦʷ+qᶦʷc'w'íya?
    then dur -say -3i Chipmunk
    Then Chipmunk said:

18. kʷint   anp'ínaʔ   məɬ {itíʔ}   itlíʔ?   anc'áʔsiqən
    kʷin   -t   an -p'ínaʔ   mɬ   itlíʔ?   an -c'asy'+qn
    take   -nt   2in -basket   and   from_there   2in -head

    kull'ínaʔntxʷ
    k+wl+l+ínaʔ -nt -xʷ
    cover   -nt -2erg
    "Take your basket, cover your head with it;

19. mi   kən   csax̌ʷt
    mi   kn   c+sax̌ʷ+t
    fut   1kn   go_downhill_cisl
    then I'll come down."

20. ixíʔ   kull'ínaʔs   iʔ   c'áʔsiqəns
    ixíʔ   k+wl+l+ínaʔ -s   iʔ   c'asy'+qn -s
    then   cover   -3erg   art   head   -3in

    spəpˤáɬaʔ
    s+pa+páˤɬaʔ
    Ape
    So Giant covered up its head.

21. uɬ   ixíʔ   scuts   t_niˤíp ilíʔ?
    uɬ   ixíʔ   s -cut -s   t_nyˤip ilíʔ?
    and   then   dur -say -3i always there

    ckull'ínaʔ[nt]   way'   kən
    c   -k+wl+l+ínaʔ -nt   way'   kn
    cust ^ -cover   -nt   yes   1kn

    ksáx̌ʷtaʔx
    k   -sax̌ʷ+t   -aʔx
    incp   -go_downhill   - ^ incp
    Then he said, "Keep it covered, I am coming down."

22. ixíʔ   scsa··x̌ʷts,   ixíʔ   sxʷət'pəncúts,
    ixíʔ   s -c+sax̌ʷ+t   -s   ixíʔ   s -xʷt'+p+ncut-s
    then   dur go_downhill_cisl   -3i   that   dur -run   -3i

    uɬ   t'i   nis
    uɬ   t'iʔ   nis
    and   evid   gone
    He came down, ran away, was gone.

23. ixíʔ   k'aʔx̌ís   ksútnaʔx,   kiʔ   c'əlxəntím
    ixíʔ   k'aʔ+x̌ís   k   -sutn   -aʔx   kiʔ   c'lx -nt -im
    that   over_there incp ^   -thing   - ^ incp   rel   hook -nt -psv

    tə   spəpˤáɬaʔ
    t   s+pa+páˤɬaʔ
    agInst   Ape
    He was going to go over there, and then he got scratched by Giant.

24. c'əlxəntím {c}   ˤáx̌ɬtəm   iʔ   sənk'míkən's
    c'lx   -nt-im   ˤax̌   -ɬt-m   iʔ   s+n+k'm+ikn'   -s
    hook   -nt-psv   scratch -ɬt-psv art   back   -3in
    He got scratched, he got scratched on his back.

25. uɬ   k'lá?   xí?   c'əm'c'úm's   i?   kəl'kíl'lxs,
    uɬ   ak'lá?   ixí?   c'm'+c'um' -s   i?   kl+kil'+l+x   -s
    and   here   that   suck   -3in art   hands   -3in
    Then he [Giant] sucked on his hands.

26. unáxʷ   x̌əx̌sáɬc'a? {i?}
    wnaxʷ   x̌+x̌s+áɬc'a?
    true   good_meat
    "It's really good meat.

27. x̌əx̌sáɬc'a?   i?   tətw'ít
    x̌+x̌s+áɬc'a?   i?   t+tw'it
    good_meat   art   boy
    This boy is really good meat."

28. ixí?   uɬ   nis   axá?   qʲʷəqʲʷc'w'íya?
    ixí?   uɬ   nis   axá?   qʲʷ+qʲʷc'w'íya?
    then   and   gone   this   Chipmunk
    Chipmunk got away.

29. xʷət'pəncú··t   i?   k'əl stəmtíma?s
    xʷt'+p+ncut   i?   k'l s+tm+tíma?   -s
    run   art   to   grandmother   -3in
    He ran to his grandma.

30. cus   sna?   sna?   sna?
    cu -s   sna?   sna?   sna?
    tell -3erg onom   onom   onom
    He said, "sna? sna? sna?."

31. snína?   t'əxʷ   mat   scutx
    sn+ína?   t'xʷ   mat   s   -cut   -x
    Owl   evidently must   ipftv^ -say   -^ ipftv
    He must have been trying to say "snína?."

32. ixí?   ckʷis {i?}   ilí?   a? cutáns   i?
    ixí?   c+kʷi   -s   ilí?   a? c -wtan -s   i?
    then   take_cisl   -3erg   there   art act -placed -3in   art
    skʷəkʷr'ína? {i?}
    s+kʷ+kʷr'+ína?
    clam_shell
    She picked up a clam shell that was lying there;

33. ilí?   t'əxʷ   i?   cnul'qən'm'ən'wíxʷ
    ilí?   t'xʷ   i?   c -n+wl'+qn'+m'n'wíxʷ
    there   evidently art   act -shell_cover
    he was covered.

34. ilí?   wíkʷəntəm,   cúntəm
    ilí?   wikʷ   -nt -m   cu -nt -m
    there   hide   -nt -psv   tell -nt -psv
    She hid him there, she said to him:

35. alá?   kʷ   wíkʷmi?st,   lut   aksután
    alá?   kʷ   wikʷ+mi?st   lut   a -ks   -wtan
    here   2kn   hide   not   2i -futl   -placed
    "You hide there, don't come out."

36. ik'lí?   wík^wəntəm   i?   k'əl   sənk'i?ína?
    ik'lí?   wik^w -nt -m   i?   k'l   s+n+k'?+ína?
    there   hide -nt -psv   art   to   pillow

    She hid him there under the pillow.

37. ixí?   uł   axá?   i?   ʕa?íck^w[ala?]
    ixí?   uł   axá?   i?   ʕa?íck^wala?
    then   and   this   art   Meadowlark

    ck'am·tíw's
    c   -k+?am+m+t+iw's
    act -perched

    Then Meadowlark landed there.

38. cúntəm   lut   akscút
    cu -nt-m   lut   a -k+s -cut
    tell -nt-psv not   2i -futl -say

    She told her, "Don't tell!

39. lut   aksm'a?yám,   lut
    lut   a   -ks   -m'ay'á   -m   lut
    not   2i -futT ^ -tell_stories - ^ futT   not

    aksənmyípm
    a   -ks   -n+my+ip   -m
    2i -futT ^ -tell_on   - ^ futT

    Don't say anything, don't tell him.

40. axá?   xáq'əntsən   t   aksq'l'íps
    axá?   xaq' -nt -s   -n   t   a -k -s+q'l'+ips
    this   pay -nt -2obj   -1erg   obj_tr 2in -to_be -medallion

    I'll pay you this medallion."

41. ixí?   uł   q'lípsəm {a·· ili}   ʕa?íck^wala?,   uł   ilí?
    ixí?   uł   q'l+ips   -m   ʕa?íck^wala?   uł   ilí?
    then   and   medallion -mdl   Meadowlark   and   there

    sk'am·tíw'sc
    s   -k+?am+m+t+iw's   -c
    dur -perched   -3i

    She put the medallion on Meadowlark, she still stayed there.

42. nt'a?   ixí?   ckicx   spəpʕáła?
    nt'a   ixí?   c+kic+x   s+pa+páʕła?
    intj   then   arrive_cisl   Ape

    Right then that Giant got there.

43. cut   uc   alá?   ckicx {i?}   ixí?   i?   tətw'ít
    cut   uc   alá?   c+kic+x   ixí?   i?   t+tw'ít
    say   dub   here   arrive_cisl   that   art   boy

    He aked, "Did that little boy get here?"

44. cúntəm   lut   kən   t'a   cwíkəm
    cu -nt-m   lut   kn   t'   c -wik   -m
    tell -nt-psv not   1kn   negfac   act-see -mdl

    She told him, "No, I haven't seen him."

45. ixí?   scuts   ʕaʔíckʷalaʔ   aʔ
    ixí?   s -cut -s   ʕaʔíckʷalaʔ   aʔ
    then   dur -say -3i   Meadowlark   art

    n'w'l'w'l'qən'mnwíxʷ   iʔ   skʷək̓ʷr'ína?
    n'+w'l'+w'l'+qn'+m'n'wíxʷ   iʔ   s+kʷ+k̓ʷr'+ína?
    clam_shell_dim   art clam_shell
    Meadowlark said, "The closed clam shell!"

46. ixí? után,   k'lənk'ahk'ʷʼíps   ixí?   iʔ   skʷək̓ʷr'ína?
    ixí? wtan   k'l+n+k'ahk'ʷʼ+íp -s   ixí?   iʔ   s+kʷ+k̓ʷr'+ína?
    that placed   open   -3erg   that   art clam_shell
    There it lay; he opened that clam shell.

47. nak'ʷʼm ilí?   nłq'ut   ixí?   iʔ   tətw'ít
    nak'ʷʼm ilí?   n+łq'+ut   ixí?   iʔ   t+tw'it
    evid   there   lie   that   art boy
    Sure enough the boy way lying there.

48. ixí?   ckʷis,   xiʔ   cus
    ixí?   c+kʷi   -s   ixí?   cu -s
    that   take_cisl -3erg   that   tell -3erg
    He took him and said:

49. stim' anx̌mínk   a   ntxʷus   ha
    stim' an -x̌m+ink   a   n+txʷ+us   ha
    what   2in -want   intj cousin   inter
    "What do you like, cousin?"

50. ixí?   scuts   t'əxʷ   sc'uʔxán
    ixí?   s -cut -s   t'xʷ   s+c'w'+xan
    that   dur -say -3i   emph   animal_hind_leg
    She said, "The leg."

51. ul   stim' anx̌mínk   ntxʷus   ha
    ul   stim' an -x̌m+ink   n+txʷ+us   ha
    and   what   2in -like   cousin   inter
    "What do you like, cousin?"

52. cut   t'əxʷ   ki··lx
    cut   t'xʷ   kilx
    say   emph   arm
    She said, "The arm."

53. stim' anx̌mínk   a   ntxʷus   ha
    stim' an -x̌m+ink   a   n+txʷ+us   ha
    what   2in -like   intj cousin   inter
    "What do you like, cousin?"

54. cut   t'əxʷ   sc'c'uʔxán'
    cut   t'xʷ   s+c'+c'w'+xan'
    say   emph   leg_dim
    She said, "The little leg."

55. stim' anx̌mínk   a   ntxʷus   ha
    stim' an -x̌m+ink   a   n+txʷ+us   ha
    what   2in -like   intj cousin   inter
    "What do you like, cousin?"

56. t'əxʷ   kilx
    t'xʷ   kilx
    emph   arm
    "The arm."

57. stim'   anx̌mínk   a   ntx̌ʷus   ha
    stim'   an -x̌m+ink a   n+tx̌ʷ+us ha
    what   2in -like   intj cousin   inter
    "What do you like, cousin?"

58. t'əxʷ   iʔ   sqiltk
    t'xʷ   iʔ   s+qil+tk
    emph   art body
    She said, "The body."

59. stim' {anx̌í}anx̌mínk   ntx̌ʷus   ha
    stim'   an -x̌m+ink n+tx̌ʷ+us ha
    what   2in -like   cousin   inter
    "What do you like, cousin?"

60. t'əxʷ   c'áʔsiqən
    t'xʷ   c'asy'+qn
    emph head
    She said, "The head."

61. stim'   a ntx̌ʷus   ha
    stim'   a n+tx̌ʷ+us ha
    what   intj cousin   inter
    "What do you like, cousin?"

62. t'əxʷ   iʔ   t'ənt'ína?
    t'xʷ   iʔ   t'n+t'ína?
    emph   art ears
    "The ears."

63. ixíʔ   kʷis {iʔ}   iʔ   spuʔús
    ixíʔ   kʷi   -s   iʔ   s+pʔ+us
    then   take -3erg art heart
    Then he took the heart;

64. ixíʔ   q'məntís   nʕam   nʕam   nʕam
    ixíʔ   q'm   -nt-is naʕm naʕm naʕm
    that   swallow -nt-3erg onom onom onom
    he swallowed it, "nʕam nʕam nʕam.

65. x̌əx̌sáɫc'aʔ iʔ   tətw'ít
    x̌+x̌s+áɫc'aʔ iʔ   t+tw'it
    good_meat   art boy
    This boy tastes good."

66. {ixíʔ s} ixíʔ   snisc,   lkʷilx itlíʔ
           ixíʔ   s -nis -c lkʷ+ilx itlíʔ
           then   dur -gone -3i leave from_there
    Then he quit, he left.

67. ixí?   i?   pəptw'ína?xʷ   c'qʷa··qʷ
    ixí?   i?   p+ptw'ína?xʷ   c'qʷ+aqʷ
    that   art   old_woman   cry
    The old lady cried.

68. ixí?   ?ú··lu?səs   i?   kəl'kíl'lx,   i?   sc'u?xán,
    ixí?   ?ul+w's -s   i?   kl'+kil'+lx   i?   s+c'w'+xan
    that   gather -3erg   art hands_dim   art animal_hind_leg

    i?   stim'
    i?   stim'
    art   whatever
    She gathered up the hands, feet, everything.

69. ixí?   ckʷnim   i?   t   skʷlis,   ixí?   k'ʷul's
    ixí?   c+kʷni+m   i?   t   s+kʷlis   ixí?   k'ʷul'   -s
    that   take_cisl   art   obj_itr kinnickinnick   that   make   -3erg

    t   kspu?úsc
    t   k   -s+p?+us   -c
    obj_tr to_be -heart   -3in
    She took the kinnickinnick berries and made a heart for him.

70. ixí?   tk'ʷítxləms,   uł   xəstwílx
    ixí?   t+k'ʷit+xn+m   -s   uł   xs+t+wilx
    then   step_over   -3erg   and   get_well
    She stepped over him, and he got well.

71. axá?   t'uxʷt   ʕa?íckʷala?
    axá?   t'uxʷ+t   ʕa?íckʷala?
    this   fly   Meadowlark
    Meadowlark flew.

72. cúntəm {kʷ}   ckʷint   ixí?   i?   sq'l'ips,   lut
    cu -nt-m   c+kʷin   -t   ixí?   i?   s+q'l'+ips   lut
    tell -nt-psv take_cisl -nt   that   art medallion   not

    akskʷním   a   kʷ   m'i?m'i?múł
    a   -ks   -kʷni   -m a   kʷ   m'y'+m'y'+muł
    2i   -futT^ -take   -^futT intj 2kn   tattler
    "Give back that locket, don't you take that, you tattle tale."

73. nis,   t'uxʷt,
    nis   t'uxʷ+t
    gone   fly
    She left, flew away.

74. ixí? {s} cus   ixí? i? tətw'ít t_niʕ'íp   kʷ   wíkʷmi?st,
    ixí?   cu -s   ixí? i? t+tw'it t_n+yʕ'ip   kʷ   wik+mi?st
    that   tell -3erg   that art boy   continuously   2kn   hide
    She told the boy, "You keep hiding.

75. lut_nixʷ   akłəłq'ʷl'íw'm {məł ti}
    lut_nixʷ   a -kł   -ł+q'ʷl'+iw'+m
    no_more   2i -futl - berry_pick_again
    Don't pick berries any more.

76. n'ín'w'i?   ikspúlstəm   ixí?   spəpˁáła?
    n'ín'w'i?   i   -ks   -pul   -st -m   ixí?   s+pa+páˁła?
    a_while, 1i -futT ^ -kill_one -st -^futT that Ape
    I am going to kill this here Giant."

77. ixí?   scxʷúys   spəpˁáła?,   uł   cut
    ixí?   s   -c+xʷuy -s   s+pa+páˁła? uł   cut
    then   dur -come -3i Ape   and   say
    Then Giant came back, he said:

78. ní··kna?,   way'   kʷ   paqaˁpíq   a {i? kʷi}   i   kʷ
    níkxna?   way'   kʷ   paq+aˁ+píq   a   i?   kʷ
    goodness yes   2kn white   inter   art 2kʷu

    isəntxʷús   a
    i   -s+n+txʷ+us   a
    1in -cousin   inter
    "Gee, but you are white, my friend.

79. uł   la?kín'   sc'kinx   úłi?   kʷ   piq
    uł   la?+kín' s+c   -?kin -x   uł+i?   kʷ   piq
    and whenever ipftvp ^ -indef -^ ipftvp and_then 2kn white
    How come you're so white?"

80. cut t'əxʷ   ałí?   ?ú··lu?sən   i? sútən {i? s}
    cut t'xʷ   ałí?   ?uł+w's -n   i? sutn
    say evidently   because   gather -1erg   art thing

    i? t'ic',   uł {i?} i? sλ'əλ'úk'ʷa?
    i? t'ic'   uł   i? s+λ'+λ'úk'ʷa?
    art pitch   and   art wood_pitch
    She said, "Because I gathered that thing, pitch from bark and wood
    pitch;

81. məł   ixí?   nłəx̌ʷúla?xʷən
    mł   ixí?   n+łx̌ʷ+úla?xʷ -n
    and then   hole   -1erg
    and then I dug a big hole.

82. axá?   cənłəx̌ʷúla?xʷ   ilí?   nutəntí··n,
    axá?   c -n+łx̌ʷ+úla?xʷ   ilí?   n+wt -nt -in
    this   act -hole   there put_in -nt -1erg
    The hole that was dug I put all that there;

83. məł   n'ín'w'i?   kc'ík'na?n,   məł   ilí?   kən
    mł   n'ín'w'i?   k+c'ík'+na? -n   mł   ilí?   kn
    and   a_while,   set_on_fire -1erg and   there 1kn

    nłt'əpmús
    n+łt'pm+us
    jump_in
    and then I'll set it on fire, and jump in.

84. xʷuyx   ctixʷ {t t t} t   sútən {t}   tə
    xʷuy -x   c+tixʷ   t   sutn   t
    go   -isimptv   obtain_cisl obj_itr thing   obj_itr

sƛ'əƛ'úkʷ'aʔ
s+ƛ'+ƛ'úkʷ'aʔ
wood_pitch
Go get some of that thing, that pitch;

85. uɬ   ƛ'aʔánt {iʔ s}   iʔ   t'ic'
    uɬ   ƛ'aʔá -nt   iʔ   t'ic'
    and   fetch -nt   art pitch
    and go get some gum pitch."

86. [ixíʔ]   kʷis {iʔ}   iʔ   yámx̌ʷaʔs
    ixíʔ   kʷi   -s   iʔ   yámx̌ʷaʔ   -s
    then   take   -3erg   art cedar_bark_basket -3in
    He took his basket;

87. uɬ   cnutəntís   iʔ   t'ic'   məɬ   ilíʔ {nutn}
    uɬ   c+n+wt   -nt -is   iʔ   t'ic'   mɬ   ilíʔ
    and   put_in_cisl -nt -3erg   art pitch   and   there

    np'ət'əntˤás,
    n+p't' -nt -aˤs
    pour_in -nt -3erg
    and put the pitch in it, and then he poured it in;

88. məɬ   iʔ   sic   iʔ   sƛ'əƛ'úkʷ'aʔ   kp'nínaʔs
    mɬ   iʔ   sic   iʔ   s+ƛ'+ƛ'úkʷ'aʔ   k+p'n+ínaʔ -s
    and   art then   art wood_pitch   put_on   -3erg
    and then he put the wood pitch on.

89. sílxʷaʔ   aʔ   cənɬx̌ʷúlaʔxʷ
    sílxʷaʔ   aʔ   c   -n+ɬx̌ʷ+úlaʔxʷ
    big   art act -hole
    It was a big hole.

90. ixíʔ   cúntəm
    ixíʔ   cu -nt -m
    that   tell -nt -psv
    And said.

91. kc'ík'naʔs {xiʔ}   iʔ   t   spəpl'ínaʔ   uɬ   uláp
    k+c'ík'+naʔ -s   iʔ   t   s+p+pl'+ínaʔ   uɬ   wla+p
    set_on_fire -3erg   art aglnst Rabbit   and   burn
    And Rabbit set it on fire and it started to burn.

92. ixíʔ   aɬíʔ   spəpl'ínaʔ   uɬ   ɬaʔt'pməncút
    ixíʔ   aɬíʔ   s+p+pl'+ínaʔ   uɬ   ɬaʔt'p+mncut
    then   because   Rabbit   and   jump_around

    tack'láʔ,
    ta+c+k'láʔ
    this_way
    Rabbit jumped back and forth.

93. cúntəm   huy   anwí
    cu -nt-m   hoy   anwí
    tell -nt-psv well   you
    She told him, "Now you."

94. nənənə,   cəm'   kən   c'w'ak
    nənənə   cm'   kn   c'wak
    onom   maybe 1kn   burn
    "I might burn."

95. cúntəm   lut, cx^wuyx,   n'ín'w'i?   k^w   piq
    cu -nt -m   lut c+x^wuy -x   n'ín'w'i?   k^w   piq
    tell -nt -psv not come -isimptv a_while,   2kn white
    She said to him, "No, come, you'll get white."

96. {xi?ns} ik'lí?   łət'pməncút   ka?   niyáx^wt *unint*
           ik'lí?   ł't'+p+mncut ki?   n+yax^w+t
           there   jump_(down) rel   fall_in
    He jumped there, fell in.

97. cus   i? sən?íma?ts   ck^wint   ixí? {a} a?
    cu -s   i? s+n+?íma?t -s c+k^win -t ixí?   a?
    tell -3erg art grandchild -3in take_cisl -nt that   art

    cənsq'íw's   i? sck^wúl'tət {ixí?}
    c -n+sq'+iw's i? sc -k^wul' -tt
    act -split   art pftv-work -4i
    She told her grandson, "Take that forked stick we made."

98. atá? {i?} ta?xílstsəlx,
    atá?   ta+?xíl   -st -s   -lx
    this   do_a_certain_way -st -3erg -pl

    nyrmnússəlx,
    n+yr+m   -nu   -st   -s   -lx
    push_down -manage -st   -3erg -pl
    They did like that, they pushed him down.

99. uł   i? t   sc'u?xáns   nix^w i? t
    uł   i? t   s+c'w'+xan   -s   nix^w i? t
    and art obj_tr animal_hind_leg -3in also art aglnst

    tətw'ít yrmíłt[əm]
    t+tw'it yr+mi   -łt -m
    boy   push_on -łt -psv
    And the boy also pushed down on his leg.

100. ná··nənənənənə,   way' kən ul áp, ná··nənənə way' kən
    nánənənənə   way' kn wla+p nánənənə way' kn
    onom   yes 1kn burn   onom   yes 1kn

    uláp   ntx^wus   a
    wla+p n+tx^w+us a
    burn   cousin   intj
    "ná··nənənənənə, I am burning, ná··nənənə I am burning, friend."

101. cúntəm   lut, ilí?   k^w spíqa?x,
    cu -nt -m lut ilí?   k^w ks   -piq -a?x
    tell -nt -psv not there 2kn incp^ -white -^incp
    She told him "No, you're going to be white;

102. n'ín'w'i? ixí? mi k^w nłət'pmítk^w axá? i? k'əl
    n'ín'w'i? ixí? mi k^w n+łt'p+m+itk^w axá? i? k'l
    a_while, that fut 2kn jump_in_water this art to

cəcw'íxaʔ
c+cw'íxaʔ
little_creek
then you'll jump in the creek;

103. məɬ   n'ín'w'iʔ   kʷ   piq   c'x̌iɬt   incá
     mɬ   n'ín'w'iʔ   kʷ   piq   c+ʔx̌iɬ+t   in+cá
     and   a_while,   2kn   white   like   I
and you'll be white like me."

104. ilíʔ   nt'qú··laʔxʷəmsəlx,   uɬ   ƛ'lal
     ilíʔ   n+t'q+úlaʔxʷ+m   -s   -lx   uɬ   ƛ'l+al
     there   poke_in_ground   -3erg   -pl   and   dead
They poked him in the ground, and he died.

105. ixíʔ   t'i   t'ukʷ   iʔ   stk'ʷƛ'ústəns
     ixíʔ   t'iʔ   t'ukʷ   iʔ   s+t+k'ʷƛ'+us+tn -s
     then   evid   pop_out   art   eye   -3in
His eye popped out;

106. uɬ   t'uxʷt   itlíʔ   iʔ   skəkˤákaʔ
     uɬ   t'uxʷ+t   itlíʔ   iʔ   s+k+kˤákaʔ
     and   fly   from_there   art   bird
and a bird flew from there;

107. t'u··xʷt, uɬ   k'əl tx̌ásəmqən t'əxʷ   mat   ixíʔ
     t'uxʷt   uɬ   k'l t+x̌asm+qn t'xʷ   mat   ixíʔ
     fly   and   to pl_name   evidently   maybe   that

     k'aʔkín'
     k'aʔ+kín'
     where_to
and flew to tx̌ásəmqən Mountain, I don't know where.

108. k'əl tx̌ásəmqən ik'líʔ   t'uxʷt   uɬ   k'am·tíw's,   uɬ
     k'l t+x̌asm+qn ik'líʔ   t'uxʷ+t   uɬ   k+ʔam+m+t+iw's   uɬ
     to pl_name   there   fly   and   perched   and

     hm   hm,   hm   hm
     hm   hm   hm   hm
     onom   onom   onom   onom
It flew to tx̌ásəmqən and lit there, and went "hm hm, hm hm."

109. cúntəm   n'ín'w'iʔ   t'alaʔxwílx   iʔ   sqilxʷ,   məɬ
     cu -nt-m   n'ín'w'iʔ   t'alaʔx+wílx   iʔ   s+qilxʷ   mɬ
     tell -nt-psv   a_while,   next_generation   art   Indian   and

     kʷ   ɬə   nx̌əl'x̌l'íltən,   kʷ   snínaʔ
     kʷ   ɬ   n+x̌l'+x̌l'+ilt+tn   kʷ   sn+ínaʔ
     2kn   one_that   scarecrow   2kn   Owl
She said to him, "The next generation of people you'll be a scarecrow, Owl.

110. ixíʔ uɬ   iʔ   naqs iʔ   stk'ʷƛ'ústəns   t'i   t'ukʷ
     ixíʔ uɬ   iʔ   naqs iʔ   s+t+k'ʷƛ'+us+tn -s   t'i   t'ukʷ
     then and   art   one   art   eye   -3in   evid   pop_out
The other of his eyes popped out.

111.ixí? {k'əl}   k'əl c'islín   k'əl c'islín   ixí? k'li?
    ixí?   k'l c'yslin   k'l c'yslin   ixí? ik'lí?
    that   to   place_name   to   place_name   that there

    k'am·tíw's
    k+?am+m+t+iw's
    perched
    It lit on c'isəlín Mountain.

112.t'i   hm   hm,   hm   hm
    t'i?   hm   hm   hm   hm
    evid   onom   onom   onom   onom
    It went "hm hm, hm hm."

113.cúntəm,   n'ín'w'i?   ixí? t'ala?xwílx   i?   sqilx^w
    cu -nt -m   n'ín'w'i?   ixí? t'ala?x+wílx   i?   s+qilx^w
    tell -nt -psv a_while,   that next_generation   art Indian
    She said to him, "When the next generation comes

114.məł   n'ín'w'i?   kmax   k^w   cənx̌əl'x̌l'íltn {səlx}
    mł   n'ín'w'i?   kmax   k^w   c -n+x̌l'+x̌l'+ilt+tn
    and   a_while,   only   2kn   act -scarecrow

    you'll be just a scarecrow."

115.{ixí? uł i?} ixí? uł   way'   t'a   cmistín
                 ixí? uł   way'   t'   c   -my   -st   -in
                 that and   all   evid cust -know - ^ cust -1erg

    That's it, that's all I know.

116.[nxixayápəlqs]
    n+xy+xayáp+lqs
    end_of_story
    End of story.

TWO GIRLS AND THEIR UNCLE

1. cwix   i?   sqilx",   uɫ {i?}   i?   stəmtíma?   uɫ   i?
   c -wix   i?   s+qilx"   uɫ   i?   s+tm+tíma?   uɫ   i?
   hab-live   art   person   and   art   grandmother   and   art

   səsí?səlx,   uɫ   tk'as?asíl   i?   xəxíw'xu?təm
   s+si? -s -lx   uɫ   tk+?as+?asíl   i?   x+xiw'+xw'tm
   uncle -3in-pl   and   two_persons   art   girls

   There lived some people, a grandmother, their uncle, and two little
   girls.

2. uɫ   ɫa?   ct'aˤpá   -m {ya l?}   i?   səsí?səlx   məɫ
   uɫ   ɫa?   c -t'aˤpá   m   i?   s+si? -s -lx   mɫ
   and   when   hab-shoot   mdl   art   uncle -3in-pl   and

   ixí?   cúntəm
   ixí?   cu -nt -m
   that   tell -nt -psv

   And when their uncle killed something he told them:

3. kʷint   axá?   i?   sc'im'
   kʷin -t   axá?   i?   s+c'im'
   take   -nt   this   art   bone

   "Take these bones,

4. məɫ   n?askʷlítkʷəntp   i?   k'əl siwɫkʷ
   mɫ   n+?askʷl+itkʷ -nt -p   i?   k'l   siwɫ+kʷ
   and   throw_in_water -nt -5erg   art   to   water

   and throw them in the water."

5. ixí?   məɫ   n?askʷlítkʷsəlx,   uɫ   i?   sútən {i?} i?
   ixí?   mɫ   n+?askʷl+itkʷ -s -lx   uɫ   i?   sutn   i?
   that   and   throw_in_water -3erg -pl   and   art   thing   art

   qʷílc[ən]
   qʷil+cn
   fir_boughs

   And they threw them in the water, and the things, the fir boughs.

6. ixí?   uɫ   cúntəm {p}
   ixí?   uɫ   cu -nt-m
   that   and   tell -nt-psv

   And he told them:

7. ixí?   p   nc'ənc'nmáˤsəm   məɫ
   ixí?   p   n+c'n+c'n+m+aˤs -m   mɫ
   then   5kn shut_eyes   -mdl   and

   n?askʷlítkʷəntp   i?   sc'im'
   n+?askʷl+itkʷ -nt -p   i?   s+c'im'
   throw_in_water -nt -5erg   art   bone

   "Close your eyes when you throw the bones in the water;

8. uł   ixí?   nixʷ   i?   qʷílcən
   uł   ixí?   nixʷ   i?   qʷil+cn
   and   that   also   art   fir_boughs
   and also the fir boughs."

9. ixí?   mat   ilí?   ła?
   ixí?   mat   ilí?   ła?
   that   maybe   there   when

   cc'íqʷstsəlx {i?}   i?   słiqʷ
   c   -c'iqʷ   -st   -s   -lx   i?   s+łiqʷ
   cust ^ -butcher   - ^ cust -3erg   -pl   art   meat
   That's there when they butcher the meat.

10. məł   ilí?   i?   qʷílcən   ixí?   nixʷ   ik'lí?
    mł   ilí?   i?   qʷil+cn   ixí?   nixʷ   ik'lí?
    and   there   art   fir_boughs   that   also   there

    n?askʷʼəlítkʷəntp
    n+?askʷʼl+itkʷ -nt -p
    throw_in_water -nt -5erg
    "And the fir boughs there, throw them too in the water."

11. ixí?   uł   ilí?   n?askʷʼlítkʷsəlx
    ixí?   uł   ilí?   n+?askʷʼl+itkʷ -s   -lx
    that   and   there   throw_in_water -3erg   -pl
    And they threw them in the water.

12. uł   lut ik'lí?   t'a   cxʷúy'ilx
    uł   lut ik'lí?   t'   c   -xʷuy'+y -lx
    and   not there   negfac   hab-go   -pl
    And they don't go there.

13. cúntməlx   uł   lut_pən'kín'   ik'lí?   ksxʷúy'imp
    cun-nt -m   -lx uł   lut_pn'+kin'   ik'lí?   ks -xʷuy'+y -mp
    tell -nt -psv -pl and   never   there   futl -go_pl -5in
    He told them, "Don't you ever go there."

14. ilí··?   uł   ixí?   mat {xa}   xƛ'áƛ'əlx
    ilí?   uł   ixí?   mat   xƛ'+aƛ'   -lx
    there   and   that   maybe   be_grown   -pl
    Then they grew up.

15. uł   ik'lí?   xʷúy'ilx {l ən}
    uł   ik'lí?   xʷuy'+y -lx
    and   there   go_pl   -pl
    And they went there.

16. ixí?   uł   mat   ilí?   n?acəcknítkʷəlx
    ixí?   uł   mat   ilí?   n+?ackn+itkʷ   -lx
    then   and   maybe   there   play_in_water   -pl
    Maybe they played in the water.

17. uł   wíksəlx   ixí?,   ní··kna? {i} i?   stməlscút
    uł   wik -s   -lx ixí?   níkxna?   i?   s+tm+lscut
    and   see -3erg   -pl that   goodness   art   beads
    And they saw them, goodness, the jewels.

18. ixí?   km'əntísəlx
    ixí?   km' -nt -is   -lx
    that   take -nt -3erg -pl
    They took them;

19. uɬ {n} nˁacˁacína?məlx   uɬ   q'lípsəmsəlx
    uɬ   n+ˁac+ˁac+ína? -m -lx uɬ   q'l+ips+m -s -lx
    and   earring   -mdl -pl and   necklace -3erg -pl
    they made earrings and put necklaces on;

20. lut_cmaylx   ilí?   ?ícacknəlx
    lut_cmay -lx ilí?   ?ic+c+kn -lx
    everywhere -pl there   play   -pl
    They played in all kinds of ways with them.

21. ixí?   uɬ   wíkəntməlx   i? t   səsí?səlx
    ixí?   uɬ   wik -nt -m   -lx i? t   s+si? -s -lx
    then and see -nt -psv -pl art agInst uncle -3in -pl
    Then their uncle saw them.

22. ixí?   cus   i? skʷuys
    ixí?   cu -s   i? s+kʷuy -s
    then   tell -3erg art mother -3in
    He told his mother:

23. way'   iksx̌ʷílməlx
    way'   i   -ks   -x̌ʷil   -m   -lx
    well   1i -futT^ -discard - ^futT -pl
    "I'm going to throw them away.

24. way'   xƛ'aƛ'əlx,   lut t'a   cníxəl'lx
    way'   xƛ'+aƛ'   -lx lut t'   c -nixl'   -lx
    well   be_grown -pl not negfac hab-listen -pl
    They are big, they don't mind."

25. {ixí?} ixí?   nis   lkʷilx
           ixí?   nis   lkʷ+ilx
           that   gone leave
    Then he went, he left.

26. k'a?x̌ís   n?aɬxʷúla?xʷ
    k'a?+x̌ís   n+?aɬxʷ+úla?xʷ
    over_there go_into_ground
    Little ways from there he went into the ground.

27. məɬ   xa?   ?í··cacknəlx
    mɬ   axá? ?ic+c+kn   -lx
    and   this play   -pl
    They played there.

28. uɬ k'əm i? t stəmtíma?səlx   stímxəx ilí?   mut
    uɬ k'm i? t s+tm+tíma? -s -lx ?   ilí?   mut
    and except art? grandmother -3in -pl ?   there sit_sg
    And only their grandmother is there still sitting there.

29. ɬyáʕpəlx
    ɬ+yaʕ+p   -lx
    arrive_back -pl
    They got back.

30. lut_stim',   way'   k'aw,   lut_stim',   ʔímxəlx,   lkʷílxəlx
    lut‾s+tim'   way'   k'aw   lut‾s+tim'   ʔim+x -lx   lkʷ+ilx -lx
    nothing   yes   gone   nothing   move -pl   leave -pl
    There was nothing, all gone, nothing, they moved, went away.

31. k'əm_kmax ixíʔ   ilíʔ   a   nʔamtús   i   la   culáp
    k'm‾kmax ixíʔ   ilíʔ   a   n+ʔamt+ús   iʔ   c   -wla+p
    only   that   there   art   sit_by   art   in   hab-burn
    Just her sitting by the fire.

32. cúntməlx   way'   mʕan   p   ɬa
    cun-nt -m   -lx   way'   mʕan   p   ɬaʔ
    tell -nt -psv -pl   well   interj   5kn   one_that

    cənt'it'ínaʔ
    c   -n+t'y+t'ínaʔ
    hab-disobedient
    She told them, "Look, you are disobedient;

33. uɬ   way'   x̌ʷíɬɬəms   iʔ   t   səsíʔmp
    uɬ   way'   x̌ʷil   -ɬm   -s   iʔ   t   s+siʔ   -mp
    and   yes   discard -5obj   -3erg   art   agInst   uncle   -5in
    and your uncle threw you away;

34. ta_nyʕ'íp,   məɬ   axáʔ   məɬ nixʷ   incá   kən   x̌ʷuy
    ta‾n+yʕ'+ip   mɬ   axáʔ   mɬ nixʷ   in+cá   kn   x̌ʷuy
    keep_on   and   this   and also   I   1kn   go
    for ever, and now I'm going to leave too."

35. [uɬ]   ixíʔ   sc'qʷc'qʷáqʷs   uɬ   cúsəlx   lut
    uɬ   ixíʔ   s   -c'qʷ+c'qʷ+aqʷ -s   uɬ   cu -s   -lx   lut
    and   that   dur   -cry_pl   -3i   and   tell -3erg   -pl   not

    aksx̌ʷúy,   tkəm'km'áməlx unint
    a   -k+s   -x̌ʷuy   t+km'+km'+am -lx
    2i   -futl   -go   hold_on   -pl
    They cried, they asked her, "Don't go!" They grabbed her.

36. uɬ   ixíʔ   iʔ   xƛ'ut ilíʔ   ct'ap,   ilíʔ   cɬax̌ʷ
    uɬ   ixíʔ   iʔ   xƛ'ut ilíʔ   c   -t'ap   ilíʔ   c   -ɬax̌ʷ
    andthat   art   rock there   hab-object_lies   there   hab -hole
    There was a rock lying there, a hole there;

37. uɬ   ixíʔ   k'əɬʔúɬxʷ   ixíʔ   iʔ   pəptwínaʔxʷ
    uɬ   ixíʔ   k'ɬ+ʔuɬxʷ   ixíʔ   iʔ   p+ptwínaʔxʷ
    and   that   go_under   that   art   old_woman
    and the old lady went under it.

38. k'aʔx̌ís   nyax̌ʷt
    k'aʔ+x̌ís   n+yax̌ʷ+t
    over_there   fall_in
    She fell in there.

39. k'lí?   ksənppílxa?xəlx
    ik'lí?   ks   -n+p+pilx   -a?x   -lx
    there   incp ^   -enter_pl   - ^ incp -pl
    They started to go in there;

40. ixí?   ck'əłpəxᵂpúxᵂəntməlx   uł unint   ?acəcqa?lx
    ixí?   c+k'ł+pxᵂ+puxᵂ   -nt -m -lx   uł   ?ác+c+qa? -lx
    that   breathe_on_cisl   -nt -psv -pl   and   go_out_pl -pl
    he brought them out and they went out.

41. ixí?   nák'ᵂəm ałí?   i?   sútən   túpəl'   i?   stəmtíma?
    ixí?   nak'ᵂm ałí?   i?   sutn   tupl'   i?   s+tm+tíma?
    that   evid   because art   thing   spider   art   grandmother
    The grandmother must be a spider.

42. ixí?   uł   axá?   ilí?   c'ax̌əlwísəlx
    ixí?   uł   axá?   ilí?   c   -?ax̌l+wis   -lx
    then   and   this   there   hab-mill_about -pl
    They were hanging around.

43. uł   c'awt   ixí?   a   cu?r'ísəlp'
    uł   c'aw+t   ixí?   a   c   -wr'+islp'
    and   extinguish   that   art   hab-fire
    And the fire went out.

44. ixí?   skəm'ntísəlx   i?   stím'səlx   ilí?
    ixí?   s   -km'   -nt -is   -lx i?   stim'   -s -lx ilí?
    then   ?   -take   -nt -3erg   -pl art   thing   -3in-pl there
    They took whatever they had there.

45. ki?   súxᵂəxᵂsəlx   nkəxkxáməlx
    ki?   suxᵂ+xᵂ   -lx n+kx+kxa+m   -lx
    rel   leave_pl   -pl walk   -pl
    They left, they walked.

46. ití?   t_tanm'ús   uł   xᵂúy'ilx
    ití?   t_tanm'+ús   uł   xᵂuy'+y -lx
    from_that   any_which_way   and   go_pl   -pl
    They went any old place.

47. xᵂu··ylx   məł   púlxəlx   məł   itlí?
    xᵂuy   -lx mł   pul+x   -lx mł   itlí?
    go   -pl and   camp   -pl and   from_there
    They went long ways, and they camped, and started again.

48. xᵂu··ylx   məł   púlxəlx   {məł}
    xᵂuy   -lx mł   pul+x   -lx mł
    go   -pl and   camp   -pl and
    They went, and camped.

49. ixí?   uł   nák'ᵂəm   t   naspəpáˤsəs
    ixí?   uł   nak'ᵂm   t   nasp+p+áˤs+s
    then   and   evid   aglnst   Sea_gull

    wíkəntəməlx   way'   t'əcxᵂúy'ilx
    wik -nt -m   -lx   way'   t'c   -xᵂuy'+y -lx
    see -nt -psv -pl   yes   habCisl -go_pl -pl
    Then Sea Gull must have seen them coming;

50. uł   xi?   cúntməlx
    uł   ixí?   cun -nt -m   -lx
    and   then   tell -nt -psv   -pl
    and he said to them:

51. {k'əl sən k'əl}   k'əl ?u?tíma?tk   k' nstaw'tíma?tk
                      k'l ?awt+íma?+tk   k' n+s+t+?awt+íma?+tk
                      to   below   to below

    ik'lí?   mi   p   cni?ák'^w
    ik'lí?   mi   p   c+n+y?ak'^w
    there   fut 5kn cross_cisl
    "Below, go below and cross there."

52. ixí?   uł   ny'ay'ák'^wəlx   ik'lí?
    ixí?   uł   n+y'a+y'ak'^w -lx   ik'lí?
    then   and   cross   -pl   there
    So they crossed there.

53. uł   ixí?   cúntəm {i? t}   i?   t   łkíkxa?s {lut a}
    uł   ixí?   cu -nt -m   i?   t   ł+kí+kxa?   -s
    and   then   tell -nt -psv   art aglnst older_sister-3in
    And the older sister said to her:

54. n'ín'w'i? {amtsís}   k^wu   ?amtím   lut
    n'ín'w'i?   k^wu   ?am -t -im   lut
    a_while,   4obj feed -nt -^3e4obj   not

    aks?íłən   t   stim'
    a -ks -?íłn   t   stim'
    2i -futl -eat obj_itr thing
    "When he gives us things to eat, don't eat anything."

55. ik'lí?   yá^ҁpəlx   uł   xi?   cúntməlx   t
    ik'lí?   ya^ҁ+p -lx uł   ixí?   cun -nt -m   -lx   t
    there   gather -pl   and then   tell -nt -psv -pl   aglnst

    naspəpá^ҁsəs
    nasp+p+á^ҁs+s
    Sea_gull
    They got there and Sea Gull said to them:

56. way'   kən   k'^wəl'cəncút   mi   p   ?ał?íłən
    way'   kn   k'^wl'+cn+cut   mi   p   ?ał+?íłn
    yes   1kn   cook   fut 5kn eat
    "I'm cooking so you can eat."

57. sq'^wuct   axá?
    s+q'^wuct   axá?
    fat   this
    It's fat.

58. uł   lut t'ə   ?íłən   i?   sx?itx
    uł   lut t'   ?íłn   i?   s+x?it+x
    and   not negfac eat   art oldest_one
    And the oldest one didn't eat;

59. uł   kmax   ixí?   i?   st?iwtx   itlí?
    uł   kmax   ixí?   i?   s+t?iwt+x   itlí?
    and   only   that   art   young_one   from_there

    c'ǝnk'ǝntís
    c'nk'   -nt   -is
    dip_finger   -nt   -3erg
    just the young one dipped her finger in it;

60. ki?   ?iłs   sǝnp't'cáˤnǝms
    ki?   ?ił -s   s   -n+p't'+caˤn+m -s
    rel   eat -3erg   dur -put_in_mouth -3i
    she ate it, put it in her mouth.

61. ilí··?   uł   ixí?   itlí?   sxʷuys
    ilí?   uł   ixí?   itlí?   s   -xʷuy   -s
    there   and   then   from_there   dur -go   -3i
    They stayed there a while, then they went.

62. cut   way'   kʷu   sxʷuyx   i?   k'ǝl sw'a?w'ása?tǝt
    cut   way'   kʷu   s   -xʷuy-x   i?   k'l   s+w'a+w'ása? -tt
    say   yes   4kn   ipftv ^ -go - ^ ipftv   art   to   aunt   -4in
    She said, "We are going to our aunt."

63. ixí?   itlí?   xʷúy'ilx,   ilí?   cǝnt'lúla?xʷ
    ixí?   itlí?   xʷuy'+y -lx   ilí?   c   -n+t'l+úla?xʷ
    then   from_there   go_pl -pl   there   hab-gulch
    Then they went; and there is a gulch there.

64. ixí?   xʷǝt'pǝncút i?   sx?itx   uł   ití?
    ixí?   xʷt'+p+ncut i?   s+x?it+x   uł   ití?
    then   run   art   oldest_one   and   from_that

    tla?x̌ís   qilt {k'ǝl}   k'ǝl sk'ʷut
    tla+?x̌ís   qil+t   k'l   s+k'ʷut
    from_there   top   to   half
    The oldest one ran down and from there got on top to the other side.

65. uł   cus   i?   łcǝc?úpsc   huy   cxʷuyx
    uł   cu -s   i?   ł+c+c?+ups   -c   hoy   c+xʷuy -x
    and   tell -3erg   art   younger_sister -3in   well   come   -isimptv
    She said to her little sister, "Hurry, come here."

66. ti?   xʷǝt'pǝncút ixí?   {la n la}   k'a?x̌ís
    ití?   xʷt'+p+ncut ixí?   k'a?+x̌ís
    from_that   run   then   over_there
    She ran down there.

67. way'   k'a   nixʷtúla?xʷ   ki?   ?am·útǝt
    way'   k'   n+yxʷ+t+úla?xʷ   ki?   ?am+m+út+t
    yes   to   underground   rel   sit_down
    At the bottom she sat down.

68. uł   t'i?   awáˤ,   awáˤ   i?   sqʷǝsqʷsí?s,
    uł   t'i?   awáˤ   awáˤ   i?   s+qʷs+qʷsi? -s
    and   evid   onom   onom   art   child   -3in

taʔxʷsqʷəsqʷsíʔ
taʔxʷ+s+qʷs+qʷsíʔ
get_baby
Her baby went "awáˤ, awáˤ." She got a baby.

69. ixíʔ   cxʷət'pəncút   iʔ   ɬkíkxaʔs
    ixíʔ   c+xʷt'+p+ncut   iʔ   ɬ+kí+kxaʔ   -s
    then   run_cisl   art   older_sister -3in
    The older sister ran down.

70. cúntəm   ixíʔ   məɬ   n'ín'w'iʔ   aláʔ   kʷ   aláʔ   lut
    cu -nt -m   ixíʔ   mɬ   n'ín'w'iʔ   aláʔ   kʷ   aláʔ   lut
    tell -nt -psv   then   and   a_while,   here   2kn   here   not

    kʷu   t'   akskxnám
    kʷu   t'   a -ks   -kxna   -m
    1kʷu   negfac 2i -futT ^ -go_along - ^ futT
    She said to her, "Now you stay here, don't go with me."

71. ixíʔ {s} cus   cxʷuyx   naspəpáˤsəs
    ixíʔ   cu -s   c+xʷuy -x   nasp+p+áˤs+s
    that   tell -3erg   come   -isimptv   Sea_gull
    She said, "Come here Sea Gull.

72. ˤác'ənt   way'   kʷ   taʔxʷsqʷsqʷsíʔ
    ˤac'   -nt   way'   kʷ   taʔxʷ+s+qʷs+qʷsíʔ
    look_at -nt   yes   2kn   get_baby
    Look, you got a baby."

73. ixíʔ   scuts   n'ín'w'iʔ   tətw'ít   mi {tx}
    ixíʔ   s -cut   -s   n'ín'w'iʔ   t+tw'it   mi
    that   dur -say   -3i   a_while,   boy   fut

    txəxt'ntíp
    t+xt'   -nt -ip
    take_care_of   -nt -5erg
    He said, "If it's a boy take care of it;

74. náx̌əmɬ   xíxuʔtəm   məɬ   nc'əq'mnítkʷəntp
    nax̌mɬ   xi+xw'tm   mɬ   n+c'q'+mn+itkʷ -nt -p
    but   girl   and   throw_in_water -nt -5erg
    but if it's a girl throw it in the water."

75. cúntəm   lut,   cxʷuyx,   way'
    cu -nt -m   lut   c+xʷuy -x   way'
    tell -nt -psv   not   come   -isimptv   yes

    akɬnáx̌ʷnəx̌ʷ   ilíʔ   kʷint
    a -kɬ   -nax̌ʷ+nx̌ʷ   ilíʔ   kʷin   -t
    2i -to_be -wife   there   take   -nt
    She said, "No, come here, that's your wife, take her."

76. itlíʔ   sxʷuys
    itlíʔ   s -xʷuy   -s
    from_there dur -go   -3i
    She started going.

77. x^wu··y úɬiʔ tk'ʷətxəlxálq^w ilíʔ a
    x^wuy uɬ+iʔ t+k'ʷtx+lx+alq^w ilíʔ a
    go and_then step_over_log there art

    cmaʕ
    c -maʕ
    hab-lie_on_ground
    She went, and then she stepped over a log laying there.

78. itlíʔ spəpl'ínaʔ cut paqaʕpíqaʔs
    itlíʔ s+p+pl'+ínaʔ cut paq+aʕ+píqaʔ+s
    from_there Rabbit say white_legs

    asaʔstám
    a -saʔ+stám
    2in -sister_in_law
    Rabbit said: "Your sister-in-law's legs are white white!"

79. ixíʔ nsp'áqsəs iʔ t t'kíkstəns {uɬ xiʔ ntəq}
    ixíʔ n+sp'+aqs -s iʔ t t'k+ikst+tn -s
    then hit_on_lip -3erg art aglnst cane -3in
    She hit him on the nose with her cane.

80. aláʔ ntəqəntís {iʔ st} iʔ sp'saqs
    aláʔ n+tq -nt -is iʔ s+p's+aqs
    here touch_on -nt -3erg art nose
    He put his hand on his nose.

81. ixíʔ sx^wət'pəncúts
    ixíʔ s -x^wt'+p+ncut-s
    then dur -run -3i
    Then he ran away.

82. itlíʔ sx^wuys, x^wu··y
    itlíʔ s -x^wuy -s x^wuy
    from_there dur -go -3i go
    Then she went on, and went.

83. mat {k'ʷ} q'sápiʔ ki kicx
    mat q'sápiʔ kiʔ kic+x
    maybe long_time rel arrive
    It took her a long time to get there.

84. iʔ l tk'əmkn'íɬx^w ilíʔ cqx̌am {iʔ iʔ s} iʔ
    iʔ l t+k'm+kn'+íɬx^w ilíʔ c -qx̌a+m iʔ
    art at outside there hab -split_wood art

    sw'aʔw'ásaʔs
    s+w'a+w'ásaʔ -s
    aunt -3in
    Her aunt was splitting wood outside the tipi.

85. aɬíʔ iʔ t sc'im' iʔ t q'ʷəmqín ka
    aɬíʔ iʔ t s+c'im' iʔ t q'ʷm+qin ka
    because art aglnst bone art aglnst horn rel

cqx̌áməlx
c   -qx̌a+m   -lx
hab-split_wood -pl
They split it with a bone, a horn.

86. təx^wslip'   t'əx^w_mat
    tx^w+s+lip'   t'x^w_mat
    get_wood   maybe
    Getting wood, I guess.

87. ixí?   uł   ití?   k'amtálq^w
    ixí?   uł   ití?   k+?amt+álq^w
    that   and   from_that   sit_on_log
    She sat on the log.

88. wi··m'   cqəx̌stís {i?}   i?   t
    wim'   c   -qx̌   -st   -is   i?   t
    in_vain cust ^ -split_wood - ^ cust -3erg art agInst

    sw'a?w'ása?s
    s+w'a?+w'ása? -s
    mother's_sister -3in
    The aunt couldn't split it.

89. ki? ʕ'ac'[əs]   nák^{'w}əm ixí?   i?   słwilts   ilí?
    ki? ʕ'ac'   -s   nak^{'w}m   ixí?   i?   s+łw+ilt -s   ilí?
    rel look_at -3erg   evid   that   art niece   -3in   there

    k'amtálq^w
    k+?amt+álq^w
    sit_on_log
    Then she saw it was her niece sitting on the log.

90. ixí?   uł   k^wis {n}   n?ułx^wsts   k'əl
    ixí?   uł   k^wi   -s   n+?ułx^w -st   -s   k'l
    then   and   take   -3erg   enter   -caus -3erg   to

    citx^ws
    citx^w   -s
    house   -3in
    She took her and took her in her house.

91. ixí?   uł   ʕax̌əntí··s   i?   sp'c'niłx^w,   stim'
    ixí?   uł   ʕax̌   -nt -is   i?   s+p'c'n+iłx^w   stim'
    then   and   lace   -nt -3erg   art tipi   thing

    t'əx^w_mat,
    t'x^w_mat
    maybe
    She laced up the tipi or whatever;

92. uł   ilí?   nilí?,   uł {axá?}   axá?   mat   i? |
    uł   ilí?   n+ilí?,   uł   axá?   mat   i? |
    and   there   be_there   and   this   maybe art at

    naspəpáʕsəs   ilí?   tʕip   ilí?   i?
    nasp+p+áʕs+s   ilí?   t_n+yʕip   ilí?   i?
    Sea_gull   there   continuously   there   art

ɬcəc̓úpsc
ɬ+c+c̓+ups   -c
younger_sister -3in

Her little sister stayed there at Sea Gull's, for good.

93. ilí··ʔ,   ilíʔ   uɬ   k̓ʷm'iɬ   uɬ   t̓i   taʔx̌ʷsqʷəsqʷsíʔ
    ilíʔ   ilíʔ   uɬ   k̓ʷm'iɬ   uɬ   t̓iʔ   taʔx̌ʷ+s+qʷs+qʷsíʔ
    there   there and suddenly and evid get_baby

    ixíʔ {iʔ}iʔ   sx̌ʔitx
    ixíʔ iʔ   s+x̌ʔiɬ+x
    that art   oldest_one

She stayed there, and all at once the older one got a baby.

94. ní··knaʔ   way'   ʕimt {iʔ}   iʔ   t   sw'aʔw'ásaʔs
    níkx̌naʔ   way'   ʕim+t   iʔ   t   s+w'a+w'ásaʔ   -s
    goodness   yes   angry   art aglnst aunt   -3in

Goodness, her aunt got mad.

95. ʕímtməntəm   ixíʔ   ɬmaʕʷs   ixíʔ   a
    ʕim+t+m   -nt -m   ixíʔ   ɬ+maʕʷ   -s   ixíʔ   a
    be_angry_at   -nt -psv that   break_again   -3erg   that   intj

    cʕax̌
    c   -ʕax̌
    hab-lace

She was mad at her, she tore down the lacing;

96. a   ckʕax̌íc'aʔs   ixíʔ   ɬmaʕʷs
    a   c+k+ʕax̌+íc'a?   -s   ixíʔ   ɬ+maʕʷ   -s
    art lace_cisl   3erg   that   break_again   -3erg

she took down the lacing.

97. ixíʔ   cus   xiʔmíx {mi}n'ín'w'iʔ   p   x̌ʷʔíltəm
    ixíʔ   cu -s   xiʔ+míx   n'ín'w'iʔ   p   x̌ʷʔ+ilt   -m
    then   tell -3erg whatever   a_while,   5kn hold_baby   -mdl

She said to them: "Any time you come and hold the baby,

98. t̓i   awá,   awá,   awá   ixíʔ {iʔ iʔ}   iʔ   sk'ʷk'ʷímǝlt
    t̓iʔ   awá   awá   awá   ixíʔ   iʔ   s+k'ʷ+k'ʷim'+l't
    evid onom   onom   onom that   art child

and the baby goes awá, awá, awá,"

99. cut n'ín'w'iʔ   t   swit   mi   k'əwpstís   ixíʔ
    cut n'ín'w'iʔ   t   swit   mi   k'w+p   -st   -is   ixíʔ
    say a_while, aglnst   who   fut   stop_talking   -caus -3erg that

she said, "Whoever makes it stop crying,

100.məɬ   way'   ixíʔ {iʔ}a   lʔiws   mat
    mɬ   way'   ixíʔ   a   lʔiw   -s   mat
    and   yes   that   art m's_father   -3in   must

that must be his father."

101.ixíʔ   úɬiʔ   sx̌ʷʔíltəms {həɬ}   həɬsútən
    ixíʔ   uɬ+iʔ   s -x̌ʷʔ+ilt+m -s   hɬ=   sutn
    then   and_then dur -hold_baby -3i   group=   thing

hałskəm'xíst,   hałsəmx̌íkən,   t'iʔ   hałsənk'l'íp
hł=   s+km'xist   hł=   s+mx̌+ikn t'iʔ   hł=   s+n+k'l'+ip
group= Bear   group= Grizzly   evid group= Coyote

So they started holding the baby, all of them, the Bear, the Grizzly, the Coyote.

102. ciyáˢ   x^wʔíltməlx
     c+yaˢ   x^wʔ+ilt+m -lx
     all   hold_baby -pl

Everybody held the baby.

103. ixíʔ   uł   t   spəpl'ínaʔ   x^wʔíltəm   uł {t} k'əwáp
     ixíʔ   uł   t   s+p+pl'+ínaʔ x^wʔ+ilt+m   uł   k'wa+p
     that   and aglnst Rabbit   hold_baby and   quiet

     I   ixíxiʔ
     I   ix+íxiʔ
     in in_a_while

And then Rabbit held it too, and for a little while it stopped crying;

104. uł   itlíʔ   c'q^waq^w
     uł   itlíʔ   c'q^w+aq^w
     and   from_there cry

and then it cried.

105. [ilí··ʔ] uł   ixíʔ   wápupxən
     ilíʔ   uł   ixíʔ   wap+wp+xn
     there   and   then   Lynx

And then Lynx.

106. ixíʔ   wápupxən ixíʔ x^wʔíltəm ixíʔ   uł   k'əwáp
     ixíʔ   wap+wp+xn ixíʔ x^wʔ+ilt+m ixíʔ   uł   k'wa+p
     then   Lynx   that   hold_baby that   and quiet

Lynx held the baby and that's when it stopped.

107. ixíʔ   [uł]   ktəm'álx^wstəm   iʔ   t
     ixíʔ   uł   k+tm'+alx^w -st   -m   iʔ   t
     then   and   strip   -caus -psv art aglnst

     sw'aʔw'ásaʔs
     s+w'a+w'ásaʔ -s
     aunt   -3in

Then her aunt stripped her;

108. kəm'łtím   iʔ stim's
     km'   -łt -im   iʔ stim' -s
     take   -łt -psv art thing -3in

she took her things;

109. uł   t'i   lut t'a   kstim'
     uł   t'iʔ   lut t'   k   -s+tim'
     and   evid not negfac have -thing

and she had nothing;

110. məł   xiʔ   iʔ   sqʷəsqʷsíʔs   ilíʔ
      mł   ixíʔ   iʔ   s+qʷs+qʷsiʔ -s   ilíʔ
      and   then   art   child   -3in   there
her baby was there.

111. ixíʔ   xaʔ   pulstsəlx   wápupᵪən
      ixíʔ   axáʔ   pul   -st   -s   -lx   wap+wp+xn
      then   this   kill_one-st -3erg -pl   Lynx
And then they killed Lynx.

112. tər'qəntísəlx   uł   t'k'ʷak'ʷ
      tr'q   -nt -is   -lx uł   t'k'ʷ+ak'ʷ
      kick   -nt -3erg   -pl and   land_flat
They kicked him and he fell down.

113. uł   xiʔ   ʔap'ʔíp'xnəmsəlx   ilí··ʔ
      uł   ixíʔ   ʔap'+ʔíp'+xn+m -s   -lx   ilíʔ
      and   then   rub_with_feet -3erg -pl   there
Then they rubbed him on the ground;

114. uł {k'am kmax} kmax_k'am {iʔ s}   iʔ   síp'iʔs   ilíʔ
      uł   kmax_k'am   iʔ   síp'iʔ   -s   ilíʔ
      and   only   art   hide   -3in   there
and there is only his skin left.

115. ciyáˤ   láqʷmiʔst,   púlstsəlx
      c+yaˤ   láqʷ+miʔst   pul   -st -s   -lx
      all   lay_about   kill_one-st -3erg   -pl
Everything was laying there, they killed him.

116. ixíʔ   skəm'xíst   məł   cxʷuy   məł   ixíʔ   ʔap'ʔíp'xnəm
      ixíʔ   s+kmx+ist   mł   c+xʷuy   mł   ixíʔ   ʔap'+ʔíp'+xn+m
      then   Bear   and come   and   then   rub_with_feet
Bear came and he rubbed his feet,

117. ałíʔ   kʷ   ksqʷəsqʷsíʔ
      ałíʔ   kʷ   k   -s+qʷs+qʷsiʔ
      because   2kn   have   -child
"Because you got a baby."

118. xiʔ   ilíʔ   mut,   ƛ'lal
      ixíʔ   ilíʔ   mut   ƛ'l+al
      that   there   sit_sg   dead
He sat there, dead.

119. uł   xiʔ   sc'qʷaqʷs   iʔ   tkəłmílxʷ,   c'qʷa··qʷ
      uł   ixíʔ   s   -c'qʷ+aqʷ -s   iʔ   tkłmilxʷ   c'qʷ+aqʷ
      and   then   dur -cry   -3i   art   woman   cry
And then the woman cried and cried.

120. uł   xiʔ   sckicxs   ˤan'
      uł   ixíʔ   s   -c+kic+x   -s   ˤan'
      and   then   dur -arrive_cisl -3i   Magpie
And then Magpie came.

121.cut way'   t'aqəltá·ˤla?[1]
     cut way'   t'aqltáˤla?
     say well   honey
     She said, "oh my dear!"

122.ixí?   məł   a   nxn'úsxəntən   k^wis
     ixí?   mł   a   n+xn'+us+xn+tn   k^wi   -s
     that   and   art   moccasin_patch   take   -3erg
     She took a patch of old moccasin;

123.məł   ixí?   txn'ína?s
     mł   ixí?   t+xn'+ína?   -s
     and   then   cover_w_patch   -3erg
     and covered her [private parts] up.

124.ixí?   məł   cx^wuy yutlx^w   məł   cut
     ixí?   mł   c+x^wuy yutlx^w   mł   cut
     then   and   come Raven   and   say
     Then Raven came and said:

125.q^waˤ   k^w   c'a?knála?k
     q^waˤ   k^w   c'a?kn+ála?k
     onom   2kn matter
     "What's the matter?"

126.məł   i   k'lá?   ł   c'əq'mís
     mł   i?   ak'lá?   ł   c'q'+mi -s
     and   art   here   ?   throw   -3erg
     Then he threw it to one side.

127.məł   xi?   scuts   ˤ'an'
     mł   ixí?   s -cut   -s   ˤ'an'
     and   that   dur -say   -3i   Magpie
     Then Magpie said:

128.ˤ'a··n'   int'aqəlt'áˤla?[2]
     ˤan   in -t'aqlt'áˤla?
     onom   1in -honey
     "Oh my dear!"

129.xi?   cəm'   mat   k^wənxásq'ət   ilí?
     ixí?   cm'   mat   k^wn+x+asq't   ilí?
     then   maybe maybe a_few_days   there
     They stayed there a few days.

130.cúntəm   ixí? {təl'}   i?   təl'   láq^wmi?st   i?   tl {a c}
     cu -nt -m   ixí?   i?   tl'   láq^w+mi?st   i?   tl'
     tell -nt -psv   that   art from   lay_about   art from

---

[1] See also utterances 128, 149, 165, 197. These, and other chanted or sung (stylized) utterances often contain phonological oddities. The phonetics of this form are unclear.
[2] See also utterances 121, 149, 165, 197.

spumts
s+pumt -s
fur   -3in

Then that hair laying there said,

131.cúntəm   kʷu   ʔú·∙luʔsəntxʷ   mi kʷu
    cu -nt-m   kʷu   ʔul+w's -nt -xʷ   mi kʷu
    tell -nt-psv 1obj   gather -nt -2erg   fut 1obj

tkʷ'ítxəlməntxʷ
t+kʷ'it+xl+m -nt -xʷ
step_over   -nt -2erg

said: "Gather me up, and then step over me."

132.ixíʔ   ʔúʔ·∙luʔsəs   ixíʔ   uɬ   xiʔ tkʷ'ítxləms
    ixíʔ   ʔul+w's -s   ixíʔ   uɬ   ixíʔ t+kʷ'itx+l+m -s
    then   gather -3erg   then   and   that step_over   -3erg

Then she gathered it up, and stepped over it.

133.uɬ   xiʔ {ɬ}   ɬx̌əstwílx   st'əlsqílxʷ
    uɬ   ixíʔ   ɬ+x̌s+t+wilx   c+t'l+s+qilxʷ
    and   that   get_well_again come_to_life_cisl

And he got well, came to life.

134.ixíʔ   cúntəm   ixíʔ   məɬ   isənkʷním
    ixíʔ   cu -nt -m   ixíʔ   mɬ   i   -s   -n+kʷni+m
    then   tell -nt -psv   then   and   1i -inten -sing

He told her, "Now I am going to sing."

135.ixíʔ   uɬ   sənkʷníms
    ixíʔ   uɬ   s -n+kʷni+m -s
    then   and   dur -sing   -3i

And he started to sing.

136.uɬ   lut_swit,   xiʔ   itlíʔ   ʔimx   ya lkʷílxəlx
    uɬ   lut_swit   ixíʔ   itlíʔ   ʔimx   ya lkʷ+ilx -lx
    and nobody   then   from_there move   art leave -pl

And there is nobody, they had all packed and gone.

137.lut_səwít   t'a   ct'aˤpám   t   sλ̕'aʔcínəm, {lut}
    lut_swit   t'   c -t'aˤpá -m   t   s+λ̕'aʔcínm
    nobody   negfac hab-shoot -mdl obj_itr   deer

Nobody can kill any deer, no.

138.laʔkí·∙n   məɬ   spəpl'ínaʔ   t   kʷ'ʷəkʷ'ʷy'úmaʔ
    laʔkín   mɬ   s+p+pl'+ínaʔ   t   kʷ'ʷ+kʷ'ʷy+úmaʔ
    sometime and   Rabbit   obj_itr small

t'aˤpám
t'aˤpá -m
shoot -mdl

Eventually Little Rabbit killed a little one;

139.uɬ   iʔ   kʷ'ʷíλ̕'ət lut_stim'
    uɬ   iʔ   kʷ'ʷiλ̕'+t lut_s+tim'
    and   art others nothing

but the others nothing.

140. aɬíʔ cqʼmíltnəlx
 aɬíʔ c -qʼm+ilt+tn -lx
 so hab-starve -pl
 They are starving.

141. ixíʔ uɬ axáʔ t sƛ̕aʔcínəm iʔ t sx̌wʼiltən
 ixíʔ uɬ axáʔ t s+ƛ̕aʔcínm iʔ t s+x̌wʼ+ilt+n
 then and this ? deer art ? drying_rack
 They dried the deer.

142. lut {iʔ} iʔ sqʼʷuct iʔ stimʼ iʔ skɬíkən' ilíʔ
 lut iʔ s+qʼʷuct iʔ stimʼ iʔ s+kɬ+ikn' ilíʔ
 not art fat art thing art rump_fat there

 cután
 c -wtan
 hab-placed
 The fat, anything, the fat on the rump that's there.

143. uɬ xiʔ cxʷu··y ʕanʼ
 uɬ ixíʔ c+xʷuy ʕanʼ
 and then come Magpie
 And then Magpie came.

144. məɬ ilíʔ ckʼəɬʔúɬxʷ
 mɬ ilíʔ c+kʼɬ+ʔuɬxʷ
 and there go_under_cisl
 And she came under the tent.

145. məɬ ixíʔ scuts ilíʔ cqaqácla?s ixíʔ iʔ
 mɬ ixíʔ s -cut -s ilíʔ c -qa+qácla?s ixíʔ iʔ
 and then dur -say -3i there hab-wheel that art

 sútən {iʔ} iʔ sənlákʷ
 sutn iʔ s+n+lakʷ
 thing art tallow
 She said, "He's wheeling something made of tallow."

146. cus, ixíʔ uɬ laʔntís
 cu -s ixíʔ uɬ laʔ -nt -is
 tell -3erg then and peck -nt -3erg
 She said, and she pecked it.

147. məɬ xiʔ ikʼlíʔ xʷətʼpəncút {ya} iʔ skʷuys
 mɬ ixíʔ ikʼlíʔ xʷtʼ+p+ncut iʔ s+kʷuy -s
 and then there run   art mother -3in
 And then his mother ran over there

148. məɬ kspʼápʼqiʔs
 mɬ k -spʼ+ap+q -iʔ -s
 and futT^ -whack_on_head -^futT -3i
 and whacked her on the head.

149. məɫ cut ʕa‥n' t'aqəlt'áʕla?[3]
mɫ cut ʕan t'aqlt'áʕla?
and say onom onom
And she said, "Oh my dear!"

150. cúntəm lut alá? akscwíkʷmi?st
cu -nt -m lut alá? a -ksc -wikʷ+mi?st
tell -nt -psv not here 2i -futPerf -hide
She told her, "Don't hide there.

151. ʕ'ác'ənt cəm' x̌ən'núntsən,
ʕ'ac' -nt cm' x̌n' -nu -nt-s -n
look_at -nt maybe hurt -manage -nt-2obj -1erg

cən?úɫxʷəxʷ
c+n+?uɫxʷ -xʷ
enter_cisl -isimptv
I might hurt you, come in."

152. ixí? uɫ i? cus, cən?úɫxʷxʷ məɫ
ixí? uɫ i? cu -s c+n+?uɫxʷ -xʷ mɫ
then and art tell -3erg enter_cisl -isimptv and

n'ín'w'i? ?amtsín
n'ín'w'i? ?am -t -s -in
a_while, feed -nt -2obj -1erg
She said to her, "Come in and I'll feed you."

153. ixí? uɫ i? t sɫiqʷ x̌ʷíc'xtəm məɫ i?
ixí? uɫ i? t s+ɫiqʷ x̌ʷíc' -xt -m mɫ i?
then and art obj_tr meat give -benf -psv and art

t sútən i? t sqʷuct
t sutn i? t s+qʷuct
obj_tr thing art obj_tr fat
She gave her some meat, something, some fat.

154. {ixí? məɫ} ixí? məɫ ɫxʷú‥y, ixí? ʕ'an' ɫkicx
ixí? mɫ ɫ+xʷuy ixí? ʕ'an' ɫ+kic+x
that and go_back then Magpie arrive_again
Then she went back, Magpie got back.

155. uɫ aɫí? ksqʷəsqʷasí?a kmúsməs i?
uɫ aɫí? k -s+qʷs+qʷasí?a k+mus+ms i?
and so have -children four_persons art

sqʷəsqʷasí?as
s+qʷs+qʷasí?a -s
children -3in
She has children, four children.

156. məɫ ixí? nq'a?q'?í‥ksəs t
mɫ ixí? n+q'a?+q'?+íks -s t
and then put_in_hand -3erg obj_tr

---

[3] See also utterances 121, 128, 165, 197.

ksc'aɬʔíɬənsəlx
ksc   -ʔaɬ+ʔíɬn   -s -lx
futPerf -eat_pl   -3i -pl
She put in their hands something to eat.

157. məɬ   ixíʔ   scuts   iʔ   knaqs
     mɬ   ixíʔ   s -cut   -s iʔ   k+naqs
     and   then   dur -say   -3i art one_person
     And one of them said:

158. ʕ'a··n'   anwí   kʷ   qʕa··y
     ʕan   anwí   kʷ   qaʕy
     onom   you   2kn   black
     "My, yours is black,

159. uɬ   incá   pi··q
     uɬ   in+cá   piq
     and   I   white
     and mine white."

160. ʕ'a··n,   uɬ   c'əqʷc'qʷáqʷəlx
     ʕan   uɬ   c'qʷ+c'qʷ+aqʷ   -lx
     onom   and   cry_pl   -pl
     My, and they cried.

161. ixíʔ   məɬ   cənɬx̌ʷp'ám   yutlxʷ   məɬ kəm'ɬtíməlx
     ixíʔ   mɬ   c+n+ɬx̌ʷp'a+m   yutlxʷ   mɬ   km'   -ɬt -im   -lx
     then   and   run_in_cisl   Raven   and take -ɬt -psv   -pl
     And Raven ran in and took it from them,

162. məɬ nis,   uɬ   ʔamʔamtís   iʔ   sqʷəsqʷasíʔas
     mɬ   nis   uɬ   ʔam+ʔam   -t   -is   iʔ   s+qʷs+qʷasíʔa   -s
     and gone and   feed   -nt -3erg art children   -3in
     and went away and fed his children.

163. ixíʔ   itlíʔ   x̌lap,   məɬ   way'   xʷuy   ʕ'an'
     ixíʔ   itlíʔ   x̌la+p   mɬ   way'   xʷuy   ʕ'an'
     then   from_there tomorrow   and   yes   go   Magpie
     Next day Magpie went,

164. məɬ way'   ik'líʔ   iʔ   l   k'əɬq'ílx
     mɬ   way'   ik'líʔ   iʔ   l   k'+ɬq'+ilx
     and yes   there   art in   lie_under
     and lay under the flap.

165. məɬ way'   ɬʔamtím   iʔ   t   t'ət'aqəltáʕlaʔs[4]
     mɬ   way'   ɬ+ʔam   -t -im   iʔ   t   t'+t'aqlt+áʕlaʔ -s
     and yes   feed_again -nt -psv   art obj_tr honey   -3in
     And she fed her that honey.

166. məɬ ɬcxʷuy
     mɬ   ɬ+c+xʷuy
     and come_again
     And she came back home.

---

[4] See utterances 121, 128, 149, 197.

167. ixí? i? t sútən {i? t} i? t
ixí? i? t sutn i? t
that art aglnst thing art aglnst

[s]qʷl'íp t'kʷmíc'a?s ixí?
s+qʷl'+ip t'kʷ+m+íc'a? -s ixí?
moss cover -3erg that

She covered it with something, with moss.

168. ixí? məł t'i ilí? ł?am?amtís
xi? mł t'i? ilí? ł+?am+?am -t -is
then and evid there feed_ again -nt -3erg

And she fed them again.

169. uł ya?x̌ís ałí? a cx?it i? xʷíc'əłts
uł ya?x̌ís ałí? a c+x?it i? xʷíc' -łt -s
and that_one so art first art give -łt -3erg

i? sənlák'ʷ
i? s+n+lak'ʷ
art tallow

And first she gave them the white tallow,

170. la_c'iwt məł ixí? łkʷən'nús i? słiqʷ
la_c+?iw+t mł ixí? ł+kʷn -nu -s i? s+łiqʷ
last_time and that take_ again -manage -3erg art meat

the last time she got hold of the meat.

171. ʕa··n' incá_kən qʷʕay⁵ anwí piq unint
ʕan incá_kn qʷaʕy anwí piq
onom I black you white

"Oh, mine is black, yours white."

172. ik'lí? ck'ək'níya? yutlxʷ [uł] nłəx̌ʷp'ám
ik'lí? c -k'+k'níya? yutlxʷ uł n+łx̌ʷp'a+m
there hab-listen Raven and run_in

Raven was listening there and ran in there.

173. axá? ʕ'an' nq'a?q'?íksəs i?
axá? ʕ'an' n+q'a?+q'?+íks -s i?
this Magpie put_in_hand -3erg art

sqʷəsqʷasí?as i? t sqʷl'íp
s+qʷs+qʷasí?a -s i? t s+qʷl'+ip
children -3in art obj_tr moss

Magpie put some moss in her children's hands.

174. cus c'axknḁ́ʕla?k' p sc'a?xkínx
cu -s c'axknḁ́ʕla?k' p s -c'a?xkín -x
tell -3erg do_what 5kn ipftv^ -do_what -^ ipftv

He [Raven] said, "What are you doing, what's the matter with you?"

---

⁵ In this stylized utterance the glottalization of qʷaʕy is lost. As stated above (p. 124, fn 1), idiosyncratic phonological changes occur in many such stylized utterances.

175.ixíʔ   scuts   t'əxʷ {kʷu sc}   x̌ast
     ixíʔ   s -cut -s   t'xʷ   x̌as+t
     that   dur -say   -3i   evidently   good

     sc'aɬʔíɬnxəlx   t   sqʷl'ip
     sc   -ʔaɬ+ʔíɬn   -x   -lx   t   s+qʷl'ip
     ipftvp ^ -eat_pl   - ^ ipftvp   -pl obj_itr moss
     She said, "They are eating some moss."

176.ixíʔ   ɬəɬʔácqaʔs   yutlxʷ, ɬxʷuy
     ixíʔ   ɬ -ɬ+ʔácqaʔ   -s   yutlxʷ   ɬ+xʷuy
     then   dur -go_out_again -3i Raven   go_back
     Raven went out, he went back.

177.nák'ʷəm   ilíʔ   ck'ək'níyaʔ,   lut t'a   ɬxʷuy   k'əl
     nak'ʷm   ilíʔ   c -k'+k'níyaʔ   lut t'   ɬ+xʷuy   k'l
     evid   there   hab -listen   not negfac go_back   to

     citxʷs
     citxʷ   -s
     house   -3in
     But he was listening there, he hadn't gone to his house.

178.cúntməlx   iʔ   t   túm'səlx
     cun -nt -m   -lx   iʔ   t   tum'   -s   -lx
     tell -nt -psv -pl   art aglnst woman's_mother -3in -pl

     k'wápwi,   lut   kst'qʷcínəmp
     k'wa+p -wy   lut   ks -t'qʷ+cin   -mp
     quiet -ipimptv   not   futl -holler   -5in
     Their mother told them, "Be quiet, don't holler.

179.way'   t'i   p   ʔaɬʔíɬən axáʔ   uɬ
     way'   t'iʔ   p   ʔaɬ+ʔíɬn axáʔ   uɬ
     well   evid   5kn   eat_pl   this   and

     nq'aʔq'ʔíksəntməlx
     n+q'aʔ+q'ʔ+íks -nt -m -lx
     put_in_hand   -nt -psv -pl
     and eat." And she put it in their hands.

180.way'   uɬ   ʕ'a·n' incá_kən piq   uɬ   anwí   qʷaʕy
     way'   uɬ   ʕan   incá_kn   piq   uɬ   anwí   qʷaʕy
     yes   and   onom I   white and you   black
     "Oh, mine is white and yours is black."

181.cənɬx̌ʷp'am   yutlxʷ unint   kəm'ɬtí··məlx   uɬ   xiʔ
     c+n+ɬx̌ʷp'a+m   yutlxʷ   km' -ɬt -im   -lx uɬ   ixíʔ
     run_in_cisl   Raven   take -ɬt -psv -pl and   then

     ɬəɬnísc
     ɬ -ɬ+nis   -c
     dur -gone_again   -3i
     Raven ran back in, took it away from them and left again.

182.uɬ   xiʔ   scuts   yutlxʷ way'   kən
     uɬ   ixíʔ   s -cut   -s   yutlxʷ way'   kn
     and   then   dur -say   -3i   Raven yes   1kn

ksx^wúya?x   ik'lí?
ks   -x^wuy   -a?x   ik'lí?
incp ^ -go   - ^ incp to_there
And Raven said, "I'm going over there."

183. ixí?   sx^wu··ys   uɬ   ilí?   k'əɬ?úɬx^w {i? l} t'əx^w
     ixí?   s -x^wuy -s   uɬ   ilí?   k'ɬ+?uɬx^w   t'x^w
     then   dur -go -3i and there go_under   evidently

     i   l   citx^w   i   l {s}   tək^wtán
     i? l   citx^w   i? l   tk^wtan
     art in house   art in   tule
So he went and went under there in the house, in the tules.

184. atá?   cx^wuy   ixí?   i? tətw'ít
     atá?   c -x^wuy   ixí?   i? t+tw'it
     here   hab-go   that   art boy
The little boy passed by there.

185. {cx^w}   cx^wuysts   i? qa?qácla?sc
             c   -x^wuy -st   -s   i? qa?+qácla?s   -c
             cust ^ -go   -caus -3erg art wheel   -3in
He was wheeling his wheel.

186. cya^ʕ   sənlák'^ʷ
     c+ya^ʕ   s+n+lak'^ʷ
     all   tallow
It's all tallow.

187. ixí?   la?ɬtís,   ixí?
     ixí?   la?   -ɬt -is   ixí?
     then   peck   -ɬt -3erg   then

     cənləq'^ʷləq'^ʷíw's ts
     c   -n+lq'^ʷ+lq'^ʷ+iw's   -t -s
     cust ^ -break_in_two   -st -3erg
He [Raven] pecked it, and broke it in two.

188. ixí?   sc'q^waq^ws   i? tətw'it
     ixí?   s -c'q^w+aq^w   -s i? t+tw'it
     then   dur -cry   -3i art boy
The little boy started to cry.

189. cut wa··y' inqa?qácla?{k^wu} k^wu   la?ɬtís   i?
     cut way'   in -qa?+qácla?   k^wu   la?   -ɬt -is   i?
     say yes   1in -wheel   1k^wu peck -ɬt -3erg art

     t   qəwláqa?
     t   qwláqa?
     aglnst   darned_thing
He said, "That darned thing took my wheel."

190. ixí?   cɬx̌^wp'am   i? sk'^ʷuys,   ixí?
     ixí?   c+ɬx̌^wp'a+m   i? s+k'^ʷuy -s ixí?
     then   run_out_cisl   art mother -3in then

sp'áp'qəs   nákʷʷəm   yutlxʷ
sp'+ap'+q   -s   nakʷʷm   yutlxʷ
whack_on_head -3erg   evid   Raven
His mother came out there, and hit Raven on the head.

191. sp'áp'qəs {iʔ iʔ}   iʔ   yutlxʷ   uɬ   xiʔ   nákʷʷəm
     sp'+ap'+q   -s   iʔ   yutlxʷ   uɬ   ixíʔ   nakʷʷm
     whack_on_head -3erg art   Raven and   there evid

     uɬ   iʔ   λ'lal   ilíʔ   t'əxʷ   qʷm'áp
     uɬ   iʔ   λ'l+al ilíʔ   t'xʷ   qʷma+p
     and   art dead   there evidently faint
     She hit Raven over the head, and he lay there dead, fainted.

192. ixíʔ   ɬənɬx̌ʷp'ám   iʔ k'əl citxʷs
     ixíʔ   ɬ+n+ɬx̌ʷp'a+m iʔ k'l citxʷ -s
     then   run_back_in   art to house -3in
     She ran back in her house.

193. ckʷis   iʔ   st'xitkʷ   iʔ
     c+kʷi   -s   iʔ   s+t'x+itkʷ iʔ
     take_cisl -3erg art   soup   art

     kc'xʷína?ɬts   ixíʔ   ilíʔ
     k+c'xʷ+ína? -ɬt -s ixíʔ   ilíʔ
     pour_on   -ɬt -3erg that   there
     She took the soup and poured it on him there.

194. {uɬ xiʔ} ilí··ʔ   ct'ak'ʷ   yutlxʷ xiʔ sqiɬts
     ilíʔ   c -t'ak'ʷ   yutlxʷ ixíʔ s -qiɬt -s
     there hab -put_down Raven then dur-awaken-3i
     Raven lay there, then woke up.

195. ixíʔ   ckʷis   ixíʔ ilíʔ {a c} kmax sqʷʷuct ilíʔ
     ixíʔ   c+kʷi -s ixíʔ ilíʔ   kmax s+qʷʷuct ilíʔ
     then   take_cisl -3i that there   only fat   there
     He took that, it was nothing but fat.

196. ixíʔ   nt'k'ʷəntís   i   l   yámx̌ʷa?s   ixíʔ
     ixíʔ   n+t'k'ʷ -nt -is iʔ l   yámx̌ʷa? -s   ixíʔ
     then   put_in -nt -3erg art in basket -3in   then

     ɬəɬxʷúys
     ɬ -ɬ+xʷuy -s
     dur go_back -3i
     He put it in his basket, and then he went back.

197. sxʷu··ys   [uɬ]   níkna   way'   kʷu
     s -xʷuy -s   uɬ   níkxna? way'   kʷu
     dur -go -3i and goodness yes   1obj

     kʷuksts   itíʔ iʔ t int'aqəltáˤn[6]
     kʷuk   -st -s itíʔ iʔ t in -t'aqltáˤn
     do_service -st -3erg that art aglnst 1in -honey
     He went and [said], "Goodness, that woman sure pleased me."

---

[6] See utterances 121, 128, 149, 165.

198. ixí?   ?amtís   i?   sqʷəsqʷasí?as
     ixí?   ?am   -t   -is   i?   s+qʷs+qʷasí?a   -s
     then   feed -nt -3erg   art children   -3in

     nək'ník's   uɬ   ?amtís
     nk'+nik' -s   uɬ   ?am   -t   -is
     cut   -3erg   and feed -nt -3erg

     So he fed his children, he cut it up and fed them.

199. ixí?   s?aɬ?íɬəns   ixí?   i?   sqʷəsqʷasí?as
     ixí?   s -?aɬ+?íɬ -s   ixí?   i?   s+qʷs+qʷasí?a   -s
     then   dur -eat_pl -3i   that   art children   -3in

     His children started eating.

200. way'   t'i   cx̌aˤp,   t'i   cx̌aˤp
     way'   t'i? c -x̌aˤ+p t'i? c -x̌aˤ+p
     yes   evid hab-draft   evid hab-draft

     And he could feel the air, the air.

201. ta··   ki   tqəntís
     nta   ki?   tq   -nt -is
     intj   rel   touch -nt -3erg

     He touched it.

202. nák'ʷʷəm   ixí?   i?   sqʷəqʷɬm'úsc'a?[s]
     nak'ʷʷm   ixí?   i?   s+qʷ+qʷɬm'+ús+c'a? -s
     evid   that   art guts   -3in

     c'aɬ?íɬtəm   i?   t   sqʷəsqʷasí?a
     c   -?aɬ+?íɬ -t -m   i?   t   s+qʷs+qʷasí?a
     cust^   -eat_pl -st -psv   art aglnst children

     It's his [own] guts that the children are eating.

203. ixí?   ɬckəm'əntí··s,   ik'lí?   ɬkʷums {n}
     ixí?   ɬ+c+km'   -nt -is   ik'lí?   ɬ+kʷum   -s
     that   take_back_cisl   -nt -3erg   there   store_again -3erg

     nutəntís {xi}
     n+wt   -nt-is
     put_in   -nt-3erg

     He took it back away and put it back where it belonged.

204. ixí?   uɬ   way'   ik'lí?   ɬa?   ɬxʷuy
     ixí?   uɬ   way'   ik'lí?   ɬa?   ɬ+xʷuy
     that   and   yes   there   when   go_back

     That was the last time he went back there.

205. ixí?   scútslx   wa··y'   uɬ   i?   t   sq'míltən
     ixí?   s -cut -s -lx   way'   uɬ   i?   t   s+q'm+ilt+tn
     that   dur -say -3i -pl   yes   and   art aglnst hunger

     kʷu   ksƛ'əxʷtm'íxa?x {xi}
     kʷu   ks   -ƛ'xʷ+t -míx+a?x
     4kn   incp^ -pl_die - ^incp

     They said, "We are just starving to death."

206.axáʔ   nkʷnim   wápupxən   uɫ   mqʷaqʷ
    axáʔ   n+kʷni+m   wap+wp+xn   uɫ   mqʷ+aqʷ
    this   sing   Lynx   and   snow_fall
    And Lynx started to sing and it started to snow.

207.məɫ   xiʔ   cniɫc   spíx̌əms
    mɫ   ixíʔ   cniɫ+c   s   -pix̌+m -s
    and   then   (s)he   dur -hunt -3i
    And he went hunting.

208.uɫ   axáʔ {cut}   cus   way' caʔkʷ   p   cx̌ʷuy   p
    uɫ   axáʔ   cu   -s   way' caʔkʷ   p   c+x̌ʷuy   p
    and   this   tell -3erg yes should   5kn   come   5kn

    ɫc'imx   ak'láʔ
    ɫ+c+ʔimx   ak'láʔ
    move_back_cisl   here
    He told them, "You better move back over there.

209.uɫ   n'ín'w'iʔ   ʔamɫúlmən
    uɫ   n'ín'w'iʔ   ʔam   -ɫulm -n
    and   a_while,   feed -5obj -1erg
    I'll feed you."

210.ixíʔ   uɫ   c'ímxəlx   ik'líʔ
    ixíʔ   uɫ   c   -ʔimx   -lx   ik'líʔ
    then   and   hab-move   -pl   there
    And they moved over there.

211.uɫ   xiʔ   iʔ tətw'it cut   way' kʷu ksxʷʔíltaʔx
    uɫ   ixíʔ iʔ t+tw'it cut   way' kʷu ks   -xʷʔ+ilt   -aʔx
    and that art boy   say yes 4kn incp ^ -hold_baby - ^ incp
    And the boy, they said, "We're going to hold the baby."

212.ixíʔ   uɫ   sxʷʔíltəmsəlx
    ixíʔ   uɫ   s   -xʷʔ+ilt+m -s   -lx
    then   and   dur -hold_baby -3i   -pl
    So they took the baby.

213.xʷaʔntí··səlx   uɫ   kʷm'iɫ   uɫ   way' k'laxʷ
    xʷaʔ -nt -is   -lx   uɫ   kʷm'iɫ   uɫ   way' k'laxʷ
    pick_up-nt -3erg -pl and suddenly and   yes   evening

    k'map
    k'ma+p
    dark
    They held the baby, all of a sudden it was getting late and dark.

214.uɫ   iʔ   kəl'kíl'lx   iʔ   t   sp'əc'níɫxʷ   cənʔuɫxʷ
    uɫ   iʔ   kl'+kil'+lx   iʔ   t   s+p'c'n+iɫxʷ   c+n+ʔuɫxʷ
    and   art   hands_dim   art   ?   tipi   enter_cisl
    Two hands came into the tent.

215.uɫ   cut {iks}   iksxʷʔám
    uɫ   cut   i   -ks   -xʷʔa -m
    and   say   1i -futT ^ -hold - ^ futT

iksxˠⁿ?í[ltm]

i	-ks	-xˠⁿ?+ilt	-m
1i	futT ^	-hold_baby - ^ futT	

And said, "I want to hold it, I want to hold the child."

216.

ixí?	ik'lí? {wi}	xˠíc'əłtsəlx		
ixí?	ik'lí?	xˠic'	-łt -s	-lx
then	there	give	-łt -3erg	-pl

They gave it to him.

217.

xi?	nc'əq'mís		i	l	p'ína?s,	ixí?
ixí?	n+c'q'+mi	-s	i?	l	p'ína? -s	ixí?
that	throw_in	-3erg	art	in	basket -3in	then

snisc,			xˠət'púsəs	
s	-nis	-c	xˠt'+p+us	-s
dur	-gone	-3i	run_away_with	-3erg

He threw it in his basket, and left, ran away with it.

218.

[nakˠˡ'əm]	ixí?	spapá ͨła?
nakˠˡ'm	ixí?	s+pa+pá ͨła?
evid	that	Ape

That's the Ape.

219.

ixí?	uł	axá?	c'əqˠc'qˠáqˠəlx	
ixí?	uł	axá?	c'qˠ+c'qˠ+aqˠ	-lx
then	and	this	cry_pl	-pl

They cried.

220.

lut	t'	ka?kíci?səlx,		wi··m'
lut	t'	ka?+kíc -i? -s	-lx	wim'
not	negfac	find -m -3erg	-pl	in_vain

They couldn't find him.

221.

uł	xi?	scútsəlx		way'	t_tanm'ús
uł	ixí?	s -cut -s	-lx	way'	t_tanm'+ús
and	then	dur -say -3i	-pl	yes	any_which_way

kˠu	{ks}	ksλ'aλ'a?ntím		
kˠu	ks	-λ'a?+λ'a?	-nt	-im
4kn	futT ^	-look_for	-nt	-4erg

They said, "We are going to look for nothing."

222.

ixí?	uł	stkˠⁿ?útsəlx		həłwápu?pxən
ixí?	uł	s -tkˠⁿ?+ut -s	-lx	hł= wap+wp+xn
then	and	dur -walk_pl -3i	-pl	group= Lynx

Lynx and his family walked away.

223.

tkˠⁿ?ú··təlx,	t'i	mat	lkˠákˠəlx {uł}
tkˠⁿ?+ut -lx	t'i?	mat	lkˠ+akˠ -lx
walk_pl -pl	evid	maybe	far -pl

They walked and went long ways.

224.

ixí?	uł	yá ͨpəlx	ixí?	i?	k'əl	pəptwína?xˠ
ixí?	uł	ya ͨ+p -lx	ixí?	i?	k'l	p+ptwína?xˠ
then	and	gather -pl	that	art	to	old_woman

They got to the old lady.

225. ilí   mut
     ilíʔ   mut
     there   be_home
     She was there.

226. ixíʔ   cúntmǝlx   ixíʔ   iʔ   t   pǝptwínaʔxʷ
     ixíʔ   cun-nt -m   -lx   ixíʔ   iʔ   t   p+ptwínaʔxʷ
     then   tell -nt -psv -pl that   art   aglnst old_woman
     The old lady told them:

227. kǝn   xíxuʔtǝm   ki   kʷu   skʷánx̌ǝns   ixíʔ   t
     kn   xi+xwʼtm   kiʔ kʷu   s+kʷan+x̌n -s ixíʔ   t
     1kn   girl   rel 1kʷu prisoner -3i that   aglnst

     spapáˁɬaʔ
     s+pa+páˁɬaʔ
     Ape
     "When I was a little girl Ape kidnapped me.

228. uɬ   wayʼ   ˁácʼǝnt   kʷu   wíkǝntp   kǝn   kʼiwlx
     uɬ   wayʼ   ˁacʼ   -nt   kʷu   wik -nt   -p   kn   kʼiw+lx
     and   yes   look_at -nt   1obj see -nt -5erg   1kn   old
     And look, you can see I'm old.

229. uɬ   ixíʔ   iʔ   sqʷsiʔmp   scpíx̌ǝx
     uɬ   ixíʔ   iʔ   s+qʷsiʔ -mp   sc   -pix̌   -x
     and   that   art   son   -5in   ipftvp ^ -hunt - ^ ipftvp
     And your boy is hunting.

230. mǝɬ unint   ilíʔ unint   tʼǝxʷ   a   cǝnmáˁyuʔs
     mɬ   ilíʔ   tʼxʷ   a   c   -n+mˁay+wʼs
     and   there   evidently   art   hab   -lay_across
     There is a log across the road.

231. kʼaɬáʔ   liʔ   mi   p   wkʷwíkʷmiʔst
     kʼaɬáʔ   ilíʔ   mi   p   wkʷ+wíkʷ+miʔst
     on_that_side   there   fut 5kn   hide_self
     You can hide a little ways from there.

232. mi cmay   wíkǝntp   iʔ   sqʷsiʔmp
     mi cmay   wik -nt   -p   iʔ   s+qʷsiʔ -mp
     fut maybe   see -nt -5erg   art   son   -5in
     Maybe you'll see your boy.

233. uɬ   wayʼ   λʼx̌ap
     uɬ   wayʼ   λʼx̌a+p
     and   yes   grow
     He's grown up."

234. uɬ   itíʔ   [s]cxʷuyx   iʔ   tǝtwít
     uɬ   itíʔ   s   -c+xʷuy -x   iʔ   t+twʼit
     and   from_that   ipftv ^ -come   - ^ ipftv art   boy
     Then the boy came along.

235. uɬ   ixíʔ   cúsǝlx   i   t   λʼáx̌ǝx̌λʼx̌áps
     uɬ   ixíʔ   cu -s   -lx   iʔ   t   λʼax̌+x̌+λʼx̌áp   -s
     and   then   tell -3erg -pl   art   aglnst elders   -3in

alá?   kʷu   alá?
alá?   kʷu   alá?
here   4kn   here

His parents said to him: "Here, we are here."

236. ixí?   uɬ   itlí?   sxʷuy[s]
     ixí?   uɬ   itlí?   s -xʷuy   -s
     then   and   from_there dur -go   -3i

He kept on going.

237. cut n'ín'w'i?   xlap   mi alá?   kən   ɬckicx
     cut n'ín'w'i?   xla+p   mi alá?   kn   ɬ+c+kic+x
     say a_while,   tomorrow   fut here   1kn   arrive_cisl_again

He said, "Tomorrow I'll come back."

238. uɬ   ta°íp   xʷuy {lut}   lut ilí?   t'   ƛ'lap
     uɬ   t_ny°'ip   xʷuy   lut ilí?   t'   ƛ'la+p
     and   continuously   go   not there   negfac stop

He kept going, didn't stop there.

239. lut sq'sápi?s   ki ití   cxi?wílx
     lut s -q'sápi?   -s   ki? ití?   c+xy'+wilx
     not dur -long_time -3i   rel from_that   travel_cisl

     spəpá°ɬa?
     s+pa+pá°ɬa?
     Ape

It wasn't long, Ape came by.

240. uɬ   ití?   ɬni?ák'ʷ   nixʷ
     uɬ   ití?   ɬ+ny?ak'ʷ   nixʷ
     and   from_that   cross_again   also

And he crossed too.

241. ixí? scuts {a sc' uɬ} sc'kinx   uɬ   ilí?
     ixí? s -cut -s   s+c   -?kin   -x   uɬ   ilí?
     that dur -say -3i   ipftvp ^   -indef - ^ ipftvp and   there

     kʷ   ma°áwtətxən
     kʷ   ma°áwt+t+xn
     2kn   sideways

He asked [the boy], "What made you twist your foot sideways?

242. ilí?   kʷ   ma°áwtətxən
     ilí?   kʷ   ma°áwt+t+xn
     there   2kn sideways

You turned your foot there."

243. cut   ilí?   i?   sútən   i?   səw'sw'á°s   uɬ
     cut   ilí?   i?   sutn   i?   sw'+sw'+a°s   uɬ
     say   there   art thing   art pheasant   and

     ikst'a°pám   ki? t'uxʷt
     i -ks   -t'a°pá -m   ki? t'uxʷ+t
     1i -futT ^ -shoot   - ^ futT rel fly

He said, "The thing there, a pheasant. I was going to shoot it and then it flew away."

244. ixí?   úłi?   cut
     ixí?   uł+i?   cut
     that   and_then   say
     That's what he said.

245. ixí? uł   s?atxílxsəlx   púlxəlx
     ixí? uł   s -?atx+ílx   -s -lx puł+x -lx
     then and   dur -sleep_pl -3i -pl camp   -pl
     They slept, they went to bed.

246. uł   axá? i?   λ'aǎ̌əǎ̌λ'ǎ̌áp   ixí?   utəntísəlx
     uł   axá? i?   λ'aǎ̌+ǎ̌+λ'ǎ̌áp   ixí?   wt   -nt -is -lx
     and this art elders   that   put_down -nt -3erg -pl
     The parents arranged it.

247. ǎ̌áq'səlx {i?}   i?   [n]sapm'átk\ʷ   uł   ití?   sx\ʷyalq\ʷ {uł}
     ǎ̌aq' -s -lx   i?   n+sapm'+átk\ʷ   uł   ití?   s+x\ʷy+alq\ʷ
     pay   -3erg -pl art water_bugs   and that   wood_worm
     i?   c'áyǎ̌a?
     i?   c'áyǎ̌a?
     art crayfish
     They paid the little wiggle worms, the wood worms, the crawfish,

248. mat   ilí?   i   l   siwłk\ʷ, ixí?   ǎ̌əq'ǎ̌á··q'səlx {ks}
     mat   ilí?   i? l   siwł+k\ʷ ixí?   ǎ̌q'+ǎ̌aq'   -s   -lx
     maybe there   art in water   that   pay_pl   -3erg -pl
     there in the water. And they paid them,

249. n'ín'w'i?   ła   nix\ʷítk\ʷ   spəpá\ʕła?
     n'ín'w'i?   ła? n+yx\ʷ+itk\ʷ   s+pa+pá\ʕła?
     a_while,   if   fall_in_water   Ape
     for Monster to fall in the water.

250. ixí?   i   l   łk\ʷk\ʷá\ʕst   uł   xi?   ití?
     ixí?   i? l   ł+k\ʷ+k\ʷa\ʕst   uł   ixí?   ití?
     then   art in early_morning and then   from_that
     łcxi?wílx   ixí? i? tətwít łcni?ák\ʷ
     ł+c+xy'+wilx   ixí? i? t+tw'it ł+c+n+y?ak\ʷ
     travel_cisl_again that art boy   cross_cisl_gain
     In the morning the boy came by again and crossed again.

251. uł {xi?} ixí?   t_s?iwt   cniłc   x\ʷət'pəncút ilí?
     uł   ixí?   t_s+?iw+t cnił+c x\ʷt'+p+ncut ilí?
     and   then   behind   (s)he   hurry   there
     ckicx
     c+kic+x
     arrive_cisl
     And right behind him the other was hurrying, and got there.

252. uł   xi?   scuts {i l}   i   l   ya\ʕ'cín   ckicx   uł
     uł   ixí?   s -cut -s   i? l   ya\ʕ'+cín c+kic+x   uł
     and then   dur -say -3i art in shore   arrive_cisl and

cut
cut
say
And he said, he got to the edge of the water and said:

253.ta?kín {ki p}   ki k^w ni?ák'^w
    ta+?kín'   ki? k^w n+y?ak'^w
    from_where   rel 2kn cross
"Where did you cross?"

254.cúntəm   t'əx^w   axá? i ta cənma∩áyu?s
    cu -nt -m   t'x^w   axá? i? t c -n+m∩áy+w's
    tell -nt -psv   evidently this art ? hab-lay_across
He said, "Over on that log."

255.ah, ixí? ití?   stqcəlxálq^ws,   púti? tm'iw's
    ah ixí? ití?   s -t+qc+lx+alq^w -s pút+i? tm'+iw's
    intj that from_that dur -run_over_logs -3i still half_way

    ki x̌^wc'ap   ixí?
    ki? x̌^wc'a+p   ixí?
    rel break_in_two   that
He ran on the log, he was in the middle of the log, and it broke.

256.i? t   sx^wyalq^w   aɬí? ?iɬs
    i? t   s+x^wy+alq^w aɬí? ?iɬ -s
    art aglnst wood_worm   because eat -3erg
The wood worms had eaten it.

257.ixí?   nix^wítk^w,   nt'a ki kəm'km'áx̌səlx   i?
    ixí?   n+yx^w+itk^w   nt'a ki? km'+km'+ax̌-s -lx i?
    then fall_in_water intj rel grab_pl   -3erg -pl art

    t   c'áyx̌a?
    t   c'áyx̌a?
    aglnst crayfish
He fell in the water and the crawfish grabbed him,

258.uɬ   i? t   sútən i ta nsapm'átk^w
    uɬ   i? t   sutn i? t n+sapm'+átk^w
    and   art aglnst thing art aglnst water_bugs
the things, the wiggle worms.

259.uɬ   ixí? t   nsapm'átk^w k^wísəlx   uɬ
    uɬ   ixí? t   n+sapm'+átk^w k^wi -s -lx uɬ
    and that aglnst water_bugs   take -3erg -pl and

    nt'qmnítk^wsəlx
    n+t'q+mn+itk^w   -s   -lx
    push_under_water -3erg -pl
And the wiggle worms grabbed him and pushed him under water.

260.ilí··? cacacá∩ uɬ   λ'lal
    ilí?   ca+ca+cá∩ uɬ   λ'l+al
    there holler   and   dead
They did that, he cried and he died.

261.ixíʔ   itlíʔ   sxʷúy'ysəlx   axáʔ,   iʔ
    ixíʔ   itlíʔ   s -xʷuy'+y -s -lx   axáʔ   iʔ
    then   from_there   dur -go_pl   -3i -pl   this   art

    sqʷsíʔsəlx
    s+qʷsiʔ -s -lx
    son   -3in -pl
    Then they went on, and their boy.

262.xʷu··ylx   uɬ   lkʷákʷəlx   úɬiʔ   wíksəlx   iʔ
    xʷuy -lx   uɬ   lkʷ+akʷ -lx   uɬ+iʔ   wik -s   -lx   iʔ
    go   -pl   and   far   -pl   and_then   see -3erg   -pl   art

    t'íkʷət
    t'ikʷt
    lake
    They went a long way, and they saw a lake.

263.ixíʔ   sutáns {iʔ}   ixíʔ   nkʷλ'álqsəm   iʔ
    ixíʔ   s -wtan -s   ixíʔ   n+kʷλ'+alqs+m   iʔ
    then   dur -placed -3i   then   take_clothes_off   art

    sqʷsíʔsəlx   k[i]   nɬət'pmítkʷ
    s+qʷsiʔ -s -lx   kiʔ   n+ɬt'p+m+itkʷ
    son   -3in -pl   rel   jump_in_water
    He put the ..., their son took his clothes off, he jumped in the water.

264.t'a   xiʔ   sk'ráms
    nt'a   ixíʔ   s -k'ra+m -s
    intj   that   dur -swim   -3i
    He swam.

265.nt'a·· uɬ   axáʔ {iʔ} iʔ   sk'ʷuys   nákʷəm ʕʷəsʕʷísxaʔ
    nt'a   uɬ   axáʔ   iʔ   s+kʷuy -s   nakʷm ʕʷs+ʕʷísxaʔ
    intj   and   this   art mother -3in   evid   Robin
    Gee, his mother is Robin.

266.t'a   cacacá··ʕ
    nt'a   ca+caʕ+cáʕ
    intj   holler
    She was hollering.

267.uɬ {iʔ} ya lʔiws   axáʔ {iʔ k'əl iʔ k'əl} iʔ   k'əl
    uɬ   ya lʔiw   -s   axáʔ   iʔ   k'l
    and   art m's_father   -3in   this   art to

    ɬúkʷlaʔxʷ   kʷəlk'lwís
    ɬúkʷ+laʔxʷ   kʷlk'+lwis
    dirt   roll_around
    And his father rolled around in the dirt.

268.ixíʔ   nákʷəm   [sw'əsw'áʕs]
    ixíʔ   nakʷm   s+w's+w'aʕs
    that   evid   pheasant
    That's a pheasant.

269.ixí? uɬ ilí? k'ʷəlk'əlwí··s
ixí? uɬ ilí? k'ʷlk'+lwis
then and there roll_around
He rolled around there.

270.uɬ axá? xʷu··y i? sqʷsí?səlx
uɬ axá? xʷuy i? s+qʷsi? -s -lx
and this go art son -3in -pl
And their son kept on going.

271.məɬ n?aɬxʷítkʷ məɬ ɬc'ácqa? məɬ cut
mɬ n+?aɬxʷ+ítkʷ mɬ ɬ+c+?ácqa? mɬ cut
and dive and come_out_again and say

xʷuxʷuxʷuxʷú, xʷuxʷuxʷú,
xʷuxʷuxʷuxʷú xʷuxʷuxʷú
onom onom
And he'd go under water and he'd say "xʷuxʷuxʷuxʷú, xʷuxʷuxʷú."

272.nák'ʷəm ixí? sútən, ?a?súɬ
nak'ʷm ixí? sutn ?a?súɬ
evid that thing Loon
That's whatchamacallit, Loon.

273.wi··m' cx̌əlítstsəlx, uɬ nis
wim' c+x̌lit -s -lx uɬ nis
in_vain call_cisl -3erg -pl and gone
They called and called him, he's gone.

274.{ixí? uɬ i?} ixí? uɬ t'əxʷ mat ƛ'axʷt i?
ixí? uɬ t'xʷ mat ƛ'axʷ+t i?
then and maybe dead_pl art

ƛ'ax̌əx̌ƛ'x̌áps, lut t'a cmistí[n]
ƛ'x̌+x̌+ƛ'x̌a+p -s lut t' c -my -st -in
parents -3in not negfac cust^ -know -^ cust -1erg
I guess his parents must have died, I don't know;

275.nis k'aɬá?
nis k'aɬá?
gone on_that_side
He kept going that way.

276.k'ra··m uɬ k'a nsqʷ'ʷut ki t'íxəlx
k'ra+m uɬ k' n+sqʷ'ʷ+ut ki? t'ix+lx
swim and to other_side rel come_to_shore
He swam, and got out of the water on the other side.

277.ilí? i? sqilxʷ way' cwix, cuxwíx
ilí? i? s+qilxʷ way' c -wix c -wx+wix
there art person well hab-live hab-live_pl
There are people there, several.

278.k'li? kicx {uɬ i? a} ixí? i? ?a?súɬ aɬí? uɬ c'x̌iɬ_t
ik'lí? kic+x ixí? i? ?a?súɬ aɬí? uɬ c+?x̌iɬ_t
there arrive that art Loon so and like

cq'iʔmíx
c   -q'y'+mix
hab-speckled
He got there, the Loon has like speckles.

279. ixíʔ   uɫ {kʷʼulʼlʼ} kʷʼulʼlʼ_t {sútən t} spuct
    ixíʔ   uɫ   kʷʼulʼ+lʼ_t   s+puc+t
    then and   turn_into   scab
And then he turned into something, scabs.

280. ixíʔ   uɫ   k'liʔ   iʔ xíxuʔtəm   cus {iʔ k'liʔ ckʷ}
    ixíʔ   uɫ   ik'líʔ iʔ xi+xw'tm   cu -s
    then and   there art girl   tell -3erg
And there the little girl, told the...

281. cúntəm {iʔ t} iʔ t   tum's
    cu -nt -m   iʔ t   tum'   -s
    tell -nt -psv art aglnst woman's_mother -3in

    xʷuyx   asw'aw'ásaʔ {ʕʼácʼənt} way'
    xʷuy -x   a -s+w'a+w'ásaʔ   way'
    go -isimptv   2in -aunt   yes

    tawskíccəlx
    taw+s+kíc+c   -lx
    have_visitors -pl
Her mother told her, "Go over to your aunt, look, they got company."

282. ixíʔ   uɫ   k'liʔ   xʷuy xiʔ   iʔ xíxuʔtəm
    ixíʔ   uɫ   ik'líʔ xʷuy ixíʔ iʔ xi+xw'tm
    then and   there go   that art girl
The girl went over there.

283. məɫ cut {k'liʔ} kən sƛ'aʔmíx   t   sʔur'ísəlp'
    mɫ cut   kn s   -ƛ'aʔ -mix   t   s+w'r'+islp'
    and say   1kn ipftv^ -fetch -^ipftv obj_itr fire
She said, "I want to get a piece of fire."

284. uɫ   ʕʼácʼəs   ixíʔ iʔ sqəl'tmíxʷ kmax spuct
    uɫ   ʕʼacʼ -s   ixíʔ iʔ s+ql't+mixʷ kmax s+puc+t
    and look_at -3erg that art man   only   scab
And she looked at the man, he's nothing but sores.

285. ixíʔ   ɫəɫxʷúys,   cus   iʔ tum's
    ixíʔ   ɫ   -ɫ+xʷuy -s cu -s   iʔ tum'   -s
    that dur -go_back -3i tell -3erg art woman's_mother -3in
She went back, and said to her mother:

286. níˑˑkna   isw'awásaʔ   ixíʔ iʔ sqəl'tmíxʷ kmax
    níkxnaʔ   i   -s+w'a+w'ásaʔ ixíʔ iʔ s+ql't+mixʷ kmax
    goodness 1in -aunt   that art man   only

    spuct   ta ctəxstís
    s+puc+t   t   c   -tx   -st   -is
    scab   ? cust^ -comb -^cust -3erg
"Gee, aunt, the man is nothing but sores and she's combing him."

287.ixí? uɬ k'li? xʷuy uɬ cus i? ɬcəc?úpsc
    ixí? uɬ ik'lí? xʷuy uɬ cu -s i? ɬ+c+c?+ups -c
    then and there go and tell -3erg art younger_sister -3in

She went there and told her younger sister:

288.ca?kʷ ilí? way' x̌ʷilstxʷ, myaɬ
    ca?kʷ ilí? way' x̌ʷil -st -xʷ myaɬ
    should there yes discard -st -2erg too_much

xʷa?spúct
xʷa?+s+púct
many_scabs

"You should throw him away, he's too scabby."

289.lut t'a ctq'a?ílsmstəm i? t
    lut t' c -ɬ+q'a?+íls+m -st -m i? t
    not negfac cust^ -pay_attention -^cust -psv art agInst

sl'ax̌ts
s+l'ax̌+t -s
partner -3in

Her partner didn't pay attention.

290.ixí? uɬ ik'lí? i? xíxu?təm ɬxʷuy,
    ixí? uɬ ik'lí? i? xi+xw'tm ɬ+xʷuy
    then and there art girl go_back

Then the little girl went back.

291.uɬ way' lut t'a kspuct ixí? i? sqəltmíxʷ
    uɬ way' lut t' k -s+puc+t ixí? i? s+qlt+mixʷ
    and yes not negfac have -scab that art man

The man didn't have any scabs.

292.ixí? x̌ʷilsts {ya} ixí? i? cucáˤwlx
    ixí? x̌ʷil -st -s ixí? i? cw+caˤw+lx
    that discard -st -3erg that art bathe

x̌ʷilsts,
x̌ʷil -st -s
discard -st -3erg

He had thrown them way, had bathed and gotten rid of them.

293.ní··kna? {t i?} wísxən {i?} i? qəpqíntəns, ixí?
    níkxna? wis+xn i? qp+qin+tn -s ixí?
    goodness long art hair -3in that

ctəxstím ixí? t tkəɬmílxʷ
c -tx -st -im ixí? t tkɬmilxʷ
cust^ -comb -^cust -psv that agInst woman

Gee, his hair is long, the woman is combing it.

294.ixí? i? xíxu?təm məɬ xʷət'pəncút cut
    ixí? i? xi+xw'tm mɬ xʷt'+p+ncut cut
    that art girl and run say

The girl ran over, said:

295. {is}isw'aw'ása?   stəxstís   ixi? i?
     i -s+w'a+w'ása?   s   -tx   -st   -is   ixí? i?
     1in -aunt   cust ^ -comb - ^ cust -3erg   that art

    sqəltmíxʷ,
    s+qlt+mixʷ
    man
    "My aunt is combing that man.

296. way'   qʷámqʷəmt   i? qəpqíntəns
    way'   qʷam+qʷm+t   i? qp+qin+tn -s
    yes   excellent   art hair   -3in
    His hair is sure nice."

297. ixí?   sxʷuys   ik'lí?, uł   cut
    ixí?   s -xʷuy -s ik'lí? uł   cut
    then   dur -go -3i there and   say
    She went there, and said:

298. ckʷint   ixí?   t   incá   istxám
    c+kʷin -t ixí?   t   in+cá i -s   -txa+m
    take   -nt that agInst I   1i -inten -comb
    "Give it here, I'll comb him."

299. cúntəm   lut,   mał   xʷa?spúct,   lut
    cu -nt -m   lut   mał   xʷa?+s+púct   lut
    tell -nt -psv   not   too_much many_scabs   not

    akstxám
    a -ks   -txa   -m
    2i -futT ^ -comb - ^ futT
    She said, "No, he's got too much scab, you can't comb him."

300. ixí?   úłi?   xəcməncútəlx,   cútəlx   way' *unint*
    ixí?   uł+i?   xc+mn+cut -lx   cut -lx   way'
    then   and_then get_ready -pl   say -pl   OK
    Then they got ready, and they said,

301. ixí?   uł   t'i?   cútəlx   way'   kʷu
    ixí?   uł   t'i?   cut -lx   way'   kʷu
    then   and   evid   say -pl   yes   4kn

    ks?alu?scúta?x   swit *unint*   i
    ks   -?al+w's+cút   -a?x   swit   i?
    incp ^ -gather   - ^ incp who   art

    ks[xast] {kiw}
    k   -s+xas+t
    to_be -best
    then they said: "We are going to gather and have a contest."

302. ixí?   uł   ?alu?scú··təlx ilí?,
    ixí?   uł   ?al+w's+cút -lx ilí?
    then   and   gather   -pl there
    And they gathered there.

303.uɬ   xiʔ   t'aˤpáməlx   iʔ t
   uɬ   ixíʔ   t'aˤpá -m   -lx iʔ t
   and   then   shoot -mdl   -pl art agInst

   t'at'aˤpíkstməlx   iʔ   t   c'q'íln'səlx {uɬ}
   t'a+t'aˤp+íkst+m -lx   iʔ   t   c'q'+iln -s -lx
   shoot_target   -pl   art agInst arrow -3in -pl
   And they shot at targets with arrow heads.

304.uɬ   ixíʔ   ƛ'x̌ʷup   ixíʔ iʔ   ʔaʔsúɬ
   uɬ   ixíʔ   ƛ'x̌ʷu+p   ixíʔ iʔ   ʔaʔsúɬ
   and   that   win   that art Loon
   And Loon won.

305.uɬ   lut t'əx̌ʷ   cm'ay'xítmiʔstəlx   məɬ   itíʔ   lut
   uɬ   lut t'x̌ʷ   c -m'ay'+xít+miʔst   -lx   mɬ   itíʔ   lut
   and not evidently   hab -tell_stories   -pl   and   that   not
   And they didn't tell stories and did not...

306.iʔ   k'ʷiƛ't   k'ərk'ráməlx   məɬ iʔ   k'ʷiƛ't   tanm'úsəlx
   iʔ   k'ʷiƛ'+t   k'r+k'ra+m   -lx   mɬ   iʔ   k'ʷiƛ'+t   tanm'ús   -lx
   art others swim   -pl   and art others   insignificant -pl
   Others swam, others did nothing.

307.lut t'a   cƛ'x̌ʷúpəlx
   lut   t'   c   -ƛ'x̌ʷu+p   -lx
   not negfac hab   -win   -pl
   They didn't win.

308.uɬ   ixíʔ   ƛ'x̌ʷup   iʔ   ʔaʔsúɬ
   uɬ   ixíʔ   ƛ'x̌ʷu+p   iʔ   ʔaʔsúɬ
   and   that   win   art Loon
   Loon won.

309.ixíʔ   uɬ   way'   a   cmistín {n}
   ixíʔ   uɬ   way'   a   c   -my   -st   -in
   that   and   all   art cust ^ -know - ^ cust -1erg

   nc'ayx̌ʷápəlqs,   kiw
   n+c'ayx̌ʷ+áplqs   kiw
   end_of_story   yes
   That's all I know, it's the end of the story, yes.

MOSQUITO

1. ixí?   ilí?   spúlxxəlx
   ixí?   ilí?   s   -pul+x -x   -lx
   then   there ipftv^ -camp -^ ipftv -pl

   həłca?sláqs {i? l}
   hł=   ca?+sl+áqs
   group= Mosquito
   The Mosquito group was camped at...

2. ilí?   t'ík'ʷət
   ilí?   t'ik'ʷt
   there lake
   There is a lake there.

3. uł   ilí?   púlxəlx
   uł   ilí?   pul+x -lx
   and   there camp   -pl
   And they camped there.

4. uł   ixí?   cxʷuy   i? sy'al'wánk
   uł   ixí?   c+xʷuy i? s+y'al'w+ánk
   and   then   come art Cricket
   And then Cricket came.

5. uł   ałí?   ksλ'əxʷəntíməlx
   uł   ałí?   ks   -λ'xʷ   -nt -im   -lx
   and   so   futT^ -kill_many -nt -psv -pl
   And he was going to kill them all.

6. uł   ilí?   ukʷwíkʷmi?st   i?   sy'al'wánk   ixí? {i?}
   uł   ilí?   wkʷ+wíkʷ+mi?st i?   s+y'al'w+ánk ixí?
   and   there hide_self   art Cricket   that

   i? l t'ík'ʷət
   i? l t'ik'ʷt
   art in lake
   The Crickets hid there in the lake.

7. uł   axá?   i? tətw'ít i? ca?sláqs
   uł   axá?   i? t+tw'it i? ca?+sl+áqs
   and   this   art boy   art Mosquito
   And the little boy Mosquito,

8. cúsəlx   xʷuyx   nmulx
   cu -s   -lx xʷuy   -x   n+mul   -x
   tell -3erg -pl go   -isimptv   dip_water -isimptv
   they told him, "Go get some water."

9. ixí?   uł   xʷu··y   nmúləm   uł   ilí?   után
   ixí?   uł   xʷuy   n+mul -m   uł   ilí?   wtan
   then   and   go   dip_water mdl and there placed
   And he went and dipped the water, and put it there.

146

10. ckʷis   iʔ siwɬkʷ {kʷ c}
    c+kʷi   -s   iʔ siwɬ+kʷ
    take_cisl   -3erg art water
    He took the water,

11. xʷətʼílx {c} tiɬx
    xʷtʼ+ilx   tiɬ+x
    get_up   stand
    and he stood up straight.

12. axáʔ   iʔ l kʼíkʼaʔt   ki   cut
    axáʔ   iʔ l kʼí+kʼaʔt   kiʔ cut
    this   art in near   rel say
    And very near somebody said:

13. wayʼ kʷínti   kəmʼkmʼáx̌ənti,
    wayʼ kʷi -nt -y   kmʼ+kmʼ+ax̌n -t -y
    yes   take -nt -tpimptv grab_by_arms -nt -tpimptv

    wayʼ kʷínti   púlskʷi
    wayʼ kʷi -nt -y   pul -skʷy
    well take -nt -tpimptv kill_one-tpimptv
    "Take him, grab him by the arm, kill him."

14. səwʼswʼílx
    swʼ+swʼ+ilx
    whisper
    They were whispering.

15. ixíʔ ɬəɬxʷúˑ·ys   uɬ cus   iʔ ɬqəqáqcaʔs
    ixíʔ ɬ -ɬ+xʷuy -s uɬ cu -s   iʔ ɬ+q+qá+qc+aʔ -s
    that dur -go_back -3i and tell -3erg art elder_brothers -3in
    He went back and he told his big brothers:

16. wayʼ ilíʔ   ksqilxʷ
    wayʼ ilíʔ   k   -s+qilxʷ
    yes   there there_be -person
    "There are people there."

17. wayʼ scutx   kəmʼkmʼáx̌ənti
    wayʼ s   -cut -x   kmʼ+kmʼ+ax̌n -t -y
    yes   ipftv ^ -say - ^ ipftv grab_by_arms -nt -tpimptv

    púlskʷi
    pul -skʷy
    kill_one-tpimptv
    They were saying, "Grab him by the arm and kill him."

18. uɬ   cut iʔ   knaqs
    uɬ   cut iʔ   k+naqs
    and say art one_person
    And one said:

19. lut, nkʼʷayxáxaʔ
    lut   nkʼʷ+ʔayxáxaʔ
    not a_while
    "No, wait a while."

20. ixíʔ   cúntəm   iʔ   t   łqáqcaʔs   ha
    ixíʔ   cu -nt -m   iʔ   t   ł+qá+qcaʔ   -s   ha
    then   tell -nt -psv   art   aglnst   older_brother   -3in   inter

    kʷ   scənx̌ílx
    kʷ   sc   -n+x̌il   -x
    2kn ipftvp ^ -fear   - ^ ipftvp
    His older brother asked him, "Are you afraid,

21. ałíʔ   kiʔ   kʷ   ctan'məscín
    ałíʔ   kiʔ   kʷ   c -tanm's+cín
    because   rel   2kn   hab-idle_talk
    that you are talking nonsense?"

22. ixíʔ   sxʷuys   ixíʔ   iʔ   caʔsl'áqs   uł   nʔułxʷ {iʔ l}
    ixíʔ   s   -xʷuy -s   ixíʔ   iʔ   caʔ+sl'+áqs   uł   n+ʔułxʷ
    then   dur -go   -3i   that   art   Mosquito   and   enter

    iʔ   l   kʷílstən   ilíʔ
    iʔ   l   kʷils+tn   ilíʔ
    art   in   sweat_house   there
    So Mosquito went, and went into the sweat house there.

23. ixíʔ   sʔitxs
    ixíʔ   s   -ʔit+x   -s
    then   dur -sleep   -3i
    He went to sleep.

24. ixíʔ   mat   ʔitx   uł   cyaʕp   iʔ   sy'al'wánk
    ixíʔ   mat   ʔit+x   uł   c+yaʕ+p   iʔ   s+y'al'w+ánk
    then   maybe sleep   and   arrive_here art Cricket
    He slept and the Crickets came.

25. cyaʕp   uł   ixíʔ {pul}   λ'əxʷəntíməlx
    c+yaʕ+p   uł   ixíʔ   λ'xʷ   -nt -im   -lx
    arrive_here and   then   kill_many -nt -psv   -pl
    They got there and they killed them all.

26. púlstməlx   uł   c'sápəlx
    pul   -st -m   -lx   uł   c'sa+p   -lx
    kill_one-st -psv   -pl   and   gone   -pl
    They killed them, all gone.

27. kmax_k'im iʔ   tətw'ít   ixíʔ {iʔ l}   iʔ   l   kʷílstən
    kmax_k'm   iʔ   t+tw'it   ixíʔ   iʔ   l   kʷils+tn
    only   art boy   that   art   in   sweat_house

    aláʔ mut   ixíʔ   ilíʔ   cxʷəlxʷált
    aláʔ mut   ixíʔ   ilíʔ   c -xʷl+xʷal+t
    here   sit_sg that   there   hab-alive
    Only the little boy that was sitting in the sweat house is left alive.

28. ixíʔ   qiłt   nt'a··   c'sápəlx   λ'əxʷəntíməlx
    ixíʔ   qił+t   nt'a   c'sa+p -lx   λ'xʷ   -nt -im   -lx
    that   awaken   intj   gone   -pl   kill_many -nt -psv   -pl
    He woke up, gee, they're all gone, killed.

29. ixí? sxʷuys i? k'əl t'ík'ʷət uɬ ilí? i? c'í?stən
ixí? s -xʷuy -s i? k'l t'ik'ʷt uɬ ilí? i? c'i?s+tn
that dur -go -3i art to lake and there art weeds_sp
He went to the lake, and there there were those jointed weeds.

30. ixí? kʷis i? c'í?stən
ixí? kʷi -s i? c'i?s+tn
that take -3erg art weeds_sp
He took the jointed weeds,

31. uɬ xi? kt'l'íw'səs
uɬ ixí? k+t'l+iw's -s
and that split_lengthwise -3erg
and split them lengthwise.

32. uɬ ilí? mˤantís i? sx̌əx̌c'í?
uɬ ilí? maˤ -nt -is i? s+x̌+x̌c'i?
and there lie_on_ground -nt -3erg art stick
He stuck a stick there [to keep the weed open].

33. ixí? skɬmuts, ixí? s?úcləms
ixí? s -kɬ+mut -s ixí? s -?ucl+m -s
that dur -sit_sg_on -3i that dur -paddle -3i
He sat down in there, then he paddled.

34. xʷu·∙y, ixí? scuts u∙∙lalá t inqaqí∙∙c
xʷuy ixí? s -cut -s ulalá t in-qa+qíc
go then dur -say -3i onom ? 1in -brothers

kʷu qalutá∙∙nkɬts i? t xəmáˤmləxqən
kʷu qal+wt+ánk -ɬt -s i? t xmaˤmlx+qn
1kʷu step_on_belly -ɬt -3erg art ? ?
He went, he said [sang]: "Oh my brothers, the Crickets stepped on my belly.

35. u∙∙lalá t inqaqí∙∙c kʷu qalutá∙∙nkɬts
ulalá t in -qa+qíc kʷu qal+wt+ánk -ɬt -s
onom ? 1in -brothers 1kʷu step_on_belly -ɬt -3erg

i? t xəmáˤmləxqən
i? t xmaˤmlx+qn
art ? ?
Oh my brothers the Crickets stepped on my belly."

36. ixí? təl' wíw'a?st uɬ {c} ckicx {i? t ix} i? tkəɬmílxʷ
ixí? tl' w'í+w'a?st uɬ c+kic+x i? tkɬmilxʷ
that from high_dim and arrive_cisl art woman
From the top of the hill came a woman.

37. cut ca?slá∙∙qs, ca?slá∙∙qs, cxʷuyx ak'lá?
cut ca?sl+áqs ca?sl+áqs c+xʷuy -x ak'lá?
say Mosquito Mosquito come -isimptv here
She said, "Mosquito, Mosquito, come here.

38. way' kʷ iks?amnám t
way' kʷ i -k+s -?amná -m t
yes 2kʷu i_ -futT^ -feed -^futT obj_itr

mm'átk'yaʔ
m+m'átk'yaʔ
blood_pudding
I am going to feed you some blood pudding.

39. ixíʔ   ik'líʔ   sxʷu··ys   uɬ   ʕacəntís   iʔ   stáɬəms
    ixíʔ   ik'líʔ   s -xʷuy -s uɬ   ʕac -nt -is   iʔ   s+taɬm -s
    that   there   dur -go   -3i and tie -nt -3erg   art boat   -3in
    He went there and tied his boat,

40. uɬ   ixíʔ {st}   sx̌íƛ'əms   ik'líʔ
    uɬ   ixíʔ   s -x̌iƛ'+m -s   ik'líʔ
    and   that   dur -climb -3i   there
    and climbed the hill.

41. {t} xáʔ   cus   iʔ   ɬsísəncaʔs   ixíʔ   iʔ
        axáʔ   cu -s   iʔ   ɬ+sí+sncaʔ   -s   ixíʔ   iʔ
        this   tell -3erg art younger_bro   -3in that   art

    tkəɬmílxʷ
    tkɬmilxʷ
    woman
    This woman told the younger brother:

42. xʷuyx   mi {n} nutənúlaʔxʷəntxʷ   yaʔ {a}
    xʷuy   -x   mi   n+wtn+úlaʔxʷ -nt -xʷ   iʔ
    go   -isimptv fut   put_in_ground -nt -2erg   art

    cxʷəƛ'xʷáƛ'   a   nƛ'əmƛ'máqs {iʔ i} iʔ   sútən   iʔ
    c -xʷƛ'+xʷaƛ'   a   n+ƛ'm+ƛ'm+aqs   iʔ   sutn   iʔ
    hab-whittle   art sharp_point   art thing   art

    slip'
    s+lip'
    fire_wood
    "Go and put in the ground these sticks that are whittled to a sharp end,
    the whatchamacall it, the wood.

43. ilíʔ   nqəx̌qx̌úlaʔxʷəntxʷ   məɬ k'ʷixʷɬtxʷ
    ilíʔ   n+qx̌+qx̌+úlaʔxʷ -nt -xʷ   mɬ k'ʷixʷ -ɬt -xʷ
    there   drive_in_ground   -nt -2erg and untie   -ɬt -2erg
    Drive them into the ground, and untie his [boat].

44. n'ín'w'iʔ   ʔí··ɬən   məɬ   k'ʷíxʷəɬtxʷ   iʔ   stáɬəm
    n'ín'w'iʔ   ʔiɬn   mɬ   k'ʷixʷ -ɬt -xʷ   iʔ   s+taɬm
    a_while,   eat   and   untie   -ɬt -2erg   art boat
    While he is eating you untie the boat."

45. ixíʔ   sxʷuys   iʔ   tətw'ít   uɬ
    ixíʔ   s -xʷuy -s   iʔ   t+tw'it   uɬ
    that   dur -go   -3i   art boy   and

    nqəx̌qx̌ú··laʔxʷs   iʔ   xəxw'íɬ
    n+qx̌+qx̌+úlaʔxʷ -s   iʔ   x+xw'iɬ
    drive_in_ground -3erg   art trail_dim
    The boy went and drove the stick in the little trail.

46. ixí? uɬ kʷ'ixʷs i? stáɬəm
    ixí? uɬ kʷ'ixʷ -s i? s+taɬm
    that and untie -3erg art boat
    He untied his boat.

47. uɬ axá? i·· cqəɬtím i? yámx̌ʷa? i?
    uɬ axá? i·· cq -ɬt -im i? yámx̌ʷa? i?
    and this intj place_down -ɬt -psv art basket art

    t mmátk'ya?
    t m+mátk'ya?
    ? blood_pudding
    And he put down the basket with the blood pudding.

48. uɬ ?í··ɬən, uɬ itlí? naqs cqəɬtím
    uɬ ?iɬn uɬ itlí? naqs cq -ɬt -im
    and eat and from_there one place_down -ɬt -psv
    And he ate it, and he set down another one.

49. itlí? ?i··ɬs, ní··kxna? way' uɬ mq'ink {uɬ}
    itlí? ?iɬ -s níkxna? way' uɬ mq'+ink
    from_there eat -3erg goodness yes until satiated
    He ate it, gee, he was full to a busting point.

50. cut níkna? sl'ax̌t astáɬəm way' uɬ kʷ'íxʷəxʷ
    cut níkxna? s+l'ax̌t a -s+taɬm way' uɬ kʷ'ixʷ+xʷ
    say goodness partner 2in -boat yes and untied
    He said, "Gee, partner, your boat came untied."

51. nt'a xi? sɬəx̌ʷp'áms ki? s?uckl'ípəms
    nt'a ixí? s -ɬx̌ʷp'a+m -s ki? s -?uckl'+íp+m -s
    intj that dur -run_out -3i rel dur -run_downhill -3i
    Gee he ran out of there and ran down the hill.

52. ixí? {a} a cənλ'əmλ'máqs{i?} ilí?
    ixí? a c -n+λ'm+λ'm+aqs ilí?
    that art hab-sharp_point there

    cənututnúla?xʷ
    c -n+wt+wtn+úla?xʷ
    hab-stuck_in_ground
    Those sharp sticks, they were stuck in the ground.

53. ixí? tr'qəntís ki? t'k'ʷakʷ ixí? {k p}
    ixí? tr'+q -nt -is ki? t'k'ʷ+akʷ ixí?
    that kick -nt -3erg rel land_flat that

    kɬəw'ɬəw'íw's uɬ λ'lal
    k+ɬw'+ɬw'+iw's uɬ λ'l+al
    poked_in_middle and dead
    He kicked him, he fell down, his body got poked, and he died.

54. t'i x̌ʕa··m {i? i?} i? ca?sláqs itlí? t'uxʷt
    t'i? x̌aʕ+m i? ca?+sl+áqs itlí? t'uxʷ+t
    evid hum art Mosquito from_there fly
    Mosquito hummed, flew from there.

55. cúntəm   n'ín'w'i?   t'ala?xwílx   i?   sqilx"
    cu -nt -m   n'ín'w'i?   t'ala?x+wílx   i?   s+qilx"
    tell -nt -psv a_while,   next_generation   art person
    He said, "When the next generation of people comes,

56. ałí?   lut   k"   t'a   n?ałna?sqílx"tən
    ałí?   lut   k"   t'   n+?ałn+a?+s+qílx"+tn
    so   not   2kn   negfac man_eater
    you won't be a man-eater.

57. kmax   n'ín'w'i?   c'ał?íłstx" {i?}   i?
    kmax   n'ín'w'i?   c   -?ał+?íł -st   -x"   i?
    only   a_while,   cust ^ -eat_pl - ^cust -2erg   art

    xi?míx_swit
    xi?míx_s+wit
    anybody
    You'll only bite any which critter."

58. [nc'ayx"ápəlqs]
    n+c'ayx"+áplqs
    end_of_story
    End of story.

a

a *intj.* In CR 49.

a (aˀ). *art.* In SF 89, CMB 16, GU 31, M 42.

a- *2i*. In CN 12, CMB 22, CR 35, GU 35.

a- (an-). *2in*. In CN 12, CMB 51, CE 37, CR 40, GU 75, M 50.

ah *intj.* In GU 255.

ak'láˀ *here.* In SF 120, CN 46, FC 8, CMB 75, CE 26, CR 10, GU 126, M 37.

alalalala *onom.* In CN 55.

aláˀ (√lˀ). *here.* In SF 76, CN 23, CMB 29, CE 62, CR 35, GU 70, M 27.

ałíˀ *because, so.* In SF 27, CN 33, FC 3, CMB 2, CE 53, CR 80, GU 41, M 5.

an- *2in*. In SF 62, CN 12, CE 44, CR 18.

anwí (√nw). *you.* In SF 40, CE 12, CR 93, GU 158.

atáˀ *this, here.* In FC 8, CMB 12, CR 98, GU 184.

atláˀ *from here.* In CMB 40.

awá *onom.* In GU 98.

awáˤ *onom.* In GU 68.

axáˀ *this.* In SF 14, CN 15, FC 4, CMB 4, CR 28, GU 3, M 7.

-aˤm (-m). *psv.* In SF 119.

-aˤs (-is). *3erg.* In SF 59, CR 87.

aˀ *art.* In CE 72, CR 32.

-aˀx *^incp.* In SF 4, CN 8, FC 23, CMB 21, CR 21, GU 39.

c

c- *cust^.* In SF 25, CN 4, FC 40, CMB 14, CE 10, GU 9, M 57.

c- *gpat.* In SF 76.

c- *hab.* In SF 1, CN 1, FC 1, CMB 1, CE 1, CR 1, GU 2, M 21.

-c (-s). *3i*. In SF 6, CN 60, CR 66, GU 181.

-c (-s). *3in*. In SF 3, CR 69, GU 92.

ca+ca+cáˤ (√cˤ). *holler.* In CE 55, GU 260.

ca+cáˤyp+m (√cˤyp). *cry.* In CE 33.

caˤʷ+lx (√cˤʷ). *bathe.* In FC 5.

caˀkʷ *should, if, would, could, as.* In CMB 126, GU 208.

caˀ+sl(')+áqs (√cˀ, √sl(')). *Mosquito.* In M 1.

c+cám'+aˀ+t (√cm'). *small.* In CE 41.

c+cw'íxaˀ (√cwx). *little creek.* In CE 10, CR 102.

citxʷ (√ctxʷ). *house.* In SF 44, CN 92, CMB 103, CE 42, GU 90.

ciˀ (√cˀ). *stop.* In CN 56.

c+kic+x (√kc). *arrive cisl.* In FC 11, CR 42, GU 120, M 36.

c+km' (√km'). *take cisl.* In SF 32, FC 28.

c+km'a (√km'). *take cisl.* In SF 93.

c+km'+km'+ax̌ (√km'). *take cisl.* In CN 92.

c+k+ʕax̌+íc'aʔ (√ʕx̌). *lace cisl.* In GU 96.

c+k+ʔwt+ímaʔtk (√ʔwt) *below cisl.* In In CMB 41.

c+k'aʔít+t (√k't). *get near cisl.* In CN 47.

c+k'laʔ *later, this way.* In CN 84.

c+k'ɬ+pxʷ+puxʷ (√pxʷ). *breathe on cisl.* In GU 40.

c+k'ɬ+ʔuɬxʷ (√ʔɬxʷ). *go under cisl.* In GU 144.

ckʷ+aks (√ckʷ). *drag.* In CN 92.

c+kʷi (√kʷn). *take cisl.* In CN 54, CR 32, GU 193, M 10.

c+kʷin (√kʷn). *take cisl.* In CR 72, GU 298.

c+k'ʷilk' (k'ʷlk'). *rolling cisl.* In CMB 42.

c+ɬx̌ʷp'a+m (√ɬx̌ʷp'). *run out cisl.* In GU 190.

c+maqʷ (√mqʷ). *mountain.* In CMB 80.

cmay *maybe.* In GU 232.

cm' *maybe.* In SF 110, CMB 22, CR 94, GU 151.

c+m'+m'aqʷ (√mqʷ). *hillock.* In CMB 11.

cniɬ+c (√cnɬ). *(s)he.* In CN 57, GU 207.

c+n+ɬx̌ʷp'a+m (√ɬx̌ʷp'). *run in cisl.* In GU 161.

c+n+wt (√wt). *put in cisl.* In CR 87.

c+n+yʔakʷ (√ykʷ). *cross cisl.* In GU 51.

c+n+ʔacqʔ+úlaʔxʷ (√ʔcqʔ). *crawl out of ground.* In CMB 119.

c+n+ʔuɬxʷ (√ʔɬxʷ). *enter cisl.* In CN 48, CE 59, GU 151.

cq (√cq). *place down.* In M 47.

cq+q+ink (√cq). *fall on back.* In CN 55.

crq+mncut (√crq). *jump.* In CN 82.

cr't+ups (√cr't). *Fisher.* In SF 4.

c+sax̌ʷ+t (√sx̌ʷ). *go downhill cisl.* In CR 19.

c+tixʷ (√txʷ). *obtain cisl.* In CR 84.

c+t'akʷ (√t'kʷ). *lay cisl.* In CE 89.

c+t'l+s+qilxʷ (√t'l, √qlxʷ). *come to life cisl.* In GU 133.

c+t'uxʷt (√t'xʷt). *fly cisl.* In CE 84.

cu (√cn). *tell.* In SF 3, CN 10, FC 24, CMB 20, CE 12, CR 34, GU 2, M 8.

cun (√cn). *tell.* In GU 13.

cut (√ct). *say.* In SF 20, CN 7, FC 4, CE 6, CR 4, M 12.

cw+caʕw+lx (√cʕw). *bathe.* In GU 292.

cwix (√(c)wx). *live.* In CE 51.

c+xy'+wilx (√xy'). *travel cisl.* In GU 239.

c+xʔit (√xʔt). *first.* In GU 169.

c+xʷt'+p+ncut (√xʷt') *run cisl.* In CMB 74, GU 69.

c+xʷuy (√xʷy). *come.* In SF 13, CMB 86, CE 26, CR 11, GU 65, M 4.

c+xʷuy+a+xʷúy (√xʷy). *come.* In SF 116.

c+x̌lit (√x̌lt). *call cisl.* In GU 273.

c+yaxʷ+t (√yxʷ). *fall cisl.* In
SF 60.

c+ya+yúxʷt (√yxʷ). *fall cisl.* In
SF 116.

c+yaˤ (√yˤ). *all.* In SF 109, CN
70, FC 35, GU 102.

c+yaˤ+p (√yˤ). *arrive here pl.*
In M 24.

c+yaˤ' (√yˤ'). *lots.* In SF 51,
CE 52.

c+ʔácqaʔ (√ʔcqʔ), *go out cisl.*
In GU 271.

c+ʔx̌ił+t (√ʔx̌ł). *like.* In CMB 6,
CR 103, GU 278.

c'

c'ar (√c'r). *onom.* In CN 36.

c'asy(')+qn (√c'sy(')). *head.*
In CMB 52, CR 18.

c'aw+t (√c'w). *extinguish.* In
GU 43.

c'axknáˤlaʔk' (√ʔkn). *do
what.* In GU 174.

c'áyx̌aʔ (√c'yx̌ʔ). *crayfish.* In
GU 247.

c'aʔkn+álaʔk (√ʔkn). *matter.*
In GU 125.

c'aʔxkín (√ʔkn). *do what.* In
GU 174.

c'ər (√c'r). *onom.* In CN 79.

c'iqʷ (√c'qʷ). *skin, butcher.* In
GU 9.

c'iʔs+tn (√c'ʔs). *weeds sp.* In
M 29.

c'l+c'al (√c'l). *trees.* In CR 10.

c'l+c'l+qin+xn+m (√c'l). *stick
legs up.* In SF 22.

c'l+c'lx+w'+aqst+xn (√c'lx).
scratch thigh. In CMB 74.

c'lx (√c'lx). *hook.* In SF 90, CR
23.

c'm'+c'um' (√c'm'). *suck.* In
CR 25.

c'nk' (√c'nk'). *dip finger.* In
GU 59.

c'q'+iln (√c'q'). *arrow.* In CMB
27, GU 303.

c'q'+m (√c'q'). *throw.* In CMB
50.

c'q'+mi (√c'q'). *throw.* In SF
30, CE 56, CR 9, GU 126.

c'qʷ+aqʷ (√c'qʷ). *cry.* In SF
52, CMB 24, CE 33, CR 67,
GU 104.

c'qʷ+c'qʷ+aqʷ (√c'qʷ). *cry pl.*
In GU 35.

c'r (√c'r). *onom.* In CN 79.

c'ris (√c'rs). *Kingfisher.* In CN
30.

c'sa+p (√c's). *gone, dry.* In FC
15, M 26.

c'sqáq+naʔ (√c'sq).
Chickadee. In SF 103.

c'um (√c'm). *suck.* In CN 23.

c'wak (√c'wk). *burn.* In CR 94.

c'yslin (√c'ysln). *place name.*
In CR 111.

c'+ʔ+ax (√c'x). *shame inch.* In
CMB 127.

h

ha *intj.* In SF 86, CR 49, M 20.

hahá *intj.* In CR 13.

hł= *group.* In SF 103, CR 1, GU
101, M 1.

hm *onom.* In CR 109.

hoy (√hy). *well, finish.* In SF
20, FC 15, CR 93, GU 65.

i

i- *1i.* In SF 29, CMB 35, GU 215.

i- *1in*. In SF 25, CN 8, CR 12, GU 128, M 35.

ik'líʔ *there, be there, to there*. In SF 7, FC 5, CMB 46, CE 24, CR 7, GU 10, M 39.

ilíʔ (√lʔ). *there*. In SF 8, CN 17, FC 2, CMB 15, CE 25, CR 21, GU 9, M 1.

-im ^*3e4obj*. In SF 41, GU 54.

-im *4erg*. In GU 221.

-im *psv*. In CN 17, CMB 46, CE 5, CR 23, GU 108, M 5.

in- *1in*. In SF 25, CN 8, GU 189, M 34.

-in *1erg*. In CN 4, CMB 126, CE 100, CR 82, GU 152.

incá (√nc). *I*. In CE 77, CR 103, GU 34.

incá kn *I*. In GU 171.

-ip *5erg*. In SF 113, GU 73.

-is *3erg*. In SF 32, CN 21, FC 28, CMB 15, CE 2, CR 64, GU 18, M 53.

itíʔ *that, from that*. In SF 103, CMB 16, CE 5, GU 46.

itlíʔ *from there*. In SF 5, CN 22, FC 11, CMB 41, CE 16, CR 18, GU 47, M 48.

ix+íxiʔ (√xʔ). *in a while*. In CN 37, FC 12, GU 103.

ixíʔ *that, then, there*. In SF 2, CN 2, FC 4, CMB 3, CE 11, CR 2, GU 2, M 1.

-ixʷ *2erg*. In CMB 29.

iʔ *art*. In SF 1, CN 1, FC 1, CMB 1, CE 1, CR 1, GU 1, M 1.

-iʔ (**-m**). ^*futT*. In GU 148.

k

k- (kɬ-). *there be, have*. In SF 2, CN 4, FC 7, CMB 6, CE 72, CR 13, GU 109, M 16.

k- (kɬ-). *to be*. In SF 114, CMB 35, CE 37, CR 40, GU 301.

k- (ks-). *futT*^. In GU 148.

k (ks-). *incp*^. In CR 21, CMB 68.

ka *rel*. In FC 40, GU 85.

kas+lipx̌ʷ+x̌ʷ+x̌ʷ+x̌ʷ (√lpx̌ʷ). *slip in*. In CE 3.

kaʔ+kíc (√kc). *find*. In CE 10, GU 220.

k+ckʷ+íc'aʔ (√ckʷ). *pull cover off*. In CMB 47.

k+c'ík'+naʔ (√c'k'). *set on fire*. In CR 83.

k+c'xʷ+ínaʔ (√c'xʷ). *pour on*. In GU 193.

ki (kiw). *yes*. In CN 95.

kic+x (√kc). *arrive*. In CN 10, FC 24, CMB 7, CE 43, GU 83.

kil (√kl). *chase*. In CMB 70.

kilx (√klx). *hand, arm*. In SF 85, CR 52.

kiw *yes*. In SF 68, FC 3, CMB 19, GU 309.

kiʔ *rel*. In SF 30, CN 64, CMB 61, CE 31, CR 23, GU 45, M 12.

k+kw'ápaʔ (√kw). *dog*. In CMB 114.

kl+kil'+l+x (√klx). *hands*. In CR 25.

k+lk'+íc'aʔ (√lk'). *wrap*. In FC 28.

kl'+kil'+lx (√klx). *hands dim*. In CR 68, GU 214.

kɬ- *there be, have*. In CN 71, CMB 94.

kɬ- *to be*. In GU 75.

kɬ- (ks-). *futI*. In CR 75.

k+ɬaʔ+ɬaʔ+qí (√ɬʔ). *lean on*. In CMB 30.

kɬ+mut (√mt). *sit sg on*. In M 33.

kɬ+pkʷ (√pkʷ). *put down*. In CN 39.

kɬ+qmi (√qm). *lay st down*. In CN 99.

kɬ+tr'q+íkiʔ (√trq). *kick ice*. In CN 98.

kɬ+t'k'ʷ+ikn' (√t'k'ʷ). *lie on ice*. In CN 91.

kɬ+t'k'ʷ+k'ʷ+ikn' (√t'k'ʷ). *fall on ice*. In CN 82.

kɬ+wtan (√wtn). *lie on*. In CN 103.

k+ɬw'+ɬw'+iw's (√ɬw'). *poked in middle*. In M 53.

k+ɬx̌ʷp (√ɬx̌ʷp). *hang up*. In CMB 57.

kmax *only*. In SF 80, CN 42, FC 2, CMB 38, CE 60, CR 113, GU 59, M 57.

kmax k'am *only*. In GU 114.

kmax k'im *only*. In M 27.

k+mus+ms (√ms). *four persons*. In CN 3, CMB 2, GU 155.

km' *or*. In SF 22.

km' (√km'). *take*. In SF 17, CN 44, FC 28, CMB 37, CE 2, GU 18.

km'a (√km'). *take*. In SF 93, CN 99.

km'+km'+ax̌ (√km'). *grab pl by arms*. In CN 92, GU 257.

km'+km'+ax̌n (√km'). *grab by arms*. In M 13.

kn *1kn*. In SF 20, CN 8, FC 36, CMB 21, CE 13, CR 13, GU 34.

knaqs (√nqs). *one person*. In SF 107, FC 11, CMB 3, GU 157, M 18.

k+naqs+mísaʔt (√nqs). *alone*. In SF 27.

k+naqs+ús (√nqs). *one berry*. In CR 4.

k+nm'+qin (√knm'). *blind*. In CE 7.

kn+xit (√kn). *help*. In CN 37.

kp' (√kp'). *place on*. In CMB 58.

k+p'n+ína? (√p'n). *put on*. In CR 88.

k+p'w'+qi (√p'w'). *shit on*. In CE 68.

ks- *futI*. In CMB 22, CR 35, GU 13.

ks- *futT^*. In SF 35, CN 12, CE 64, GU 221, M 5.

ks- (ks-). *incp^*. In SF 4, CN 8, FC 23, CMB 21, CE 54, CR 101, GU 39.

ks+c- (ks-c). *futCust*. In FC 40.

ksc- (ksc-). *furPerf*. In GU 150.

k+stim' (√tm'). *do what*. In FC 23.

k+tɬ+tɬp+ína? (√tɬ). *braids*. In FC 18.

k+tm'+alxʷ (√tm'). *strip*. In GU 107.

k+t'l+iw's (√t'l). *split lengthwise*. In M 31.

k+wl+l+ína? (√wl). *cover*. In CR 18.

k+wt+wtan (√wt). *put on.* In
CMB 27.

kxna (√kxn). *go along.* In GU
70.

k+ʕax̌+íc'aʔ (√ʕx̌). *lacing.* In
GU 96.

k+ʔam+m+t+iw's (√ʔmt).
perched. In CR 37.

k+ʔamt+álqʷ (√ʔmt). *sit on
log.* In GU 87.

k+ʔwt+ímaʔtk (√ʔwt). *below.*
In CMB 41.

k'

k' *to.* In SF 40, CN 8, FC 36,
CMB 11, CE 2, GU 51.

k'aɬáɬxaʔ (√k'ɬx̌ʔ). *a ways.* In
SF 77.

k'aɬáʔ (√k'ɬʔ). *on that side.* In
SF 46, FC 206, GU 231.

k'am *except.* In SF 92, CMB 23.

k'aw (√k'w). *gone, not there.* In
SF 80, CMB 17, CE 45, GU
30.

k'aw+cn (√k'w). *stop talking.*
In FC 30.

k'aʔít+t (√k't). *get near.* In CN
47, CE 15.

k'aʔ+kín' (√kn'). *how, where
to.* In SF 62, FC 25, CE 29,
CR 107.

k'aʔ+x̌ís (√x̌s). *over there.* In
SF 10, CN 23, CE 80, CR 23,
GU 26.

k'í+k'aʔt (√k't). *near.* In CN
34, M 12.

k'i+k'm (√k'm). *nearly, soon.*
In CE 86.

k'ip' (√k'p'). *pinch.* In SF 76.

k'iwlx (√k'w). *old.* In GU 228.

k'+k'níyaʔ (√k'nyʔ). *listen.* In
CMB 115, GU 172.

k'+ɬq'+ilx (√ɬq'). *flap, lay
under.* In GU 164.

k'l *to, for, on, about, at, until.* In
SF 4, CN 8, FC 6, CMB 5,
CE 9, CR 29, GU 4, M 29.

k'laxʷ (√k'lxʷ). *evening.* In GU
213.

k'l+k'lk+íc'aʔ (√k'lk). *bundle.*
In FC 9.

k'ɬ+c'q'+mi (√c'q'). *throw.* In
SF 84.

k'ɬ+kc'+ikst (√kc'). *?* In SF 15.

k'ɬ+kʷl+iwt (√kʷl). *sit pl
under.* In SF 16.

k'ɬ+mut (√mt). *sit sg.* In SF 38.

k'ɬ+nik' (√nk'). *cut out.* In SF
131, CN 15.

k'ɬ+n+k'ahkʷ+íp (√k'hkʷ).
open. In CR 46.

k'ɬ+p+pilx (√plx). *enter under.*
In SF 21.

k'ɬ+p+pil'+x (√plx). *crawl
under.* In SF 12.

k'ɬ+pxʷ+puxʷ (√pxʷ). *breathe
on.* In GU 40.

k'ɬ+q'aʔ (√q'ʔ). *stick in.* In
CMB 26.

k'+ɬq'+ilx (√ɬq'). *lie under.* In
GU 164.

k'ɬ+q'ʔ+alqs (√q'ʔ). *stick
under clothes.* In CE 65.

k'ɬ+q'ʔ+ax̌n (√q'ʔ). *stick under
arm.* In CMB 52.

k'ɬ+tkʷip+c'aʔ (√tkʷp). *set
fire.* In SF 44.

k'ɬ+t'akʷ (√t'kʷ). *lay under.* In
SF 125.

k'ɬ+x̌ʷil+l (√x̌ʷl). *lots.* In FC 2.

k'ɬ+ʔác+c+qaʔ (√ʔcqʔ). *exit from under*. In SF 42.

k'ɬ+ʔamt+íp (√ʔmt). *sit by door*. In CMB 106.

k'ɬ+ʔim (√ʔim). *wait for*. In CN 87.

k'ɬ+ʔuɬxʷ (√ʔɬxʷ). *go under*. In GU 37.

k'm *except*. In GU 28.

k'm kmax *only*. In GU 31.

k'ma+p (√k'mp). *dark*. In GU 213.

k'ra+m (√k'r). *swim*. In CMB 53, GU 264.

k'r+k'ra+m (√k'r). *swim*. In GU 306.

k's+us (√k's). *ugly*. In FC 19.

k'wa+p (√k'w). *quiet*. In GU 103.

k'w+p (√k'w). *stop talking*. In GU 99.

k'y'l+ilxʷ (√k'y'l). *tree bark*. In CMB 15.

kʷ

kʷ *2kn*. In CMB 23, CE 12, CR 35, GU 70, M 20.

kʷ *2kʷu*. In SF 25, CMB 77, CR 12, M 38.

kʷára *onom*. In FC 36.

kʷi (√kʷn). *take*. In SF 30, CN 15, FC 32, CMB 56, CR 86, GU 90, M 13.

kʷils+tn (√kʷls). *sweat house*. In M 22.

kʷin (√kʷn). *take*. In CMB 51, CR 18, GU 3.

kʷl+iwt (√kʷl). *live, dwell, sit pl, be home*. In SF 99, CN 7, FC 2, CMB 83.

kʷl+kʷil (√kʷl). *red*. In CE 39.

kʷƛ'up *onom*. In CMB 64.

kʷm'iɬ *suddenly*. In CE 84, GU 93.

kʷn (√kʷn). *take, receive*. In CE 66, GU 170.

kʷni (√kʷn). *buy, take*. In CE 54.

kʷn+ikst+m (√kʷn). *abuse*. In CN 56.

kʷni+m (√kʷn). *take*. In FC 39, CR 69.

kʷriʔ (√kʷrʔ). *yellow*. In CN 93.

kʷr+xan (√kʷr). *Crane*. In FC 33.

kʷu *1kʷu*. In CMB 35, GU 70, M 34.

kʷu *1obj*. In CMB 129, GU 131.

kʷu *4kn*. In SF 40, CN 64, CMB 68, GU 62.

kʷu *4obj*. In SF 41, GU 54.

kʷuk *do service*. In GU 197.

kʼʷ

kʼʷaʔ+kʼʷúl' (√kʼʷl'). *work*. In SF 25.

kʼʷilk' (√kʼʷlk'). *rolling*. In CMB 42.

kʼʷiƛ'+t (√kʼʷƛ'). *rest, others*. In CN 41, CMB 27, GU 139.

kʼʷixʷ (√kʼʷxʷ). *untie*. In M 43.

kʼʷixʷ+xʷ (√kʼʷxʷ). *untied*. In M 50.

kʼʷ+kʼʷínaʔ (√kʼʷnʔ). *small*. In CN 72, FC 2.

kʼʷ+kʼʷy+úmaʔ (√kʼʷy). *small*. In GU 138, SF 64.

kʼʷlk'+lwis (√kʼʷlk'). *roll around*. In GU 267, SF 20.

kʼʷlʼ+cn+cut (√kʼʷlʼ). *cook.* In SF 24, CN 18, CMB 131, GU 56.

kʼʷn+kʼʷin (√kʼʷn). *study.* In SF 106.

kʼʷnx+asqʼt (√kʼʷnx). *a few days.* In GU 129.

kʼʷnʼ+ásaʔqʼt (√kʼʷn). *a few days.* In CN 29.

kʼʷulʼ (√kʼʷlʼ). *work, make, do, fix, train, practice, treat.* In CN 65, CMB 14, CE 37, CR 69.

kʼʷulʼ+cn+m (√kʼʷlʼ). *cook.* In CN 76.

kʼʷulʼ+lʼ t (√kʼʷlʼ). *turn into.* In CMB 73, GU 279.

kʼʷulʼ+m (√kʼʷlʼ). *build, work, use.* In CMB 82.

kʼʷʔ+ap+q (√kʼʷʔ). *bite head.* In CMB 13.

kʼʷʔ+ap+qn (√kʼʷʔ). *bite head.* In CMB 126.

l

l *in, on, at, for, with.* In SF 36, CN 18, CMB 26, CE 42, GU 31, M 1.

la c+ʔiw+t (√ʔwt). *last time.* In GU 170.

laqʼís (√lqʼ). *cut off.* In SF 128.

láqʷ+miʔst (√lqʷ). *lay about.* In CE 92, GU 130.

laʔ (√lʔ). *peck.* In GU 146.

laʔ+kín (√kn). *when, whenever, wherever, how, from time to time, sometime.* In GU 138.

laʔ+kínʼ (√knʼ). *whenever.* In CR 79.

laʔɬ *and, with.* In SF 2.

lipx̌ʷ (√lpx̌ʷ). *slip in.* In CE 3.

lipx̌ʷ+x̌ʷ+x̌ʷ (√lpx̌ʷ). *slip in.* In CE 6.

lkip (√lkp). *pit cook.* In CMB 83.

lkʼ (√lkʼ). *tie.* In CN 72.

lkʷ+akʷ (√lkʷ). *far.* In GU 223.

lkʷ+ilx (√lkʷ). *leave.* In CMB 110, CR 66, GU 25.

lkʷut (√lkʷ). *far.* In SF 5, CN 81.

lu *onom.* In SF 31.

lut (√lt). *not.* In SF 5, CN 4, FC 2, CMB 22, CE 10, CR 13, GU 12, M 19.

lut cmay (√lt). *everywhere, every which way.* In GU 20.

lut nixʷ (√lt). *no more.* In CR 75.

lut pnʼ+kinʼ (√lt, √knʼ). *never.* In GU 13.

lut s+timʼ (√lt, √tmʼ). *nothing.* In SF 50, CE 6, GU 30.

lut swit (√lt, √wt). *nobody.* In GU 136.

lut+st (√lt). *refuse.* In FC 16.

-lx *pl.* In SF 7, CN 2, FC 2, CMB 5, CE 45, CR 1, GU 1, M 1.

lʔiw (√lʔw). *m's father.* In CN 37, CE 44, CMB 20, GU 100.

ɬ

ɬ- *dur.* In CN 27, CMB 48, GU 176, M 15.

ɬ- (s-). *inten.* In SF 29, CN 59.

ɬ (ɬaʔ). *if, when.* In CN 44.

ɬ (ɬaʔ). *one that.* In CR 109.

ɬ *subord.* In SF 40, FC 32.

ɬax̌ʷ (√ɬx̌ʷ). *hole.* In GU 36.

ɬaʔ *if, when.* In GU 2.

ɬaʔ *one that.* In CMB 133, GU 32.

ɬaʔt'p+mncut (√ɬt'p). *jump around.* In CR 92.

ɬ+c+cʔ+ups (√cʔ). *younger sister.* In GU 65.

ɬ+c+kic+x (√kc). *arrive cisl again.* SF 23, GU 237.

ɬ+c+km' (√km'). *take back cisl.* In GU 203.

ɬ+c+n+lipx̌ʷ (√lpx̌ʷ). *slip in cisl again.* In CE 4.

ɬ+c+n+yʔakʷ (√ykʷ). *cross cisl again.* In GU 250.

ɬ+c+xy'+wilx (√xy'). *travel cisl again.* In GU 250.

ɬ+c+xʷuy (√xʷy). *come again.* In GU 166.

ɬ+c+yaˤ+p (√yˤ). *arrive here again pl.* In CE 72.

ɬ+c+ʔácqaʔ (√ʔcqʔ), *come out again.* In GU 271.

ɬ+c+ʔimx (√ʔmx). *move back cisl.* In GU 208.

ɬc'+apɬ+x̌n+m (√ɬc'). *hit with wing.* In CE 77.

ɬix̌ʷ+p+t (√ɬx̌ʷ). *slipped away.* In SF 123.

ɬk+cin (√ɬk). *bowl.* In CN 18.

ɬ+kic+x (√kc). *arrive again.* In SF 50, GU 154.

ɬ+kí+kxaʔ (√kxʔ). *older sister.* In GU 53.

ɬ+k'l'+l+ilx (√k'l). *hide again.* In CE 75.

ɬ+kʷi (√kʷn). *take again.* In SF 107.

ɬ+kʷ+kʷaˤst (√kʷˤst). *early morning.* In GU 250.

ɬ+kʷn (√kʷn). *take again.* In GU 170.

ɬ+kʷum (√kʷm). *store again.* In GU 203.

ɬ+ɬaxʷ (√ɬxʷ). *dress.* In CMB 90.

-ɬm (-ɬulm) *5obj.* In GU 33.

ɬ+maˤʷ (√mˤʷ) *break again.* In GU 95.

ɬ+nis (√ns). *gone again.* In CN 60, FC 10, GU 181.

ɬ+n+ɬx̌ʷp'a+m (√ɬx̌ʷp'). *run back in.* In GU 192.

ɬ+nyʔakʷ (√ykʷ). *cross again.* In CMB 49, GU 240.

ɬ+n+ʔuɬxʷ (√ʔɬxʷ). *enter again.* In CE 58.

ɬ+pix̌+m (√px̌). *hunt again.* In SF 29, GU 207.

ɬ+qá+qcaʔ (√qcʔ). *older brother.* In CN 8, CE 90, M 20.

ɬq+mi (√ɬq). *put.* In CE 49.

ɬ+q+qá+qc+aʔ (√qcʔ). *elder brothers.* In M 15.

ɬq'+ilx (√ɬq'). *lie.* In CE 95.

ɬ+qʷl'+íw'm (√qʷl'). *berry pick again.* In CR 75.

ɬ+sí+sncaʔ (√sncʔ). *younger bro.* In M 41.

-ɬt *ɬt.* In SF 131, CN 15, FC 10, CMB 21, CE 5, CR 24, GU 108, M 34.

ɬ+t+k'iw+lx (√k'w). *climb again.* In CMB 78.

ɬt'p+m+ncut (√ɬt'p). *jump (down).* In CR 96.

ɬt'+p+m+us (√ɬt'p). *jump in.* In CR 83.

ɬúkʷ+laʔxʷ (√ɬkʷ). *dirt.* In GU 267.

-ɬulm *5obj.* In GU 209.

ɬw+ɬwn+ikst (√ɬwn). *let go pl.*
In CMB 68.

ɬw' (√ɬw'). *poke.* In CMB 57.

ɬw'+ɬw'+tan (√ɬw'). *poker.* In
CMB 67.

ɬ+xʷuy (√xʷy). *go back.* In CN
27, FC 37, GU 154, M 15.

ɬ+xʷuy+st (√xʷy). *take st back.*
In CN 26.

ɬ+x̌s+t+wilx (√x̌s). *get well
again.* In GU 133.

ɬx̌ʷp'a+m (√ɬx̌ʷp'). *run out.* In
M 51.

ɬ+yaʕ+p (√yʕ). *arrive again pl.*
In GU 29.

ɬ+ʕ'ac' (√ʕ'c'). *look at again.* In
SF 47.

ɬ+ʔácqaʔ (√ʔcqʔ). *go out
again.* In GU 176.

ɬ+ʔam (√ʔm). *feed again.* In
GU 165.

ɬ+ʔam+ʔam (√ʔm). *feed
again.* In GU 165.

λ'

λ'axʷ+t (√λ'xʷ). *dead pl.* In CE
48, GU 274.

λ'aʔ (√λ'ʔ). *fetch.* In GU 283.

λ'aʔá (√λ'ʔ). *fetch.* In CR 85.

λ'aʔ+λ'aʔ (√λ'ʔ). *look for.* In
GU 221.

λ'aʔ+λ'ʔ+ús+m (√λ'ʔ). *look
for.* In SF 52, FC 34.

λ'l+al (√λ'l). *dead.* In SF 60, CN
55, CMB 135, CE 80, CR
104, GU 118, M 53.

λ'la+p (√λ'l). *stop.* In GU 238.

λ'l+λ'l (√λ'l). *dead pl.* In CMB
13.

λ'xʷ (√λ'xʷ). *kill many.* In CMB
17, M 5.

λ'xʷ+t (√λ'xʷ). *pl die.* In GU
205.

λ'xʷu+p (√λ'xʷ). *beat, win.* In
GU 304.

λ'x̌a+p (√λ'x̌). *grow.* In GU
233.

λ'x̌+x̌+λ'x̌a+p (√λ'x̌). *parents,
elders.* In GU 274.

m

-m *^futT.* In SF 35, CN 12, CMB
35, CE 64, CR 39, GU 23, M
38.

-m *mdl.* In SF 15, CN 66, CMB
46, CE 4, CR 6, GU 7.

-m *psv.* In SF 3, CN 10, CMB 22,
CE 13, CR 24, GU 2, M 20.

-m (-um) *2obj.* In SF 25, CE 37.

mał (myał) *too much.* In CN
22, CMB 22, GU 299.

mat *maybe, must.* In SF 60, CN
29, CMB 103, CE 89, CR 31,
GU 9, M 24.

maʕ (√mʕ). *lie on ground.* In
GU 77, M 32.

maʕáwt+t+xn (√mʕwt).
sideways, turn foot. In GU
241.

máʕ+mlaʔ (√mlʕ). *maggots.*
In CE 98.

maʔ+mí (√mʔ). *send away.* In
FC 14.

mi *fut, then.* In SF 25, CN 13, FC
29, CMB 29, CE 37, CR 19,
GU 51, M 42.

-mix *^perf.* In GU 283.

-míx+aʔx *^incp.* In SF 101, GU
205.

mł *and.* In SF 23, CN 77, FC 5,
CMB 5, CE 2, CR 2, GU 2,
M 43.

m+mátk'ya? (√mtk'y?).
blood pudding. In M 47.
m+m'átk'ya? (√mtk'y?).
blood pudding. In M 38.
mnik (√mnk). *shit.* In CMB 96.
mniml+tt (√mnml). *us, we.* In
CN 61, CMB 6.
-mp *5in.* In CN 37, GU 13.
mq'+ink (√mq'). *satiated.* In
CMB 93, M 49.
mqʷ+aqʷ (√mqʷ). *snow fall.* In
GU 206.
mut (√mt). *sit sg, be home.* In
CN 10, FC 38, CMB 31, GU
28, M 27.
my (√my). *know.* In CN 4,
CMB 126, CE 100.
myal *too much.* In SF 64, CMB
21, GU 288.
my+p (√my). *learn.* In CN 102.
mˤ'an *mind you, interj.* In CN
104, GU 32.

m'

m'ay'á+m (√m'y'?). *tell
stories.* In CR 39.
m'ay'+xít+mi?st (√m'y'). *tell
stories.* In GU 305.
m'a?+m'ás+lqs+m (√ms).
feel dress. In CMB 107.
m'y'+m'y'+mul (√my').
tattler. In CR 72.

n

-n *1erg.* In SF 25, CMB 76, CE
37, CR 40, GU 151.
nakʷ+á *not.* In SF 25.
nakʷm *evid.* In SF 30, CN 80,
FC 32, CMB 38, CE 7, CR 7,
GU 41.
nánənənə *onom.* In CR 100.

nánənənənə *onom.* In CR 100.
naqs (√nqs). *one.* In SF 11, CR
110, M 48.
nasp+p+áˤs+s (√nsp). *Sea
gull.* In GU 49.
nax̌ml *but, however, so.* In SF
11, CMB 7, GU 74.
nax̌ʷ+nx̌ʷ (√nx̌ʷ). *wife.* In GU
75.
naˤm *onom.* In CR 64.
n+c'ayxʷ+áplqs (√c'yxʷ). *end
of story.* In SF 133, CN 106,
GU 309, M 58.
n+c'l+c'lx+?+ups (√c'lx).
scratch bottom. In CMB 76.
n+c'n+c'n+m+aˤs (√c'ˤn).
shut eyes. In GU 7.
n+c'n+c'nq'+us (√c'nq').
gouge eyes. In CE 31.
n+c'q'+mi (√c'q'). *throw in.* In
GU 217.
n+c'q'+mn+itkʷ (√c'q'). *throw
in water.* In GU 74.
nənənə *onom.* In CR 94.
níkxna? *goodness.* In SF 49,
CN 24, CMB 97, CE 19, CR
78, GU 17, M 49.
nik' (√nk'). *cut.* In CN 54.
n+ilí? (√l?). *be there.* In GU 92.
nis (√ns). *gone, as far as one
can see.* In SF 31, CN 60, FC
10, CMB 79, CR 22, GU 25.
nixl (√nxl). *hear, understand,
mind, listen.* In CR 6.
nixl' (√nxl). *hear, understand,
mind, listen.* In GU 24.
nixʷ *also, more, again.* In SF 87,
CR 75, GU 8.
n+kcn+ikn (√kcn). *overtake.*
In CMB 122.

n+kxa+m (√kx). *go on foot.* In SF 37.

n+kx+kxa+m (√kx). *walk.* In GU 45.

n+kʷl+wt+itkʷ (√kʷl). *live in water.* In SF 57.

n+kʷni+m (√kʷn). *sing.* In GU 134.

nk'+nik' (√nk'). *cut.* In GU 198.

n+k't'+us (√k't'). *cut off head.* In CMB 47.

n+kʷa?+kʷín (√kʷn). *pick.* In CE 62.

n+kʷƛ'+alqs+m (√kʷƛ'). *take clothes off.* In GU 263.

nkʷ+s+pin+tk (√nkʷ, √pn). *one year.* In CE 89.

n+kʷul'+mn (√kʷl'). *custom.* In CN 61.

nkʷ+?ayxáxaʔ (√nkʷ, √?yx). *a while.* In M 19.

n+lipx̌ʷ (√lpx̌ʷ). *slip in.* In CE 4.

n+lk'+w's+us (√lk'). *tie in middle.* In CN 69.

n+lp+lpx̌ʷ (√lpx̌ʷ). *slip in.* In CE 32.

n+lp'x̌ʷ+ups (√lp'x̌ʷ). *stuck in anus.* In SF 118.

n+lqʷ+lqʷ+iw's (√lqʷ). *break in two.* In GU 187.

n+ɬc'+c'+úlaʔxʷ (√ɬc'). *hit ground.* In CE 88.

n+ɬc'+úlaʔxʷ+m (√ɬc'). *throw on ground.* In CE 67.

n+ɬq'+ut (√ɬq'). *lie.* In CR 47.

n+ɬt'p+m+itkʷ (√ɬt'p). *jump in water.* In CN 36, CMB 53, CR 102, GU 263.

n+ɬt'p+m+úlaʔxʷ (√ɬt'p). *jump in hole.* In CMB 104.

n+ɬt'pm+us (√ɬt'pm). *jump in.* In CR 83.

n+ɬw'+ɬw'+ups (√ɬw'). *poke anus.* In CMB 67.

n+ɬx̌ʷ+iɬc'aʔ (√ɬx̌ʷ). *hole.* In SF 92, CMB 103, CR 81.

n+ɬx̌ʷp+us (√ɬx̌ʷp). *boil.* In CN 19.

n+ɬx̌ʷp'a+m (√ɬx̌ʷp'). *run in.* In GU 161.

n+ƛ'm+ƛ'm+aqs (√ƛ'm). *sharp point.* In M 42.

n+mul (√ml). *dip water.* In M 8.

n+my+ip (√my). *tell on.* In CR 39.

n+mʕay+w's (√mʕy). *lay across.* In GU 230.

n+pkʷ+us (√pkʷ). *put on fire.* In CE 47.

n+p+pilx (√plx). *enter pl.* In FC 8, GU 39.

n+p+plx+úlaʔxʷ (√plx). *crawl in.* In SF 70.

n+pqʷ+us (√pqʷ). *sprinkle.* In SF 53.

n+p'c'+aʕtkʷ (√p'ʕc'). *squirt in water.* In CN 20.

n+p'ƛ'm+qs+iɬxʷ (√p'ƛ'm). *tipi top.* In CN 35, FC 36.

n+p't' (√p'ʕt'). *pour in.* In CR 87.

n+p't'+caʕn+m (√p'ʕt'). *put in mouth.* In GU 60.

nq+nqs+ilxʷ (√nqs). *neighbor pl.* In FC 3.

n+qx̌+qx̌+úlaʔxʷ (√qx̌). *drive in ground.* In M 43.

n+q'a?+q'a? (√q'?). *stick in pl.*
In CMB 91.

n+q'a?+q'?+íks (√q'?). *put in*
hand. In GU 156.

n+qʷa?+qʷ?+ípna? (√qʷ?).
cheek pocket. In CN 73.

n+q'ʷic'+t (√q'ʷc'). *full.* In SF
103.

n+q'ʷm (√q'ʷm). *put in.* In SF
94.

n+q'ʷm+q'ʷm+us (√q'ʷm).
plug hole. In SF 109.

n+sapm'+átkʷ (√spm'). *water*
bugs. In GU 247.

n+sp'+aqs (√sp'). *hit on lip, hit*
on nose. In GU 79.

n+sq'+iw's (√sq'). *split.* In SF
66, CR 97.

n+sq'ʷ+ut (√sq'ʷ). *other side.*
In GU 276.

n+st+ils (√st). *think.* In SF 131,
CE 83.

n+s+t+?awt+íma?+tk (√?wt).
below. In GU 51.

-nt *nt.* In SF 3, CN 10, FC 28,
CMB 15, CE 2, CR 18, GU
2, M 5.

nta *intj.* In GU 201.

n+tq (√tq). *touch on.* In GU 80.

n+tq+us (√tq). *put on.* In CN
16.

n+txʷ+us (√txʷ). *cousin.* In CR
49.

nt'a *intj.* In SF 19, CN 68, CMB
62, CE 55, CR 42, GU 257,
M 28.

n+t'k'ʷ (√t'k'ʷ). *put in.* In GU
196.

n+t'k'ʷ+itkʷ (√t'k'ʷ). *throw in*
water. In CN 19.

n+t'l+úla?xʷ (√t'l). *gulch.* In
GU 63.

n+t'p+qs+a+m (√t'p). *tip head.*
In SF 57.

n+t'q+mn+itkʷ (√t'q). *push*
under water. In GU 257.

n+t'q+úla?xʷ+m (√t'q). *poke*
in ground. In CR 104.

n+t'y+t'ína? (√t'n?).
disobedient. In GU 32.

-nu *manage.* In SF 107, CN 102,
CMB 13, CE 66, CR 98, GU
151.

n+wa?l+íls+m (√w?l). *admire.*
In SF 89.

n+wis+t (√ws). *high.* In CE 2,
CN 35.

n+wl'+qn'+m'n'wixʷ (√wl).
shell cover. In CR 33.

n+wt (√wt). *put in.* In CMB 91,
CR 82, GU 203.

n+wtn+itkʷ (√wtn). *put in*
water. In CN 20.

n+wtn+úla?xʷ (√wtn). *put in*
ground. In M 42.

n+wt+wt (√wt). *put pl obj.* In
CMB 40.

n+wt+wtn+úla?xʷ (√wtn).
stuck in ground. In M 52.

n+xlak (√xlk). *be in circle.* In
FC 34.

n+xƛ'+p (√xƛ'). *complete.* In SF
107.

n+xn'+us+xn+tn (√xn').
moccasin patch. In GU 122.

n+xw+xw+p+aqs (√xw). *air*
in nose. In SF 127.

n+xy+xayáp+lqs (√xy). *end of*
story. In CR 116.

n+x̌il (√x̌l). *fear.* In M 20.

n+x̌ił (√x̌ł). *afraid.* In CN 55.

n+x̌l+p+us (√x̌l). *aware*. In CN
102.

n+x̌l'+x̌l'+ilt+tn (√x̌l).
scarecrow. In CR 109.

n+x̌^w+x̌^wc'+úsa⁷ (√x̌^wc').
stump. In SF 63.

n+yax^w+t (√yx^w). *fall in*. In CR
96, GU 38.

n+yaˤ'+p+ncút (√yˤ'). *stuck*.
In CE 95.

n+yq'p+alqs+tn (√yq'p). *belt*.
In CMB 26.

n+yr+m (√yr). *push down*. In
CR 98.

n+yx^w+itk^w (√yx^w). *fall in
water*. In CE 24, GU 249.

n+yx^wt+itk^w (√yx^w). *in water*.
In CMB 53.

n+yx^w+t+úla⁷x^w (√yx^w).
basement, underground. In
GU 67.

nyˤ'ip (√nˤ'p). *always*. In CR
21.

n+y⁷ak'^w (√yk'^w). *cross*. In
CMB 10, GU 51.

n+y'a+y'ak'^w (√yk'^w). *cross*. In
GU 52.

n+ˤac+ˤac+ína⁷ (√ˤc).
earring. In GU 19.

n+⁷ackn+itk^w (√⁷ckn). *play in
water*. In GU 16.

n+⁷ałx^w+íp (√⁷łx^w). *go inside*.
In CMB 61.

n+⁷ałx^w+ítk^w (√⁷łx^w). *dive*. In
GU 271.

n+⁷ałx^w+úla⁷x^w (√⁷łx^w). *go
into ground*. In GU 26.

n+⁷amt+ús (√⁷mt). *sit by*. In
GU 31.

n+⁷ask'^wl+ítk^w (√⁷sk'^wl).
throw in water. In GU 4.

n+⁷uc+xn (√⁷c). *track*. In SF
35.

n+⁷ułx^w (√⁷łx^w). *enter*. In CN
48, FC 11, CMB 30, CE 51,
GU 90, M 22.

n'

n'i+n'k'+mn' (√nk'). *knife*. In
CN 14.

n'ín'w'i⁷ *a while,*. In SF 131,
CR 76, GU 54, M 44.

n'u (n'ín'w'i⁷) *a while*. In CN
34.

n'+w'l'+w'l'+qn'+m'n'wix^w
(√wl). *clam shell dim*. In
CR 45.

p

p *5kn*. In SF 4, GU 7.

-p *5erg*. In CMB 85, GU 4.

paq+aˤ+píq (√pq). *white*. In
CR 78.

paq+aˤ+píqa⁷+s (√pq). *white
legs*. In GU 78.

pax̌^w+px̌^w+łp (√px̌^w). *pussy
willow*. In CE 13.

piq (pq). *white*. In CR 79, GU
159.

piq'^w (pq'^w). *onom*. In SF 13.

pix̌ (√px̌). *hunt*. In GU 229.

pix̌+m (√px̌). *hunt*. In SF, GU
207.

pk^w (√pk^w). *pour solids*. In CE
49.

p+ptwína⁷x^w (√ptw). *old
woman*. In SF 2, FC 24,
CMB 14, GU 37.

p+ptw'ína⁷x^w (√ptw). *old
woman*. In CR 67.

pul (√pl+st). *kill one, beat*. In CMB 35, CR 76, GU 111, M 13.

pul+x (√pl). *camp*. In GU 47, M 1.

púl'+la?xʷ (√pl'). *Gopher*. In CN 6.

put *just, exact*. In CMB 125, CE 66.

**pút+i? ** *still*. In CE 98, GU 255.

p'

p'aˁc'+lqʷ+aˁw'st+xn (√p'ˁc'). *Squirted leg*. In CN 5.

p'c' (√p'c'). *squirt*. In SF 59.

p'ína? (√p'n?). *basket*. In CR 18, GU 217.

p'lk'+mncut (√p'lk'). *turn around*. In SF 117, CN 23.

p's *onom*. In CMB 64.

p'y'+p'ay'áqa? (√p'y'q). *ripe*. In CR 4.

q

qal+wt+ánk (√ql). *step on belly*. In M 34.

qa+qácla?s (√qcl). *wheel*. In GU 145.

qa+qíc (√qc). *brothers*. In M 34.

qa+qxʷ+lx (√qxʷ). *fish*. In CN 34.

qax̌ʷ (√qx̌ʷ). *break*. In CR 6.

qaˁy (√qˁy). *black*. In GU 158.

qa?+qácla? (√qcl). *wheel*. In GU 189.

qa?+qácla?s (√qcl?s). *wheel*. In GU 185.

qic+lx (√qc). *run*. In CMB 70.

qil+t (√ql). *top*. In SF 46, CMB 45, GU 64.

qił+ł+t (√qł). *wake up*. In FC 35.

qił+t (√qł). *awaken*. In SF 75, FC 33, CE 94, GU 194, M 28.

qm+qmin (√qmn). *lie*. In CE 52.

qp+qin+tn (√qp). *hair*. In CN 71, GU 293.

qwláqa? (√qwlq?). *darned thing*. In GU 189.

qx̌ (√qx̌). *splil wood*. In GU 88.

qx̌a+m (√qx̌). *split wood*. In GU 84.

qy'axʷ (√qy'xʷ). *smell*. In SF 11.

qy'xʷ (√qy'xʷ). *smell*. In SF 132.

q'

q'a?+íls+m (√q'?). *pay attention*. In SF 129, CMB 43.

q'a?+lqʷs+íslp'+tn (√q'?). *fire rod*. In CMB 66.

q'l+ips (√q'l). *medallion, necklace*. In CR 41.

q'l+ips+m (√q'l). *medallion, necklace*. In GU 19.

q'm (√q'm). *swallow*. In CR 64.

q'm+ilt+tn (√q'm). *starve*. In GU 140.

q'+q'ax̌ (√q'x̌). *clearing*. In CE 75.

q'+q'sápi? (√q'sp?). *little while*. In SF 98.

q'sápi? (√q'sp?). *long ago, long time*. In SF 56, GU 83.

q'y'+mix (√q'y'). *speckled*. In
GU 278.

q^w

q^wamq^wmt (√q^wm). *excellent*.
In GU 296.

q^wa^ʕ *onom. Raven's sound when
he talks*. In GU 125.

q^wa^ʕy (√q^wy). *black*. In GU
171.

q^wil+cn (√q^wl). *fir boughs*. In
GU 5.

q^wl+min (√q^wl). *ashes*. In SF
53, CN 16, CE 46.

q^wma+p (√q^wm). *faint*. In GU
191.

q'^w

q'^wast+ínk (√q'^wst). *Coyote
magic*. In CMB 81.

q'^wa^ʕy (√q'^w^ʕy). *black*. In
CMB 59.

q'^wic't (√q'^wc'). *full, fat*. In
CMB 97.

q'^wl'+iw'm (√q'^wl'). *berry pick*.
In CR 3.

q'^wm+qin (√q'^wm). *horn*. In
GU 85.

q'^w+q'^wc'w'íya? (√q'c'w'y?).
Chipmunk. In SF 2, CR 1.

q'^wuc'+t (√q'^wc'). *fat*. In FC 19.

q'^w+?+uł (√q'^wł). *black*. In
CMB 62.

s

s- *?* In CN 78.

s- (c-). *cust^*. In GU 295.

s- *dur*. In SF 6, CN 7, FC 2, CMB
11, CE 34, CR 2, M 22.

s- *inten*. In GU 134.

s- *ipftv^*. In FC 4, CMB 86, CE
86, CR 31, GU 62, M 1.

-s *2obj*. In CR 40, GU 151.

-s *3erg*. In SF 19, CN 11, FC 10,
CMB 8, CE 2, CR 1, GU 9,
M 8.

-s *3i*. In SF 6, CN 7, FC 2, CMB
11, CE 34, CR 2, GU 35, M
15.

-s *3in*. In SF 3, CN 2, CMB 1, CE
2, CR 1, GU 1, M 20.

sax^w+t (√sx^w). *go downhill*. In
CR 19.

sa?+stám (√stm). *brother in
law, sister in law*. In GU 78.

s+c- *ipftvp^*. In FC 40, CMB 83,
CR 79, GU 175, M 20.

s+c+ca^ʕsnt (√c^ʕsnt). *little
stars*. In CE 27.

sc+q'^wl'+iw's (√q'^wl'). *picking*.
In CR 9.

s+c'+c'w'+xan' (√c'w'). *leg
dim*. In CR 54.

s+c'im' (√c'm). *bone*. In GU 3.

s+c'w'+xan (√c'w'). *animal
hind leg*. In SF 82, CR 50.

sic (√sc). *new, then*. In FC 19,
CMB 77, CR 88.

sílx^wa? (√slx^w?). *big*. In SF
126, CR 89.

síp'i? (√sp'?). *hide*. In CN 53,
CMB 47, GU 114.

siwłk^w (√swł). *water, liquor*. In
SF 56, CN 34, CE 19, GU 4,
M 10.

siw+st (√sw). *drink*. In CE 24.

siwst+a?x (√swst). *dinking
water*. In CE 9.

síya? (√sy?). *saskatoons,
service berries*. In CN 20.

s+kic+c (√kc). *visitor.* In CN
12.

s+k+kˁáka**ʔ** (√kˁ**ʔ**). *bird,
animal, chicken.* In CE 25,
CR 106.

s+k+lkʷt+ilt (√lkʷ). *distant
child.* In CMB 3.

s+kł+ikn' (√kł). *rump fat.* In
GU 142.

s+kmxist (√kmxst). *bear.* In
CN 8, GU 116.

s+km'xist (√km'xst). *bear.* In
GU 101.

s+k'awíla**ʔ**x (√k'wl**ʔ**x). *Addy.*
In SF 96.

s+k'l+cnił (√cnł). *to the side.*
In SF 21.

-skʷ *tsimptv.* In CN 56, CMB 36,
M 13.

s+kʷan+x̌n (√kʷn). *prisoner.*
In GU 227.

s+kʷ+kʷr'+ína**ʔ** (√kʷr'). *clam
shell.* In CR 32.

s+kʷ+kʷusnt (√kʷsnt). *stars.*
In CE 27.

s+kʷ+kʷ**ʔ**+iłp (√kʷ**ʔ**). *rose
bush.* In CE 18.

s+kʷlis (√kʷls). *kinnickkinnick.*
In CR 3.

s+kʷls+iłmlx (√kʷls).
kinnickkinnick. In CE 37.

s+kʷr+xan (√kʷr). *Crane.* In
FC 6.

s+kʷs+kʷist (√kʷst). *name pl.*
In CN 4.

-skʷy *tpimptv.* In M 13.

s+kᵚ+kᵚim'+l't (√kᵚy).
child. In GU 98.

s+kᵚúma+lt (√kᵚm). *virgin.*
In FC 4.

skᵚut (√kᵚt). *half, other side.*
In GU 64.

s+kᵚuy (√kᵚy). *man's mother.*
In CE 44, GU 22.

s+lip' (√lp'). *fire wood.* In M
42.

s+l'ax̌t (√l'x̌t). *friend, partner.*
In SF 24, GU 289, M 50.

słiqʷ (√słqʷ). *meat.* In FC 9,
GU 9.

s+ł+łw'+il't (√łw). *nephew dim.*
In CR 12.

s+łw+ilt (√łw). *niece.* In GU
89.

s+ƛ'a**ʔ**cínm (√ƛ'**ʔ**cnm). *deer.*
In SF 123, GU 137.

s+ƛ'+ƛ'úk'ᵚa**ʔ** (√ƛ'k'ᵚ**ʔ**). *wood
pitch.* In CMB 58, CR 80.

s+ma+m**ʔ**ím (√m**ʔ**m). *women.*
In SF 80, FC 4.

s+mx̌+ikn (√mx̌). *grizzly.* In
CMB 5, GU 101.

s+m'a+m**ʔ**ím (√m**ʔ**m).
women. In SF 32, CMB 83.

s+m'a**ʔ**+m'áy' (√m'y'). *story.*
In SF 110.

sna**ʔ** *onom.* In CR 30.

sn+ína**ʔ** (sn). *Owl.* In CR 31.

s+n+kstíya**ʔ** (√ksty**ʔ**). *skunk,
m's name.* In SF 13.

s+n+k'l'+ip (√k'l'). *Coyote.* In
CN 2, CMB 1, CE 1, GU
101.

s+n+k'm+ikn' (√k'm). *back.* In
CR 24.

s+n+k'**ʔ**+ína**ʔ** (√k'**ʔ**). *pillow.*
In CR 36.

s+n+lak'ᵚ (√lk'ᵚ). *tallow.* In
GU 145.

s+n+p's+aqs+tn (√p's). *nose.*
In SF 126.

sn+sínca⁷ (√snc⁷). *younger brothers.* In CMB 21.

s+n+wl+wl+músa⁷s+tn (√wl). *arrow points.* In CMB 14.

s+n+⁷am+⁷ím·a⁷t (√⁷mt). *grandchildren.* In SF 2.

s+n+⁷íma⁷t (√⁷m⁷t). *grandchild.* In CR 1.

s+pa+páˤła⁷ (√pˤł⁷). *ape.* In CR 7, GU 218.

s+plim+cn (√plm). *mouth.* In CMB 97.

s+p+pl'+ína⁷ (√pl'). *rabbit.* In CR 1, GU 78.

s+puc+t (√pc). *scab.* In GU 279.

s+pumt (√pmt). *fur.* In CE 92, GU 130.

s+p⁷+us (√p⁷). *heart.* In CR 63.

sp'+ap'+q (√sp'). *whack on head.* In GU 148.

s+p'c'n+iłx\w (√p'c'n). *tipi.* In CE 42, GU 91.

s+p's+aqs (√p's). *nose.* In SF 131, GU 80.

s+qil+tk (√ql). *body.* In SF 91, CR 58.

s+qilx\w (√qlx\w). *person, Indian.* In SF 1, CN 1, FC 1, CMB 6, CE 53, CR 109, GU 1, M 16.

s+ql'+tmix\w (√ql'). *man, husband.* In CE 76, GU 284.

s+q'l'+ips (√q'l). *medallion.* In CR 40.

s+q'm+ilt+tn (√q'm). *hunger.* In GU 205.

s+q\wl'ip (√q\wl'p). *moss.* In GU 167.

s+q\w+q\włm'+ús+c'a⁷ (√q\włm'). *guts.* In GU 202.

s+q\wsi⁷ (√q\ws⁷). *son.* In CMB 4, GU 229.

s+q\ws+q\wasí⁷a (√q\ws⁷). *children.* In CN 2, CMB 1, CE 72, GU 155.

s+q\ws+q\wsi⁷ (√q\ws⁷). *child.* In GU 68.

s+q'\wuct (√q'\wct). *fat.* In GU 57.

s+si⁷ (√s⁷). *uncle.* In CR 13, GU 1.

-st *caus.* In SF 21, CN 26, CMB 17, GU 90.

-st ^*cust.* In SF 25, CN 4, FC 40, CMB 14, CE 10, GU 9, M 57.

-st *st.* In SF 60, CN 14, FC 16, CMB 8, CE 62, CR 98, GU 288, M 26.

s+tałm (√tłm). *boat.* In CMB 49, M 39.

s+tim' (√tm'). *what, what thing, something, thing, whatever.* In SF 86, CN 13, FC 9, CMB 15, CE 12, CR 49, GU 44.

s+tkcx\w+iłp (√tkcx\w). *red willow.* In CE 22.

s+t+k'\wλ'+k'\wλ'+us+tn (√k'\wλ'). *eyes.* In CE 2.

s+t+k'\wλ'+us+tn (√k'\wλ'). *eye.* In CR 105.

s+t+ml+scut (√ml). *stock, wealth, beads.* In GU 17.

s+tm+tíma⁷ (√tm⁷). *grandmother, grandchild.* In SF 3, FC 7, CE 35, CR 15, GU 1.

s+t+taq (√tq). *Squirrel.* In SF 2.

s+tx+min (√tx). *comb.* In CE 52.

s+t²iwt+x (√t²wt). *young one.* In GU 59.

s+t'a²+t'á²p+w's+tn (√t'p). *place name.* In SF 55.

s+t'l+s+qilxʷ (√t'l). *earth people.* In GU 133.

s+t'mk²+ilt (√t'mk²). *daughter.* In CMB 6.

s+t'x+itkʷ (√t'x). *soup.* In GU 193.

s+t'²i² (√t'²²). *grass.* In SF 93.

sut+n (√st). *thing.* In SF 118, CN 20, CMB 3, CE 92, CR 23, GU 5, M 42.

suxʷ+xʷ (√sxʷ). *leave pl.* In CE 45, GU 45.

swit (√swt). *who, indef, somebody, anybody.* In SF 8, CMB 94, GU 99.

s+wy'+wy'+numt+x (√wy'). *handsome pl.* In FC 4.

s+w'ar'ák'+xn (√w'rk'). *Frog.* In FC 17.

s+w'ar'+íps (√w'r'). *stink bug.* In SF 86.

s+w'a+w'ása² (√w's²). *aunt.* In GU 62.

s+w'r'+islp' (√wr'). *fire.* In GU 283.

sw'+sw'+aˤs (√sw'). *pheasant.* In CE 41, GU 243.

sw'+sw'+ilx (√sw'). *whisper.* In M 14.

s+x²it+x (√x²t). *oldest one.* In GU 58.

s+xʷa²+xʷa²+nk+íłp (√xʷ²). *thornbush.* In CMB 72.

s+xʷip+lp (√xʷp). *rug.* In CMB 35.

s+xʷuy+nt (√xʷy). *ice.* In CN 93.

s+xʷuy+tn (√xʷy). *step, travel, track.* In SF 52.

s+xʷy+alqʷ (√xʷy). *wood worm.* In GU 247.

s+x̌as+t (√x̌s). *best.* In GU 301.

s+x̌w'+ilt+n (√x̌w'). *drying rack.* In GU 141.

s+x̌+x̌c'i² (√x̌c'²). *stick.* In CMB 57, M 32.

s+yum+cn (√ym). *partner.* In CE 91.

s+y'al'w+ánk (√yl'w). *Cricket.* In M 24.

s+y'al'w'+an'k (√ylw). *Cricket.* In M 4.

s+ˤ'an' (√ˤ'n'). *Magpie.* In SF 104.

s+ˤ'an'íxʷ (√ˤ'n'xʷ). *Muskrat.* In CMB 3.

t

t *?* In SF 49, GU 28, M 34.

t *agInst.* In SF 3, CN 11, CMB 16, CE 35, CR 23, GU 21, M 20.

t *obj itr.* In SF 93, CN 33, CMB 130, CE 71, CR 3, GU 54, M 38.

t *obj tr.* In CN 20, CMB 14, CE 37, CR 40, GU 153.

-t (-nt). *nt.* In CN 13, CR 18, CMB 51, GU 3, M 13.

-t (-st). *st.* In GU 178.

t n+yˤ'ip (√yˤ'p). *continuously.* In FC 37, CMB 14, CR 74, GU 238.

t s+ʔiw+t (√ʔw). *behind*. In GU 251.

t tanm'+ús (√tnm'). *any which way*. In GU 46.

ta variant of **t** before words that begin with resonant or **c-** *hab*.

ta n+yˤ'ip (√yˤ'p). *keep on, forever*. In GU 34.

ta wnix^w (√wnx^w). *for sure*. In CMB 101.

ta+c+k'lá? (√k'l?). *this way*. In CR 92.

tałt (√tł). *surely*. In CMB 125.

tanm's+cín (√tn'ms). *idle talk*. In M 21.

tanm'ús (√tnm's). *insignificant*. In GU 306.

taw+s+kíc+c (√tw, √kc). *have visitors*. In GU 281.

ta+ʔkín' (√ʔkn'). *from where*. In GU 253.

taʔlí? *very much*. In SF 98.

taʔx^w+s+q^ws+q^wsí? (√tx^w, √q^ws?). *get baby*. In GU 68.

taʔxí (√ʔxl). *do that*. In CN 54.

taʔxíl (t?xl). *do a certain way*. In SF 76, CN 14, CMB 8, CE 62, CR 6.

taʔ+xl+xíl (√ʔxl). *do that pl*. In CN 52.

tił+x (√tł). *stand*. In M 11.

tix^w (√tx^w). *obtain*. In CR 84.

tix^wk^wún+m (√tx^w, √k^wn). *talk*. In CE 87.

tiʔxíl (√ʔxl). *do so*. In CN 64.

t+kaʔłl+ús (√k?łs). *three berries*. In CR 5.

tki? (√tk?). *pee*. In CN 94.

tkłmilx^w (√tkł). *woman, wife*. In CN 11, CMB 55, GU 119, M 36.

t+km'+km'+am (√km'). *hold on*. In GU 35.

t+k+ʔasl+ús (√?sl). *two berries*. In CR 5.

tk+ʔas+ʔasíl (√?sl). *two persons*. In GU 1.

t+k'iw+lx (√k'w). *climb*. In CN 78, CR 8.

t+k'm+kn'+iłx^w (√k'm). *outside*. In SF 36, CMB 30, GU 84.

t+k's+ils (√k's). *bad stomach*. In CE 69.

t+k^wl+wt+isxn (√k^wl). *sit pl on rock*. In SF 58.

t+k^wr'+k^wr'+akst+xn (√k^wr'). *Yellow leg*. In CN 5.

tk^wtan (√tk^w). *tule*. In GU 183.

tk^w?+ut (√tk^w?). *walk pl*. In GU 222.

t+k'^wit+xn+m (√k'^wt). *step over*. In CE 93, CR 70, GU 131.

t+k'^wr+k'^wrc'+aqst+xn (√k'^wrc'). *bow legs*. In FC 20.

t+k'^wtx+lx+alq^w (√k'^wt). *step over log*. In GU 77.

tl (√tl). *break*. In SF 82.

tl *of, from, than*. In CE 37.

tla+ʔxís (√?xs). *from there*. In GU 64.

tl' *of, from, than*. In CN 6, CMB 2, GU 130, M 36.

tmx^w+úlaʔx^w (√tmx^w). *country, land, ground*. In CMB 116.

tm'+iw's (√tm'). *half way*. In GU 255.

tq (√tq). *touch*. In GU 201.

t+qc+lx+alqʷ (√qc). *run over logs.* In GU 255.

t+q'a?+íls+m (√q'?). *pay attention.* In GU 289.

tr'q (√tr'q). *kick.* In SF 96, GU 112, M 53.

-tt *4i.* In CR 97.

-tt *4in.* In CN 61, GU 62.

t+tiɬ+táɬ+lqʷ (√tɬ). *Straight leg.* In CN 5.

t+tq (√tq). *touch dim.* In CN 23.

t+tw'it (√twt). *boy.* In CMB 12, CE 26, CR 27, GU 73, M 7.

tul'+mn (√tl'). *paint powder.* In CE 60.

tum' (√tm'). *woman's mother.* In CMB 61, GU 178.

tum'+tm' (√tm'). *mother.* In CE 87.

tupl' (√tpl'). *spider.* In GU 41.

tw'+tw'it (√tw). *boys.* In CN 3, CMB 4.

tx (√tx). *comb.* In CE 55, GU 286.

txa (tx). *?* In CN 47.

txa+m (√tx). *comb.* In FC 5, GU 298.

t+xlak' (√xlk'). *go around.* In CMB 80.

t+xn'+ína? (√xn'). *cover w patch.* In GU 123.

t+xt' (√xt'). *take care of, owe, aim, pregnant.* In GU 73.

txʷ+s+lip' (√txʷ, √slp'). *get wood.* In GU 86.

t+xʷuy (√xʷy). *go up to.* In GU 47.

t+xʷuy+m (√xʷy). *go towards.* In CN 15.

t+x̌asm+qn (√x̌s). *pl name.* In CR 107.

t+x̌ʷayq (√x̌ʷy). *pile.* In CE 93.

t'

t' *negfac.* In SF 5, CN 4, FC 37, CMB 43, CE 10, CR 13, GU 12, M 56.

t'akʷ (√t'kʷ). *brush.* In CE 16.

t'ak'ʷ (√t'k'ʷ). *put down.* In CN 101, CE 89, GU 194.

t'ala?x+wílx (√t'l?). *next generation.* In CR 109, M 55.

t'ap (√t'p). *object lies.* In GU 36.

t'aqltáˤla? (√t'qlt). *honey.* In GU 121.

t'aqltáˤn (√t'qlt). *honey.* In GU 197.

t'a+t'aˤp+íkst+m (√t'ˤp). *shoot target.* In GU 303.

t'aˤp (√t'ˤp). *shoot.* In CMB 16.

t'aˤpá (√t'ˤp). *shoot.* In GU 2.

t'a?+c+?x̌il (√?x̌l). *do like.* In CMB 108.

t'c *actCisl.* In CN 67, CR 7, GU 49.

t'ic' (√t'c'). *pitch.* In CR 80.

t'ik'ʷt (√t'k'ʷt). *lake.* In GU 262, M 1.

t'ix+lx (√t'x). *come to shore.* In GU 276.

t'i? *evid.* In SF 13, CN 16, FC 10, CMB 7, CE 6, CR 6, GU 68, M 54.

t'k+ikst+tn (√t'k). *cane.* In GU 79.

t'kʷ+t'akʷ (√t'kʷ). *brush.* In CE 11.

t'k'ʷ (√t'k'ʷ). *put down, set in place.* In CN 17.

t'k'ʷ+ak'ʷ (√t'k'ʷ). *land flat, lie.* In CN 84, GU 112, M 53.

t'k'ʷ+m+íc'a? (√t'k'ʷ). *cover.* In GU 167.

t'l+s+qilxʷ (√t'l, √qlxʷ). *come to life.* In GU 133.

t'n+t'ína? (√t'n?). *ears.* In CR 62.

t'p+ink (√t'p). *fat belly.* In FC 20.

t'ql+imx (√t'ql). *move.* In FC 36.

t'qʷ+cin (√t'qʷ). *honk, holler.* In GU 178.

t'+t'aqlt+áˁla? (√t'qlt). *honey.* In GU 165.

t'+t'um'+s (√t'm'). *little smile.* In CMB 46.

t'ukʷ (√t'k'ʷ). *pop out.* In CR 105.

t'uxʷ+t (√t'xʷ). *fly.* In SF 88, CN 35, CE 5, CR 71, GU 243, M 54.

t'xʷ *emph, evidently.* In SF 60, CN 4, FC 2, CMB 15, CE 13, CR 14, GU 175.

t'xʷ **mat** *maybe.* In SF 104, GU 86.

t'xʷ+t+lwis (√t'xʷ). *fly around.* In CE 25.

u

uc *dub.* In CMB 85, CE 101, CR 43.

ulalá *onom.* In M 34.

uł *and, until, up to, then.* In SF 2, CN 2, FC 4, CMB 1, CE 1, CR 1, GU 1, M 3.

úł+i? *and then.* In SF 42, CMB 53, CE 61, CR 79, GU 77.

w

wa *onom.* In CMB 76.

wap+wp+xn (√wp). *lynx.* In GU 105.

way' (√wy'). *well, yes, OK, all, finish, hello, quit.* In SF 11, CN 8, FC 11, CMB 9, CE 15, GU 30, M 13.

wckl'+ip+m (√wckl'). *go downhill.* In SF 48.

wik (√wk). *see.* In SF 89, CN 93, CMB 85, CE 1, CR 44, GU 17.

wikʷ (√wkʷ). *hide.* In CR 34.

wikʷ+mi?st (√wkʷ). *hide.* In SF 36, CR 35, GU 150.

wim' *in vain.* In CMB 88, CR 16, GU 88.

wis+xn (√ws). *long.* In GU 293.

witk'x (√wtk'x). *vomit.* In CE 70.

wix (√wx). *live.* In SF 1, CN 1, FC 1, CMB 1, CR 1, GU 1.

wkʷ+wíkʷ+mi?st (√wkʷ). *hide self.* In GU 231, M 6.

wla+p (√wl). *burn.* In SF 45, CMB 58, CR 91, GU 31.

wnaxʷ (√wnxʷ). *true.* In CR 26.

wr'+islp' (√wr). *fire.* In GU 43.

wt (√wt). *put down.* In CN 21, CMB 15, GU 246.

wtan (√wtn). *placed.* In CN 80, FC 21, CMB 62, CR 32, GU 142, M 9.

wx+wix (√wx). *live pl.* In GU 277.

-wy *ipimptv.* In CN 88, CMB 71, GU 178.

wy'+wy'+cin (√wy'). *finish eating pl*. In CN 43.

w+ʔ+ham (√whm). *bark inch.* In CMB 114.

w'

w'í+w'aʔst (√ws). *high dim*. In CMB 45, CE 71, M 36.

w'í+w'aʔx (√wx). *living place dim*. In CE 58.

x

-x *?* In CMB 128.

-x ^*incp*. In CE 54.

-x ^*ipftv*. In SF 40, FC 4, CMB 86, CE 86, CR 31, GU 62, M 1.

-x *isimptv*. In SF 77, CN 37, CMB 9, CE 26, CR 12, GU 65, M 8.

xc'+m (√xc'). *tight*. In SF 113.

xít+miʔst (√xt). *run*. In SF 122.

xi+xw'tm (√xw'tm). *girl*. In GU 74.

xiʔ+míx (√xʔ). *whatever*. In FC 29, CMB 15, GU 97.

xiʔmíx swit (√xʔ, √swt). *anybody*. In M 57.

xki (√xk). *do something*. In SF 60, CN 41.

xlk+mncut (√xlk). *turn*. In SF 120.

xƛ'+aƛ' (√xƛ'). *be grown*. In GU 14.

xƛ'ut (√xƛ't). *rock*. In SF 30, CE 78, GU 36.

xmaˤmlx+qn (√xmˤ). *?.* In M 34.

-xt *benf.* In CE 37, GU 153.

xt+xít+miʔst (√xt). *run around*. In CE 41.

xwił (√xwł). *road*. In CE 75.

xw+xwa+p (√xw). *deflate*. In SF 110.

x+xiw'+xw'tm (√xw'tm). *girls*. In GU 1.

x+xw'ił (√xw). *trail dim*. In M 45.

xy'+wilx (√xy'). *travel*. In GU 239.

x+ʔkin (√ʔkn). *how*. In SF 81.

xʷ

-xʷ *2erg*. In CN 26, CMB 96, CE 79, CR 18, GU 131, M 42.

-xʷ *isimptv*. In GU 151.

xʷaʔ (√xʷʔ). *pick up*. In GU 213.

xʷaʔ+s+púct (√xʷʔ, √pc). *many scabs*. In GU 288.

xʷic' (√xʷc'). *give*. In CN 28, FC 10, CE 38, GU 153.

xʷic'+x+m (√xʷc'). *give to*. In SF 107.

xʷist (√xʷy). *walk, hurry*. In CMB 71.

xʷl+xʷal+t (√xʷl). *alive*. In M 27.

xʷƛ'+xʷaƛ' (√xʷƛ'). *whittle*. In M 42.

xʷt'+ilx (√xʷt'). *get up*. In M 11.

xʷt'+p+ncut (√xʷt'). *hurry, run*. In SF 50, CMB 69, CE 33, CR 22, GU 64.

xʷt'+p+us (√xʷt'). *run away with*. In GU 217.

xʷust (√xʷst). *hurry*. In CMB 68.

xʷuxʷuxʷú *onom*. In GU 271.

xʷuxʷuxʷuxʷú *onom.* In GU
271.

xʷuy (√xʷy). *go, time go by,*
behave. In SF 4, CN 8, FC 5,
CMB 5, CE 1, CR 2, GU 34,
M 8.

xʷuy'+y (√xʷy). *go pl.* In SF 7,
GU 12.

xʷy+lwis (√xʷy). *wander.* In
CE 8.

xʷʔa (√xʷʔ). *hold.* In GU 215.

xʷʔ+ilt (√xʷʔ). *hold baby.* In
GU 97.

xʷʔ+ilt+m (√xʷʔ). *hold baby.*
In GU 101.

xʷʔit (√xʷʔ). *many, much.* In
FC 3.

x̌

x̌aq' (√x̌q'). *pay.* In CR 40, GU
247.

x̌as+t (√x̌s). *good.* In SF 114,
CN 16, GU 175.

x̌aʕ+m (√x̌ʕ). *hum.* In M 54.

x̌aʕ+p (√x̌ʕ). *cool, draft.* In GU
200.

x̌c+mncut (√x̌c). *get dressed,*
get ready. In FC 5, GU 300.

x̌il (√ʔx̌l). *act so.* In CN 104.

x̌iƛ'+m (√x̌ƛ'). *climb.* In CMB
33, M 40.

x̌la+p (√x̌l). *morning,*
tomorrow. In SF 28, FC 31,
CR 2, GU 163.

x̌l+ína? (√x̌l). *cache.* In SF 9.

x̌lit (x̌lt). *call, summon.* In GU
273.

x̌l+wis (√x̌l). *travel, fool*
around. In CMB 60.

x̌m+ink (√x̌m). *want, like.* In
FC 40, CR 49.

x̌n' (√x̌n). *hurt.* In GU 151.

x̌q+x̌aq (√x̌q). *hole.* In SF 109.

x̌q'+x̌aq' (√x̌q'). *pay pl.* In GU
248.

x̌s+t (√x̌s). *good.* In CN 58, CR
70, GU 133.

x̌s+t+wilx (√x̌s). *get well.* In
CN 58, CR 70,

x̌s+x̌s+qin+xn (√x̌s). *good*
knees. In SF 22.

x̌w'+aw' (√x̌w'). *dried.* In FC 9.

x̌w'+x̌w'+aw' (√x̌w'). *dry pl.*
In CMB 68.

x̌+x̌aq (√x̌q). *empty dim.* In SF
83.

x̌+x̌s+áɫc'aʔ (√x̌s). *good meat.*
In CR 26.

x̌ʷ

x̌ʷc'a+p (√x̌ʷc'). *break in two.*
In GU 255.

x̌ʷil (√x̌ʷl). *discard.* In GU 23.

x̌ʷl+x̌ʷil (√x̌ʷl). *discard.* In
CMB 39.

x̌ʷy+x̌ʷay+t (√x̌ʷy). *sharp.* In
CN 14.

x̌ʷʕ+ilxʷ (√x̌ʷʕ). *fox.* In CE 90.

y

-y *tpimptv.* In CN 88, M 13.

ya *art.* In SF 63, CN 37, CMB
20, CE 11, GU 136.

yámx̌ʷaʔ (√ymx̌ʷʔ). *cedar*
bark basket, basket. In CR
86, GU 196, M 47.

yaxʷt (√yxʷ). *fall.* In SF 60, CE
78, 87.

yax̌ (√yx̌). *?* In SF 81.

ya+yúxʷt (√yxʷ). *fall.* In SF
116.

yaˤ+p (√yˤ). *arrive pl.* In CMB 5.

yaˤ+yáˤt (√yˤt). *all.* In FC 16, CMB 99.

yaˤ' (√yˤ'). *arrive, gather.* In SF 99.

yaˤ'+cín (√yˤ'). *shore.* In GU 252.

yaˤ'+p (√yˤ). *arrive pl.* In FC 8.

yaʔx̌ís (√ʔx̌s). *that one, back then, over there.* In CMB 34.

ylmixʷm (√ylmxʷ). *chief.* In SF 25.

yl+yal+t (√yl). *run away.* In SF 124.

yr+mi (√yr). *push on.* In CR 99.

yutlxʷ (√ytlxʷ). *raven.* In SF 88, CE 5, GU 161.

yxʷ+ut (√yxʷ). *below.* In CMB 75.

yʔaˤ+p (√yˤ). *arrive.* In SF 7.

y'

-y' ^*futT.* In SF 132, GU 148.

ˤ

ˤac (√ˤc). *tie.* In M 39.

ˤalapúl (√ˤlpl). *Gopher.* In CN 2, CMB 2.

ˤan *onom.* In GU 128.

ˤapnáʔ *now.* In CMB 101.

ˤax̌ (√ˤx̌). *lace.* In GU 91.

ˤay+ncút (√ˤy). *laugh.* In SF 34.

ˤay+ˤáyn+k (√ˤyn). *tickle.* In SF 18.

ˤaʔíckʷalaʔ (√ˤʔckʷlʔ). *meadowlark.* In CR 37.

ˤim+t (√ˤm). *angry.* In GU 94.

ˤim+t+m (√ˤm). *be angry at.* In GU 95.

ˤ'

ˤ'ac' (√ˤ'c'). *look at.* In CN 66, CMB 34, CE 27, CR 7, GU 72.

ˤ'ac'+m (√ˤ'ac'). *look.* In CN 46.

ˤ'an' (√ˤ'n'). *Magpie.* In GU 120.

ˤ'ax̌ (√ˤ'x̌). *scratch.* In CR 24.

ˤ'ay+ncút (√ˤ'y). *laugh.* In SF 14, CMB 60.

ˤ'ay+ˤ'ay+ncút (√ˤ'y). *laugh pl.* In FC 22.

ˤ'ʷ

ˤ'ʷs+ˤ'ʷísxaʔ (√ˤ'ʷsxʔ). *Robin.* In GU 265.

ʔ

ʔác+c+qaʔ (√ʔcqʔ). *go out pl.* In SF 43, CN 38, GU 40.

ʔácqaʔ (√ʔcqʔ). *go out.* In SF 81, FC 10, CMB 32, CE 54.

ʔaks+wíx (√wx). *stand.* In CMB 76.

ʔakʷ+ʔakʷt+l+ílx (√ʔkʷt). *crawl around.* In CE 98.

ʔal+w's+cút (√ʔl). *gather.* In GU 301.

ʔał+ʔíł (√ʔłn). *eat pl.* In GU 202, M 57.

ʔał+ʔíłn (√ʔłn). *eat pl.* In SF 26, CN 28, GU 56.

ʔam (√ʔm). *feed.* In CN 13, GU 54.

ʔam+m+út+t (√ʔmt). *sit down.* In GU 67.

ʔamná (√ʔmn). *feed*. In CN
12, M 38.

ʔam+ʔam (√ʔm). *feed*. In GU
162.

ʔap'+ʔíp'+xn+m (√ʔp'). *rub
with feet*. In GU 113.

ʔaqʼʷ (√ʔqʼʷ). *scrape*. In CE
46.

ʔasíl (ʔsl). *two*. In SF 9.

ʔatx+ílx (√ʔtx). *sleep pl*. In SF
75, GU 245.

ʔawt+íma?+tk (√ʔwt). *below*.
In GU 51.

ʔax̌+lwis (√ʔx̌l). *mill about*. In
GU 42.

ʔayx̌ʷ+t (√ʔyx̌ʷ). *tired*. In SF
20.

ʔaʔsúł (√ʔsl). *Loon*. In GU
272.

ʔic+c+kn (√ʔckn). *play*. In GU
20.

ʔił (√ʔłn). *eat*. In FC 40, CMB
96, GU 60, M 49.

ʔiłn (√ʔłn). *eat, feast*. In CN 22,
CMB 86, GU 54, M 44.

ʔimx (√ʔmx). *move*. In CMB
113, GU 30.

ʔiskʼʷl+m (√ʔskʼʷl). *pitch*. In
CE 2.

ʔitx (√ʔtx). *sleep*. In SF 72, CE
95, M 23.

ʔkin (√ʔkn). *indef*. In CMB 83,
CR 79, GU 241.

ʔuckl'+íp+m (√ʔckl'). *run
downhill*. In M 51.

ʔucl+m (√ʔcl). *paddle*. In M
33.

ʔul+w' (√ʔl). *gather*. In CE 92.

ʔul+w's (√ʔul√w's). *gather*. In
CE 93, CR 68, GU 131.

ʔx̌il (√ʔx̌l). *do like*. In FC 40.